more . . .

"With his blend of intriguing characters, vivid imagery, and earthy humor, the author never loses balance or momentum. If Olympic medals were given for narrative athleticism, Urrea would get the gold."

— Allison Block, *Chicago Sun-Times*

"Nothing short of miraculous. . . . Urrea's portrayal of the people who live on the land is unusually complex. . . . The story of the saint is told with such love and care that it will make a believer out of anyone."

— Leila Lalami, *Oregonian*

"A charmingly written manifesto. . . . These 500 pages slip past effortlessly, with the amber glow of slides in a magic lantern, each one a tableau of the progress of earthly grace. . . . Teresita is a saint we could really use right now."

— Stacey D'Erasmo, *New York Times Book Review*

"Beautifully composed. . . . The book constantly stirs a readers own sense of wonder. The sights, the sounds, the smells, the passions of Teresita's life and her times all come bidden at the masterly calling of the novelist."

— Alan Cheuse, *Chicago Tribune*

"Nothing in this review will convey the richness and raw beauty of the writing, or just how accessible and intensely entertaining a story this is. . . . I would gladly wait 20 more years for a book that affected me as deeply as *The Hummingbird's Daughter* has. . . . A profound and transcendent achievement."

— Lynda Sandoval, *Denver Post*

The
HUMMINGBIRD'S
DAUGHTER

Other Books by Luis Alberto Urrea

NONFICTION

The Devil's Highway: A True Story
Across the Wire: Life and Hard Times
on the Mexican Border
By the Lake of Sleeping Children: The Secret
Life of the Mexican Border
Nobody's Son
Wandering Time

FICTION

In Search of Snow
Six Kinds of Sky

POETRY

The Fever of Being
Ghost Sickness
Vatos

The

HUMMINGBIRD'S DAUGHTER

A Novel

LUIS ALBERTO URREA

BACK BAY BOOKS
Little, Brown and Company
NEW YORK   BOSTON

Little, Brown and Company

Time Warner Book Group
1271 Avenue of the Americas, New York, NY 10020
Visit our Web site at www.twbookmark.com

Originally published in hardcover by Little, Brown and Company, May 2005

First Back Bay international edition, January 2006

Printed in the United States of America

10 9 8 7 6 5 4 3 2 1

For Cinderella

Truth is everything.
Of truth I have no fear.
In truth I see no shame.

— TERESITA URREA

Truth, for the tyrants, is the most terrible and
cruel of all bindings: it is like an incandescent iron
falling across their chests. And it is even more
agonizing than hot iron, for that only burns the flesh,
while Truth burns its way into the soul.

— LAURO AGUIRRE

Book I

THE INITIATION
OF THE DREAMERS

*Daughter of Amapola, daughter of Marcelina.
Marcelina begat Tula, Tula begat Juana. Juana
begat Anastasia, who begat Camilda. Camilda
de Rosalío begat Nicolasa; Nicolasa, Tolomena;
and Tolomena, Rocío. Rocío begat Dolores, who
begat Silvia María. Silvia María, Dominga, who
begat Epifania, who begat Agustina, and Agustina
begat María Rebeca, who begat that* puta *Cayetana,
who begat Teresa, named "of Cabora."*

— BRIANDA DOMECQ,
*La insólita historia de la
Santa de Cabora*

One

ON THE COOL OCTOBER MORNING when Cayetana Chávez brought her baby to light, it was the start of that season in Sinaloa when the humid torments of summer finally gave way to breezes and falling leaves, and small red birds skittered through the corrals, and the dogs grew new coats.

On the big Santana rancho, the People had never seen paved streets, streetlamps, a trolley, or a ship. Steps were an innovation that seemed an occult work, stairways were the wicked cousins of ladders, and greatly to be avoided. Even the streets of Ocoroni, trod on certain Sundays when the People formed a long parade and left the safety of the hacienda to attend Mass, were dirt, or cobbled, not paved. The People thought all great cities had pigs in the streets and great muddy rivers of mule piss attracting hysterical swarms of wasps, and that all places were built of dirt and straw. They called little Cayetana the Hummingbird, using the mother tongue to say it: Semalú.

On that October day, the fifteenth, the People had already begun readying for the Day of the Dead, only two weeks away. They were starting to prepare plates of the dead's favorite snacks: deceased uncles, already half-forgotten, still got their favorite green tamales, which, due to the heat and the flies, would soon turn even greener. Small glasses held the dead's preferred brands of tequila, or rum, or rompope: Tío Pancho liked beer, so a clay flagon of watery Guaymas brew fizzled itself flat before his graven image on a family altar. The ranch workers set aside candied sweet potatoes, cactus and guayaba sweets, mango jam, goat jerky, dribbly white cheeses, all food they themselves would like to eat, but they knew the restless spirits were famished, and no family could afford to assuage its own hunger and insult the dead. Jesús! Everybody knew that being dead could put you in a terrible mood.

The People were already setting out the dead's favorite corn-husk cigarettes, and if they could not afford tobacco, they filled the cigarros with machuche, which would burn just as well and only make the smokers cough a little. Grandmother's thimble, Grandfather's old bullets, pictures of Father and Mother, a baby's umbilical cord in a crocheted pouch. They saved up their centavos to buy loaves of ghost bread and sugar skulls with blue icing on their foreheads spelling out the names of the dead they wished to honor, though they could not read the skulls, and the confectioners often couldn't read them either, an alphabet falling downstairs. Tomás Urrea, the master of the rancho, along with his hired cowboys, thought it was funny to note the grammatical atrocities committed by the candy skulls: Martía, Jorse, Octablio. The vaqueros laughed wickedly, though most of them couldn't read, either. Still, they were not about to lead Don Tomás to think they were brutos, or worse — pendejos.

"A poem!" Tomás announced.

"Oh no," said his best friend, Don Lauro Aguirre, the great Engineer, on one of his regular visits.

"There was a young man from Guamúchil," Tomás recited, "whose name was Pinche Inútil!"

"And?" said Don Lauro.

"I haven't worked it out yet."

Tomás rode his wicked black stallion through the frosting of starlight that turned his ranch blue and pale gray, as if powdered sugar had blown off the sky and sifted over the mangos and mesquites. Most of the citizens of Sinaloa had never wandered more than 100 miles; he had traveled more than anyone else, 107 miles, an epic journey undertaken five days before, when he and his foreman, Segundo, had led a squad of armed outriders to Los Mochis, then to the Sea of Cortés beyond. All to collect Don Lauro Aguirre, arriving by ship from far Mazatlán, and with him, a shipment of goods for the ranch, which they contracted for safe delivery in a Conducta wagon train accompanied by cavalry.

In Los Mochis, Tomás had seen the legendary object called "the sea."

"More green than blue," he'd noted to his companions, already an expert on first sight. "The poets are wrong."

"Pinches poets," said Segundo, hating all versifiers and psalmists.

They had gone on to greet the Engineer at the docks. He fairly danced off the boat, so charged with delight was he to be once again in the rustic arms of his *bon ami très enchanté!* Under his arm, carefully wrapped in oilcloth, Aguirre clutched a leather-bound copy of Maxwell's *Treatise on Electricity and Magnetism.* In Aguirre's opinion, the Scotsman had written a classic! Don Lauro had a nagging suspicion that electricity, this occult force, and magnetism, certainly a force of spirit, could be used to locate, and even affect, the human soul. In his pocket, a greater wonder was hidden: a package of Adams's Black Jack chewing gum — the indescribable flavor of licorice! Wait until Tomás tasted that!

The ship looked to Segundo like a fat bird with gray wings floating on the water after eating some fish. He was delighted with himself and pointed to the boat and told one of the buckaroos, "Fat bird. Ate some fish. Floating around." He lit a little cigar and grinned, his gums and teeth clotted with shreds of tobacco.

Segundo had the face of an Aztec carving. He had Chinese eyes, and a sloping Mayan forehead. His nose was a great curving blade that hung down over his drooping bandido mustache. He thought he was handsome. But then, Aguirre also thought himself handsome, though he seemed to have inherited the penchant for fat cheeks that was supposed to be the curse of the Urrea clan. He tried to remember to suck in his cheeks, especially when he was being compared to his friend Tomás Urrea. Where had Tomás's cheeks gone? In bright light, you could see his cheekbones casting shadows as if he were some Indian warrior. And those eyes! Urrea had a ferocious gleam in his eyes — a glare. Men found it unnerving, but women were apparently mesmerized. They were the only green eyes Aguirre had ever beheld.

"You have much work to do, you lazy bastard," said Tomás.

The Urrea clan paid Aguirre handsomely to exercise his education for them in elaborate hydrological and construction plans. He had designed a network of vents to carry odors from the house's revolutionary indoor toilet. He had even astounded them all by designing a system of pipes that carried water uphill.

With liquid on the mind, it was not long before they

found the notorious El Farolito cantina. There, they ate raw shellfish still gasping under tides of lime juice and hot sauce and great crystals of salt that cracked between the teeth of the men. Naked women writhed to a tuba-and-drum combo. The men regarded this display with joy, though Aguirre made the effort to feel guilty about it. Lieutenant Emilio Enríquez, in charge of the Conducta wagon train, joined them at the table.

"Teniente!" Tomás shouted. "What do you hear?"

"Gentlemen," said Enríquez, arranging his sword so he could sit. "Unrest in Mexico City."

Aguirre had to admit to himself that this soldier, though an enforcer of the oppressors, was a dashing figure in his medallions and the bright brass fittings on his tunic.

"What troubles are these, sir?" he said, always ready to hear the government was being overthrown.

Enríquez twirled the ends of his upswept bigote and nodded to the barkeep, who landed a foaming beer before him.

"Protesters," he sighed, "have dug up Santa Anna's leg again."

Everybody burst out laughing.

The old dictator's leg had once been blown off by a cannonball and buried with full military honors in the capital.

"Every year, somebody digs it up and kicks it around," Enríquez said.

Tomás raised his glass of beer.

"To Mexico," he said.

"To Santa Anna's leg!" Lieutenant Enríquez announced.

They all raised their glasses.

"The Canadians," Enríquez said, as he poured himself a

fresh glass of beer, "have launched a mounted police force. They control their Indians."

"And bandits?" Tomás interjected.

Tomás Urrea's own father had been waylaid by bandits on the road to Palo Cagado. The bandits, a scruffy lot said to have dropped out of the Durango hills, had been after silver. Tomás's father, Don Juan Francisco, was well known for carrying casks of coin to cover the wages of the three hundred workers on his brother's great million-acre hacienda south of Culiacán. When the outlaws discovered no silver, they stood Don Juan Francisco against an alamo tree and executed him with a volley of ninety-seven bullets. Tomás had been nine at the time. Yet his subsequent hatred of bandidos, as he grew up on the vast ranch, was so intense it transformed into a lifelong fascination. Some even said Tomás now wished he were a bandido.

"It goes without saying, caballeros. Bandits!" said Enríquez. "Besides, we have already started the rural police program here in Mexico to accost our own outlaws."

"Gringos! They have copied us again," Tomás announced.

"Los Rurales," Enríquez continued. "The rural mounted police force."

"To the Rurales," Tomás said.

They raised their glasses.

"To the bandits," said Segundo.

"And the Apaches," Enríquez said, "who keep me employed."

They drank the hot brew and pissed out the back door and tossed coins to the women to keep them dancing. Tomás suddenly grabbed a guitar and launched into a ballad about a boy who loved his schoolteacher but was too shy to tell her. Instead, he wrote her a love note every day and tucked it in a tree. One day, while he was placing his latest testimonial in the tree, it was hit by lightning, and not only did this poor boy die, but the tree with its enclosed epistles of love burned to the ground. The teacher ran to the tree in time to behold this disaster. The ballad ended with the melancholy schoolteacher, lonely and unloved, brushing the ashes of the boy's unread notes from her hair before turning out her lamp and sleeping alone for yet another night. The naked dancers covered themselves and wept.

Early the next morning, the men left the thunderously hungover barkeep and dancers behind and began their long ride inland, to where the hills started to rise and the iguanas were longer than the rattlesnakes. They began to forget the color of the sea.

Cayetana greeted that dawn with a concoction made with coffee beans and burned corn kernels. As the light poured out of the eastern sea and splashed into windows from coast to coast, Mexicans rose and went to their million kitchens and cooking fires to pour their first rations of coffee. A tidal wave of coffee rushed west across the land, rising and falling from kitchen to fire ring to cave to ramada. Some drank coffee from thick glasses. Some sipped it from colorful gourds, rough clay pots that dissolved as they drank, cones of banana leaf. Café negro. Café with canela. Café with goat's milk. Café with a golden-brown cone of piloncillo melting in it like a pyramid engulfed by a black flood. Tropical café with a dollop of sugarcane rum coiling in it like a hot snake. Bitter mountaintop café that thickened the blood. In Sinaloa, café with boiled milk, its burned milk skin floating on top in a pale membrane that looked like the flesh of a peeled blister. The heavy-eyed stared into the round mirrors of their cups and regarded their own dark reflections. And Cayetana Chávez, too, lifted a cup, her coffee reboiled from yesterday's grounds and grits, sweet with spoons of sugarcane syrup, and lightened by thin blue milk stolen with a few quick squeezes from one of the patrón's cows.

On that long westward morning, all Mexicans still dreamed the same dream. They dreamed of being Mexican. There was no greater mystery.

Only rich men, soldiers, and a few Indians had wandered far enough from home to learn the terrible truth: Mexico was too big. It had too many colors. It was noisier than anyone could have imagined, and the voice of the Atlantic was different from the voice of the Pacific. One was shrill, worried, and demanding. The other was boisterous, easy to rile into a frenzy. The rich men, soldiers, and Indians were the few who knew that the east was a swoon of green, a thick-aired smell of ripe fruit and flowers and dead pigs and salt and sweat and mud, while the west was a riot of purple. Pyramids rose between llanos of dust and among turgid jungles. Snakes as long as country roads swam tame beside canoes. Volcanoes wore hats of snow. Cactus forests grew taller than trees. Shamans ate mushrooms and flew. In the south, some tribes still went nearly naked, their women wearing red flowers in their hair and blue skirts, and their breasts hanging free. Men outside the great Mexico City ate tacos made of live winged ants that flew away if the men did not chew quickly enough.

So what were they? Every Mexican was a diluted Indian, invaded by milk like the coffee in Cayetana's cup.

Afraid, after the Conquest and the Inquisition, of their own brown wrappers, they colored their faces with powder, covered their skins in perfumes and European silks and American habits. Yet for all their beaver hats and their lace veils, the fine citizens of the great cities knew they had nothing that would ever match the ancient feathers of the quetzal. No cacique stood atop any temple clad in jaguar skins. Crinolines, waistcoats. Operas, High Mass, café au lait in demitasse cups in sidewalk patisseries. They attempted to choke the gods with New York pantaloons, Parisian petticoats. But still the banished spirits whispered from corners and basements. In Mexico City, the great and fallen Tenochtitlán, among streets and buildings constructed with the stones of the Pyramid of the Sun, gentlemen walked with their heads slightly tilted, cocked as if listening to this puzzling murmur of wraiths.

They still spoke a thousand languages — Spanish, too, to be sure, but also a thicket of songs and grammars. Mexico — the sound of wind in the ruins. Mexico — the waves rushing the shore. Mexico — the sand dunes, the snowfields, the steam of sleeping Popocatépetl. Mexico — across marijuana fields, tomato plants, avocado trees, the agave in the village of Tequila.

Mexico. . . .

All around them, in the small woods, in the caves, in the precipitous canyons of copper country, in the swamps and at the crossroads, the harsh Old Ones gathered. Tlaloc, the rain god, lips parched because the Mexicans no longer tortured children to feed him sweet drafts of their tears. The Flayed One, Xipe Totec, shivering cold because priests no longer skinned sacrifices alive and danced in their flesh to bring forth the harvest. Tonántzin, goddess of Tepeyac, chased from her summit by the very Mother of God, the Virgen de Guadalupe. The awesome and ferocious warrior god, Hummingbird on the Left, Huitzilopochtli. Even the Mexicans' friend, Chac Mool, was lonely. Big eared and waiting to carry their hopes and dreams in his bowl as he transited to the land of the gods from the earth, he lay on his back watching forever in vain for the feathered priests to return. Other Old Ones hid behind statues in the cathedrals that the Spaniards had built with the stones of their shattered temples. The smell of sacrificial blood and copal seeped out from between the stones to mix with incense and candles. Death is alive, they whispered. Death lives inside life, as bones dance within the body. Yesterday is within today. Yesterday never dies.

Mexico. Mexico.

The pain in her belly kicked Cayetana Chávez over. She dropped her cup. She felt a cascade of fluids move down her bowels as the child awoke. Her belly!

It clenched. It jumped. It clenched.

At first, she thought it was the cherries. She had never eaten them before. If she had known they would give her a case of chorro . . .

"Ay," she said, "Dios."

She thought she was going to have to rush to the bushes.

They had come for her the day before. The Chávez girls were known by everybody. Although Santana Ranch was divided into two great lobes of territory — crops to the south and cattle to the north — there were only fifty workers' households, and with the children and grandparents added up, it made for fewer than 150 workers. Everybody knew better than to bother Cayetana's older sister, Tía. Good Christ: the People would rather move a rattlesnake out of their babies' cribs with a stick than go to Tía's door. So when they came from the northern end of the rancho with news that one of the Chávez sisters' cousins had killed himself, they'd asked for La Semalú.

Ay, Dios. Cayetana was only fourteen, and she had already learned that life was basically a long series of troubles. So she had wrapped her rebozo around her head and put on her flat huaraches and begun her slow waddle through the darkness before the sun rose.

She wondered, as she walked, why the People called her Hummingbird. Was it because she was small? Well, they were *all* small. Everyone knew semalús were holy birds, carrying prayers to God. She also knew she had a bad reputation, so calling her Semalú was probably some kind of joke. They loved to make jokes. Cayetana spit: she did not think anything was funny. Especially now. Her poor cousin. He had shot himself in the head. Her mother and father were dead, shot down in an army raid in Tehueco lands. Her aunt and uncle had been hanged in a grove of mango trees by soldiers that mistook them for fleeing Yaquis near El Júpare. The men were strung up with their pants around their ankles. Both men and women hung naked as fruit. Some of the Mexicans had collected scalps. She sighed. Aside from her sister, she was alone in the world. She put her hands on her belly as she walked along the north road. It was three miles to the cattle operation. The baby kicked.

Not yet, not yet.

She didn't mind being called a hummingbird.

Hours later, she pushed through the shaky gate of her cousin's jacal. He was still lying on his back in the dirt.

Someone had placed a bandana over his face. His huaraches were splayed. His toes were gray. The blood on the ground had turned black. He didn't stink yet, but the big flies had been running all over him, pausing to rub their hands. A rusty pistola lay in the dirt a few inches from his hand.

The neighbors had already raided her cousin's shack and taken all his food. Cayetana traded the pistola to a man who agreed to dig a hole. He dug it beside a maguey plant beside the fence, and they rolled the body into it. They shoved the dirt over him and then covered the grave with rocks so the dogs wouldn't dig it up.

Inside the shack, Cayetana found a chair and a bed frame made of wood and ropes. There was a machete under the bed. A pregnant girl from distant Escuinapa was there, waiting. Cayetana didn't know her, but she let her move in, since the girl was afraid that she would lose her infant to coyotes if she had it outside. Cayetana accepted the girl's blessing, then swung the machete a few times. She liked the big blade. She started to walk home.

The sun was already setting. She didn't like that. The dark frightened her. That road was also scary. It wound between black cottonwoods and gray willows. Crickets, frogs, night birds, bats, coyotes, and ranch dogs — their sounds accompanied her through the dark. When she had to pee — and since the child had sprouted inside her, she had to pee all the time — she squatted in the middle of the road and held the machete above her head, ready to kill any demon or bandit that dared leap out at her. An owl hooted in a tree behind her, and that made her hurry.

She came around a bend and saw a small campfire off to the side of the road. It was on the south side. That was a good omen — north was the direction of death. Or was it west? But south was all right.

A man stood by the fire, holding a wooden bowl. He was chewing, and he watched her approach. A horse looked over his shoulder, more interested in the bowl than in her. Her stomach growled and her mouth watered. She hadn't eaten in a day. She should have hidden in the bushes, but he had already seen her.

"Buenas noches," she called.

"Buenas."

"It's dark."

He looked up as if noticing the darkness for the first time.

"It is," he agreed. Then: "Don't hit me with that machete."

"I won't."

"Gracias."

"This is for bandidos."

"Ah!"

"Son cabrones," she explained. "And I'll kill the first one that tries anything."

"Excellent," he said.

"And ghosts."

He put food in his mouth.

"I don't think you can kill a ghost," he said.

"We'll see about that," she said, flashing her blade.

The small fire crackled.

"What are you eating?" she asked.

"Cherries."

"Cherries? What are cherries?"

He held one up. In the faint fire glow, it looked like a small heart full of blood.

"They come from trees," he said.

"Son malos?" she asked. "They look wicked."

He laughed.

"They are very wicked," he said.

"I am going home," she said.

"So am I."

"Is this your horse?"

"It is, but I like to walk."

"You must have good shoes."

"I have good feet."

He spit out a seed and popped another cherry in his mouth. She watched his cheeks swell as his jaw worked. Spit. Eat another cherry.

"Are they sweet?" she asked.

"Sí."

He spit a seed.

He heard her belly growl.

"You will bring a child to light soon," he said.

"Yes."

"A girl."

"I don't know," she replied.

"A girl."

He handed her the bowl.

"Eat," he said.

The cherry juice in Cayetana's mouth was dark and red, like nothing she had ever tasted.

She spit out the seed.

"I have to go now," she said, "it is late."

"Adios," he said.

Cayetana replied in the mother tongue: "Lios emak weye." God go with you. She walked into the night. Funny man. But one thing she knew from experience — all men were funny.

She'd gotten a restless night's sleep with the bellyache she blamed on the stranger's fruit. Now the morning brought increased tumult inside her. Cayetana thought she could make it to the row of outhouses that Tomás had built between the workers' village and the great house where the masters slept. But the child within her had decided it was time to come forth, announcing the news about halfway to the outhouses when the pain dropped Cayetana to her knees and the strange water broke from her and fell into the dust.

Two

HUILA HATED THE WAY her knees popped when she stood. *Crack! Crack!* She sounded like a bundle of kindling.

She made the sign of the cross, fetched her apron, and took up her shotgun. Huila's mochila of herbs and rags and knives was packed and ready, as always. She put its rope-loop handle over her left shoulder. She packed her pipe with tobacco, lit a redheaded match from one of her votive candles, and sucked in the flame. She had stolen some good rum-soaked tobacco from Don Tomás when she'd cleaned his library. He knew she stole it — on several occasions, she had smoked it right in front of him.

The masters called her María Sonora, but the People knew she was Huila, the Skinny Woman, their midwife and healer. They called the masters Yoris — all whites were

Yori, the People's greatest insult Yoribichi, or Naked White Man. Huila worked for the Big Yoribichi. She lived in a room behind the patrón's kitchen, from which Tomás believed she directed the domestic staff, but from which the People believed she commanded the spirits.

She felt in her apron pockets for her medicine pouch. Everybody knew it was made of leather — man leather, they said, gathered from a rapist's ball sack. The rumor was that she had collected it herself back in her village of El Júpare. When one of the pendejos working around her or her girls started to give her grief, she'd pull the awful little warty-looking blackened bag out of her apron pocket and toss it and catch it, toss it and catch it, until the man quieted down and started watching. Then she'd say, "Did you have something you wanted to say to me?"

She felt her way out of her room at the back of the kitchen, and felt her way along the edge of the big tin table where the girls chopped up the chickens, and she went out the back door. She paused for a moment to offer up a prayer to the Maker. As María Sonora, she prayed to Dios; as Huila, she prayed to Lios. Dios had doves and lambs, and Lios had deer and hummingbirds. It was all the same to Huila. She hurried around the house, heading for Cayetana's shack.

❋

Cayetana heard the men on horseback laughing. Their voices came through the ragged blanket that served as her front door. She was on all fours, panting like a dog. Stuff leaked down the backs of her thighs. Two village girls knelt at the door and soothed her brow, combing her hair back with their fingers, offering her sips of water.

"Does it hurt?"

"Unh."

She was beyond small talk.

"You will be all right, Semalú."

They moved her back onto her sleeping mat, where she poured sweat and clutched herself and moaned. The girls had never looked between anybody's legs, and La Semalú was too gone to worry about what she was showing them. They looked into the folds of her and feared that the baby's face would pop out and glare at them. They made the sign of the cross over their own brows, and over Cayetana's belly.

Cayetana grunted.

One of the girls said, "I thought it would be beautiful."

She felt it would be helpful to dribble water from the jarrito onto Cayetana's belly. She jumped. Kicked. They patted her hands.

"Huila's coming. Don't worry, compañera, Huila's coming."

⁂

Huila could see the men now, in the scant fire of dawning, tall on their horses. Well, no: the patrón was tall. The others were squat on their mounts beside him. He was like a giraffe among burros. Fools all. The People called Tomás El Rascacielos — the Sky Scratcher. And there he was with his idiot friend Aguirre and his pinche henchman, Segundo, out by the main gate, waiting for their goods to arrive. Well, Huila didn't mind the goods. She liked lilac soap, and she liked the new tooth powders to clean her teeth, and she liked canned coffee and peppermints. She liked a quick snort of anís in a shot glass, and she liked cotton underpants. She did not like jujubes. The Sky Scratcher loved them, bought jujube in huge colorful sheets, and cut out little plugs of it that he fed to his horses. Jujube, in Huila's opinion, would only pull out your teeth, and if you sucked it, it turned nasty — swampy and slick as a snail on your tongue. Damn the jujube! she decided.

Huila made her way up the low drybank where Cayetana's ramada stood, crooked and seemingly empty. If you didn't know a cute girl lived here, you would kick it apart as a ruin, try to use its walls as firewood. A cute girl mounted and forgotten. Huila knocked the glowing coal out of her pipe and added to her thoughts: Damn the men!

She pushed the awful blanket aside and bent into the hut. She was greeted by the same smell she always breathed when the little ones came. Old cooking smoke, and sweat, and a shitty smell, and all kinds of tang in the air. Thank Lios there was no smell of rot or infection or death in the air. Midwives did their work in many ways, in their own styles, but for Huila, it always began with the nose. Huila had seen terrible things in these huts — and every time she had, she had first smelled death.

Two little monkey girls huddled beside the mother.

"You," Huila said. "Fetch me clean water."

The girls scrambled out of there and ran.

"Do not fear, child," Huila said. "Huila is here. Huila brought your mother into the world, and Huila brought you into the world. Now Huila will bring your baby into the world as well."

"I am not afraid."

Huila dropped her mochila in the dirt. She got down on her knees. *Crack! Pop!*

She said, "Yes you are."

Three

TOMÁS OPENED HIS POCKET WATCH and said, "Where is this damned Conducta?"

"It's coming, boss," said Segundo.

Segundo was known as Ojo del Buitre. Buzzard Eye. With that droopy beak of his, he even looked like a vulture. They said he could spot things so far in the distance that mere mortals could not see them at all. Often, Tomás would see a distant dot that could be a tree or a cow, and Segundo would proclaim, "Why, it's old Maclovio, and he's wearing his stupid red hat!" Or, "Those Indians might be Apaches."

Ojo del Buitre. As if Segundo didn't already have enough names. He was Antonio Agustín Alvarado Saavedra, Hijo. Hijo was, of course, "the Second," which led to his nickname of Segundo. He was the son of the *caballero de estribo,* the top hand, from Don Miguel Urrea's great rancho — his father had scoured the hundreds of worker women for juicy concubines for the great man. Segundo and Tomás had grown up together. Neither one would ever admit such a thing, but they were nearly brothers.

"Buitre," said Tomás, "do you see it?"

"Not yet."

"Then it is truly at a far remove," Tomás noted.

Don Lauro was utterly asleep in his saddle. He listed to the right, starting to approach a forty-five-degree angle.

"I hope that cabrón doesn't fall off his horse," Tomás said.

"It would make an impression," Segundo replied. "That head of his would knock a hole in the earth."

"Now, now," muttered Tomás.

Tomás had never fallen asleep on a horse in his life. He had eaten on horses, stood on horses, vomited on horses, and in 1871 had made love while trotting on a horse. Ajúa! Viva el amor! Someday he would try it at a dead run.

They all said he was the best horseman in the region. From his uncle Miguel's million-acre ranch to the restaurants of Ocoroni, everybody talked about Tomás Urrea and his horses. This particular mount, El Mañoso, was legendarily cranky. That morning, in fact, in the stable, Segundo had been inspired to kick it in the head when it bared its teeth and turned to bite his knee. Tomás loved the horse, mistaking the horse's pathological hatred of Segundo for loyalty to himself. After all, the horse had never tried to bite him.

"Buitre! Ojo!" shouted Tomás. "What do you see now?"

Segundo shrugged.

"Where is the wagon?"

Segundo languidly rolled a cigarette.

"Who knows, boss," he said.

He adjusted his hat and stared off. He cleared his throat and made his report.

"I see a rabbit and a ground squirrel. The ground squirrel is getting a seed. There's a pile of horse turds in the middle of the road just at the foot of the grade, and it looks to me like a big fly is really enjoying that." He fished a match out of his hatband, struck it on his saddle, lit up. "Over by Los Mochis, there's a pelican flying south."

"You blasted liar."

"Sorry, patrón. The pelican is flying north."

Segundo blew a puff of smoke. He had an infuriatingly mild expression on his face. His patrón worked the black stallion in a circle.

"This kind of insolence vexes me every day," Tomás told Aguirre, who had roused from his slumber, a dollop of drool pressed into his beard.

A faint, shrill scream carried over the distance. They craned around.

"What the devil was that?" Don Lauro said.

"Let's go look," Tomás replied.

Segundo put out one leg and held his boot against El Mañoso's black chest to hold him back.

"Wait," he said. "It is only one of the girls having a baby."

Tomás reined in his mount and gawked.

"How did you know that?" he demanded. "Don't tell me you have the ears of a coyote to go with your eyes!"

Segundo grinned.

"I saw that old midwife walking behind us," he said.

Tomás saw Cayetana's ramada in the distance.

"Huila," he said.

"Sí."

"Whose shack is that?"

"Quién sabe?" Segundo replied. Who knows?

Tomás wanted to know. He wanted to know everything. Especially if it had to do with women.

He'd always wanted to see a human child come to light, for example. He'd watched the cows and horses and pigs and dogs slide out of their mothers. Surely, a woman wasn't that bloody, was she? The doctor in Ocoroni had told him he did not want to see it — he would be afraid of women forever after. It was the women of the poor ones, and the Indias, who did el parto in front of the doctor. Even the doctor was always locked out in the hall when the Yori women like Mrs. Urrea gave birth, where he listened at the door and shouted in his directions.

"Whose shack is that?" Tomás asked again.

"Some little she-dog." Segundo shrugged. "Workers. They're always making babies."

Tomás wished he could leave these men and see what Huila was doing. But Segundo tapped him on the arm and said, "Boss, I see the wagons coming over the ridge."

"Remember, Lauro," Tomás said. "Look for women. Eye contact, that's the key."

The Urrea wagon was accompanied by Lieutenant Enríquez and his troop. The good lieutenant, upon seeing Tomás and his gents, reached into his tunic and presented a flask. Tomás and Segundo responded with flasks of their own. Aguirre, alone among them, carried no liquor.

"To Santa Anna's leg!" they cried, and took sharp swallows.

Cayetana's wailing floated over them on its way west.

"Are you flogging today?" Enríquez asked.

"No, no," Tomás said, waving his hand. "A childbirth."

"Ah. Well." Enríquez did not care about a childbirth.

The train was twelve wagons in length.

"No women?" said Tomás.

"Women!" Enríquez removed his cap and wiped his brow on one sleeve.

"My friend the Engineer is seeking his true love."

"Ah."

Tomás had first instructed Aguirre in the ways of love

when they were eleven, in boarding school in Culiacán. Aguirre had been a spindly-legged little scholar, and a bunch of rough boys from Caimanero knocked off his spectacles and roughed him up behind the big fruit stalls downtown. Tomás, fresh from stealing candied yams from the candy stalls in the open-air market, was wandering down the street to see if the parochial-school girls were outside the cathedral so he could offer them a few choice compliments. He had heard Aguirre sobbing first, and then had come around the corner to find Fausto Hubbard and Popo Rojas kicking him as he cowered.

Tomás was taller than the two boys put together. One thing he'd learned at Don Miguel's hacienda was that he should protect the weak. Not that Don Miguel cared about the weak, but some of the old-timers among the People had told him that, and it seemed like the sort of thing to repeat to youngsters. And besides, Tomás was so enamored of the damned People that Don Miguel had christened him with a nickname: he called Tomás Nariz de Apache, Apache Nose. All the more reason.

Tomás waded into the boys and pounded both of them, sent them running with hard boots to the ass. Only then did he discover what he'd rescued: Aguirre in short pants and a beanie lying in a mash of rotten oranges and sniveling.

Aguirre had looked up at him, his green eyes and his tawny cowlick, and he said, "What are you, a German?"

Interesting, Tomás thought. This kid might not be much of a fighter, but he had already noticed something nobody but his rescuer was aware of: Tomás happened to know that he was a Visigoth. Actually, he didn't know what a Visigoth was — only that they had brought blond hair into Spain. The connection seemed clear.

"Get up," he said.

After picking peels and seeds off Aguirre's embarrassing short pants, he led him to the cathedral.

"We are going," he explained, "to go look at women."

※

"Women?" Enríquez craned around and beheld the wagon train. "Here?"

"Surely, you must have women in this Conducta!" Tomás insisted. "Do you want Aguirre to die a virgin?"

"Now wait a minute —" Aguirre blustered, but they ignored him.

"Back there," Enríquez said. "At the rear of the Conducta, there is an Arab. In the buggy. He has a woman, I think."

"Fantástico!" Tomás enthused. "Let's go."

He had taught Aguirre on the steps of the Culiacán cathedral: look into the faces of every group of young women he encountered. Eye contact, that was the secret. As soon as a girl made eye contact, Aguirre was ordered to smile at her. If she smiled back, she was his true love. They were only eleven and twelve, but they gazed without flinching into the limpid mysterious eyes of sixteen- and seventeen-year-old Catholic girls in their blue skirts and white blouses.

He had tried this stratagem for fifteen years, but no one who had smiled back had ever even given him a kiss.

They trotted down the line of wagons.

Behind the Conducta train they discovered a buggy with a man darker than the Mexicans.

Enríquez said: "The troublesome Arab."

"An Arab!" sighed Aguirre. How fascinating.

"I am Antonio Swayfeta," the Arab said. "I go to El Paso, Texas. This is the most beautiful city in the world."

Swayfeta's boy, squatting beside his father, shrugged. El Paso, Culiacán, it was all the same to him. Suddenly, a mysterious creature covered in black cloth from head to foot rose out of the back of the buggy, a noonday ghost. The horses stepped back.

"Caray!" exclaimed Tomás.

This phantasm peered at them through a slit in the cloth.

Aguirre smiled at her burning black eyes.

He was astounded when the ghost's eyebrows wiggled at him.

"El Paso, you say," Aguirre said to Swayfeta, unsure if he had committed adultery right in front of him.

"Yes, yes! Streets. Trains. Gringos. Money."

The phantom extruded a hand from the folds of cloth and adjusted a wrinkle — dark skin, pink nails, and a copper bracelet. Aguirre felt the bracelet was intended as some sort of message. The hand vanished.

"Have you been there?" he asked to camouflage his spying.

"No."

"Do you know where it is?"

"No."

"Excellent!" said Tomás.

"May you find your way," Aguirre called as he backed his horse away.

"*Inshallah,*" said Swayfeta.

"Pendejo," said Segundo.

As the wagon train rumbled north, away from his gate, and his wagons of goods peeled off and entered the gate, Tomás kicked a leg over his pommel and flew off the saddle, landing flat-footed with his hands in the air. He clapped them happily. Every day was full of amazements! Even here, outside of Ocoroni! He could hardly wait to get out of bed each day to see who had died, what had happened, what worker girl would lift her skirt, what bandit had been lynched, what gringo or soldier or renegade warrior – imagine an Arab! — might wander through his ranch. Already, this boring day had been full! He directed the driver of his first wagon to rip off the canvas top and reveal the goods.

A Singer sewing machine.

Cans of peaches, pears, and stewed prunes.

Bolts of cloth.

A case of new repeater rifles.

One thousand rounds of long bullets.

One slightly rotten burlap bag of the new Burbank potatoes.

Jujubes wrapped in wax paper.

Twenty pounds of sugar.

Five huge tins of lard.

A tin of Nestlé's Infant Food: the newest sensation of advanced science!

Cotton unmentionables, parasols, stockings, hankies, a straw hat with silk roses on the brim, facial powder, three dresses, and five pairs of French knee boots for Loreto, Urrea's wife.

A sample board of ten of the new barbed wires from Chicago.

Bacon.

Coffee.

Blue pots and pans for cooking.

White cloth bags of Pillsbury's XXXX Flour.

A Montgomery Ward catalogue.

Dark bottles of beer, clear bottles of tequila, colored bottles of various liquors but especially cognac — all Sinaloan gentlemen sipped cognac after great meals. Wobbly-looking clay tanks full of evil pulque and mezcal. Huge aromatic tobacco leaves wrapped in cloths that looked like big diapers.

A huge crystalline block of sea salt.

Among the other small boxes, bags, and crates, Tomás found his prize. A boxed set of Jules Verne's great adventures: *Vingt mille lieues sous les mers,* and the newest, *Voyage autour du monde en quatre-vingts jours.*

"You will translate," Tomás told Aguirre, who was trying to chew through a sheet of jujube.

"Claro que sí," Aguirre replied as Cayetana's siren call of agony rose and fell, making the ears of the horses swivel. Far in the distance, the carefully wrapped bride of Swayfeta raised one hand and waved.

Huila vigorously rubbed her hands together to make her palms hot. You had to have hot hands in this line of work if you were going to do any good.

Cayetana was lying there naked, her belly run all over with red marks like dead rivers in a desert. Huila had seen two thousand like Cayetana. She put her hot hands on the girl's belly, and Cayetana gasped. Huila rubbed.

"There," she said. "Does that feel good?"

Cayetana could only grunt.

Huila nodded.

"Calma," she said. "No te apures." You had to talk to

them as if they were skittish horses. "No problems," Huila assured her. "No worries at all."

"My sister," Cayetana gasped, "calls me a puta."

"A puta!"

"She says I'm a whore."

"Hmm." Huila reached behind her and took a soggy mass of cool wet leaves and pressed it into Cayetana's opening. "Too bad you aren't. You'd have some money. A better house to live in than this!"

"Then I'm not a puta?"

"Do you believe you are a puta?"

"No."

"Then you are not a puta. Push."

"Ay!"

"Push!"

"Ay, ay!"

"Rest."

"But Huila —"

"Rest now."

"Huila — I have been bad."

Huila snorted.

"Who hasn't?"

"The priest said I was a sinner."

"So is he. Now rest."

These girls, when the pain started, how they babbled! Huila preferred the old women of twenty-nine or thirty, those pushing out their sixth and seventh babies. They were mostly quiet. Pain was no discovery to them. These little girls, they thought they were the first to ever feel a twinge! It made them go insane. Ay Dios. Huila was getting old and tired of all of it.

They heard uproar outside, male voices laughing, singing. The wheels of the wagon going by. Cayetana craned up.

"Just men," said Huila. She patted Cayetana back down. "Just those damned men. Pay them no mind." She heated her hands again, and moved them in circles upon the child's belly. "One day," she said, "the world will be ruled by women, and things will be different."

This comment shocked the two observers more than the birth itself.

"Forgive me!" Cayetana wailed.

"For what?"

"For my sins."

"I'm no priest. Go to confession for that. Now let's have a baby."

"Huila!"

Huila put her hands beneath Cayetana, and thought for the two-thousandth time that it was like catching a fresh egg coming from a hen.

"Your child," she said, "is here."

And in a moment that seemed like forever and no time at all, Teresita came falling into the world. She did not cry. As Huila wiped her face, she looked, as she always must, very closely. She had seen few signs of late, and she didn't expect a sign here in this poor shack with this poor little Hummingbird. Yet the infant had a red triangle on her forehead. Red triangles, Huila knew, were reserved for the powerful ones. She herself had been so marked.

Teresita opened her eyes and stared at the old woman.

"Hello," said Huila. "Go to your mother."

She laid cloths soaked in herbs between the young mother's legs. The cloths shaded pink and Huila pulled them away and put a new pad in their place. She had manzanita tea to clean out Cayetana's birth canal. She had a flask of cotton-root tincture to slow the bleeding. Vervain would open the black nipples. And now, as the baby's mouth sought her mother's breast, Huila wiped the new mother with a soothing yerba mansa.

Huila fished a banana out of her mochila and peeled it, sitting in the dirt. "Ah," she said, "a banana." She took a huge bite and chewed it happily. Later, she would offer up thanksgiving prayers to God and to her patron saints. But right now, she needed her breakfast.

"Are you happy, child?" Huila asked.

The two girls had closed in on Cayetana, and were fussing over the infant.

"Happy?" said Cayetana. She had never thought of the word as it related to her. Happy? What would happiness feel like?

"I think so," she replied, finally. "I think I am . . . happy."

Huila wondered if Tomás had remembered to have chocolates shipped to the ranch. Cómo me encantan los pinches chocolates! she thought. When women ran the world, the palaces would be made of chocolate!

She said nothing of the red triangle.

Four

TIME! AY, DIOS. Cayetana kept asking herself where the time went. This year, that year, almost two years gone.

Now she couldn't even remember giving birth, though she did remember deciding to never do it again. She was careful to take the dark potions Huila brewed from roots that served to keep her womb hollow.

At sixteen years old, she was old enough to be married and to be facing the appalling ancientness of her twenties. And yet her own fate seemed almost secondary. The old ones warned that the new century was coming, and with it, the end of the entire world. 1900! Cayetana could not imagine such a frightening date — all those empty zeros. Lutheran missionaries had said Jesus Himself was riding out of Heaven on a fiery horse, and, apparently, all the dead would leap out of the ground and kill everybody. A wandering Lipan held a short council with the People and told them that the end would be different: the white men would all die and the dead Indios and the buffalo would return. He had given Huila three buffalo teeth and promised that these awesome beasts would be back. The People had never heard of buffalo. "We didn't know they'd left," noted Don Teófano.

"What of the mestizos, like us?" asked Don Nacho Gómez-Palacio. The Lipan had pondered it and said, "Half of you will probably die." The question of the day, after that, was: will half of all of us die, or will half of each of us die? The men were comforted by the thought of their bottom halves living.

Cayetana didn't think she would live long enough to see the century turn — how long was it? She counted on her fingers, lost count, said, "It's a long time." Her daughter, crawling on her dirt floor, heard her voice and said her favorite word: "Cat!"

"Be quiet," Cayetana said.

"Cat!"

The child spoke early, and when she did speak, it was often that word. She called Cayetana a cat, she called pigs cats and trees cats, and the mockingbird was also a cat.

"Cat! Cat!" the baby shouted.

At four months, she had wanted to explore, but could only manage to crawl backward. With a deep red face, the triangle on her forehead turning a ruddy carmine with her exertions, she would roll onto her belly and back out of the ramada and find herself outside, and she would start to wail. Cayetana could not help herself. This was funny. She had finally found something to laugh about.

But the pissing, the caca — first black, then green, then yellow — and the vomit. Por Dios! Fúchi! The child sucked at her teat for long slurpy gulping sessions, then turned her head and puked burning hot whey all over Cayetana's front. She did not appreciate that. And the nursing! Ay, ay, ay! Qué barbaridad! Her nipples were chafed, cracked. Her hardened breasts were constantly aching. And the blasted child popped out little teeth almost immediately, and she bit Cayetana hard. And the disgrace of the milk, sometimes running down her front in two long stains before she even noticed it, everybody, she was sure, looking at her and snickering. The baby, the baby, the baby — it was always the baby. Uy, la niña! She's so cute. She's so strong. Look how she stares in my face! Look at her little red triangle on her little head! Not a word to Semalú — not a good morning, a how are you, a how are you feeling.

Cayetana peeked out the blanket door and looked at the rancho. The corn and maguey were green as far as she could see. The distant cotton and squash and bean fields were emerald, egrets and ibis walked among the rows like little blots of snow. Of course, she had never seen snow, but she had heard someone mention it, so she made a point of repeating the word often so she would seem wise and knowledgeable.

How she wished she could be out there picking some chiles and feeling the sting of the juices making her hands swell. The nightmare of the sun and the burning in your eyes were not as bad as the slavery of motherhood. She looked back at her daughter and relented. The child was lying there kicking happily, holding a ball of cloth and babbling at it.

Sometimes, a feeling came over her, a feeling like wanting to weep, but not for sadness. This happened when she nursed, after she winced from the pain and the child closed her eyes and made small fists and suckled. But like happiness, love was a thing Cayetana guessed at.

She had named the baby Rebecca. Names, everyone agreed, were important — look at Segundo. Like prayers, Cayetana imagined names built spirit ladders that led to the heavenly realms, that with enough names, you could simply rise, like Segundo, to a position of power. She made an excellent long name for her daughter, but since she had not yet baptized her, and because she couldn't write, she had to repeat the name to herself to keep it straight.

Niña García Nona María Rebecca Chávez.

"Afuera?" said the child. "Sí?"

"You are not going outside."

"Afuera? Afuera!"

"Quiet."

"Cat?"

"No," Cayetana said.

To her horror, her daughter's hair was showing light streaks — almost blond.

Cayetana had tried, at first, to pluck all the light hairs, but they spread, a weed, an incrimination, a combination of her mother's obsidian curls and the golden and auburn straight hair of Tomás. Cayetana could not imagine what might happen to her if Tomás took note of this poor bastard girl. Even worse, what if Doña Loreto, his elegant wife, noticed?

Chela, also known as the Little Cactus Fruit, La Tunita, was hanging wet clothes on the bushes in the sun.

"Tunita," Cayetana called.

"Qué hubo, Semalú?" Tunita said. She had three girls of her own.

"I'll take down your laundry for you if you'll watch the child," Cayetana said.

Tunita wiped sweat from her brow with the back of one wrist and said, "All right." She sent her girls running up to Cayetana's hut, and they pushed past Cayetana like little geese, squealing.

"Gracias," Cayetana called as she stepped down the dry-bank and crossed the creek. She crept up on a big apricot tree outside the corrals and watched Tomás and the vaqueros work a pinto in the ring. She often spied on the men of the ranch, watching them talk and smoke and laugh. She crouched in the dusty berry bushes and pushed away from her face a drooping branch with nasty little rocky apricots, dangling like earrings.

Segundo came forth, leading an old man with no hat.

"Jefe," he called.

Tomás sat on the top rail and laughed as the pinto bucked off another vaquero. His kind of horse.

Loreto had given Tomás a smart pair of tight black trousers with silver conchas arrayed down the outsides of his legs. He wore a short leather vest and white shirt, his black boots with silver and gold spurs, and a big Montana-style gringo cowboy hat he'd bought off a buckaroo riding through the country with a posse in a futile hunt for the horse-thieving bandit Heraclio Bernal, the Sinaloan Thunderbolt.

"I look too good," he told Segundo, "to mount a hard-headed horse today."

"Boss, I have somebody here."

Tomás glanced at the old man. He was in sorry shape. His peasant's pants were tattered, his lips sunburned and peeling. The back of his shirt was black.

"This cristiano has seen better days," Tomás noted.

He hopped down from the rail and stepped forward. The reek from the old man pushed him back.

"Tell him your story," Segundo said.

"Ay señores," said the old man, so used to begging for mercy from powerful hacienda bosses that he wrung his hat in his hands before him even though there was no hat. "Mine is a tale of woe." His head shook, and his eyes looked half-crazy to the vaqueros. Cayetana settled in comfortably. A story!

Tomás offered him a small, obligatory smile.

"And?"

He had come walking from across the Sonoran border. He had lived in his ranchería near the Yaqui River since he was born there, sixty-six years before. Military men appeared one day with a deed from the government that his land had been sold to a gringo investor who intended to run sheep on the land and harvest peaches irrigated with

Yaqui River water. When the old man had resisted, he had been tied to a fence and horsewhipped. He and his wife had been sent forth on foot, and their ranchería was now the home of an Irishman from Chicago.

Tomás and Segundo looked at each other.

"You walked here from Sonora?"

"Ehui."

"Ehui?" said Segundo.

"It means yes," Tomás said. "In their tongue."

"Indians." Segundo spit.

"How many days?"

"Many."

"Have you eaten?"

"Not for days."

Tomás put his hands on his hips.

"And your wife, old man?"

"Dead, señor. I left her beside the road three . . . no, four days ago."

Tomás whistled. He took off his hat and put it on the old man's head. It sank past the man's ears.

He said, "I am sorry."

Tomás gripped the old man's arm — it felt like a stick with some flan pudding flung over it.

"Can you help me?" the old man asked.

"Of course, of course. You are welcome here."

"My wounds, sir . . ."

Tomás turned him, looked at his blackened shirt.

"Let's see," he said.

He and Segundo pulled the shirt away from the welts left by the whip, and the flesh made a soft ripping sound, and clouds of hideous stench escaped, and cascades of fat white worms fell out of his shirt.

Segundo skipped away.

Tomás said, "Jesus Christ!"

The old man sank to his knees, as if the shirt and the worms were the only things keeping his wound sealed, and indeed, blood began to drip off his back, falling on the ground behind him as he knelt.

"Boys," said Tomás, "get this pilgrim to Huila right now."

"He's going to die," said Segundo.

"If he dies — but you're not going to die, are you, my friend, you are too strong to die, you've come too far to die, cabrón! — but if he dies, bury him well and . . . bury him with my hat!"

This was a gesture that would be of more interest in the bunkhouse and the workers' village than the pestilence of worms raining from the old man's back.

Two of the buckaroos brought a wagon and loaded him on it muttering, "Easy," and, "There you go, viejo." The wagon headed for the house, and the old man weakly waved his hat and cried, "Gracias! Gracias!"

"I'd like to find that Irishman," Segundo noted.

"You just want to whip a gringo," said Tomás.

"That's true," said Segundo.

Tomás's head was tingling. His bride, Loreto, in league with the house girls, had assured him that if he put lemon juice in his hair, it would turn even blonder in the sun. But so far, all he had was an irritated scalp and the tangy scent of a salad.

"Is my hair more blond yet?" he asked.

"Not quite," said Segundo.

"Don't be negative."

Now, a rider came from the west. He wore a straw hat

that was almost conical, and he had a sad old shotgun tied across his back with twine. Rope sandals.

"Now what!" Tomás cried.

Cayetana, her movements making shushing noises in her bush like the breeze, shifted to see the next amazement.

"That rider is on a mule," Segundo said.

A straw hat and a mule: this was a guaranteed laugh getter for the vaqueros.

"Don Tomás Urrea!" the man called.

Tomás stepped forward.

"At your service, caballero," he said.

The boys giggled. Horseman. Haw! Muleman, maybe. Tomás cast a surreptitious glance back at them to silence them.

"I bring a message from your uncle, Don Miguel Urrea."

"Yes?"

"The Rurales approach!"

"Rurales!"

"Mounted Mexican rural police, sir!"

"Will wonders never cease."

The rider nodded.

"You're not from here," Tomás said. "I hear an accent."

"I am from the land near Pátzcuaro," the man replied.

"Which town?"

"Parangarícutirimícuaro, sir."

All the giggling cowpokes fell silent and stared.

"What did you say?"

"Parangarícutirimícuaro," the rider replied.

This won a round of applause from the assembled men. As the rider and his mule headed back toward Ocoroni,

Tomás took up his favorite topic. He always had a favorite topic. These days, he was fascinated by bees.

"These Mormons," he told Segundo, "in the land of Ootah."

Christ, thought Segundo, not the bees again.

They climbed back on the fence. The vaqueros recommenced their torment of the spirited pinto pony. It was as if the last two apparitions had never materialized at all.

"Yes," Tomás said, "bees."

Nobody gave a shit about bees.

"They have tamed bees."

"Right."

"Tamed bees, docile as cows. They provide honey, you see, and wax. They are tame. They probably come when the Mormons whistle."

"Such miracles," Segundo offered.

Presently, two riders came down the road. Ocoroni, Tomás mused, must be the crossroads of the world.

"Ah! Los Rurales, at last!" said Tomás.

They were a sight, these two. They came forward on huge sorrel mounts, their fancy saddles flashing silver in the sun. They wore full charro outfits — tight tan pants, tight tan jackets, red bandanas, and vast Mexican sombreros worked with silver thread.

"What are these pendejos going to do, sing us a serenade?" Tomás said.

They wore crossed gunbelts across their chests, and they had Winchesters in their scabbards. Segundo thought their spurs were the biggest he'd ever seen.

"Greetings," Tomás called out.

They reined and stared down at the patrón.

"We are Rurales," one of them said. "I am Gómez, and this is Machado."

Tomás nodded.

"So you are the mighty Rurales," he said. "Lieutenant Enríquez of the cavalry told us you would be coming one day. It has been two years, my friends!"

"He's Captain Enríquez now," said Gómez. Machado just sat on his horse and said nothing. "It is better not to see us," Gómez boasted. Machado smirked.

"Good for Enríquez," said Tomás. "Would you care to dismount? Have some water, or some tequila? A bite to eat."

Gómez shook his vast sombrero.

"We do not drink on duty," he intoned. "Nor do Rurales fraternize."

Fraternize, Tomás thought. He doesn't even know what that word means.

"We are accompanying a prisoner."

"Oh?" said Tomás, looking around.

"He's coming," said Gómez. "In a wagon."

"Who is it?"

"El Patudo." Bigfoot.

The men looked at each other. El Patudo. They found El Patudo? The famous bandit?

"Where did this big-footed fellow make his home?" Tomás asked.

"Guamúchil."

They all knew the patrón's limerick, *There was a young man from Guamúchil, whose name was Pinche Inútil*. To the consternation of the Rurales, the men all broke out laughing. "Viva Guamúchil!" one of them cried. Gómez thought they were laughing at him, and he put his hand on his revolver. Tomás didn't help when he said, "Gómez, my good man, did you say El Patudo hails from Parangarícuti-rimícuaro?"

The vaqueros started laughing again.

"I don't hear anything funny," Gómez said.

He was starting to think this Urrea smelled like lemons.

Segundo said, "Son pendejos, estos cabrones."

Gómez understood that: he and Segundo were clearly cut from the same cloth. Gómez nodded. Rich men and their little cowboys. He grinned.

"I can see that," he said.

Soon enough, the wagon came around the bend. A fat Rural sat on the bench and worked the reins on two stoop-shouldered mules whose heads nodded sadly with each hoofclop. The wagon was a flatbed, and something was tied in the back, but there was no cage on it, nor a prisoner chained to the boards.

"Where is our miscreant?" Tomás asked, still jolly in spite of the visit from the maggoty pilgrim.

"In the wagon," said Gómez, sounding as if he were addressing a moron. "In the jar."

"Oh hell," said Segundo.

"Jar — surely you're joking," Tomás said.

"I never joke, Mr. Urrea. We cut off El Patudo's head and put it in a chemist's jar. In rum." He lit a crooked cigarette. There was no regulation that said he couldn't smoke. "We are touring the province with it. A lesson."

All the vaqueros crowded around. They had not seen a cut-off head before. Cayetana wanted to look away, but like all Mexicans, was eerily appeased and relieved by death.

Gómez continued: "Let the people see we are serious. And the bandits."

The wagon came forth, and they could clearly see a large apothecary's jar made of glass, with a glass lid that looked like a Russian church spire, all held down by crisscrossed ropes. Within, a dreadful soup of pale gold rum and the bouncing bobbing black head of El Patudo.

"There's meat hanging off it!" one of the boys shouted.

The bandit's head was still turned away from them, looking as if El Patudo was staring back along the road he had just traveled, remembering Ocoroni with fond nostalgia and hoping to return to it one day. A frilly lace of gray and pink flesh hung in tatters from the stump of his neck.

The wagon stopped, and the mules shuddered, and the rum sloshed, and the head slowly turned to regard Rancho Santana. Cayetana yelped. It was the man with the cherries from that night years ago.

"So," Tomás finally said. "If this poor fellow was known as Bigfoot, why did you bring us his head?"

Five

AS HE SAT IN HIS OFFICE tallying the payroll — how was he supposed to feed all these people? — Tomás turned over a leaf of his fat ledger and jotted his new favorite word, *Parangarícutirimícuaro*. It would become one of his cherished lessons: his children would be tormented with that word for years, having to pronounce it without hesitation to prove to Tomás that they had mastered their oratorical skills. He composed a greatly hilarious poem:

> *There was a young man from Parangarícutirimícuaro,*
> *Oh to hell with it.*

A servant girl spoke from the doorway:

"Patrón? It is time for supper."

"Supper!" He looked out the window. It was dark already! He'd been sitting there squinting by the blubbery light of an oil lamp, and he had not noticed.

"Allí voy," he said.

"Sí, señor."

She left a small cloud of cinnamon in her wake.

Tomás took a fine house coat from a wall hook and flung a few drops from his washing bowl onto his face. He slicked back his lemony hair and smoothed out his whiskers. He poured himself a token copa of rum, in honor of the beheaded bandit, and walked into the dining room. There, he was startled to find the long table set for one.

"And my bride?" he called.

The cinnamon girl appeared and said, "She was not feeling well, sir. Things of women."

He nodded sagely. These things of women were apparently terrible and unpredictable. The tossings of the baby within, no doubt. His first child was already asleep in a cunning little wooden rocking bed that reproduced the soothing rolling of the sea and was painted pale blue with orange seashells along its sides. A squat girl from Leyva was paid solely to sit and rock the child at night.

Tomás regarded his supper. The girls lit candles. He sipped his rum. He wondered if the old man with the wormy back had survived — he had forgotten to ask Segundo.

Tomás looked at the servants and the cooks and the empty room and the long table.

He raised his glass to them all.

"Cheers," he said.

The child was asleep, wrapped in a rebozo and lying on the straw mat in the dirt. Cayetana huddled in the middle of the floor, eating a bit of rice and a chicken neck from a wooden bowl. She dug the tiny wads of meat out of each vertebral compartment, thinking of them as small presents at some fantastic birthday party. When she was small, chicken necks were haciendas, and she was a giant, pulling out Yoris and eating them as they screamed between her molars.

She glanced at her child. If she didn't do it now, she would never do it.

When she finished eating, she wiped her fingers on her skirt, and she put the bowl on the rough wooden table one of the vaqueros had made for her. He had recently been traumatized by hearing that American cowboys called Mexican vaqueros "buckaroos.". It made him feel sad, philosophical even, and he had turned momentarily generous.

Cayetana's things were bundled in the tatty door blanket of her ramada. She blew out the candles and gathered her child in her arms. She didn't even look around — there was nothing to see. She hurried to her sister's house.

❊

Tomás called, "Excuse me!"

The girls charged out of the kitchen to attend to him. "Sir!" they cried in a panic. What if the meat was rotten? What if the tortillas were cold? What if the coffee was weak?

"Call Huila, would you?"

"Sir!"

They hurried back to the kitchen and tapped on her door. Her small room was beside the back entrance of the house.

"What!" she shouted.

"It is the patrón," the cinnamon girl said. "He has asked for you."

Huila went out to the table, limping a little. Her hip was inflamed. She could see the bones in her mind: they glowed red like fireplace pokers. Oh well! The hills are old, too, and they are still covered in flowers.

"What do you want?" she said.

Tomás smiled at her. Her insolence was somehow correct and appealing to him.

"María Sonora," he said.

"Huila."

"Huila, yes, of course. I am lonesome."

Huila scratched her hip and said, "Huh." She looked at all the food on the table. "Soon, you'll be lonesome and fat if you keep eating like this."

"Join me?"

She scraped a chair back and fell into it.

She shouted, "Another plate!"

A girl stumbled forward and set china and silverware before her and almost tripped hurrying out.

"They fear you more than they fear me," Tomás said.

Huila poured herself some coffee. Five spoons of sugar, a splash of boiled milk.

"They *respect* me," Huila said.

She pointed at his glass of rum and crooked her finger. He handed it over. She sipped.

He grinned and spooned beans onto her plate.

"Y yo?" he asked. "Do they respect me?"

She forked one of the thin steaks from the platter and ripped off a piece, wrapped it in a tortilla. Ate. Dipped a rolled tortilla in her soup, nipped off the end and chewed. Slurped her coffee. Picked up a yellow chile with two fingers and bit it: her brow instantly popped out beads of sweat. She collected some beans on the tattered tortilla and ate them, licked her fingers. She was delighted to discover a saucer of white goat cheese, and she pinched up a pyramid of it and shook off the drooling fluids and popped it in her mouth. A spoonful of soup: bananas! With lime and chile and chicken broth! She grunted.

More coffee.

She finally looked at him.

"Have you done anything respectable?" she asked.

"I saved the wormy pilgrim," he said.

"Well, you sent him to me. I saved him."

Tomás hated the sound of chewing, and Huila chewed like some machine.

"How is he, by the way?"

"Smelly."

She slurped her coffee, leaned back, closed her eyes,

and belched almost inaudibly, letting the gas escape through her teeth in a snakelike hiss: "Tssssst!"

"And you," she said, "what do you care if an old ranchero lives or dies? Why do you like the People so much? Aside from the girls. Everybody knows why you like the girls."

He cleared his throat. This girl business was best left unanswered. But the rest of it. At last! Something to talk about!

"The People!" he said.

"That's what I said. Are you deaf?"

"Don Refugio," he finally replied.

Don Refugio Moroyoqui never explained himself. Even when he was teaching little Tomás how to tie a rope, or how to carve a pair of pistol grips out of twin windfall branches, or when he taught Tomás how to make jerky in sun racks that they could hammer apart later for feasts of machaca, he stayed quiet even while speaking. A particular knot could be tied but one way. The grain of the wood allowed but one shaving. Some roads, despite appearances, went in only one direction. Don Refugio did not speak of dried-out riverbeds.

Tomás followed the old Indio around and studied his curious ways. He had learned to ask simple questions, like "What is that?" *A ball-peen hammer.* "Where did these blue eggs come from?" *Quail.* "How do Indians say water?" *Bampo.*

Don Miguel, the great patrón, found it somewhat odd, though he had also learned to rope cows from an old Indio in the 1820s. What boy didn't have his old Indian to teach him? What girl did not have the old washerwoman to teach her to make teas from weeds? How many hacienda babies had been nursed by old Guasave and Tehueco nannies? Besides, Don Miguel had been far too busy running the ranch and raising his own boys to worry about what Tomás did to keep himself busy. As long as the Indian kept Tomás out of his way, Don Miguel was grateful.

No one, not even Don Miguel, would have asked Don Refugio to explain himself, anyway. He had survived Bácum — that was enough to make them shy around Don Refugio, even afraid. It had already been ten years, but the screams still seemed to echo in the valleys. Massacres were nothing new, but this one had been infected with a kind of genius that made it worm its stench and its crackle into the dreams of the People for years. He was tiny and black as old walnut wood, with snowy tousled hair and white whiskers that hung over his mouth and were shaded yellow and brown at the ends from his smoking. Frail, perhaps, but he had survived.

Little Tomás was up before dawn, as usual, investigating. A roulette wagon was still parked outside the house, its mounted gambling apparatus standing erect like a big wooden pinwheel. It was only half-covered by a white cloth and was a fascination: machinery of any kind was still miraculous. Cigar butts and empty cognac bottles lay about the wagon in a scuffle of mess. Tomás collected bottles: one red, two green, and one blue. He looked through the blue bottle at the world. He hid a few cigar butts in his pockets to share with Segundo after lunch.

These roulette wagons went from hacienda to hacienda, bringing gambling and liquor with them. They didn't dare roll through the countryside in the dark. Their strongboxes enticed deadly attention, and highwaymen could spring out at any moment, guns blasting away. So the wagons tied off at a main house and kept the party going all night.

The cavalry had been riding past with a few prisoners from the city when they had seen the lights and heard the uproar — their officers were snoring now on the patrón's couches. Their nasty little horses were standing, heads drooped, already flicking their tails at the biting flies. One cavalry rider sat astride his mount, asleep. The women prisoners were squatting in the dirt, a chain running from neck to neck. They were covered by their rebozos, so they looked like small lumps, or a sort of cattle waiting to be herded to market. Tomás gazed at them through the blue glass. He knew they were being dragged north to Guaymas or south to Culiacán or to some field somewhere to be executed. This was the way of the world — Tomás didn't know yet to feel bad for them.

As Tomás looked at their hunched forms in the blue light, he saw Don Refugio come striding his way.

Don Refugio had heard the racket all night, the idiotic shouts and forced laughter of the damned Yoris. Don Refugio didn't like yelling. He knew that Yoris having a high time could quickly turn, and it paid to keep an eye on them.

The soldiers at Bácum had rounded up the townsfolk at gunpoint. They'd kicked the People, shoved them. The church doors were open, and the People trusted Christ, so they went in, thinking they had been offered refuge. The soldiers made strange jokes: "Praise Jesus," one said. A mother at the far edge of the crowd could not control her screaming child. The little boy jumped and kicked. A soldier shouted, "Silencio!" But the boy would not cease his screaming. The soldier stepped forward and smashed the mother in the face with the butt of his rifle. She fell like dropped laundry, and the boy, suddenly silent, bent to her and poked at her still form.

Don Refugio said, "Captain? May I retrieve that child so he doesn't get away?"

And he had been waved on, to collect the small victim. Don Refugio took the boy in his arms. He backed through the cactus hedge behind them, a solid wall of twenty-foot-high nopales, silently, never getting a thorn, and there he held the boy and watched as the soldiers slammed the doors and nailed them shut and the people within began crying out as they realized their fate and buckets of burning pitch were flung into the shattered windows and the cries rose to insane shrieks and frantic pounding as the 450 bodies within ignited.

He often told Tomás that Bácum had taught him one lesson: sinners were not the only ones fated to burn.

But mostly, Don Refugio talked to Tomás about hammers and horseshoes.

He came forward. "Muchacho," he called. "Qué hay aquí?"

Tomás shrugged.

"Nada," he said.

The maidens stood up, like the horses, hobbled by their neck chains, clinking and shuffling, looking at the ground. Don Refugio saw that each of the young women had filthy bandages on her left arm, matted and stuck to a stump. Jesucristo! He had heard of this. Scalps, ears, noses, hands. These were salted and shipped away in wooden crates, though nobody knew where they went. Some son of a dog in an army office opened a ledger and counted each arm and made a little red check. No doubt his handwriting was beautiful. Don Refugio spit. He cursed.

Tomás scurried after him when he trotted off.

"Go away."

"Why?"

"Leave me."

"Why?"

Don Refugio went in his shack and exited, dragging a rickety wooden chair along the ground. He carried a small red can.

"What's in the can?"

"Go away."

"What did I do to you, old man?"

"Go away now."

"Why are you mad at me?"

"I am not mad at you."

Don Refugio went to a scraggly old cottonwood and set the chair beneath it. Tomás dawdled, wondering what Don Refugio could possibly think he was doing. It was almost time to get to work. This was no time to sit beneath a tree.

"What are you doing?" he called.

"Nothing. Sitting. I'd like a cigar," he said. "Do you have one?"

"I do."

Tomás pulled one of the cavalrymen's cigar butts out of his pocket.

"You shouldn't steal," Don Refugio said. "And you shouldn't smoke. Toss it here."

Tomás pitched it underhanded. It fell in the dirt, and Don Refugio rose from the chair, bent to it, looked at it, flicked off some dust. He wiped the wet end on his sleeve.

"Yori spit," he said. He made a monkey face of distaste. Tomás smiled.

Don Refugio pried the cap off the red can and poured the kerosene over his head. He smelled sharply of juniper and fever. He put the cigar in his mouth. Pulled out a wooden match. He stared at Tomás, who was already starting to shout. "You, boy," he said. "Don't be like your fathers." He struck the match and exploded in flame.

The heat knocked Tomás down. He sat up and stared as Don Refugio burned without moving, his hand held up and holding the burned match as it charred. The cottonwood caught on fire, its trunk blackening, the branches over Refugio's head snapping and sparking. Startled locusts exploded in flame and flew from the tree in a halo of comets.

Tomás stood and screamed. But the roosters were crowing. The chickens and the turkeys and the ducks were making their morning racket. The dogs were barking, the burros were braying. The crows were squabbling. It took the People a long time to hear him. Inside the big house, the patrón and his guests never awoke.

Huila had let her coffee go cold. She stared at him with her mouth slightly agape.

"Puta madre," she exclaimed.

"No one knows that story," Tomás said. "Not even my friend Aguirre."

He shifted in his seat, wiped his eyes.

"So!" he said. "What do you think?"

She patted him on the arm.

"What's for dessert?" she asked.

Six

THE GIRLS OF THE RANCHO revered Huila. Any one of them would have gladly been her daughter, though Huila was famously without child, or man. They said she had lost her betrothed in one of the great killings, but no one knew because no one would dare to ask. Her shadow could reach all the way across the ranch when she walked, and children rushed to cool their bare feet in the darkness of her passing.

Daily, the People were amazed that this holy woman with her yellow shawl and double-barreled shotgun, and her petrified balls of a buckaroo in her mysterious apron, was merely a servant to Tomás and Doña Loreto. They could not imagine those hands, which could bring babies forth from the womb, which could drive wicked spirits from the insane with an egg and some smoke, the same hands that castrated pigs and made teas that offended tapeworms so severely that they tumbled out of the guts of men and cows, that those sacred hands picked up Urrea plates, washed Urrea shirts, or carried out Urrea wads of soiled paper from the indoors excuse-me closet. The thought of genteel Loreto Urrea giving the great one an order was so deeply offensive that none of the People could bear to think about it much. If you were born to be a burro, they sighed, you can't be an eagle.

Cayetana thought about Huila as she walked through the dark. The baby was heavy in her arms, and at one point she snuffled and jerked, and Cayetana whispered, "Don't wake up! Please, don't wake up."

She pushed through the reeds on the far side of the pigpen. The big old sow hove to her feet and watched Semalú pass. She wiggled her flat plate nose, sniffing the air. Having launched hundreds of piglets into the world, the sow recognized a mother and a little one going by. She grunted a soft greeting.

Cayetana stopped outside her sister's door and collected herself. She knocked. The door scraped open, and one of her nieces peered up at her.

"Get your mother," she said.

Even though the house was only one room, and Cayetana could clearly see her sister, Tía, in the corner, her sister called out, "¿Quién es?"

"Soy yo," Cayetana replied. "La Semalú."

"Pinche Cayetana," Tía cursed softly, already exasperated by whatever idiocy the little tramp had thought up now.

Tía pulled open the door and stared. She was only twenty-three, but she was already old. She had three children of her own. Her teeth had started to go bad, and they hurt her all the time. She smoked every piece of cigarette and cigar she could find. Cayetana had never seen someone smoke so much. And Tía, who could not possibly ingest enough cigarettes, had developed a habit that at once fascinated and terrorized Cayetana. She used her own open mouth for an ashtray, smoke rising from her nostrils as if she were some strange beast in a fireside storyteller's cuento, before she opened her mouth and tapped the hot ash from her cigarette onto her tongue. It hissed.

"Tía," Cayetana said, taking in a deep breath and holding her back straight. "I have been called across the ranch to work."

"Work? Now?"

Tía sucked in some smoke, then studied the end of her cigarette: apparently, there wasn't yet enough delicious ash for her.

"Yes. There is a . . . a pregnant cow, you see. I have to go help."

Tía administered her ashes: *Ssss!*

"Liar," she said.

"No, it's true!"

"When will you be back?"

"By morning, I swear it."

"Give me the girl."

Tía took the bundle from Cayetana and accidentally dropped her cigarette. It was only an old hand-rolled, and it was only a stub, but the paper broke and the tobacco scattered at their feet.

"Goddamn it!" Tía shouted. "The baby knocked it out of my hand!"

"Sorry."

"Look what you did, pendeja!"

"Sorry, sorry."

"You're not working. You're going whoring."

"I —"

"Who are you going to see now? Another Yori?"

Cayetana backed away one step.

"I —" she said.

"Lárgate," her sister snapped, which was as rudely as the People could say *go away*.

"I will," Cayetana said.

On her way, she stopped and picked up her bundle of

things she had hidden beyond the pigsty. She would be afraid on the road, but she had been on the road before. She blessed Huila, and she appealed to the spirits to watch over her as she walked. She said a prayer for her child. When she got to the fence, she followed it to the big gate and slipped out onto the road to Ocoroni.

She walked fast. She never looked back. All she could think of were cherries. El Patudo's head. The dead. She was going to walk until she could think of nothing at all.

Seven

THE CHILDREN OF THE RANCHO were up before Huila, sitting in the cool dirt of their doorways, playing with marbles if they had them, small stones if they did not, chewing the crusty rind of an old tortilla, holding cunning little dolls twisted together from maize husks, unaware of God or the spirits; or they were killing doves with stones and slings and bringing the slaughtered birds to their mothers, who would pluck them and cook them. The doves' breasts on the greasy plates looked like the noses of Indians cut off by marauding Rurales. The Urrea children and Doña Loreto were the last to rise.

It was a good, bright day — the breeze carried high peach clouds with blue bellies, and the smell of salt drifted to the People all the way from the invisible sea. Huila had seen wraiths crossing the far hills, lines of the dead walking home. Others might have seen the passing shade of clouds on the hills, but Huila was not fooled. Those shadows were dead Comanches and dead gringos and a few Mexicans leading their sad ghost horses. Some of those poor bastards were going to find the road that led to Hell. Oh, well — you should have been better children to your Father, and better fathers to your children. Cabrones! Ay Dios! Huila had quartered an orange and left it under her special tree. It never hurt, for example, to leave the Maker a snack. And not some rotten onion you were throwing out, either! It didn't bother her that the coyote gobbled them as soon as she'd finished her prayers and walked away. Who was she to say that God did not use the coyote's teeth to chew His gifts?

She rocked along like the pendulum of the main-house clock, her bad hip singing inside her. Her rebozo was pulled about her head, her great black hair spiked with lightning bolts of white was twirled in a tight bun — no man ever saw her hair hanging free. Huila knew, even at this old age, even skinny as she was, with her belly pooched loose and empty above her rocky hips, that if any man saw her hair flying loose, he would be overcome with desire for her. A love that might never die out. Bola de bueyes! The girls of the rancho said you could see the stars in Huila's hair. Huila kept her devastating secret hidden as an act of charity.

Oh, but her back hurt when she bent to pass through the fences.

As she was bent nearly double, getting her leg through and pulling her skirt along so none of the vaqueros could look up in there and see her bloomers, she saw the tall girl lying in the dirt. Huila went to her and looked down. "Child," she said.

The girl looked up at her. She was barefoot, as all the children of the workers' village were. Her legs were scabbed with old mosquito bites, scratches, and holes from where she'd yanked out ticks. None of the children wore undergarments until they were older than seven, and they squatted wherever they were and flared out their rough dresses to make puddles in the dust.

"What are you doing?"

"Ants!" the girl said. "I'm watching ants!"

Huila squinted and finally saw the ants. Well now, her eyes were weaker, too. She hadn't even noticed the ants.

"Mochomo," Huila said.

"Ehui," the girl replied.

So she knew the mother tongue.

"You don't look like an Indian, child."

"What do Indians look like?"

Huila laughed.

"Us," she said.

The girl shrugged and turned back to the ants.

"Who is your mother?" Huila asked.

"The Hummingbird. She is gone."

"Ah! You're Nona Rebecca Chávez."

"I am Teresa."

Huila looked down at her. "I remember a different name."

Teresa rolled over and looked up at Huila. Her front was filthy, and she had dirt on her chin. "Huila," she said.

"Yes."

"I see you in church."

"Oh?"

"The Father told us about Saint Teresa. In church. Remember?"

"Yes. Wasn't she the one who flew? Did she smell like flowers?"

"She loved God more than anyone else in the world, and God let her do miracles. Now I love God more than anybody in the world. I like Saint Teresa. I am going to be her."

Huila smiled.

"You don't love God more than I do," Huila said.

"God loves you as much as He loves me," Teresita said. "But I love Him more than you do. I do."

"Mira, nomás," said Huila. "Pues, qué bueno."

"Yes, it is good."

"Don't kill those poor ants, then."

"Oh Huila! I am not killing them. I am praying for them."

Huila laughed.

"All right, then," she said. "Good luck."

"Thank you."

Teresita turned back to the ants.

"You seem more like Saint Francis to me than Saint Teresa," Huila said.

"No," said Teresita. "He's a boy. I'm a girl."

Huila turned to walk away, paused, and said, "How old are you, child?"

"Six."

"And is your life good since La Semalú left?"

"No, Huila."

This life was only meant for us to endure, not to enjoy, Huila thought. Joy was for rich men and Yoris. Huila pulled her rebozo tighter. If you were born to be a nail, you had to be hammered.

"Be strong . . . Teresa."

"I am."

Huila walked on, pausing just once to glance back.

Tía had one egg. "One fucking egg for all you fat pigs?" she yelled. The children all knew to say "Sí, Mamá." She sent her boy out to the mango huerta to steal one of the Urreas' iguanas. She could possibly be flogged for it; she didn't know — it couldn't be as bad as stealing a chicken. But what was she supposed to do? And when the boy came back with a writhing green lizard that whipped them all with its tail, and Tía took her rusty meat-cutter's knife to saw at the lizard's neck, Teresita scrambled out from her small spot and rushed out the door. She didn't understand why, with mangos and peaches, prickly-pear fruits and plums and leftover beans in the buckaroos' tin plates, Tía could never find anything to eat. Segundo, the big mean vaquero, once even showed her which flowers you could eat. Even if she wasn't allowed to steal squash from the gardens, nobody cared if she stuffed her mouth with yellow petals. They'd laugh and say she looked like a deer.

Tía had stopped waiting for word from Cayetana long ago, and she had even abandoned her hope that one day a letter might come with money in it. That little whore! She had left this half-breed bitch in her house and hadn't had the decency to leave a pound of beans or a chicken. Nothing. What was she supposed to do, boil rocks?

Teresita peeked in the door to find Tía stirring a pot. Tía studied the ash clinging to her cigarette, and tapped it onto her tongue. *Ssss!* "What do you want?" she said.

"Is that the iguana?" Teresa asked.

"What the devil do you think it is, you idiot? Did you see any other food here? Did you think I'd murdered my own children to make stew to feed you?"

"No, Tía."

"No, Tía."

"Am I an Indian?"

"We are the People."

"But what am I?"

"A little pig that eats too much."

"Tía . . ."

"Don't bother me with stupidity. What am I, what am I! What kind of ridiculous question is that?"

"I just want to know, Tía."

"If you're so curious, go ask your good friend Huila! Can't you see I'm busy?"

Ssss!

"Does it taste good, Tía? The cigarette?"

Tía studied the crooked cigarette and smiled.

"This mierda is the only good thing in my life," she said.

Teresita had learned to put her body to sleep at night. Her smacks and bruises ached when she lay down — Tía liked to spank, and she wasn't shy about using the wooden spoon. Teresita had to take charge of the uproarious parts of herself too naughty to be quiet at bedtime. Each night, Teresita would concentrate first on her feet, tired and sore from walking on rocks and hot dirt all day. She would order them: *Feet, go to sleep.* Feet were the least of her problems — you can always get your feet to sleep. She could feel the golden glow come over her toes and spread to her heels, and the pain would be replaced by the soft tingle of sleep. Once the feet were becalmed, she could bring the glow up her legs, smoothing it like cream over her sore spots. *Legs, go to sleep.* And the legs, too, would sleep. *Hips, belly, go to sleep.* And now the glow was inside her, warm as a full meal, heavy in her gut, and it throbbed a little with her heartbeat. She would go this way up herself and down her arms. It was the hands that caused the most trouble, those bad twins, always inciting each other to misbehave. She would have to be cross with them, scold them a little to get them to stop fidgeting and plucking and scratching. *Hands! I told you, get to sleep!* The hands were such a task that she fell asleep soon after, tired and happily numb.

On the day when Teresita set out to discover who she was, she by chance went to the same fruit tree her own mother had once leaned against. Teresita's hands went to the spots below where Cayetana had first gripped the trunk, and she looked out at the same corral, where Tomás was perched atop the same rail with the same vaqueros. Segundo was breaking a nasty little bronco, and the boys were laughing and shouting and waving their hats at the horse when it got too close to the fence. Above Teresita's head, furious cicadas assaulted the high branches of the fruit tree, fondling its fuzzy globes.

The next development of the day announced itself with a hiss.

"Psssst!"

At first, she thought Tía had discovered her and was eating a cigar. She glanced over — a gray cowboy-hat crown appeared over the edge of the watering trough. It looked as if the hat was floating along by itself, or being held aloft by a ghost.

"Hey!" the hat said.

"What!"

A freckled face atop a gangly neck appeared beneath the hat, now revealed to be ridiculously huge on the boy's head. It looked to Teresa as if his jug ears were the only things keeping the hat from falling to his chin.

The boy nodded at her once, then cut his head toward the corral, then made some kind of O shape with his mouth.

"What?" she repeated.

The kid wiggled his eyebrows, then jutted his chin at the corral.

She sniffed dismissively and moved back around to her side of the tree. What a strange and rude boy! She wanted to look at Don Tomás again. Don Tomás had never spoken to her, but he did wink once when she was walking into church. He never attended Mass, but he accompanied his fine wife and their children to the church, then spent the morning sitting in the little plazuela of Ocoroni, eating sliced fruit with chile powder that came in cones of wax paper.

"Oye, tú!"

"What?"

"Girl!"

She looked around the trunk. The boy's head rose and fell, the hat casting a reflection in the green water of the trough. He looked like some kind of puppet show.

"Is that him?" he said.

"Him?"

"Is that him, I said. Him. You know, the Sky Scratcher. The patrón."

"It is," she said.

"I knew it."

The boy turned his eyes back to Tomás and stared raptly. Teresa had never seen a look like that. She decided to investigate.

She walked over to the trough and squatted beside him and nudged him with her elbow.

"Hey!" he said. "Watch it."

He moved an inch away from her.

"You don't live here," she said.

"Hell no. Don't live here. Don't live anywhere."

"Ocoroni?"

"No."

He spit.

"You mean you're just — wild?"

She loved him.

"That's right," he sneered. "I'm wild, like that bronco, and don't forget it."

They watched the cowboys together.

"Why are you here?" she finally asked.

"Him. Urrea." He put a twig in his mouth like a cigarette and said, "That son of a whore is my father."

"No!"

"Yes."

"No!"

"Don't be stupid."

Teresa looked back at Tomás. He kicked one leg over the top of the rail and jumped down, landing with his arms in the air and bowing as the vaqueros applauded. "Ahora, chavos," he announced, "I am going to my little house for a little bottle of beer and some sweet little kisses from the little lips of my little wife."

"To go with your little pecker," Segundo said.

The boys whistled at Tomás as he walked away.

Teresita said to the skinny kid with the hat: "Stay here."

Fifty yards ahead of Teresita, Tomás was diminished in perspective, and he looked like a doll. She held up her hand and squinted her eye and it looked as if she held him in her grip. She smiled.

He was worried. She could see it all around him. She only caught the vaguest suggestion of color around some people, and then only as she looked askance at them. It was sometimes this way with her, but when she had asked Tía why she saw these penumbras, the response was a kick and a glare. She did not raise the topic again.

Tomás had worry leaking out from under his hat like smoke. Along with these purple clouds were some baffling vibrations that, for reasons she couldn't explain, looked to her as if they came from a lemon. He clutched his hat and yanked it off his head, and a great polychromatic up-welling spiraled into the sky. It wobbled as he drew his sleeve across his brow, and then he was charging up the porch steps and vanishing into the shadows of the big house. The door slammed.

Teresita knew she was not allowed to follow. She knew that a field worker caught inside the house would be in real trouble. But she was not there to steal. She would simply go in the door and call for him, and when he came, she would tell him she needed to talk to Huila. Like Tía said.

She put her bare foot on the first step and tried it. It seemed solid enough. The only steps she had ever climbed were the solid stone stairs that led into the church. She stepped up, and stepped up, and was on the porch without incident. She was amazed by the technology of the door-knob. It was clearly a fine object, a thing of shining brass and an egg shape made of some white thing that could have been a stone or a giant pearl or that thing they called ivory. She grabbed the doorknob and pulled. Nothing hap-pened. She pushed. She tried turning it, and there was a click that alarmed her, and then the door seemed to open of its own volition, and she followed it as it swung inward, its greasy hinges silent and fluid, and she was inside.

She was amazed to see that the patrón didn't have a dirt floor, and she stood fascinated by the wood planks under her feet. In the village, the really good housekeepers sprinkled lemon juice to wet down the ground dust and make every-thing smell fresh. But this floor was beyond any juicy sand. It shone, too, as if there were a thin flood of creek water upon it.

And there was perfume in the air, not lemons. Teresa slid the door shut and took inventory of the many fabulous objects before her. She did not know what Yoris called the fluttering white things that hung in the windows, but they were gauzy, and she could see light through them, as if they had been made of moth wings or ashes.

The walls were white. Pale green geckos moved across them and vanished behind a series of framed paintings of burros. These were Doña Loreto's melancholy studies, each burro endowed with huge teary eyes that bespoke a sorrow and a nostalgia for better times. Candles and oil lamps flut-tered, even though it was midday. Teresita didn't know if she should blow them out to save the patrón the cost of fresh oil and new wicks.

She reached out her foot and touched a thick carpet. Teresita had never felt anything like it. She stepped onto it and sank her toes into its plush surface. Gold and red designs twined their way around its edge, and its rich blue had roses and vines somehow woven into it.

A harried-looking woman suddenly appeared and said, "You, child, dump this and replace it!," shoving a sloshing chamber pot into her hands and then vanishing down the hall. "Fúchi!" Teresa said, and she put it down on the nearest couch.

A muted heartbeat arrested her attention. She looked around for the source of the sound. She saw a tall wooden tower in one corner, and it had a narrow glass door, and a swinging gold pendulum flashed inside. She walked to this strange square tree and looked up at its face. It was round, and across it, a blue moon seemed to float, followed by a swirly yellow sun. She did not know numbers, so the icons on its face meant nothing to her. She put her hands upon the wood column and felt it ticking. She put her ear to it to listen to such a wondrous thing.

Tomás came hurrying out of his office, waving a letter of credit over his head, already starting to call out for someone to fetch Segundo, and remembering that his spurs were still on and Loreto did not allow spurs in the house, when he skidded to a halt and beheld Teresita in congress with his big clock.

"How in the devil did you get in here?" he demanded.

She looked up at him serenely. "I followed you." She turned back to the clock. "This tree has a heart," she said.

He blinked. Looked at her more closely. He knew he'd seen her before. If Loreto saw her dirty bare feet on the rug — well!

"What, might I ask, are you doing?"

"I have been talking to this tree, but it won't answer me."

He smiled.

"It must be a very rude tree," she said.

He laughed.

He stepped up to the clock and looked at it. "I suppose you're right," he said. "Clocks are rude."

"This is a clock?"

"Yes, it is. It is a grandfather clock."

She seemed delighted by this information.

He thought he should be having her whipped or something, but he reached into his vest pocket instead. He didn't know why. "Look here," he said. He pulled out his pocket watch and clicked open its lid. It played a small bit of Mozart. She gasped.

"It is the grandson watch!" Teresa exclaimed.

He laughed once more.

"Make the music again."

He clicked the lid shut and reopened it.

"Be careful," she warned. "When it grows big like the grandfather, it won't fit in your pocket."

What an amusing little creature, Tomás thought.

Teresita looked around the room.

"Patrón?" she said.

"Yes?"

"Where do you keep your chickens? Do they sleep here?"

"No, no. They sleep in the henhouse."

"Your chickens have their own house?" she whispered.

He noticed the appalling chamber pot on the couch. His eyebrows rose. His household was, apparently, falling apart. He would have words with the maids about it as soon as he dealt with this small invader. He clapped his hands twice.

The harried woman stormed out of the hall and cried, "Sí, señor?"

"This young lady," he said, "seems to have wandered into the house by mistake. Could you fetch her a cool glass of juice, then see her out?"

The maid goggled at Teresita.

"I like juice," Teresita said.

"It looks like this is your lucky day," Tomás said.

The maid stepped forward to grab Teresita.

"Sir?" Teresita said.

He looked at her.

"Does Huila live here?"

He bent to her and said, "Huila. What do you want with Huila?"

"I need to ask her something."

He squatted before her, careful not to impale his buttocks with the starry rowels on his spurs.

"What do you need to ask her?"

"I don't know who I am," Teresita said. "My aunt told me Huila would know who I am."

Tomás stared into the face of this strange little girl. Then he looked up at the maid. Then he looked back at Teresita.

"What is your name?" he asked.

"Teresa."

"All right, Teresita," he said, rising. "Let us go find Huila for you. Let's find out who you are."

He took her hand and led her down the hall toward the kitchen.

She said, "Do you have any cookies? I like cookies."

He laughed again.

Teresita was amazed to see huge black cooking pots hanging from hooks on the walls of the kitchen. Tía had one big pot, one dented small tin pot, and a pan. Here, there were skillets, and there were pots as small as coffee cups, pots as large as bathtubs. A metal ring hung from the ceiling, and on hooks all around it hung more pots.

Tomás looked around and said, "Where is Carmela?"

"Carmela the cook, sir?" one of the girls asked.

"Right. Is she sick?"

"She no longer works here, sir," the girl said. "She left us three years ago."

He stood there and tried to hide his surprise.

"Oh," he said.

Teresita looked around with her mouth open. A mesh sack of onions dangled from an iron hook, yellow as tallow. Beneath this galaxy of pans and onions was a white metal table. This was where the girls chopped up the chickens and the meat with great cleavers that hung in rows on nails in the wall.

Tomás pulled a chair up to this table and helped Teresita climb up. The frazzled house girl from down the hall ladled a measure of tamarind juice from a clay barrel and poured it in a glass. She set the glass before Teresita.

"Gracias," Teresita said.

"Cookies, please," said Tomás.

A plate appeared with two fat gingerbread pigs lying on a folded cloth napkin. Teresita saw that among the rich, even food got a blanket. She bit off one pig's leg and chewed.

"Thank you," she said to Tomás.

"Oh, it's my pleasure," he replied.

They shook hands.

"I must get back to work," he said. "But the girls will

attend to you. Girls? Huila, please." He patted Teresita's shoulder and said, "Do call again."

They listened to him jingle as he went back down the hall.

The maid scrunched her nose at Teresita, then went to Huila's door at the back of the kitchen and knocked.

Eight

ONCE, OVER BREAKFAST, Tomás had told Huila his dream of the night before: he had fallen from the roof of the barn, and just as he was going to hit the ground, he had begun to fly. And he flew like this, only a foot above the ground, as if he were scuttling along in shallow water, only occasionally touching the ground to propel himself along. Then, as he glided over the tomato and cotton fields, he had come upon a giantess dressed all in white with a red skirt, and he had swum under her hem and up her great white legs. Loreto was upstairs, so he felt free to say such barbarities: barbarities, after all, were a fine art among the witty gentlemen of Sinaloa.

Huila had answered him with a baffling tale based on disturbing evidence that the flesh was the dream, and that death was the awakening, and then she had demanded to know details even he was not willing to discuss over scrambled eggs: had he actually entered the giant woman's privates, and if he had, did he find them to be meaty, or a starry void? Huila had not relented. "I didn't have the dream," she said, "and I'm not the one who is prancing around with his chile in his hand." Tomás had nearly spit coffee then, and he cried "Huila!" in his most affronted voice. Seemingly deaf to his outcry, she demanded an accounting of all the places in his life where the numbers four and six had revealed themselves.

Tomás, forever after, reminded himself to keep his dreams a secret.

Now, Huila beheld the small one eating her cookies and thought twice about how she should proceed. Ah, Saint Teresa herself. In the Urrea house, many ears were always listening. While this child, she could see right away, had the Hummingbird's hair — in spite of its strawberry-blond streaks — the rest of her was all Tomás. She glanced around the kitchen. The girls were watching the child as they worked, making eyes at each other. Surely, they were all thinking Teresita should be spanked, and her family charged with an offense for letting her in the main house. Some haciendas right there in Ocoroni would shoot trespassers and even their mothers and fathers.

Huila herself wondered how the child came to be in the kitchen and not back in the yard. Tomás, she thought, was soft. Perhaps, in some way he did not even suspect, he had recognized the child as his own. If he had been paying attention, he would have seen his own eyes staring right back at him. But the Yoris, they didn't notice the things right before their faces. They were too busy looking over the horizon.

"Teresita," she said.

"Yes?"

"How do you like your cookies?"

"Good."

"No," Huila corrected her. "When an adult asks you a question like that, you must answer politely, and say thank you." It was a child's job to learn.

Teresita watched her lips, watched the small vertical wrinkles that went up to the base of her nose.

"The cookies are good, thank you," she said.

"Very nice."

Huila finished her coffee.

"Give me a bite," she said. Teresita held her cookie to the old one's lips. "Gracias," she said.

"De nada," Teresita replied, already having absorbed her first lesson.

Huila rose.

"Can I talk to you?" Teresita asked.

"Let's take a walk," said Huila.

❈

Huila carried a great straw basket.

"I have a hankering for agua de jamaica," she said.

Teresita matched her stride for stride as they walked into the trees.

"I've never had agua de jamaica."

"Never?"

"No."

Had these people never taught her anything?

"What do you drink at Tía's house?" Huila asked.

"Water. Nothing."

"No wonder you don't know who you are," Huila said. "People like that." She bent through the rails of a fence and pointed. "The hibiscus tree." They went there and Huila said, "Pick the flowers. We'll fill the basket, then set the flowers out in the sun to dry."

Teresita plucked a red hibiscus from the lowest of the branches. She pinched off the bottom of the flower. She licked the bead of nectar from it. Huila smiled. She had done that when she was a girl.

"When the flowers are dry," Huila said, "we boil them with sugar. That's agua de jamaica."

"How much sugar?"

"How much do you like?"

"A lot."

Huila smiled.

"Me too," she said. "So we'll put in a lot of sugar! It needs sugar. It's like this pinche life, you see — so tart. It stings your mouth. You have to feel around inside it with your tongue to find the sweetness."

This was Teresita's second lesson.

Late in the day, Teresita made her way back to Tía's shack. She had saved one pig cookie for her auntie, and it was crumbly but still whole in Teresita's one pocket. The tired cotton pickers were hauling their heavy sacks of bolls out of the dusty fields, their prickled hands bloody and scabbed. The chile pickers had red eyes and runny noses, their eyelids puffy from the burning juice. Butchers lay together in the shade of a cottonwood, stinking of blood and fat, passing a cigarette and a clay jug of pulque. "Adios!" they called, and Teresita called back, "Adios!" Nobody but those Sinaloans said good-bye instead of hello when they saw each other.

Don Teófano, the handyman and occasional mule skinner, carried three planks over his old shoulder and walked along the track, bouncing as the ends of the wood bounced, making a rhythm that made his whole body bob as he walked. "Adios," she told him. He raised a hand off the boards, then slapped it back down when they started to tip off his shoulder. His sharp sweat smelled almost exactly like the leaky pine boards, and Don Teófano made his way into the distance in a cloud of turpentine and pitch.

Teresita watched the girls older than she was: girls with jugs of water balanced atop their heads; weary laundry girls, smelling of soaps and salts, their boiled hands and feet white as mushrooms, and their hair escaping from under their tightly bound scarves; the evening cook on her way to the main house, her best church clothes on her back, and frazzled huaraches on her feet — her only good shoes hung off her fingers as she rushed to work. "Adios!" Teresita knew that the cook's boyfriend, one of Segundo's buckaroos, would be there at ten at night to greet her and walk her back to her house seven doors down from Tía's.

"Adios!"

The ones with sick children and dying old ones brought them out into the gentle sunset. They'd been locked inside their stifling houses all day, and it was their first chance to feel a cool breeze. A curled old woman lay huddled in a wheelbarrow, wrapped in her rebozo and looking like a puppy. Writhing young men tied to chairs with hemp rope raised their palsied hands and pointed at the birds with their knuckles. Great cascades of drool fell from their chins, and they shrieked and laughed at the crows, the donkeys, the scampering children, the astonishment of the reddening sun. Mothers smoothed their unruly hair with old stiff-bristled brushes. "Adios!" Teresita called to them, and they called back, "Os!" and "Dos!" and "Awoss!" and reached for her as she went by.

And there was Segundo, slouched on his mount, and watching it all with a small smile on his lips. "Adios!" she called to the big vaquero. His dark hat turned toward her, and one finger rose and touched the brim.

Teresita had told Huila that Tía called her mother a whore. "That is not correct," Huila told her. And Tía also called Teresita a whore. "That is a sin," Huila said.

Teresita pushed through the crooked door of the shack. Tía was sitting in the one chair at her small table. Teresita's bedding was wadded up against the wall. Tía's children were still outside.

"I wish I had a cigarette," Tía said. "Did you see any cigarette butts lying around out there?"

Teresita shook her head.

"No, Tía. But I brought you something else."

She pulled the cookie out of her pocket, brushed off some lint, and handed it to her auntie.

"Oh?"

Tía actually smiled for a moment. She grabbed the cookie and bit off its head and closed her eyes. She knew she should save the rest for her children. Any mother would save it. She took another bite. The children were small — they'd need less of the cookie than she did. Didn't she deserve it? A little bit of cookie after all this shit she had to live with? One last nibble, and — ah cabrón! — the cookie was gone.

"Do you have another?"

"No, Tía."

Tía drummed her fingers.

"Where did you get it?" she asked. She was thinking that perhaps La Tunita might have a cigarette. She knew women who traded kisses to the vaqueros for smokes, but she was not going to do something like that. Not kisses.

"Huila gave it to me," she said.

"Where did you see Huila?"

"I went and found her."

Tía looked at her.

"What do you mean you went and found her?"

"You told me to go ask Huila who I was, so I did."

"*What do you mean you went and found her?* Did you go to her at her work? Was she visiting someone?"

"No."

Tía was scaring her a little. The crumbs of the cookie were still in the corners of her mouth. Her eyes were too bright. She bent to Teresita and grabbed her arms.

"What do you mean, then? What do you mean?"

"Tía. Tía, stop. I went there. To the house."

Tía simply froze. Her eyes seemed to look far beyond Teresita. Then she looked back into her eyes.

"The house," she whispered.

Tía let her go. "You Goddamned idiot," she said. "Oh, you little fool."

"I —"

"Shut up!" Tía tore at her own hair. "Shut up!" She turned in every direction, as if she could find a hidden door in one of her walls. "Goddamn you!"

Her boy came through the door. She wheeled on him and screamed: "Get out! Now, pendejo!" He glanced once at Teresita and ran back outside.

Tía took up her heavy wooden spoon.

"You stupid little shit," she said.

"Tía?"

Tía snagged Teresita's hair as she tried to escape, and she twirled her hand in it, forming a painful knot that pulled Teresita's scalp taut.

"Ay!" she cried. "Ay, ay!"

And the spoon fell.

❊

Hitting the ground awoke her.

Tía had carried her outside and tossed her over the top of the pigpen fence.

"If you are going to act like a pig, then live with the pigs. I'm through with you!"

The People did nothing. They stepped back into their huts and dropped their blankets over the doorways. Tía ushered her children inside. Teresita rolled over and got up on her knees. Pig shit burned in her welts.

Tía reappeared.

"And don't you die on me!" she said. "Do you hear? That's all I need, more trouble like that!"

The rough door slapped shut.

Teresita felt golden ants swarm her. A rush of tickling up her arms and legs, relentless feet strumming her tissues like guitar strings. Her eyes closed.

Then she was falling. Falling through the earth, through the spaces between the stones, into the deeper nothing of the sky. Falling, where the sky itself became small again and was contained inside her own eye. Falling through her eye into the place where dreams harden into stones and become the ground.

Corridors of flame.

Obsidian rooms.

Her days rose about her, from womb to playtime, from this moment to far ahead of herself: womanhood and mirrors. Rings of light fell through houses she did not know.

She sparked inside herself, her brain sputtered like a roman candle, whirling, fire, whirling, sparks —

— rebozo spun tight as a cinnamon roll, on her head, heavy water jug balanced upon it, riding her skull as if she were a donkey —

— fat bullets, cold as lizards, cold and greasy, cold and sliding on their grease into the receivers of rifles, and hands, dark hands, working the levers —

— laundry, stretched on river stones, foam moving down, down, down the river, white islands of foam, going down —
— maize dough in a ball, slapped by women's hands, taking shape, disk of the sun, flesh of the sun —
— down —
— cottonwood fluff going
down —
— Huila, walking
through trees —
down —
— the Hummingbird, though she had no memory of seeing the Hummingbird, she knew who it was. "Mother," she whispered, as the Hummingbird watched rain above a churning sea, coming
down.

In the dream, she traveled far.

Nine

HUILA HAD SAT ON A ROCK, and she had used a small knife to peel an orange: the peel had curled out and fallen to the ground in one endless piece, and Huila had spoken. *Your mother, child, was the prettiest girl on the ranch. She could make birds land on her fingers. It's true. And they called her Hummingbird, Semalú, and she spoke the mother tongue but learned Yori when the troubles came and her own family was scattered. Your grandmother and grandfather were good people. Poor people. Your grandmother was funny, and she had the gift come down from her own mother. What gift? The only gift there is, child. The birthing and working of the plants. That gift. Your grandfather was Catholic, and your grandmother followed the old ways. She was Mayo, and her own mother was Yaqui. Your grandfather was Tehueco, and the soldiers put him in a tree before you came.*

Your father? Ah, your father. You're too young now to hear the story. But find Huila later, when you can hear what Huila has to say, and I will tell you about your father. Do you hope he is a prince, child? A king? I will tell you this much — your father is not a bad man. Just silly. You will soon learn that almost all men are silly. Even the priests are silly. But your father is a kind man, and he has many acceptable traits, and he even owns many wonderful things that someday you might have.

And he is very, very handsome.

Teresita lay awake, leaning against the redolent flank of the she-pig. The old sow's vast heart thumped deep inside her, like the relentless tock of the grandfather clock she had seen in the main house. It seemed like weeks ago. The old pig, on her side, lazily offered her fourteen nipples to this small human shoat, and she drowsed happily, feeling the warmth of the child against her gut and her sides. One foot stirred slightly in her sleep as she dreamed of finding a broken door in the great storeroom larder across the road, and it sped up as in her dream she discovered sweet potatoes and gobbled them while her hundreds of lost piglets regrouped around her.

Teresita had tried to call up the sleep glow to stop her bruises from aching, but it was no use. Clumps of mosquitoes landed on her legs, but she didn't even feel them feeding on her. The heavy air above her choked off the celestial light, but slow throbs of lightning pulsed red and gold far to the west, over the invisible sea. And the moon was up there, parted and orange, and a lone star burned near the curve of lunar glow. Teresita lay back against the sow and tried to see ghosts — the old women said you could see them out of the corners of your eyes — but concluded the flittering shadows above her were only bats.

"Hey!"

She looked around in the dark.

"Oye, tú!"

She looked over the pig.

"Who is it?"

"Me."

"Who?"

"Me!"

He stood up. It was the skinny boy from the horse trough with the ridiculous big hat.

"Me!" he said. "Buenaventura!"

In spite of the stiffness in her back and legs, and the ache of her beaten body, she giggled.

"What kind of name is Good Luck?" she said.

"It's *my* name," he said.

He stood among weeds and small bushes, and his hat was glowing grayly in the moonlight. His arms were longer than his sleeves, and his wrists hung out from the frayed cuffs.

"Are you all right?" he asked.

She started to cry.

"Oh, don't do that," he said.

He went to step forward, but a tree branch knocked his hat off. He scrambled to retrieve it, and he slammed it on his head. This made her laugh again. She was laughing and crying, wiping her nose on her dress.

He crouched by the fence and looked in at her.

"It stinks."

"I know."

"You should get out of here."

"I don't know where to go."

He rested his arms on the crosspiece.

"I saw what happened," he said. "You should get away in case she wakes up."

"You were there?"

He held up a skinny little revolver. "I'll shoot her next time."

"No, Good Luck, no."

"I'm an outlaw, you know. I'm not scared of shooting

people!" He brandished the gun and tried to look fierce. "Soy un pistolero!"

"No."

He stuck the gun back in his belt.

"You let me know if you want some cabrones shot," he said. He sat with his back to the pig fence. "Me los acabo!" he boasted.

She sat against her side of the fence with her back pressed to his, only a plank between them. She started to cry again.

"Pinche life!" he said. He looked over his shoulder at her. "What are you called?"

"Teresita."

He reached back over his shoulder. "All right, Teresita, try this."

She reached up. He dropped a chunk of horehound candy in her palm. She put it in her mouth. They sat there sucking their candy together, not saying anything.

"I stole it," he finally said.

And, after a while: "Pinches mosquitoes! Let's get out of here!"

"I don't know if I can get up."

He got up and hopped over the fence and prodded the sow away with one worn boot and looked at Teresita.

"I been beat before. This was barely a spanking. You can always get up!"

"I can't."

"All right."

He bent to her and heaved her from the ground and over his shoulder.

He blew air out of his nose.

"You peed on yourself!"

"Sorry."

He handed her his hat.

"Take this."

He managed to climb over the fence without dropping her.

The pig asked him, "Grut?"

"Where am I taking you?"

"I don't know."

"Better decide."

"Take me to Huila."

"The witch?"

"She's no witch."

"She's a bruja desgraciada," he insisted.

Teresita spanked him with his own hat.

"She is no witch!"

"Hnf," he grunted as he started out.

His big hands wrapped around her calves as she bounced head-down over his shoulder.

"You're fat," he said.

She smacked him again with his hat.

"Don't make me shoot you," he warned.

They passed under the deep shadows of the peach trees.

"I wish I was dead," she said.

"No you don't," he replied.

"I want my mamá. I want my papá."

"That's what everybody wants."

The house was a great black hump against the night. No lights burned in any windows. He bent down and slid her off his shoulder like a sack of beans.

"Dad's house," he said. "Give him my regards."

Dad? she thought.

"Don't go!"

"Can't stay."

"Just a minute."

He squatted down beside her and stared at the house.

"These rich men," he said. "They don't care about you or me."

"He's not like that."

"They're all like that."

He picked up some pebbles.

"Where does the witch sleep?"

She pointed. He went to the black window beside the back door. He tipped his hat to Teresita and pitched a bunch of pebbles to rattle against the glass. He ducked down, but nothing happened. He threw more pebbles. Nothing. He took up a bigger rock and threw it hard: it smacked into the wall beside the window with a sound not unlike a rifle shot. "Son of a whore!" Huila's voice came from within. "What hijo de la chingada is at my window!" Buenaventura whipped another handful of pebbles, and a match flared inside, and the wobbly yellow of lamplight resolved itself through the curtains. "Stay right there, cabrón! Stay right there! I have my shotgun, and I'm going to give you both barrels!" Buenaventura pantomimed broad laughter, putting both hands on his gut and rocking back and forth. "Just wait right there, buey! I'm coming! I'm coming out right now, and when I come out, I'm going to let you have it!" He scampered around like a monkey, making Teresita laugh. He did this little dance until the latch on the back door clacked loudly. He bent nearly double and ran into the bushes with a wave.

The door banged open, and Huila emerged, hair a wild tangle, lamp in one hand and shotgun in the other, veering in every direction.

"Show yourself, desgraciado!"

Teresita called out.

"Huila!"

The shotgun aimed in her direction. Huila raised the lamp and squinted out.

"Who is that?"

"Over here," Teresita said.

"Quién es?"

"It is I, old woman," Teresita called. "The Hummingbird's daughter."

Huila let the twin hammers down on her shotgun, and she set it against the wall. She stepped down from the small porch and said, "Child?"

"Here."

Huila held out the lamp and walked to her.

"Oh, no," she said. "What have they done to you?"

"I got spanked."

"Yes," said Huila. "Yes, you surely did."

She pulled Teresita up and lifted her in one arm. Teresita wrapped her legs around the old woman, and she rode her hip back to the house. Buenaventura, watching from the bushes, nodded when the door slammed and the light was extinguished. Then he ran to the porch and stole the shotgun Huila had left behind.

"Apparently," the old woman said, "I can't escape you."

She set Teresita on the white metal table in the kitchen. It was cold to the touch, but it felt good against the welts and bruises.

"Did you pee on yourself?"

"Sí, Huila."

"Ay, niña," Huila said, shaking her head. "No matter what

happens to you, don't ever pee on yourself. They always know they've won when you pee on yourself. I've seen grown men, when they're tied to the post, pee down their legs in fear. I've seen them, when the noose is on their necks, letting water escape. Fear kills you twice, and it gives your enemy pleasure." She lifted lids on clay pots and sniffed at their openings. "That's why I don't like pinches dogs! They fall over and wag their tails and pee all over themselves to let you know you're the master. Pah! We have no masters!" She pointed at Teresita. "So no peeing!"

"I promise."

"Good."

Huila dipped some water from a bucket and went to the fire, which was a pulse of banked coals. She put the water in a pot and hung the pot on a black iron hook, then built a small pyramid of sticks beneath it. The fire sprang up when she blew on it.

"Nobody can build a fire like old Huila!" she said.

Doña Loreto had ordered some cherry pies from Guaymas. They had arrived in flat wooden cases, and only one of them had spoiled — it was alive in its slim shelf with maggots, and Loreto had sent it to the pigpen. But the other six pies were in fine shape, and Huila now took a long knife and cut a drooling wedge and put it on a plate and set the plate on the table beside Teresita. She handed the girl a fork.

Teresita sniffed the pie. It was red. For some reason she did not understand, it made her nostalgic for her mother.

"Eat."

"Sí, Huila."

Teresita grabbed the fork in her fist and ripped a glob of pie loose and stuffed it in her mouth.

"God," Huila sighed.

"What?"

The old one took the fork away from Teresita and opened her fist and turned her wrist and put the fork back in her hand, balanced on her fingers.

"This is how you hold a fork," she said.

And: "You don't have to eat the whole pie in one bite! Nobody's going to take it away from you."

And: "Chew with your mouth shut. If you want to live with donkeys, eat like a donkey. If you want to live among human beings, eat like a human being. You chew like a churn making butter."

"Sí, Huila."

"Milk?"

"Yes, please."

"More pie?"

"Yes, please."

"Well, I might have a small bite of pie myself."

Together, they scraped the whole pie tin clean.

※

"It hurts," Teresita said.

"Yes."

Huila cleaned the black pig mud out of the wounds. She had wrapped crushed cuasia in a cheesecloth, then soaked it in the hot water from the hanging pot.

"Don't squirm."

"Ay."

Huila felt — what? What was it she felt in her fingertips? A flash of the golden sparks, perhaps. A sudden onrush of heat through the skin.

"Do that again," she said.

"I did nothing," Teresita replied.

Huila put down her cuasia and put her fists on her aching hips for a moment.

"Give me your hands," she said.

Teresita put out her hands, palm down. Huila placed her palms against Teresita's.

"Make them hot," Huila said.

Teresita didn't even think about it. She told her palms to warm, and they heated immediately upon Huila's out-stretched hands.

"Mira, nomás," Huila said.

She pulled up a chair and sat, looking up at Teresita. She fished a cigar stub out of her apron and lit it with a red-headed kitchen match.

"My hands are always hot," Teresita said.

"I see."

Huila smiled. One never knew where the gift would appear. God, too, has His jests.

Loreto came into the kitchen in a long white gown with a lacy frill at her chest, her voluminous hair wild around her head in a nimbus, her scents coming upon Teresita like a fog from the coast: oranges, lilacs, ginger. Teresita had never seen teeth that white.

Huila stood with her head bowed and said, "Doña."

Although she was cruel to Tomás, she deferred to Loreto with a kind of love no man could understand. Loreto knew the rules imposed on the woman with no medicine by the light of the day, the endless despair of suspecting her man was also the man of a hundred more, none of them as kind or lovely or strict or clean, and she knew the agonies of the birthing bed too well.

"I heard voices," Loreto said, pulling her hair back. "I thought for a moment that a ghost was in the house, or a bandit."

Teresita smiled at this apparition.

"Hello," said Loreto.

"Do you clean your teeth?" Teresita asked.

Loreto didn't know what to say to that, so she simply said, "Yes."

"We had a small problem," Huila said.

Loreto bent to Teresita's lacerated thighs.

"Ay Dios," she said. "Who did this?"

"My aunt," Teresita said.

"And why on earth would she do this?"

"I got caught in your house this morning," Teresita said.

Huila remained quiet. She wished that the child would keep her mouth shut. But God arranged the scene and had His plans for the outcome. Huila was still learning to allow fate to flow unimpeded.

Loreto sat in Huila's chair.

"I suppose that was very naughty of you," she said. "Coming inside uninvited."

"She was looking for me," Huila said.

Loreto raised her eyebrows and leaned toward Teresita.

"Huila," she said, "is very, very naughty! No wonder you got in trouble."

Teresita giggled. Loreto smiled and stared up into those curious eyes. She looked at the sleepy eyelids, the slightly drooping left eye. They looked so familiar. And the pointed nose, and those lips, with their slight pout.

She turned to Huila. Her face was eloquent, though her

mouth remained shut. Huila flicked some lint from her dress, looked around the kitchen, sighed. When she finally made eye contact with Loreto, she shrugged.

Loreto knew the features of the Urrea face. She was not only wife and lover to Tomás. It was a tradition on the haciendas to keep the bloodline clean, and cousins often married cousins. Wives were chosen like good mares, for bloodline and looks. Don Miguel, the great patriarch, dreamed of siring whole lines of Urreas whose lineage was all Urrea on each side. He dreamed of a baptism certificate that would read: Fulano Urrea Urrea Urrea Urrea! Loreto was cousin as well as wife. She had been looking at those lips all her life.

Terrible questions burned in her, awful doubts and heavy sorrows, and she could not voice them, and she would not think about them.

She rose. She patted Teresita on the head. She was five years older when she rose than when she'd sat down.

"Of course," she said, "you will stay with us. I will fetch you a nightgown. And then we will all sleep. Let's sleep late, eat a nice big breakfast, and forget all about this night."

When she left the kitchen, her smell hung in the air and slowly faded away to nothing.

Teresita could not believe you wore a nice pink dress to bed, and she was startled by the underdrawers. Huila had made her sponge herself off, and had made her pay special attention to her nalgas and her fundillo. Huila herself had washed Teresita's feet. Teresita was startled to see the water in the bowl looking like chocolate frothing in a cup when Huila was through. She had no idea she had been so dirty.

Her legs were still sore and shaky, so Huila carried her to bed. Teresita had never felt sheets. She ran her hands over them, slid her legs across the delightful coolness of their whiteness. Huila pulled her chamber pot out from under the bed and said, "If you have to pee, pee in here. If you have to make caca, then go outside. I don't want to be smelling caca all night!" She blew out the candle. "What's left of the night," she grumbled.

Teresita thrilled to the weight of the old woman when she lay down beside her. The bed sank and squealed. Teresita waited to see if it would break, but it did not. Huila rolled on her side. Teresita rested against her back.

"Is the pillow all right?" Huila said.

"Yes," Teresita answered. "It's very soft."

"I always like a good pillow," said Huila. Immediately thereafter, she began to snore.

Teresita lay there as if resting in a cloud.

She thought she was awake, but she was not.

This time she dreamed of a great field of blue flowers. She was barefoot. Three old men watched her from a distance. They were of the People. She recognized their nut-brown skin and their white clothes, their straw hats. One old man raised a hand and waved to her once. His voice was small — she could barely hear him. He called out a mysterious word to her: "Huitziltepec."

He pointed.

She turned and saw a hill covered in blossoms.

She walked up the hill. Her feet hurt from the pebbles in the ground, and the path turned to a clear stream of water, and the water cooled her feet and the rocks were yellow and purple and round as eggs. She thanked the ground for its mercy.

At the summit, she discovered a white rock.

She sat.

She heard a hum above her head. She looked up: a hummingbird made of sky came down from the heavens. It was too small to be seen, yet she could see it. Its blue breast reflected the world as it descended. Its wings were white, made of writing. Although she did not have words, she recognized them. The hummingbird's wings had been written with a quill pen.

It landed on her knee. It had its back to her. It turned to the left. When it faced her, it had a small white feather in its mouth. She knew to reach out to it. The semalú dropped the feather into her hand.

Soon, the roosters were crowing.

※

Teresita opened her eyes.

Huila was kneeling in prayer before a low altar built against the wall. A picture of the Virgen de Guadalupe stood on the altar, and a tall wooden crucifix. Stones, shells, a few bundles of sage and incense grass, and a paper-wasps' nest. Small figures of Huila's saints stood on either side of the cross. Teresita recognized Saint Francis, because he had doves on his shoulders and head. To one side of the altar stood a lone glass of water.

"Huila?" she said.

The old one held up a finger.

Teresita waited.

When Huila was through praying, she braced herself on the altar and rose.

"Yes, child?"

"What is the water for?"

"It is the soul," Huila said. "It is the soul, cleansed of sins."

"Is it your soul?" Teresita asked.

"I wish it were, child." Huila stretched. "I wish it were."

She picked up Teresita's mud-stained smock. It looked, in this morning light, terrible and ratty and filthy. Teresita was suddenly ashamed.

"This won't do," said Huila.

She went out into the house. Teresita slipped from bed and looked at Jesus on the cross. She shyly touched Guadalupe's dress. She picked up the water glass and turned it, looking through it at the sun. There were little flecks of dirt in it, floating back and forth as she turned the glass.

When Huila came back, Teresita said, "I think you missed some sins."

Huila had brought her a dress from Loreto's daughter. She pulled it over Teresita's head.

"Qué bonita," she said.

Teresita posed.

Huila took up her brush, and in spite of many complaints, dragged the knots out of Teresita's hair.

She then made Teresita put on a pair of huaraches. Teresita hated them. But Huila insisted.

"Ladies," she said, "wear shoes."

"Then I don't ever want to be a lady."

Huila nodded.

"What you don't want, child, is to be an old lady like Huila."

Teresita tried the sandals, scuffing her feet on the clay tile floor.

"Huila?" she said. "How old are you?"

Huila thought.

"I must be . . . I must be fifty years old now."

Teresita was astounded at this great tower of years, but she remained still and followed the old one into the kitchen.

Huila poured her a cup of coffee and stirred in five spoons of sugar and some boiled milk. She served herself the same. They ate bolillo rolls that they dipped in the coffee cups. The coffee turned the rolls into mushy bread pudding, and Huila slurped hers like a mule at a trough. Then they ate bananas and stale bits of sweet rolls.

Huila tucked a bolillo in her pocket and said, "Let's go pray."

"You already prayed."

"Oh," said Huila. "You never finish praying."

She opened the back door and stood there.

After a moment, she yelled: "Who the hell took my shotgun!"

At the sacred spot, Huila showed Teresita how to light the sage and the incense grass in her old seashell, and which way to turn when she offered up the smoke to the four directions. "It's easy to pray in the morning," she said. "That way you can always start with the east, then all you do is turn to your left every time you pray."

Itom Achai received Huila's smoke and seemed to be in a good mood that day.

They broke the bolillo into halves and left it on a rock.

"Should we have brought God coffee?" Teresita asked.

This caught Huila up short. Did God take coffee? And if He did, would He want it black, or did He enjoy sugar and milk — all items He, in His own wisdom, had made in the first place? It was obvious that God enjoyed wine — only red wine — but coffee, that was altogether a mystery. And everyone knew God accepted tequila — God loved magueys, after all — and tequila was made with prayers to the Virgin Mary, when the juices were still milky and being strained through white sacramental cloths — and tequila was clear and everybody knew God loved a good clear liquid for all its symbolic power — but coffee would require study.

Huila made her rarest confession that day: "I don't know."

They walked back to the workers' village. The People were already out of their houses. When they saw Huila coming, and Teresita — just last night lying in pig mess — now in a radiant Yori dress — and *shoes* — they stepped back into their homes and shut their doors.

"Wait," Huila said.

She knocked at Tía's door.

When Tía opened it and saw Huila, she fell back a few steps.

"Good morning!" Huila bellowed as she shoved her way in, then slammed the door.

It took a while. Teresita waited. The big she-pig poked her nose through the slats and whiffed Teresita's dress. Teresita scratched her drippy snout.

When Huila came back out, she was smiling benignly. "Good day!" she called back into the hut, as if they had just taken tea. She patted Teresita on the shoulder and said,

"I have chores to do." She walked off, singing to herself. Teresita looked back at the house. Tía stood before her, white in the face. She had sweat on her lip, and her lids fluttered, as if a stiff breeze were blowing in her eye.

"Would you —" Tía began. She swallowed. "Would you like something to eat?"

"No thank you, Tía," she said. "I had breakfast at the main house."

She pushed past her aunt and went inside.

The People stared at Tía.

She said, "Don't look at me!"

But she knew Huila had cursed her, and forever more, they would all stare like ghosts, and none of them would ever say a word.

Ten

THE ENGINEER DON LAURO AGUIRRE arrived in a flurry of dust and rattling. He was driving a smart cabriolet pulled by a handsome black horse. Gómez and his Rurales saw him through the gate of the ranch, then rode on, in search of wanderers to bushwhack.

Tomás greeted his old friend atop his massive palomino, El Tuerto. El Tuerto wasn't one-eyed, even though his name implied it, but his troubling habit of going sideways was cured by giving him a single blinder, which forced him to follow just one of his badly crossed brown eyes.

This solution meant that he was blind on his right side when wearing his eye patch, and Tomás had to rely on precise spur work to keep him from tumbling off hillsides or falling into bogs. But once controlled, El Tuerto was a magnificent stallion, taller than all the other horses on the ranch, with the hair of a French courtesan. Any other rancher would have made El Tuerto into a plow horse, or would have shot him, but Tomás had seen his glory right away. "If he were a woman," he'd told Segundo, "I would marry him."

"Sure, boss," Segundo had replied. "Everybody likes blonds."

Aguirre steered the little wagon toward the house, and Tomás rode beside him, regaling him with tales of the quotidian wonders of his life. "Yes, yes," Aguirre repeated, "yes, yes." Huila passed before him, her new shotgun under her arm. She didn't even glance at him, but trudged into the distance.

"The curandera," Aguirre offered.

"That's the one."

"She looks cranky."

"When doesn't she?"

"Say, Urrea, my dear cabrón. I've been meaning to ask you. Are there Indians hereabouts? Do you have the red man working for you?"

"Claro," Tomás replied. "It's their land." He thought better of that comment and amended it: "It was their land."

"Apaches?"

"No."

"Yaquis?"

"A few. But we're pretty far south for too many Yaquis."

"Who, then?"

Tomás blew air out of his mouth.

"Quién sabe. Let's see — Ocoronis, some wandering Pimas, I think, or Seris — far from home if they are here. I know there are Tehuecos and Guasaves in the bunch. The Guasaves come up from Culiacán looking for work. We have Mayos."

"Mayas?" cried Aguirre. "I thought the Maya to be in the far south! A jungle people! Are these not the realms of the barbarian Chichimeca? The Dog People who laid waste to the temples and the pyramids? Are there Mayan ruins here?"

These fucking lectures.

"Not Mayas, pendejo. Mayos. O! May-*o!*"

Aguirre drew up before the main house and put his reins down on the seat and set the foot brake.

"Good Lord, man," he sniffed, "there is no need to get huffy."

By the time Tomás had collected his thoughts to insult Aguirre again, the Engineer was knocking at the door and calling for Loreto.

Inside, Loreto had already lined up her children. Aguirre had never really noticed them, except to note that there were several. He had not counted them, and he couldn't remember their names. "Yes, yes, good to see you, how do you do," he intoned, like a priest unloading wafers or shaking hands after Mass. Children, yes, certainly. He moved on to Loreto and clutched her hands, crying, "You remain as lovely as peach blossoms in spring!" He then baffled yet delighted Loreto by slipping into Italian for a moment, calling her a *fiore di pesca*. He lifted her hands in his and kissed them, taking the opportunity to smell her skin.

Loreto! Blossom of warm sugar! Sprinkled with cinnamon and vanilla! Loreto! Angel of Ocoroni!

"My," she said.

"Aguas," Tomás warned, which was his way of letting them know he was watching, invoking the ancient and honorable warning offered in Iberia when Spanish maids were about to toss the chamber-pots' contents out the windows.

"Pardon me," Aguirre said, taking a final surreptitious sniff: garlic and bacon! "I always lose my head when confronted with your lovely bride." Loreto felt a rush of embarrassed joy, for in claiming to be powerless over himself in the face of her beauty, he had not only absolved himself of adulterous guilt, but complimented her so deeply that she could never explain it even to herself, while equally complimenting Tomás as the most macho man in the region — the man who had landed this astounding powerhouse of beauty and grace, the delicious Loreto! Aguirre basked in this small coup as he stood straight and beamed at everyone.

Tomás slapped him on the back, which was a signal to all others to vanish into the far regions of the house. "Who can blame you, my beloved son of a whore?" Tomás said, all the while implying that he would indeed blame — forever — should lips meet anything other than back of the hand. He led Aguirre into his study and decanted brandy. Aguirre, sitting back in a red-gold chair beneath the library shelf, accepted the snifter and, silently, raised it in a toast to his friend.

"I'm glad you're here, old friend," Tomás said.

"I was afraid I'd miss your party," Aguirre said. "Things are complicated on the roads."

"Did you see bandits?"

"Only in the form of government agents."

"That sort of talk could stretch your neck," Tomás said.

"Oh? Are there spies even in your house?"

Tomás smiled.

"The bandits are all dead," Aguirre informed him. "And many Indians. Americanos are buying land in Chihuahua and Sonora on deeds from Mexico City." He waved his hand before his face. "There are *department stores*."

"What is this?"

"Germans selling coats and underpants and pots and toys all in one great store."

"No meat?"

"No."

"No steaks?"

"No! No meat at all."

"What kind of a store sells no meat?"

"Tomás! Por Dios! Pay attention! A department store."

"What do they sell?"

"I just told you what they sell."

"No meat."

"Correct."

"German underpants."

"Well. As a figure of speech."

"Ah."

"Things, in other words."

"Ah!"

"It is very North American."

"No meat," said Tomás. "It is the end of ranching."

"No, no," the Engineer said. "There will be department stores of meat!"

Tomás raised his glass.

"Let us drink a toast, then, to the future!"

A girl brought in a tray with fluted glasses filled with seviche, and a bowl of the delightful raw shellfish known as pata de mula. Tomás had ordered it sent from Los Mochis. The seafood had arrived in tunnels bored into blocks of ice that were wrapped in burlap and buried in mounds of sawdust. Beside the seviche, there was a glass bowl of toothpicks, a small plate of lime slices, a pinch bowl of crushed salts, and a cup filled with salsa borracha.

Aguirre immediately drenched a disk of pata de mula in lime, skewered it on a toothpick, and began the long wrestling match that passed for chewing when eating the recalcitrant shellfish. Tomás, not to be outdone, slurped up fish and lime juice from his glass, then spooned salsa borracha directly into his mouth. He turned bright crimson and his nose began running. Aguirre slopped salsa onto his seviche and spooned out a great burning gob. Tears came to his eyes. They were both sweating profusely.

"Chingue a su madre," Tomás said, but he said it the way the men said it, as one Asiatic ululation: "Heeng-yasumá!"

"Yes," Aguirre concurred, "it is tasty."

Segundo stopped by and said, "Pata de mula!"

"Dig in," Tomás invited.

When the chiles hit his tongue, Segundo sighed: "Hijo de su madre."

It was so painful they had no further words for its wonder.

There was a long pause before Aguirre spoke again.

"This election will affect you, my reckless friend," the Engineer prophesied.

Tomás absorbed this quietly.

The great dictator of Mexico, the President for Life, General Díaz, the Grand Don Porfirio, onetime hero of

Liberation, ally of the great Benito Juárez, pinche Indio general to boot, had been seduced by power, Aguirre said. The People said he'd been whitened once ensconced in the presidential palace of far Tenochtitlán, transformed into a wicked scorpion. Díaz had sent his troops forth to kill Indians and rebels as he sold away the nation for bags of European and Yanqui gold; now he was closing his fist over the states around Sinaloa. His reign was so complete that it went by his own first name: El Porfiriato.

Díaz had sent his men into the land to run in elections for control of every state. But this governor of Sinaloa, with the help of Tomás and the Masons, had won the election. The general in his palace in the Aztec capital had sent the army to Culiacán for a recount. And when they got the ballots, the count reversed itself as if by magic.

"Díaz has taken Sinaloa!" Aguirre announced.

"Are you sure?" Tomás asked.

"I am."

"Is it trouble for us?"

"It is."

Segundo looked to them and shrugged.

"Watch," Aguirre warned, "for punitive actions. For revenge. See if lands are seized for obscure reasons. See if opposition politicians vanish between Ocoroni and Guaymas — it will be a quiet thing. A trip that seems to evaporate into thin air. Tragic accidents, or mysterious bandit attacks that suddenly wipe out certain homes on the outskirts."

Tomás rubbed his face.

"Well," he said. He nodded. He had always been afraid of ruining the ranch, and now, in the one gesture he had been sure would preserve it forever, he might have annihilated everything.

Tomás leaned in and, in a conspiratorial tone of voice, inquired, "Do your department stores sell honey?"

"Honey?"

"Claro que sí! Honey! Have I told you of my experiments with the honeybee and the golden honey?"

Tomás rushed to his desk and produced a candle that was decorated along its entire length with small hexagons.

"Honeycomb!" Tomás cried.

"Rolled like a small burrito," noted the Engineer.

"Honey is the grand industry," Tomás sighed, sitting back.

After a while, they began sketching designs for new, scientific beehives, the brandy making all lines curved and crooked and possible.

Eleven

IF THERE WAS EVER UPROAR on the ranch, Teresita seemed to be in the middle of it. She ran in a pack of little ruffians, and they bedeviled the bulls in their paddocks, climbed trees, hid in bushes and pelted Rurales with rocks. Teresita already rode horses — albeit on the saddles of the buckaroos. All the wranglers seemed to enjoy her scrappy company, and they taught her naughty corridos on their guitars. She could strum — badly — and sing ditties about lonesome cows and bandits and wicked city women who left their sweethearts broken and drunk in countless cantinas from Yucatán to Nogales. Lately, Teresita's favorite game was piling six children on the back of a long-suffering donkey and sliding down its backside before scrambling aboard to do it again. In this way, they passed many minutes of hilarity, while the burro idly imagined the pleasure of kicking them over the fence.

That morning, when Huila made her move on Teresita, the sun was not yet risen. Huila carried her new double-barreled shotgun, and she had her objects in her apron pockets: tobacco, a folding knife, her apocalyptic man pouch, red matches, a bundle of sage, a bone, and her three buffalo teeth. She puffed a pipe Don Tomás had given her — its tobacco, cured in liquor, was as tasty to her as a cake.

She stepped up to Tía's door and rapped on it three times.

"Quién es?" Tía called.

"Huila."

Silence.

"What do you want?"

"The girl."

More silence.

The door scraped open, and Teresita came out.

"It is time," Huila said.

Teresita took her hand, and they walked away.

They passed the swampy pool of donkey pee in the road. They walked quietly through the scattering of workers' shacks. Huila's shotgun cut back and forth before her like some queen bee's antennae, seeking evildoers. Around them, the muffled sounds of women rising in dark homes, unfolding their envelopes of wax paper and butcher paper and, for the poorest, their banana leaves. They took green coffee beans and threw them on heated skillets with a handful of sugar if they had it, so the sugar would burn and char the beans brown. The tinkle and dark scent filled the air, both sweet and bitter.

All these women, Huila thought: Mothers of God. These skinny, these dirty and toothless, these pregnant and shoeless. These with an issue of blood, and these with unsuckled breasts and children cold in the grave. These old forgotten ones too weak to work. These fat ones who milked all day. These twisted ones tied to their pallets, these barren ones, these married ones, these abandoned ones, these whores, these hungry ones, these thieves, these drunks, these mestizas, these lovers of other women, these Indians, and these littlest ones who faced unknowable tomorrows. Mothers of God. If it was a sin to think so, she would face God and ask Him why.

"The Virgin came to your people," Huila said.

"My people?"

"Oh yes. The Mayos saw La Virgencita before the priests came."

Teresita stopped and stared up at her teacher in the dark. "What happened?"

Huila puffed her pipe. It was good. It was very, very good.

"It was before. Before you, and before me."

Teresita was astonished by this revelation: there had been a time before Huila.

"The Mother of God appeared to a group of warriors who were out in the desert, hunting. And they looked up, and there she was, descending from the sky."

Teresita gasped.

"She was, I imagine, all in purple. The Mother of God likes purple! So she came down to them from Heaven, and they were stunned and shaking with fear."

"What did they do?"

"They ran away and hid behind bushes."

"What did she do?"

"Well, she had an accident."

"What happened?"

"She landed on top of a cactus."

"Oh no!"

"Oh yes. The Mother of God was stuck on top of a huge cactus, and the warriors started throwing rocks at her and shooting arrows at her, but they could not hit her. You see, they had never seen a Yori before, and they had never seen a flying Yori, or a magnificent creature like her! So they tried to kill her. Pendejos, los hombres!"

Teresita put her hands over her face.

"And then what?" she cried.

"Then the Mother of God spoke to the warriors from atop her cactus."

"What did she say? What did she say?"

"She said — 'Get me a ladder!'"

Teresita said, "What!"

"Get me a ladder, that's what she said. Holy be her name."

Teresita burst out laughing. So did Huila.

"It's true," Huila said.

They walked on.

"What did they do?" Teresita asked.

"I imagine they fetched her a ladder!"

The sun was coming up.

"You see," Huila explained, "this is how Heaven works. They're practical. We are always looking for rays of light. For lightning bolts or burning bushes. But God is a worker, like us. He made the world — He didn't hire poor Indios to build it for him! God has worker's hands. Just remember — angels carry no harps. Angels carry hammers."

❦

Teresita sat on a rock in the morning light and watched Huila go from plant to plant, muttering to them. She actually said "Good morning" to a miserable little quince tree. Teresita giggled. Huila shot her a stern glance before turning back to the tree. "May I borrow your fruit? I promise to eat it with gratitude, and then the child and I will scatter your seeds for you over by the creek bank. Your children will live long after you!" She unfolded her knife and cut off a plump quince and sliced it and handed Teresita some of the fruit. "Me gusta el membrillo," she said as she ate the pungent fruit and it puckered her lips. "Save the seeds. I reached an agreement — we have to honor it." This very well might have been theater on Huila's part, but it worked.

"Do the plants talk back?" Teresita asked.

Huila stretched her back, grimaced. The orange sun was igniting the hilltops with thin etchings of hot copper. Quail rushed through the brush, leading lines of babies that looked like beads on a rosary.

"Everything," Huila said, "talks."

"I never heard it."

"You never listened."

Huila pointed around herself with her pipe.

"Life. Life. Life," she said. She was pointing at everything: tree, hill, rock.

"Life in rocks?" Teresita said.

"All is light, child. Rocks are made of light. Angels pass through rocks the way your hand passes through water."

Teresita wondered if angels were passing through the rock on which she sat.

"Every rock comes from God, and God is in every rock if you look for Him."

This was pretty strange talk, in Teresita's opinion.

"In a rock."

"Yes."

"In a . . . in a bee?"

"Certainly."

"In a taco?"

"You think you're funny."

Huila was irked. A tortilla, made of holy corn, corn made of rain and soil and sun, that tortilla, round as the sun itself! Was God not in the rain? Did the corn not come from God? What of the sun? Was the sun simply some meaningless accident in the sky? Some ball of light meaning nothing, signifying nothing? No! Only a heretic would fail to see God in the sun!

And the meat of the goat, and the flowers the goat ate, and the chiles in the salsa, and the guacamole, and the hands of the fine woman who slapped the tortilla into shape then laid the sizzling meat into it, and the fire, and the fire ring, and the house in which the fire ring burned, and the ancestors who raised the generation that led to the woman making the taco. Only an idiot would fail to see God in a meal!

"If you are too blind to see God in a Goddamned taco," she exclaimed, "then you are *truly* blind!"

Teresita said, "Then everything is God?"

"Don't be a heathen," Huila said. "God is everything. Learn the difference."

"I have dreams, Huila."

"We all have dreams, child."

"I dreamed of a hummingbird made of sky."

"Ah."

"He was too small to see, but I could see him."

"Yes?"

"And he landed."

"But of course."

"And he turned to me and he had a feather in his mouth."

"A feather."

"Yes, Huila. A white feather."

"You're sure it was white. It is very important, child."

"White."

"And which way did he turn, right or left?"

"Left."

"Oh!"

"Is that good, Huila?"

"Left is the direction of the heart. Did you know that? The heart is on the left."

"I thought the heart was in the middle."

"On the left. That's why wedding rings are on the left hand, you see. The heart side."

"Well, the hummingbird turned to the left."

"And what did he do with the white feather?"

"He put it in my hand."

"Yes. Good. Excellent."

"What does it mean, Huila?"

"Well — the hummingbird is the messenger of God."

"He is?"

"You didn't know that?"

"No."

"Has no one taught you anything?"

"Only you, Huila."

"Oh, child. Well, he is the messenger. He brings messages from Heaven to us on earth. And he carries our requests to the ear of God. Do you see? So he came from Heaven."

"And the feather?"

"Feathers are sacred. A white feather — I would say that was a key."

"A key to what?"

"Why, child, a key to whatever. Spirit. Heaven. I don't know what. It was your dream, not mine."

That was enough education for one day.

Huila walked her back home.

The next morning, Teresita watched Huila collect leaves and stems and put them in a cloth bag slung over her shoulder. More muttering. Asking a clavo plant to forgive her for being greedy.

When this was over, she set her bag on the ground and said, "Now, your lesson."

"I am ready, Huila."

"You must learn to feel the life in things."

"Feel it?"

"Correct. To work with plants, you must know plants. But what if you don't already know a plant? Then you must know how to feel its life force. It will tell you who it is, or at least who it is related to."

"Why?"

"What if it is poison? What if, for example, that bastard Segundo gets the chorro?"

Teresita laughed. Huila had used the country word for diarrhea: the gushing stream.

"So poor Segundo has crap in his pants —"

"Huila!"

"— and he comes to you for a healing. You must rush out to find plants to make him a tea to plug his culo —"

"Ay, Huila!"

"— but you are in some new place, and you don't know which plants are which. Do you see? There is no one to ask, and Segundo is farting like a sick cow —"

"Ay Dios, Huila!"

"— so it's urgent that you find a plant. You must go out and feel their life. You can tell which might be soothing and which might make him sicker."

"Do I feel it in my heart?"

Teresita was trying to sound religious.

"I am not the priest," Huila sniffed. "Don't try to sound like a nun. I mean feel it, *feel* it." She grabbed Teresita's wrist and ran her finger across her palm. "Feel it with your hands."

"How?"

"I will show you."

They walked out across the stubbly field where old cotton plants had been chopped down and plowed under. They reached a creosote bush, one of the heralds of the deserts not far to their north. The bush the People called Stinky — Hedionda.

"Stinky is best for training," Huila said. "It has a strong life in it. Anybody can feel it. Even Yoris."

"Really?"

Huila nodded. "Never teach a Yori all the things I am going to teach you. They have stolen enough from us.

Don't give them our souls. But you may teach Yoris to do this. Everybody should do this."

She took Teresita's wrists and positioned her hands above the bush. Teresita touched the leaves. Huila pulled her hands back.

"Don't touch," she said.

Teresita stayed quiet. Sometimes, asking Huila questions was a bad idea. The old one repositioned her hands above the bush about four inches from the leaves.

"Now what?" Teresita said.

"Wait."

A few minutes passed.

"How long do I wait?"

"We could wait all night," Huila said.

Teresita sighed.

Huila said, "Are your hands hot?"

"My hands are always hot."

"Do this."

Huila clapped her hands together three times, then rubbed her palms briskly. Teresita copied her. Huila put her hands above the plant. "Now," she said.

Teresita put out her hands. Nothing.

"Close your eyes," Huila said.

"I don't feel anything."

"Don't talk, feel!"

"But Huila —"

"Feel!"

After another interminable minute, Huila told her to slap her hands together again. Very tiresome. Teresita clapped three times, rubbed, put out her hands, already thinking about how wonderful it was going to be to escape from the old madwoman and play donkey slide with the kids in the village. Then it happened.

She gasped.

The little ugly bush began to push against her hands. It was as if cool smoke had billowed from the leaves. Cold smoke. Fog. And it rolled softly against her palms, trying to lift her hands. She laughed.

"You feel it."

"I do!"

She opened her eyes. She clutched her hands to her chest. She gazed down at the homely little hedionda bush. It was one of many, almost invisible, a lowly weed. A trash plant cluttering any landscape. Cows wouldn't even eat it. Around its base, small grasses wobbled in the breeze, and quail tracks formed small Y shapes in the yellow dust. Small blue blossoms in its shadows, and beyond them, cacti with red flowers. Down the arroyos, wild melons twined their vines around rogue mango trees. Sunflowers. Dandelions. She gawked. She grew dizzy with color. Color filled her mouth like agua de jamaica.

"Everything speaks, child," Huila said.

Teresita was laughing.

"Everything is singing."

One of Huila's mysteries was: "You are not always meant to understand, only to accept."

"I want to understand," Teresita replied.

"Only Itom Achai truly understands. It is our job to wonder. Wonder and obey."

Teresita wondered how she was to obey what she didn't understand.

Huila told Teresita to pierce her ears. Teresita was thrilled that Huila was interested in making her pretty. But Huila didn't care if she was pretty or not. Huila told her: "You must pierce your ears to show God you are no longer deaf. You have not only been blind, but deaf. Punch holes in your ears to show God they are open, and you are ready to listen. God doesn't care if you think you're pretty!" But she gave her two beautiful gold hoops to wear once she had done the ritual.

Twelve

THE MYSTERIES OF THE MAIN HOUSE were as inde-cipherable to the People as Huila's commandments were to Teresita. Commands, ideas, plans, and whims wheeled over their heads like the constellations. Even Huila was periodically baffled by the world of the Yoris. She some-times looked to Segundo when her own understanding failed her. Between them, they could usually make out a pattern.

Saturday morning, Segundo rode over to the village and he parked his horse in the middle of the street and smoked until the workers came forth and gawked. Huila made her way quickly from her sacred spot and looked up at him, too.

"Do you know what?" he said.

They were immediately afraid. Why would Segundo

come to address them? Was there to be a flogging? Had there been a massacre? Were the Apaches coming back? Was everybody fired? Had war broken out? A Mennonite missionary had moved through the ranchos assuring them that Jesus Christ would return to earth by 1880 — maybe He was early.

"The bandits are gone," he said. "Except in the north."

The north. Nobody liked the north.

"The warrior Indians are also gone. Except . . ."

"In the north," they murmured.

Segundo shifted in the saddle, and it made its three hundred leather sounds. Teresita stood next to the horse and held Segundo's boot and looked up at him. She spun his spur. It sounded like tiny Christmas bells.

Buenaventura was hiding in a thicket, trying to brush fat biting ants off himself.

"Bandits. I kind of miss them," Segundo said. "Have you heard tell of La Carambada?"

"No."

"This is a true story."

Tía tipped ash into her mouth and tapped her foot: this was a waste of her time.

"She was my favorite bandit of all," he said. "She held up wagons and coaches. She carried a great Colt forty-five, and when she had the men out of the coach and lined up, stripped of their gold and even their pants, she would pull out one of her chichis." The crowd gasped. "Oh yes. She would show the men her chichi, and she'd hold the gun to their heads, and she'd say, 'What do you think of this, cabrón?'" The People looked at each other uneasily. Huila made a mental note: La Carambada — heroine of Mexico.

Segundo laughed. "Can you imagine? All those idiotas trying to think up the right thing to say."

"I hope she shot a few of them," Huila said.

Segundo smiled.

"What a woman!" he said. "Maybe they have more like her up north."

Don Teófano said, "Excuse me, but I have work to do."

"Not today, you don't."

"Why? Is it Easter already?"

"No. The patrón has given you all the day."

"For what?"

"To reflect."

"On what?"

Segundo flicked his cigarette away.

"You need to decide your own fates."

"Fate?" said Teófano.

"Fate!" said Huila.

Segundo delivered a sober version of the elaborate story of the recent elections and the debacle of the Sinaloan candidate and his unexpected fall at the hands of Don Porfirio Díaz. Buenaventura wandered closer, amazed more by Segundo's spurs and black saddle and pistolas than by the story.

"What's that got to do," he called, "with anything?"

"Don Tomás has been in meetings for days with Don Miguel and the engineer Aguirre," Segundo said.

Aguirre. Segundo and Buenaventura together sneered at each other. Buenaventura was so delighted by this that he nearly did a little jig.

"And they have decided that the rancho must be evacuated. Tomás and Doña Loreto and the herds of cattle and horses, and the vaqueros, of course. We're going to have to move to where it's safer. They're after our patrón. Se lo van a chingar," he noted.

"Go?" said Huila. This was all news to her. "Go where?"

Segundo turned in his saddle, offering a touch of drama to the crowd. He looked beyond the main house into the distance, beyond the trees.

"What do you think?" he said.

"North!" shouted Teresita. Thanks to Huila, she was used to answering spot quizzes by now.

They rocked back on their heels, touched their hearts, their foreheads. *North!*

Segundo nodded down at them.

"North, to Sonora. You must decide which of you will go with us. You have today and tomorrow. Go to church. Pray. Decide."

He turned his horse.

"Whoever braves the journey will find work when we arrive in Sonora. Those of you who stay will be under a new patrón." He spurred his mount and said, "Good day."

"Segundo!" Huila called.

He stopped and looked back.

"Where in Sonora?" she demanded.

"Don Miguel has a great home in Alamos. A city. Loreto and the children will go there. The rest of us are going to one of the ranches. Probably Cabora."

Cabora!

Nobody had heard that word before.

They rolled it on their tongues as Segundo rode away.

Cabora . . .

Those who had not heard Segundo speak knew what he'd said before they ate breakfast. For the first time, the lives of the workers of the rancho were about to change. Knowing this gave them all an instant and deep nostalgia for the smallest of details that they had previously ignored. It was the only life they knew, in the only place they knew, and now they had to change.

"I have squandered my days," Don Teófano announced, then went to ponder the stock pond. He had not looked at a dragonfly in thirty years. He was certain there would be no dragonflies in Sonora.

Tía collapsed in her shack and shook.

Huila marched to the main house. Sonora! By God, there was plenty of work to do before they went to Sonora! She had to pack her saints, her herbs, steal some more pipe tobacco from Tomás, get some more shells for her shotgun. Sonora! Yaquis!

Teresita wandered off with Buenaventura.

"You going?" he asked.

"Yes. Of course."

"I'm going," he said.

"Good."

All over the ranch, the People were looking as baffled as infants or young monkeys. Even vaqueros were to be found in odd corners, tossing lariats at fence posts and fingering the ropes, as if ropes were fated to become arcane objects of the ancient past. Segundo was discovered on Sunday joining several little girls in a game of hopscotch.

On Monday, they were amazed to find men already shutting down the ranch. The patrones moved so fast! Things happened as if by themselves, or by invisible agents of change. Tools and goods were going into boxes.

Seeds filled burlap sacks. Favorite fruit trees were dug up and mounted on wagons, their root balls wrapped in old blankets and wetted down with buckets of water.

Women swept out their dirt floors each dawn, thinking this might be the last dawn of the world. The dust flew from their doors with tenderness. They meditated on the dirt. Even Tía, one day, said, "Dust. It is probably mentioned in the Psalms."

Padre Adriel arrived that week with flagons of holy water, and he blessed things until he was weary. He blessed the wagons and the two-wheeled carts. He blessed donkeys and mules, horses and goats. He even blessed the she-pig. He blessed hoes, shovels, axles, children, hats, metates, shoes. He did not bless pistolas, though he did bless rifles. "Rifles hunt deer," he said, "but pistolas hunt men." He heard confession in the barn.

When he saw Tomás, he said, "Do you wish to make a confession, hijo?"

"Padre," Tomás replied, "my only confession is that I do not believe in confession."

Eggs and tortillas became a new astonishment. The Sinaloans had heard that Sonorans indulged in the unspeakable atrocity of eating flour tortillas. Flour! Any human being knew that tortillas were made of corn. So they regarded their pieces of tortillas with sorrow — serving as spoon and fork and napkin all at once, their humble little maíz tortillas, with their loose skins and their delicious burned spots, had revealed themselves at last to be family members more loyal than sisters or brothers. Long after a fight with a brother, even after a funeral for a sister, you could scoop up some fried beans with a tortilla de maíz. And when you didn't have beans, a pinch of salt in a tortilla was a great meal. How could you eat salt in a wad of flour? Did not Padre Adriel say they were "the salt of the earth"? Nobody was sure what it meant, but it clearly related to the tortilla.

For a time, men stopped kicking their dogs. Once they allowed themselves this kindness, emotions without number flooded their chests. These feelings convinced some men that they were dying of hideous ailments like heartworms or the evil eye. Soon, making love became so overwhelming that their flutes drooped. The men feared weeping in front of their women so deeply that their bones would not rise. The women, however, wanted loving more than ever. Now that they were being torn away from their homes, they wanted to be pressed to the earth and worked upon it like masa on the comal, they wanted to feel the rocky flanks of the earth grow soft in that mysterious moment when the ground opened them and swallowed them. They would lift their skirts high and offer the men the tender promise of their legs, but the only ones who bit their flesh were fleas. The men merely hung their heads and scratched the dogs behind their ears.

The vaqueros were not overconcerned. They spun the occasional spur, scratched their names on the walls of the bunkhouse. They were more than willing to offer their services to the frustrated women of the village. They enthusiastically kicked every dog in sight.

Book II

WHERE THE SKY
FORGOT TO RAIN

*We should say that what most powerfully
caught the attention of the people were the
moral and intellectual qualities of the girl.
They intensified the power of her virtues, the
powers of her soul; at the same time, these
features caused the people to see in her a
saint, a celestial messenger. These moral and
intellectual qualities were a living, palpable
contrast to the vice and ignorance in
which she had been raised.*

— Lauro Aguirre,
La Santa de Cabora

Thirteen

EVERYONE PREPARED for the great leaving.

Segundo lent Buenaventura fifty pesos. Segundo had also given the boy a swayback horse that was destined for the rendering plant and a job herding cows and mules and horses to far Sonora.

"Your pistol is a piece of shit," Segundo told him.

"I will buy a new one."

"You would have to work for a whole year to pay me back my fifty pesos and also buy a new gun," Segundo told him.

"I will work."

"And what will you do until you earn the money to buy a good gun?"

"If my pistol does not shoot, I will beat them over the head with it."

Segundo laughed.

"Them!" he said. "Who?"

"Everybody."

"Eres bien machito, cabrón," he said.

He took a rust-pitted Colt from the armory and put it in one of his abandoned holsters. He tossed the pistol across Buenaventura's frayed old saddle.

"Now," he said, "you must work for two years."

"I need bullets."

"Two and a half years."

Tomás and Aguirre loaded Loreto and the children on a

carriage aimed for Don Miguel's home. "I will write to you," she promised, a gesture recognized as symbolic, since there would be no place to send a letter if she could write. Still, Tomás was no fool in romance, even with his wife, and he vowed: "I shall lie awake every night until your letters come to me, my angel. And even when they come, I shall not sleep, for I will be breathing in your scent and kissing your precious tears from the pages!" Segundo nudged Aguirre in the ribs and tipped his head at the ejaculations of the master. "Es suave, este hijo de puta," he noted.

Loreto caused a white hankie to flutter at her slightly swollen nose like a trapped moth as she sniffled. Secretly, she was thrilled: she was through with horses and the stench of cattle. Au revoir, picturesque vaqueros! Adieu, pigs, Indians, scorpions, and dust! She and her children would live in a city from now on, with cobbles, signs, schools, stores, parasols, china. Restaurants! Certainly, there would be restaurants in Alamos! She already saw herself perching on a wrought-iron chair and sipping an exotic tea, while all about her, people spoke in the intoxicating if baffling manner of Lauro Aguirre.

Loreto mopped at her eyes gently as the carriage pulled away. Everyone waved until they were small with distance and vanished to each other, except for Segundo, who saw them until they were over the crown of the hill.

"At last," Tomás startled the Engineer by saying, "we are free!"

Segundo seconded his boss's sentiments with a pious pronouncement: "The hardships of the journey are not for fine ladies or children."

Aguirre noted that behind them, scores of women and

children were tearing their small homes apart and fastening their sad scraps onto two-wheeled carts.

They had studied the route for days. Don Miguel had ordered great topographical maps from Mexico City, and they were printed in vivid colors on oiled sheets that flopped heavily and hung from the edges of the dining room table. Aguirre attacked these maps with rulers; he charted useless radii with a silver compass. The trail seemed clear enough to Tomás and Segundo. They would skirt the western edge of the Sierra Madre, heading north until they could veer to the left and enter the safety of the mining city of Alamos, or they could veer right and enter into wilder lands of the Urrea ranchos. There, marked in black oil pencil by the Patrón Grande before the maps arrived at the house, were the vague empires of the northern Urrea confederacy: Cabora, Santa María, Las Vacas, and Aquihuiquichi.

"By God," Aguirre said. "You own the entire world."

"Four ranchos!" Tomás said. "I have four ranchos!"

"And a silver mine," the Engineer reminded him.

Segundo, gobbling all the snacks the cooks could carry, smiled. He ate nanchis, sun-dried fish, pig cookies, skinny fired taquitos, orange slices with red pepper powder and salt, prunes, chicken gizzards. He grabbed two cups of coffee and stood with one in each fist, trading sips from either one. He was going to be rich. Four ranches! Surely, he'd find a way to end up with one of them.

A silver mine was what Aguirre was thinking about. With his engineering genius, they'd be pulling huge chunks of ore from the ground! He would settle in the fine city of Alamos, attending balls with Loreto. And then he'd finance a revolution with the riches.

"Alamos," sneered Tomás. "That's a town for women and priests. Give me horses."

"He loves horses," noted Segundo.

"He is a horse," said Aguirre.

"Mines!" said Tomás. "I won't spend the rest of my life in a hole with my ass sticking up in the air! Cows. Land. Bulls."

"Yes, yes," said Aguirre, waving his hand over his head as he walked his compass over the distances on the map and jotted notes in his notebook. "You are as one with your horse. You are a Mongol."

"He's an Apache," noted Segundo as he bit into a fried banana wrapped in a corn tortilla with mole sauce on it.

※

Although very detailed, each map still had substantial swaths of the occult north seemingly erased. Frightening white spaces, some of them marked with the dreadful phrase "Unknown Territory." Other regions were pale yellow, and marked with the hardly more comforting legend DESIERTO, both desert and deserted. It was the dark continent. And all along the top of the maps, the empty space known as "Los Estados Unidos Norte Americanos."

Even the place-names disturbed them. Eerie, alien in their mouths, the northern names seemed violent, shocking, remnants of some loathsome Chichimeca antiquity. The names brought to mind eldritch barbarians, skeletal hordes whooping down from the black banshee-haunted rock spires of the uncharted wastes. Old gods surely slumbered beneath the north's tortured mountains, terrible wraiths from before Christendom, entombed but dreaming of wreaking their havoc once again. If Tomás could have stomached the cliché, he would have made the sign of the cross.

Tomás read the names aloud for Segundo, who could not read them, and they were more frightening hanging in the air like wasps than writhing on the page like crushed ants.

Bavispe.
El Júpare.
Cocorit.
Guatabampo.
Tomóchic.
Temosachic.
Tepache.
Teuricachi.
Nacatóbari.
Moteporé.
Aigamé.

"Are you sure," Segundo quipped, "that there isn't a place called Tiliche?" Which was, of course, hilarious to the men, being the name of the human pecker.

Undaunted, Aguirre charted a sure course.

They would move out early in the morning that Monday — he expected to progress about twelve miles the first day.

"A farewell Mass tomorrow," Aguirre said.

"I don't go to Mass," Tomás replied.

"I don't either."

"Protestant monster."

"Godless wretch."

"I'm going to have sex," Segundo interjected.

They would head north, to El Fuerte, where they could ford the Río Fuerte at a shallow crossing. Into the haunted Mayo valleys, and across the bottom of the Yaqui lands. They would stick to the western paseos along the foothills. Then they would cross yet another big river, the Navojoa.

They would pass the lovely city of Alamos on the trail to Guaymas that cut through the empty drylands to the northwest. There, about forty miles from Alamos, and roughly one hundred fifty miles southeast of the seaport of Guaymas, they should, in a watered valley, find the rancho of Cabora.

❋

The People tied their miserable bundles. They were amazed that they had less than they thought they had; it was a wonder to them that it took so long to pack nothing. Women trembled; men wept into their sleeves. "The north," they said, "is full of ghosts."

Sad packets of dried beans were attached with strings to the slack sides of burros. A cask of vinegar here, an oiled bag holding salt or sugar there. Knives. Tattered dresses.

❋

While the People and the buckaroos were at Mass, Tomás wandered around the town plazuela. The olmos trees and the alamos had been painted halfway up their trunks. Whitewash. Benches and rocks were also white. Aguirre slumbered on one of these benches. Lazy bastard!

Tomás bought a wax-paper cone filled with diced mango, papaya, orange, and shaved coconut. He sprinkled chile powder over it and ate the tart cubes with a toothpick. He was bored enough to feel relief when the church bells rang and all the hypocrites swarmed out of the church, men putting their hats back on, and women casting off their head coverings. Scuttling little people just as venal and superstitious as when they'd gone in. Liars trying to look pious for each other. And that damned Padre Adriel, no doubt eyeing the young girls of the rancho and stirring under his ladylike robes. All a big show to somehow fool an absent God into overlooking their sins. Tomás wadded up his wax paper, tossed it angrily into the bushes, and headed over to the front steps of the church, where that irritating papist was squatting with Teresita.

Adriel said: "Are you consorting with Huila, my child?"

"Consorting?"

"Studying with her?"

"Yes, Padre."

"Beware, child," he admonished. "The heathen ways are fraught with danger. Many have thought they walked with angels and have awakened with devils."

"What?"

"You see, Satan is not a monster. We don't see him when he comes, because he has disguised himself in beauty."

"What?"

"The devil is, after all, an angel of light. The Morning Star. Do not allow yourself to be seduced by the beautiful side of evil."

"Huila is evil?" she asked.

"Huila is beautiful?" interrupted Tomás.

Adriel stood.

"Ah, Tomás."

"More propaganda, Padre?" Tomás said. "The Mass wasn't enough for you to twist this young woman's mind?"

Teresita stared up at them with her mouth open.

"Go play," Tomás said.

"All right."

She skipped away.

"Protecting the innocent from Satan," said Adriel.

Tomás slapped him on the shoulder.

"Very noble!" he said. "Any tips for me?"

"Don't look in the mirror," Padre Adriel replied.

Tomás laughed out loud.

He extended his hand.

Adriel looked at it for a moment, then took it.

"I will miss you, pinche Padre," Tomás said.

"And I you."

"Care to come to Sonora?"

"Oh no," Adriel said. "That's Jesuit territory. The Society of Jesus will take care of you."

They shook hands again, then stood there looking at the ground.

"Well!" Tomás said, finally.

"Yes!"

"I suppose it's time."

"Yes, well. Go with God."

Tomás startled the priest by saying, "You too, Padre. You too."

He reached out with his right hand and laid it on the priest's arm and gave him a gentle squeeze.

He stopped in the middle of the street and turned back. He walked back up the steps to the young priest and said, "Padre?"

"Yes?"

"If I ask you a question, will you answer me honestly?"

Adriel didn't know if it was one of his tricks or not.

Still, he said, "If I can. Certainly."

Tomás sighed.

"Doesn't all this . . ." he said. "Don't you ever . . ."

"What, Tomás?"

"Don't you ever just get tired of religion? Isn't it all just exhausting?"

Padre Adriel considered him for a moment. He crossed his arms, then put a finger to his lips.

"My friend," he said, "no one is more tired of religion than a priest."

Tomás was startled. He smiled. Nodded.

"Thank you," he said.

"Don't mention it."

He started back down the steps.

"If you think of it," he said, "say a little prayer for us."

Adriel watched him walk away.

Tomás called over his shoulder:

"If you do mention me to God, be kind!"

And these were the ones and these were the things that would go into the desert:

Tomás.

The Engineer Lauro Aguirre.

Huila.

Three cooks, two housemaids, and a milkmaid. Three laundrywomen. Their children.

Antonio Alvarado Segundo with a full complement of cowboys and hired riflemen. Also, Guerrero and Millán, two miners from Rosario, in case Tomás decided to attempt a new enterprise. They rode borrowed horses, Millán famous for his good looks and ferocity, Guerrero famous for his long hair, said to be longer than any Indian's, both men drunk.

Buenaventura on his swayback nag.

Forty of the best horses and three hundred head of cattle, twenty-three dogs, one wagon-riding cat, thirteen pigs, twenty herded goats and six tagalongs, three Brahman bulls, an army of recalcitrant mules, jolly burros, mindless oxen, ducks, turkeys, chickens, and roosters in wicker cages, an evil-tempered and half-bald swan, a turtle in a washtub, and one llama appeared from nobody knew where. And the People.

Fourteen

THE MAIN HOUSE'S CARRIAGE was followed by the ranch wagons, in turn trailed by more than fifty overloaded carts. Each wagon and cart had a driver, including Huila's wagon, whose mule driver was Don Teófano. There was also a wagon with one hired cook, to spare the household help any undue strain on the journey.

Wagons carried beds, stoves, the sewing machine, weapons, salt, slabs of jerked beef, wheat, maize, several hundred pounds of beans, salt cod, dried shrimp, chile peppers, bags of brown sugar, pots, pans, soap, tubs, water, vinegar, olives, rice, green bananas, limes, oranges, candy, tobacco, medicines, Huila's vast storehouse of herbs, onions, garlic cloves, clothes, guitars, machetes, trumpets, caged parrots, dolls, rifles, huaraches, underpants, spyglasses, love letters, Tomás's library packed in crates, picks, shovels, scythes, whetstones, bridles, harnesses, a rocking chair, the grandfather clock.

Straggling along behind this mobile flea market came the ragged children who could ride, some of them on ponies, one or two on old plow horses, one on a big pig, and Teresita, on a burro.

The edges of day were pouring mercury, burning, upon the hills.

Don Tomás, at the head of the column, sat tall on his horse and felt, like arrows, like bullets, the eyes of all his people focused on his back. He had never felt so alone.

Behind them all, a flatbed wagon whose mule driver was covered in a tent of mesh. It was the fellow from Parangarí-cutirimícuaro. Whining and humming behind him, seven hives full of bees. Tomás had concocted a smoker that pumped marijuana fumes into the hives, and the bees were relaxed and enjoying the ride. The wagon driver had red eyes and a foolish grin on his face, and he occasionally bent down and pumped a blue-white cloud of smoke into his own face.

Falls, then. Tripped horses, peones falling off their carts and splitting their heads. Ten escaped cows thundering through the willows. A wheel fallen off a wagon.

By noon, several of the cowboys had spied a lone coyote running down a dry wash, and they set out after him, firing their rifles as if to kill the devil himself. Spooking the cows, yet unable to stop, they flew over the hills like maniacs, like frantic dogs, only to slink back to the master, their heads bowed and their tails dragging. Nobody hit the coyote.

Over the hills until the ranch was out of sight. Every mind full of what it loved the most, each person certain he had lost that thing forever. Fresh mango. January sixth, the Day of the Three Kings. The Day of the Dead. Tejuino, the fermented maize beer. Fried coffee beans. Sex in the sugarcane field. Sex in the barn. Sex in the stock pond.

They made only nine miles that first day, and when they stopped, they felt as if they had traveled one hundred or more. They could have walked home and been there before midnight, yet they felt as if they were cast adrift in the most foreign land. They were grim and pale with trail dirt, their massive cloud of heraldic dust leaning far ahead of them on the evening breeze, already traveling three times the distance they had been able to go.

Crows, attracted by the stink and the tumult, spied on them from the treetops, hopping along from tree to tree, peeking out from between the ragged leaves. And buzzards, attracted by the flapping crows, hypnotized by all the wandering meat beneath them, circled and dreamed of putrescence and death, the deliciousness of rot. And unknown and unseen, to the north of the trail only five miles away from the rancho, three dead men grinned under the soil, shot by Rurales for their scant gold and their boots, buried hastily and half-eaten by beetles and voles, tunneling wildcats and foxes, these three leathery travelers vibrated underground as the people passed, shook in their paltry graves as if they were laughing, giggling, their yellow mouths wide in toothy hilarity. And in the trunks of the oldest trees, among the stones in the creek beds, buried in the soil, lying among the chips of stone kicked aside by the horses, the arrowheads of long-forgotten hunters, arrowheads misshot on a hot morning, arrowheads that passed through the breast of a raiding Guasave, gone to dust now like the bowman and scattered, arrowheads that brought down deer that fed wives and children and all of them gone, into the dirt, blowing into the eyes and raising tears that tumbled down the cheeks of Teresita.

Tomás, far ahead, weary and troubled, stopped with his head down. He raised one hand, and the group started to draw themselves around him. Segundo and the cowboys automatically rounded up the herd and moved the protesting animals toward the small seep in the field to the south. The wagons collected around the patrón: the cook pulling into the middle beside Loreto's former carriage. The various big wagons circled, and the carts after them, all collecting around Tomás, layers of home shutting out the world. And out, beyond the ring of wagons, the bees stirred and exited their hives, delicately raiding the flowers of the fields, sipping the water of the green seep in the grass. Everyone dismounting, everyone asking, "Where are we?" The fires already lit, the smoke rising all around, the guitars starting to play, the darkness only a suggestion, a blue drip of shadows from the hills coming their way from the west, and a bruise spreading through the tissue of the sky from the east.

The children settled their steeds at the outermost edge of the encampment. They tied their animals to trees or to wagons, those who thought to take care of things. Others just dropped their reins and their ropes and went off crying for their mothers and begging for food. They were sun-burned and dust choked and thirsty and bottom sore.

Teresita, so sore from riding her little donkey Panfilo, could barely walk. She made her way through the wagons, peeking at the families, greeting her friends, petting the dogs, smelling the smells. She worked her way through the maze to Huila's camp. Huila was seated in her chair, a pillow fluffed under her buttocks. "My nalgas hurt," Huila said. Teresita collapsed at her feet. Don Teófano had lit a small campfire, and he was brewing coffee in a blue white-flecked pot.

"Why must we suffer?" a woman said.

Don Teófano replied, "If you were born to be an anvil you must bear many blows."

Everyone nodded wisely.

"If you were born to be a nail, you cannot curse the hammer," he intoned.

More nodding.

"If you —"

"Ya pues, hombre!" Huila scolded.

She prodded Teresita with her foot.

"Bring me that jug."

"What jug?"

"The jug I want. You'll know which one."

Teresita got up and looked in the wagon. There was a jug under the edge of a blanket. She grabbed it and carried it to the old woman.

"For every bad thing in life, mezcal." Huila uncorked the jug. "And for every good thing, too."

The People laughed and said, "Ay, Huila!"

She took a swig, then passed it on. More laughter soon sprouted among them, and Don Teófano gave Teresita mug of steaming coffee rich with goat milk and sugar. The fires crackled all around them. Teresita lay back, listening to the sayings everyone began to pronounce: *A little poison won't kill you,* and *I'd rather be happy and poor than worried and rich,* or *Honey wasn't made for the mouths of donkeys.*

There came a stirring among the campers, and suddenly Tomás appeared among them.

"Are we all right?" he asked. "Everyone in one piece?"

"Sí, señor," the People replied, looking away. "We're fine, thanks be to God."

"Huila," he said, pleased to see her. "How are you holding up?"

"Don't worry about me," she said.

Tomás put his hand on Teresita's head.

"I packed your clock," he told her.

She laughed.

"I'm glad."

"Well," he said, "off to the next wagon."

"Good night," they called. "Buenas noches" and "Adios."

Teresita was astounded to see Buenaventura trailing Tomás. She had looked for him all day, unable to spot him in the teeming flow.

She said, "Buenaventura, what have you done?"

He was wearing the most appalling suit she'd ever seen. His pants were too short, and his buttoned jacket was too tight. And a bowler hat squatted on his head like a dirty turtle. It was simply too outrageous.

He tipped his hat to her.

"I got a job," he said.

She could say nothing — her mouth hung open.

He grinned at her. Then he leaned over and whispered, "I'm in."

"They took you in?"

He held up the flaps of his silly little gentleman's coat.

"You know it."

He pulled a doll out from under his coat and tossed it to her.

"I stole it."

Huila pretended not to hear this.

He stepped around Teresita and started into the gloom between the wagons. His head popped back out into the light, and he pointed at her. Then he winked. Then he left.

Tomás had spread out a bedroll by the fire. He leaned back on his saddle, his boots off and his socks soaking up heat from the coals. He sipped brandy and smoked a cigar and stared at Aguirre and shook his head. "What have we done?" he said.

"You have done what you must," said the Engineer.

Tomás tipped another dollop of brandy into his friend's cup.

"Salud, cabrón," he said.

"Salud," Aguirre replied, clacking his cup against Urrea's.

"To a new life, Lauro."

"To a new Mexico."

Segundo stepped up to them and squatted.

"Engineer," he said. "Boss."

"Good evening."

"Buenas."

Tomás offered him a drink. Segundo pushed his hat back and smiled. "I shouldn't," he said. "But I will." He took a swig from the bottle. Gasped lightly. "Ah. That's rich." He handed the bottle back to the patrón. "Everything's settled," he finally said. "I put out pickets to stand guard. I'll take a shift at midnight. The People are settled. Todo 'sta bien."

"Thank you, Segundo," said Tomás.

"Doing my job," Segundo replied. He stood, brushed off his trousers, and said, "I'll sleep now, if you don't need me."

They waved him away.

"Sweet dreams," Aguirre said.

Segundo turned back and said, "Be sure to shake your boots out in the morning. Scorpions."

And soon, with the bottle drained, the two old friends pulled their blankets around them and fell into a deep, aching sleep.

Fifteen

THE SECOND DAY WAS SLOWER than the first. Tired, sullen, frightened, bored, sleepy, sore, chewing grit between their teeth, raising a monumental stench of offal and piss, spoiling grease and sweat, pig stench, horse stench, mammalian breath stench, dog pelt, droppings of every hue and size, burning trash, beans, charcoal, the Exodus recommenced even more slowly than it had launched itself. Wagons creaked into line, banging into other wagons. Children fell to the ground, hungover vaqueros slipped off their saddles and were kicked by the horses. The cows tried to go back to Ocoroni. The whole enterprise wobbled like some headless snake.

The third day started well, but it collapsed into chaos when they reached the Río Fuerte. True to its name, it was the Strong River. Unexpectedly, it was running high after summer's great rains, and the carts and wagons stalled and sank in mud, then started overturning in the flood. The vaqueros were able to whistle and harry and drive the livestock across the river, but the wagons were stuck. Cows and horses hove onto the opposite bank a half mile downriver. Aguirre enlisted the aid of a ferry raft that pulled across the river by means of a thick hawser strung between cottonwoods on the opposing banks. The raft could carry only one wagon at a time. Tomás paid the ferryman with coin, beans, a mule, and one rifle.

Already exhausted, they settled on the banks and watched all day and all night as the raft crept back and forth across the water. It took twenty-five hours to get them all across — the last two hours mostly taken up by Aguirre and Tomás arguing with the ferryman that he could carry the bee wagon without being killed. He demanded some of the bees' marijuana to do it, and he insisted on wearing an entire bee suit, all heavy canvas and mesh veils.

"If you fall off the raft," Aguirre warned, "you will assuredly drown."

But no one fell off and nobody drowned.

They made camp by ones and twos and all fell asleep as the chocolate waters of the Río Fuerte shouted and gibbered beside them. It sounded mad, possessed. Water had never sounded so wicked to the People.

※

Before bed, Tomás was roused by a pair of Rurales. They asked if he had a doctor in his camp. He had Huila, which was as good. Teófano hooked his cranky mules back up, and Huila climbed aboard, and Aguirre and Segundo joined them, and they all went west.

There, under the last red explosions of sunset, they found a minuscule village called San Xacinto. It was a mere scattering of huts and a broken old adobe that was once a trading post. Now, it was a slumping and charred ruin. Black vigas crumbled in shattered mud walls.

"Apaches," said the Rurales.

"Note the propensities of the savages," Tomás intoned.

Beyond San Xacinto, on the outskirts, if there could be an outskirt to a town of seven huts spread out over a dusty mile, there stood a forlorn mud shanty with a roof apparently made of planks, palm fronds, and banana leaves. Huila thought there were sacks of beans lying in the dirt before the house, but she soon realized they were bodies.

Segundo whistled.

Huila peeked into the house. Inside, there was a still-smoking brazier filled with whitened charcoal. She shook her head. Made the sign of the cross.

She addressed a Rural.

"Sir," she said. "The healer tried to do a limpia."

"Some limpia!" he said. "What kind of cleansing kills everybody?"

"Well, he didn't realize the charcoal would poison them. The house was closed when you came, correct?"

"Closed."

She raised her hands.

"He meant to cleanse them, and he killed them."

The Rural said, "I hope they paid him well. This family will never have another worry."

Huila prayed for the dead all the way back to the camp, and for the soul of the inferior curandero. It was not her place to say if he belonged in Hell. Many of the People believed you came back after you died. She would watch for him, see if she recognized him.

⁂

Huila had been trying to teach Teresita to dream.

Dreamers, Huila said, held great knowledge, and much medicine was worked in the dream time. But it was hard to learn to dream, or at least to dream beyond the confines of the peasants' dreams. It was nothing to dream of plates of food, or of great beasts that chased you slowly across the hills, or of flying like a lazy butterfly. Even to dream of such things as realizing you had gone to church with no clothes, and everyone was looking at your bottom, but the priest had not yet noticed and you were hoping to get out before he did — everyone had these dreams.

But Huila was talking about something wholly other, some dream that no one could explain. Where you could walk into tomorrow, or visit far cities. Having never seen a city, Teresita could only imagine it was tall and shiny, like mountains of quartz, and many Yoris hurrying around on trains, though she had also never seen a train. They were like oxen, Huila had said, only dark and terrible, with clanging bells in their heads and fire in their bellies, and they screamed and spit smoke and sparks.

"I do dream," Teresita complained.

"Not these dreams."

"How will I know what kind of dream it is?"

Huila smiled.

"Child," she said, "when you dream a dream that is not a dream, you will know."

Dream a dream that is not a dream, Teresita thought. More of Huila's riddles. It meant nothing.

"Everyone," Huila said, "is given these dreams. Even unbelievers. Even those not learning what you are learning. Even Yoris are given these dreams! The secret is, not everyone learns to enter the dream and work with it. We must — we have no choice. It's simple: without the dreams, we cannot converse with the secret."

The secret. What secret?

When you wake up crying, Huila said, you have been there. When you wake up laughing. When the dead come to you. When you have miscarried, and you dream that you have met a strange young person who might often reach for you and touch you, you have been there. Not only have you been there, but you have met your child's soul. When you dream of hummingbirds. When your lover is far from you, and for a moment you open your eyes and you can see the room where he sleeps, you have gone. When your ancestors come for you, and you travel with them to another town. When your dead father forgives you; when your dead mother embraces you. When you wake up and smell a foreign odor in your bedroom, a strange perfume, or smoke, or a scent of mysterious flowers, then you have been there. You might awaken with dew on your skirt, or with feathers in your hands. You might still taste a kiss on your lips.

"Angels travel these regions," Huila said. "And souls. God can speak to you there."

Don Teófano warned: "Or the devil himself."

Huila nodded.

"Or the devil."

This sounded entirely too complicated to Teresita. Not for the first time, she felt Huila was asking too much of her. She was starting to want to forget being a girl at all, much less a healer. She spent idle moments thinking about what fun it would be to dress up like one of the vaqueros and ride a big horse all day, jumping fences, chasing bandits and steers, fording rivers, shooting her trusty six-gun.

She felt guilty, but she stayed away from Huila's wagon for a day. She ate with Antonio Alvarado Cuarto's family, happily cuddling with her mother's old friend Juliana Alvarado, listening to stories about what her mother had been like. Wondering if this was what a family was.

And now they were north of the Fuerte, in the lands that so vexed them, and they learned an alarming lesson: the landscape of their fears looked exactly like the land they had left behind. The mountains asserted themselves gradually. They were learning to travel, so that their mornings were faster, and their passage more sure. By the time the landscape started to transform, they felt more ready, aware of where the riders were spaced, or where the riflemen rode, fully practiced in swirling into a circular encampment.

Still, the carts yowled and moaned, formed voices that wailed as if the souls burning in Hell were shouting. Axles swollen from the river ground steadily against the wood frames that held them, and as the grease wore away, the hideous screeches grew louder and more prolonged. A blue haze began to spread among the wagons, and someone said, "Do you smell something burning?" The third cart in the straggling conglomeration of carts that wobbled behind the last big wagon burst into flames as the axle overheated. "Caray!" the driver hollered, standing on his seat and gesturing at the fire. "Caray!"

"Get off, you idiot!" the cowboys called as they first tried to swish water from their canteens on the flames, then rode in circles looking for water to carry in their hats. The driver unhitched his ox and stood aside as the wagon exploded into a bonfire.

"Caramba," he said, shaking his head.

Somewhere, they crossed into Sonora.

The air changed around them. The heavy wetness of Sinaloa bled away gradually, until, one night, they found themselves sneezing and blowing their noses, blood in the cloths. They had never felt air as dry as this, and the women's hair and the cat's fur crackled with small lightning as if they were all enchanted. Segundo sidled up to Tomás and said, "Boss, the men, they have rocks in their noses."

"This wind," Urrea said, "it dries your snot."

Somehow, Segundo understood that the soul could be next.

Everyone watched everything. It was as if they had lived their entire lives with their eyes closed. Each rock in the path seemed as new as the mud and stones of Genesis.

They saw cacti grow tall as giants, shaped like purgatorial souls raising their arms to the mercy of God. They saw skeletal slaughtered wagons rotting beside the road. They passed through and around tiny squalid pueblos, and the naked children of these villes ran from them in terror or ran to them in hunger. Dogs fought their dogs.

They crossed a shallow stream, its water curling away from the wheels of the wagons, throwing wobbling patterns of light onto the horses' bellies. Teresita jumped from side to side of Huila's wagon, staring at each exciting new detail of the land around her. A field of yellow blossoms. A stand of sunflowers taller than the horses. A vast nopal cactus, big as a tree. "Get me a ladder!" Huila and Teresita said at once. Fine black bulls behind a fence. A startled deer breaking and running, the various straggling dogs trailing the riders speeding away behind it, caterwauling. Gusts of butterflies blew out of the bean fields as if the wind had been painted and had shattered into white chips.

"Sit down, child," Huila scolded. "You don't see the other children squirming around like worms."

And, later, "Teresa! You'll fall out and break your neck!"

But Teresita could not sit still. And Huila herself was lost in the morning, hypnotized by the rolling of the wagon, the hips and breasts of the hills around her, the heat of the sun. Huila, in her mind, was seventeen. She had not yet been burdened with medicine and cures. She was dancing in the arms of her first love, his breath hot in her ear under the orange light of a rising moon. She smoked her cigar and thought of his hands, thought of him naked, felt him throb within her as if a great heartbeat had fallen between her legs . . . gone now, lost all these long thirty years. Gone to dust. But alive in her chest, strangely alive on her body, as if his touch had tattooed her skin, ghost love.

"Girl!" She puffed. "What did I tell you?" Puff. "Don't come crying to me if you fall and kill yourself!"

Huila. Chugging through the morning like a little flesh

locomotive, leaving gray whorls of smoke behind her in the haunted air. Then they heard the approaching whine of a thousand buzzing wings.

⁂

Huila's wagon came around a bend to a scene of great wailing.

Doña Loreto's old carriage was pulled off to the side of the road, and Don Tomás sat astride his horse, looking down with vague curiosity. Don Lauro Aguirre held a small pair of eyeglasses before his small eyes and peered down. Segundo had dismounted and stood, bent at the waist, also peering down at Buenaventura as he kicked and screamed, rolling around in the dust with his arms wrapped around his head.

Buenaventura bellowed curses: his famous new bowler hat lay in the dirt, out of reach.

They had ridden into a fast-moving swarm of yellow jackets. The wasps had come down the road in a buzzing, golden cloud, expanding and contracting as they came. For some reason, they had widened around the front riders, then clapped together like great hands around Buenaventura's head. They had stitched his head with stings and exploded away, cutting west and veering over the mustard blossoms.

"Bees!" Tomás said. He shrugged. "I get stung every week."

He and Lauro muttered to each other as Buenaventura sobbed and cussed.

Huila had Teófano pull her wagon over. She creaked down off the bed and took Segundo's hand to hop to the ground.

"I'm getting older than the sun," she said.

"Domestic bees," Tomás lectured, "would know better than to sting a boy like this."

Buenaventura sucked in a hitching breath and let loose a pathetic wail.

"Good God," said Tomás, "you'd think this cabrón had been shot."

"He's just a child, compadre," Don Lauro said. "His wounds are urticant."

"They're what?" said Tomás.

"What did he say?" said Segundo.

Huila bent over the boy.

"Move your hands," she said.

"No."

"Take your hands off your face."

"No!"

"Desgraciado," she said.

He took his hands away from his face.

"Good," she said.

She took his chin in her hand and turned his head back and forth. She wiped the tears and snot off his cheeks and lips with her cuff. The stings were red and swelling.

"Hurts," he said.

"You were born to suffer," she said. "Your only choice is to endure it."

Tomás raised his eyebrows at Aguirre. Aguirre nodded appreciatively.

Huila took a few more puffs of her cigar, then took it out of her mouth and held it in front of her. "Go ahead and cry," she said. "It's all right." Then she extended the cigar toward his face. He screamed in panic. The horses shied away.

"You're going to burn me!" he squealed.

Teresita stood in the wagon, staring at this scene in a strange kind of rapture. She couldn't move. She forgot to breathe.

Huila did not burn Buenaventura.

She pressed the spit-soggy end of the cigar onto each sting, holding it there for a moment before moving on, leaving small prints on each welt, like brown watercolors of flowers.

Buenaventura immediately stopped crying.

"Remarkable," said Aguirre.

Buenaventura sat up. "Doesn't hurt," he said.

"Tobacco juice," said Huila, looking up at Don Lauro. "Always good for bug stings." She grimaced, held her hands to the small of her back, stretched. They could hear it crackle. "Ay. My backbone is getting rusty."

Buenaventura jumped to his feet.

"Hey, it doesn't hurt," he said.

"Don't wash your face," she ordered him.

Segundo offered Huila his arm as she turned to the wagon.

"Can I give you an arm up?" he asked.

"Why the hell not," she replied.

The parade resumed.

In a blighted field of white grass, a hundred crows bowed to them over and over, cawing, bowing as they passed, over and over.

The travelers crossed themselves.

Rumor spread that one of the trees along the trail was heavy with yellowed corpses hung with ropes, their necks snapped and forming awful L's, but nobody saw any such tree, though they came upon an exploded church, and standing before it an old madman with a white shirt, no pants at all, his long and astounding sex dangling in front, blood or some other black splash dried on his belly.

Then the Sierras chopped the bottom out of the eastern sky. The riders brought back deer, limp and bloody, hung across their saddles. Huila told the old story of the Yoem hunter who shot a doe and followed the trail of blood to a pool, where he found a beautiful maiden with her breast pierced by his arrow. People nodded, sighed. True, it was true. They called the deer the old name, in the old tongue: tua maaso.

They saw badgers, a lion on a rock. Eagles and hawks swooped down the terrible canyons, ruins vibrated with rattlesnakes. Small demons that the patrón called coatimundis glared at them with their hellish eyes, twitching their striped tails as they ran and giggled. People crossed themselves again and again. Unbelievable creatures and spirits stalked them and watched them and fled from their ruckus: red wolves and gray wolves; shaggy bears and jaguars. Layer upon layer of mountain rose beside them, mountains that could have exploded with Apaches at any instant, or soldiers, or bandits, or Americans. Demons slumbering in the narrow caves whispered their names, moaned in the night and vomited storms of bats. The rocks were blue, or red, or black, or golden. Then blue again, brown, white — or was that snow? Could that be snow? Millán the miner from far Rosario said it was the shit of seabirds, but he was shouted down. What pelicans could there be in the Sierra Madre?

Rabid dogs fled across the land, kicking up pale gusts of

dust as they spun and snarled, turned sideways at speed and tore their own flanks with their spuming jaws.

Goggle-eyed faces peered down from yellow cliffs, scratched into the stone, or painted with red-berry dye, their grim mouths yawning or set in angry lines, fading with the centuries, but still rageful as the peregrinos hurried away.

They broke open sun-dried turds, pulled apart the hairy scats and found, among the long whiskers and mottled fur, small bones. The bright orange teeth of a gopher. Tiny skulls. A five-fingered foot that looked like a human hand, with long dark nails on each finger, smaller than Huila's thumbnail.

"Coyote," she said, "ate a devil."

They hurried away, offering up puffs of breath with prayers in them small as the bones: "Jesús," they gasped, "Ave María." Huila took up the minuscule devil's hand and wrapped it in a bit of tissue and slipped it in the pocket of her apron.

Owls visited them at night. Some thought the owls were witches. Some thought they were the angels of death. Some thought they were holy and brought blessings. Some thought they were the restless spirits of the dead. The cowboys thought they were owls.

One day, Buenaventura brought Teresita the most marvelous object of all. The tobacco stains were still upon his cheeks like huge freckles. He clutched in his fist a small stone, and on this stone was the imprint of a fish. She grabbed it and squinted hard at it, rubbed it, licked it.

"A stone fish," Buenaventura said.

Huila took one look and said, "This is a miracle of God," and made the sign of the cross, by now the favorite gesture of the Exodus.

Don Teófano said, "The work of the devil," and also made the sign of the cross.

Old men insisted it was left over from Noah's flood.

Aguirre had proclaimed it an excellent example of ancient Chichimeca stone carving.

Segundo had insisted a witch made it.

Tomás had simply walked away, telling him not to bother him with foolishness.

Buenaventura said, "I think it's the seed of a fish."

"What!" Teresita laughed.

"I'm going to put it in a bottle of water, see if it sprouts."

"Fish don't sprout!"

"What if they do?" he insisted. "I'll be a rich man."

"You're already rich," Huila said. "You don't even know it."

Buenaventura looked down at his rumpled suit and grimaced.

"What do shoes feel like?" Teresita asked.

"It's like your feet went to jail," Buenaventura said.

She made a face, too.

Huila, who didn't have to go barefoot anymore, said, "It's not so bad. You can step on stickers and not feel a thing."

Teresita smiled.

"That's what huaraches are for."

"True." The old woman nodded. "But shoes are more hard. Your toes are safe, the tops of your feet."

"Like having hooves," Teresita said.

And they mounted up, into Indian country: passing small

as fleas on a rumpled blanket. The Río Navojoa, though broad, was shallower than the Fuerte and Segundo scouted a fine fording spot near another ferry raft. They made camp and watched the wagons cross the water like strange blocky ships, and the buckaroos played cards with a small company of gringo horse-hunters, come down to steal their herd back from a Mexican thief. And the leaves above their heads were turning yellow, something quite marvelous to see. Yellow and red, then falling like moths, spinning through the air.

This night's camp was on a dry plain. Three Indian men walked into camp and hailed Tomás, asking for a meal. He fed them beans and steak and fried potatoes on pewter plates and fried brains in scrambled eggs. They ate with their fingers and triangular pieces of tortillas. They drank cocoa — it made them laugh. When they were done, they smoked with the men, then stood and said, "Lios emak weye," and walked into the night without another word.

"Go with God," Teresita translated.

Tomás called out, "God bless you!" but they said nothing. He shrugged. "If there is a God, it can't hurt to stay on His good side."

Teresita and Huila walked toward their camp, holding hands.

"Spies," Huila said.

The peaks grew heavy with night, the points flaring orange, then impossible molten copper. Red like a deep infection crept down the cliffs and the arroyos, heavy and somehow fluid, until it spilled purple across the plain, drowning wagon after wagon, crawling up the legs of horses until only their backs were left in light, like small oblong islands in a shallow sea. Horse by horse, night conquered the plain. Fires blinked to life, and soon the stars above and the fires below looked the same, as if a slice of the sky had been stretched out on a drying rack so they could eat it in the morning.

All around the llano, the Urrea ranch camped, pitching tents and laying blankets on the shadows of the ghosts who had gone before. Aguirre, unknowing, lay on the spot where riders of the Glanton gang had once laid out a line of salted scalps to dry in the sun; the spot where shell traders from the Sea of Cortes had slept in 1764, and near his left foot the spot where the leader of that party had copulated silently with his third bride; the same spot where Spaniards, searching for El Dorado, had rested before they'd walked ignorantly into a storm of Yaquis and died, punctured and slashed, tormented to death with fire and knives and thorns and ants.

Loreto's fine tent — now housing Tomás's kitchen — was pitched over the graves of infants, dead of the coughing sickness, buried here by Jesuit missionaries. Segundo would have been deeply offended to know he slept on an old toilet trench. Only Huila spread her blankets on a clean patch of ground: no bones, no ghosts, no copulations or abandoned stale dreams spoiling in the dirt.

Tomás led a young woman by the hand and walked up into the foothills. Millán, the miner from Rosario, had introduced her to the patrón, already buying points for himself. He was no fool. And the girl, no fool either, lifted her skirts for Tomás as he knelt before her, licking his way up her thighs — brown and sweet as candy, at the same time tart and salty, musky, silken and cold in the warm air, refreshing as the sorbet he'd licked in Culiacán back when he was a student. She was amazed that this small bit of her body could bring the great master to his knees before her. She was perhaps the most beautiful girl on that whole plain, but he did not know her name and felt no need to ask. He pressed his face to her underwear, redolent with the burning scent of her, and he pulled the cotton down, over the bright points of her hips, the shadowy curve of her belly, until the fog of dark hair came into his sight, soft in the moonlight, tickling his face as he bent to her again. He pressed his lips to the mound of her, breathing her in, tasting her like a dog, as her skirts fell over his head and her fingers pulled his head tighter to her, her legs moving apart in the dark, her beauty falling around him, her greatest gift to him, this flavor, this smell, her secret.

Teresita lay about ten feet away from Huila's feet. The wagon rose above the old medicine woman, like the greatest headboard ever built, and her mattress was the earth itself. Snoring mounds snuffled and shifted all around her.

Teresita lay back and pulled the blanket to her chin. Her bottom hurt, though not as much as it had on the first days of her ride. Her thighs and calves were burned from rubbing bare across the burro's fur. Her neck was sunburned, as were her cheeks. The ground hurt her back.

She sighed.

She focused on her legs, as she so often had, and the glow ignited softly there, the golden honey feeling she summoned from no one could say where. She pulled it up slowly, filling her lower legs with it, tingling warmly, the pain draining out of her, the glow filling all the tissues of her body.

There was no way to know when the dream began. She didn't know, even, if she really was dreaming. It seemed to her that she'd lain there for a time staring up at the stars when something caught her eye. Far up there, some strange little flicker, some bit of gray color moving across the stars.

As she watched, that fleck grew larger, grew more solid, more colorful, until she realized that it was Huila, walking down the sky as if it were a stairway.

She sat up and rubbed her eyes.

Huila's skirt blew out behind her — she was smoking her pipe, and the smoke ripped away behind her in the dry breeze. She walked down in a spiral, coming from a place far up in the night, and she saw Teresita and smiled down at her.

"Huila!" Teresita whispered.

"Child."

"What are you doing?"

"I'm flying."

Teresita put her hands over her mouth.

"You shouldn't be watching me. It's rude to watch people fly," Huila scolded. "Look over there."

Teresita looked toward the tents, and she saw skinny men in white running from sleeper to sleeper.

"Who are they?" she asked.

Huila hovered above the wagon, looking down at herself asleep on the ground.

"Son los Yaquis," she said. "The Indians are dreaming about us again."

Huila bent down and took hold of her own shoulders.

She shuddered once, as if stepping into cold water, and pulled herself toward her own body. The body kicked once and rolled over. Huila was inside, hidden from view within Huila. Teresita watched her sleep.

The body said, "Good night, girl."

"Good night, old woman," Teresita said. Then, "Is this the dream?"

"It is."

Huila started to snore.

Teresita sat there thinking, feeling the strangeness of it. She looked around the plain: sputtering fires, the Yaqui dreamers flickering out of view, the sleeping bodies, the pale white lozenges of the tents. She turned and stared. There was a small glowing patch in the air, like mist. She saw people there, holding books and newspapers. Reading . . . and she knew they were reading about her. She leaned toward the light and looked in their faces. The readers were far from her, yet right beside her. She said, "Hello?" But they were too far in time to hear her.

Later, she awoke.

Sixteen

THEY MADE CAMP IN A GOOD VALLEY. A stream came out of the foothills, and it was shaded by cotton-woods. A fallen old trunk had formed a dam across the water, and the pool behind it was green and cool. The branches of the fallen tree had taken on a life of their own, and the rotting dam had a row of thin trees rising from it. Fat black fish lurked in the green pool, and the outflow of the dam watered a wide green swath of grasses and wild-flowers.

Teresita parked her burro beside Aguirre's horse and looked up at him.

"Engineer?" she said. "What year is it?"

"1880," he said.

"Is that a good number?" she asked.

She did not yet know that Yoris did not count the numbers the way the People did, and they did not pay attention to fours or sixes, sevens or nines.

Aguirre thought for a moment, then replied: "It is the year of the exodus!" This greatly pleased him. She went off to ask Huila what that word meant.

Their lives were changing every day as they traveled. They did not know that the world all around them was changing, as well. General Sherman, to the north, had just wearily proclaimed, "War is hell." Settlers in the state of Oklahoma, like Yoris in Mexico, had begun stealing Indian land. American companies not busy embezzling the Indian Territories were heading south and buying vast land holdings from the Díaz regime.

Thomas Edison had been experimenting with long-burning filaments. Wabash, Indiana, had recently become the first city entirely lit with electric lamps. Within a year, New York City would follow. George Eastman had patented the first roll of film.

The Irish gave the world the word *boycott*. France took Tahiti. Singer sold 539,000 sewing machines to replace its older models, one of which already awaited Doña Loreto in the great house in Alamos: a housewarming present from the Urreas of far Arizona. Alexander Graham Bell placed the first telephone call.

In New York, Thomas's English Muffins appeared. Ice cost $56 a ton and 890,364 tons of it were sold to tropical countries like Mexico. Philadelphia Cream Cheese was invented.

It was beside the green trout pool that the People first noticed the pilgrims. Don Tomás had declared two days of rest to feed and water the animals, to attend to the axles, and to do a little hunting and fishing. The buckaroos immediately set out to slaughter deer, quail, turtles, fish. Meat smoked and sizzled on crude spits over nearly every campfire. The sound of singing and laughter combined with the lowing of the cattle. Tomás, lying in the shade of the horizontal cottonwood grove, idly watched the smoke rise, took in the lulling music of his rolling rancho, and nibbled the delicate meat of a trout.

"Truchas," Huila said, spitting right and left, "are full of bones."

Walkers passed the camp in small groups. They never accepted offers of hospitality. Segundo called them rude bastards for turning down his rum and beans. After the tenth scuttling crowd passed by, he took to siccing dogs on them and aiming rifles at them to make them trot.

"We are going to the messiah!" one tattered Indian called, as if this explained everything.

"The messiah!" Segundo bellowed. "What messiah?"

"Chepito!"

"Who the hell is Chepito?"

"Niño Chepito, the messiah!"

Huila listened to this with great interest.

Niño Chepito, eh?

"I will go inspect this messiah," she proclaimed.

"Ay, Huila," Tomás said. "Another pendejo with magic tricks getting the other pendejos excited."

"I should see," she said.

"A messiah?" Aguirre asked. "A heretic, perhaps. An Antichrist! There is but one messiah."

Huila eyed him.

"Yes, well," she said.

Certain members of the rancho had already started to walk into the foothills. They were converting before they even saw Chepito. Tomás watched this with some alarm.

"Why are they going?" he asked Huila.

She shrugged.

"Curious," she said. And, "If you were them, would you live like this?"

"Like what?" he asked.

Huila shook her head.

"I will return tomorrow," she said. "Do not leave without me."

She set about gathering her bundle of things for the walk, her shotgun and some shells. Old Teófano loaded his shotgun as well, and he threw a roll of blankets over his shoulder. Teresita, uninvited, joined them.

"Where are we going?" she asked.

"Into the hills," Huila replied. "A place they are calling Sal Si Puedes."

Get Out If You Can. It seemed like the wittiest name Teresita had ever heard for a place.

Teófano made a face and shook his head. "These desert and mountain people are crazy," he said. "We don't have messiahs in Sinaloa!"

They started walking along the obvious path cut through the grasses by the pilgrims. All kinds of interesting things lay along the path. An abandoned huarache. A bloody cloth. A length of hair tied to a tree, left as a manda to some saint — a woman trading her long mane for the health of a child, or the safety of a mate. Huila saw cast-off religious pictures of former messiahs the People had turned against.

They came upon a small camp with seven Mexicans gathered around a fire. Teresita was astounded to find Tía squatting here with her children.

"Auntie!" she cried.

Tía smiled.

"Isn't it wonderful?" she said.

Teresita thought she was very strange. As if she were dreaming. Her eyes stared off over Teresita's shoulder. Teresita turned to see what Tía was looking at, but she was staring at nothing.

"Isn't what wonderful, Auntie?" she asked.

"Deliverance!"

The pilgrims hunched near Tía laughed and clapped and said, "Amen."

Tía rose and tossed her cigarette makings into the flame.

"Deliverance," she repeated.

"Adios!" Huila said and pulled Teresita along the path. "Está loca. Don't look back, child. Let us go see for ourselves."

"We should go back," said Teófano.

"Don't be a coward," Huila muttered.

They went uphill, and then the path forked down into a steep canyon. They could smell the camp before they saw it. A stench of sweat and smoke rose out of the canyon.

The little piñon pines were twisted in the midafternoon light, and smoke curled through their branches like little banners. Before they knew they were near, they broke through the trees and were in the camp. It wasn't huge, but it was a mess. Broken carts and untethered mules filled the bottom of the canyon, and lean-to shacks seemed to collapse among busted wagons and drooping tents. Only about three hundred pilgrims were gathered. Huila strained and saw the Promised One seated on a small stage at the center of a moiling crowd. He looked like a fat boy sitting on a pillow with his legs crossed.

She grabbed Teresita's hand and pulled her into the crowd, Don Teófano on guard behind them with his shotgun held across his chest. People parted easily to let them pass; blissful and starry-eyed, they hummed and rocked on their heels, said "Amen" quietly, and occasionally broke into giggles. Teresita's neck hairs stood on end.

Near the stage, a small group of dancers whirled and whirled. Three men lay facedown in the dirt; one of them twitched and trembled as if he were being whipped by a savage wind.

"Does that man need help?" Huila asked.

A woman said, "No, hermana. He has seen God!"

"Ah, cabrón!" said Huila.

Niño Chepito was sitting on a small bit of carpet in the shade of a scraggly tree. His stage had raised him about three feet above their heads. His long hair was gathered behind his head and held in place by red ribbons. He had a generous double chin. He wore white peasant pants and a brightly colored blouse covered in woven designs: birds, cacti, black mountains, deer.

"If God is everywhere, my children," he was saying,

"then He is in everything. If He is in everything, then He is in me, then He is me. And I am God."

Wood flutes were twittering away. Drums sounded an endless heartbeat.

"I am the God of this world, my children. The last time I came, you killed me on the cross. I have come back to this flesh to lead you to truth."

A dancer shouted once and fell on his back — his feet kicked and hammered the dirt.

"He's going to pee," Huila noted.

And he did.

Chepito droned on. It was obvious he had been talking now for hours. Perhaps for days. Those around them were asleep on their feet.

"God is not God. I am God. The God who made this world, the God who rules you now, the Yori God, He is the evil one. This world is a trick. Only through devotion to Niño Chepito will this wicked incarnation end! The white man will die! The dead will then rise! A flood will cover the earth, and new soil thirty feet deep will sprout new corn and flowers! Have I not told you of the flood? Have I not promised to reincarnate all the dead? The deer will be fat on the flowers, and she will offer all true believers her sweet flesh!"

"Niño Chepito!"

"Chepito, Chepito."

"The Yori must die. The mestizos must die. The angels will eat these souls, for Niño Chepito will not guide them to salvation, my children. No."

"May we leave now?" whispered Teófano.

"Death is life," Chepito said. "Do you see? Death is life. Death is life. Death is life."

The drums sped up. Voices began to chant along with him.

Huila stared up at the messiah for a moment, then shook her head. "Let's go," she said.

As they pushed their way back out of the crowd, people laid hands on them, weakly grabbed at their clothes, tried to hold them, saying, "Where are you going?" and "The dark angels wait outside this valley to consume you."

Teresita was frightened when she saw Tía weeping openly, raising her hands to the sun, crying, "Death! Death! Death!"

Tía saw Teresita and rushed to her, threw her arms around her and kissed her on the cheek.

"La muerte!" she hissed. "Niño Chepito nos lleva a la muerte!"

Teresita pulled herself out of her aunt's grasp and ran after Huila.

She looked back. Tía fell to her knees and put her face in the dirt and rolled her head back and forth. The drums fell back to a heartbeat rhythm, and Chepito's voice was small and dry, like the call of a distant crow.

She never saw Tía again.

Seventeen

THOUGH SOME STAYED BLISSFUL and delivered with the peregrinos of Niño Chepito's evangelical camp, the rest of the People felt lean and ready to travel on. They had grown used to the road and the ground and the open sky. They had grown disciplined, awakening quickly at first light, starting their many fires and cooking faster every day, and they leapt to their wagons and carts and fell into order without speaking. Like children in a classroom, they had each found their spot among the many, and they did not deviate from it. Their new sense of organization was a joy to them. The Urrea ranch had transformed itself, again, into a morning spiral that curled and curled and then opened to spill them away from each encampment in a long steady flow. They were as synchronized as ants.

"Perhaps," Don Teófano suggested, "in Cabora, the milk is sweet as honey."

"What if," an old woman offered, "the honey tastes like milk?"

"I don't think I'd like that, comadre," he said.

They all voted: sweet milk was better than milky honey.

"Where does this land of milk and honey come from?" Teresita asked in the wagon one day.

"The Bible," said Huila.

"Can we read it?"

"The priest can read it," Huila said. "We don't read it."

"Why not?"

"We just don't."

"Priests," said Teófano, "go to school to read that book."

"Why can't we?" Teresita insisted.

"We're not priests," said Huila.

"But you said we do holy work. We work medicine and pray to the saints and the Virgin and the four directions."

"Don't be a pest, child."

"Aren't we the same as a priest?"

"Who?"

"Curanderas!"

"You are not a curandera, child."

"Medicine women!"

Huila laughed.

"Women," she said. "You're just a sprout. And when you are a woman, *you won't read that book!*"

"Why not?"

"Ay, niña! Women are not *priests*. Now stop this silliness."

Teresita just sat there, staring.

"Do you read?"

"Are you crazy, child? Why would I read?"

"But —"

"Reading," Huila said, "is for men. Like babies are for women, books are for men."

"White men," Don Teófano said. "I don't read."

"Rich men," Huila corrected. "Lauro Aguirre isn't any whiter than you are!"

"Doña Loreto?" Teresita asked. "Does she read?"

Huila shook her head.

"The patrón reads for her. He reads to her from books, or he reads to her from the newspaper when he thinks she can understand it."

Teresita laughed out loud. That was just stupid.

"You are learning what you need to know," said Huila. "Who needs books? Who needs to learn Yori foolishness?"

"I do."

"Why?" The old one laughed. "Do you hope to become president of the republic?"

"Why not?" Teresita insisted. "I could."

"God in Heaven," Huila sighed.

After all this talk about God, all this struggle to learn

sacred secrets, here was a book God had written for them to study, and they didn't think she would read it? She stared at Huila, the most perfect old woman she had ever known. Huila, of the cigars, of the shotgun, of the terrible black sack of men's balls in her apron. Huila, the source of power. Yet imperfect after all, made stupid by the rules of some Yori man — Teresita imagined him, whoever he was, riding one of those phantom trains they talked about, making rules and reading newspapers. She looked Huila in the eye, turned, and spit over the edge of the wagon.

"Girl!" the old woman said, but Teresita had already hopped down off the wagon.

She shuffled along beside it and untied her burro. She mounted him, saying, "You want me to be as stupid as little Panfilo!" The burro waggled his ears upon hearing his name and trotted off to the side, steered by Teresita between wagons, walkers, riders, cows, toward the edge of the great cattle drive, where she could flank the slowest cows and make believe she was a vaquero.

"I will read," she said out loud.

She kicked her burro in the ribs: he bucked up his heels once and charged ahead, long ears laid back along his blocky skull. "Go, Panfilo!" she ordered.

Soon she found Segundo. Her head was about as high as his boot as she trotted along beside him. He looked down and was startled to see her staring up at him.

"What," he said.

"What is in books?"

He scratched his head. Shrugged.

"Stories, I guess. Poems? Things like that."

"I want to read!" she shouted.

He laughed.

"You're a girl," he said. "Besides, *I* don't even know how to read. Reading isn't for people like us."

"Hmm." And she galloped away.

Books, Segundo thought. What's next?

When Teresita found Buenaventura, she told him, too, that she wanted to read. He said: "You're just an Indian. Indians don't read! If they don't teach white girls to read, what makes you think they're going to teach a little Indian anything?"

He waved her off with one hand.

She fell away from the crowd, letting her little Panfilo slow down and wander off to the side again. She let his rope reins fall loose, and he stood there confused for a moment. When he realized she wasn't prodding him along anymore, he was more than happy to drop his head into the grass and weeds beside the path. He let out a long contented sigh and ripped up mouthfuls of dandelions.

Teresita sat on his back and watched them go. Huila's big wagon was already around the bend. The carts and horses and wagons rattled along. She wasn't going to cry. She would just wait there and starve, die all alone and let the buzzards take her apart. Nobody would know what had happened to her.

Or maybe a warrior would come along.

Yes, a warrior from one of these ferocious northern tribes. She could probably join them, forget she'd ever learned Spanish. Learn to hunt. Marry a young man of the tribe. Disappear. Nobody cared anyway.

She sat on Panfilo until the entire cattle drive was down the road, and she watched them diminish, and they went around the bend and vanished, until the only things to mark their passage were the clouds of dust and the fading noise. The last to vanish was the bee wagon. Its happy beekeeper reclined at a comfortable angle on the seat and waved as he rolled along. Panfilo raised his head and looked around. He swung his head back and stared at her. He snorted.

After a while, when the land had become silent, Teresita picked up the reins and nudged him with her heels. He reluctantly pulled his lips away from the weeds and shuffled down the trail, his head nodding as he walked. "I'll show them," she promised. "I'll show everybody."

A coyote in the hedionda bushes yipped and yodeled.

Panfilo started to trot.

※

Ahead, at least six miles away from Teresita and Panfilo, Tomás rode beside the Engineer Aguirre.

"Tell me," said the patrón, "you who are a world traveler."

Aguirre pushed off this epithet with a sound like *Pah!* "Texas," he interjected, "and Mexico City are hardly the world!"

"It's enough of the world for our purposes," said Tomás. "What I'm curious about is the differences between Sinaloa and the north. Have you an opinion, my dear hijo de puta?"

"I have a certain fame for my repertoire of opinion."

Tomás smiled. "Although it is true that you are insufferable and irritating, and rightly famed for your endless posturing and platitudinous pontificating —"

"Bastard!"

"— I still would like to ask you: in your experience, what are some of the differences between ourselves and the blasted north?"

"Ah," said Aguirre, as if this were too vast a subject to

broach. "Differences." He raised his hands in a symbolic surrender. "Where could I begin?"

"Anywhere."

Aguirre regarded him.

"Have you noticed, my dear Urrea," he said, "that you Sinaloans are provincial rubes?"

"No."

"Oh well, you are bumpkins. And here is an example, since you asked. In Sinaloa, you might have noticed, you have the habit of adding the prefix 'el' or 'la' to people's names. For example, you call your dear bride 'La Loreto.'"

"So?"

"El Lauro," said Aguirre, touching his own chest.

"So?"

"La Huila, El Segundo. That peculiar little girl — La Teresita."

"So?"

"So it is wrong. Incorrect. Bizarre, in fact. It's as if all of you give yourselves some royal singularity. The Tomás Urrea has arrived. The Lauro Aguirre is here."

"Doesn't everybody talk like that?"

Aguirre shook his head.

"Have you not read a book?" he asked.

"Books are one thing," Tomás sniffed. "Talking is another. Books don't ever say 'chingado,' for example. Aguirre chingado."

"Just wait, you imbecile. They will when the minds of the population are freed. But they will never refer to anyone as 'The Tomás.' Pendejo."

Tomás clopped along for a while, thinking.

"That's interesting," he said.

"I thought so," Don Lauro replied.

Clop clop cloppa clop.

"Whereas the North Americans," Aguirre announced, "have no gender in their language."

Aghast, Tomás let out a small puff of air.

"No 'el'?" he said. "No 'la'?"

Aguirre, quite satisfied with his latest astonishment, said: "No. They have the following word: *the.*"

"As in tea?"

"Not té! The!"

"No male, no female?"

"The!"

"C'est bizarre, mon ami!"

"Los gringos," Aguirre lamented, "are hermaphrodites."

They had noticed, over the last few miles, columns of biblical smoke rising over the hills before them.

"What do you suppose that is?" Tomás asked.

They stopped and unfolded their small maps and studied the horizon.

"Volcano?"

"Not on the map," Aguirre said. "Perhaps a grass fire."

Now, as they moved ahead, the smoke columns grew darker and more solid. Segundo, who had seen these columns miles before anyone else, trotted up to them and tipped his hat.

"Gents," he said.

"Good old Eye of the Buzzard," said Tomás. "What have you to report?"

"Looking at that smoke," Segundo said.

"What do you see?"

"Smoke."

"You are a fountain of information," Aguirre said. He stopped his nag and pulled the heavy big map out of his bag. The other two reined in beside him, and they each sat within a puddle of shadow cast by their own hats. "Look here," Aguirre said. "We're near the ranch."

Segundo was staring into the distance.

"Crows," he said. "Lots of crows circling around the smoke."

"This is Cabora?" Tomás asked the Engineer.

"This valley ahead of us." His companion nodded. "I believe we are home."

Tomás turned in his saddle and peered into the distance behind them.

"We've gotten a bit ahead of the wagons," he said. "I hate to ride into the ranch without them."

"They'll catch up," Segundo said.

They could smell the smoke when the wind whipped a slender banner of it over the hill.

Aguirre spoke up: "Let's just ride up there and look," he said. "Let's see the great Cabora. Investigate this conflagration."

Tomás flicked his reins once, and his great dark steed bobbed its head and paced away.

"Let's go," he said.

"Jefe!" Segundo called. "Let me gather a few of the riflemen. This is Yaqui territory — we ought to be careful."

"We don't need any riflemen," Tomás called back. "How many days have we been on the road? The only Indians we've seen have been beggars and children. There's no danger here!" His horse seemed to engage some soft gear within itself, and it moved away smoothly, speeding up gradually as it approached the slopes.

Aguirre followed.

Segundo said: "We ought to have rifles."

❀

Teresita came upon a wagon pulled to the side of the road. A fat mule skinner sat up on the box, his floppy hat smashed on his head like a collapsed brown cake, portions of tattered brim melting down his face and sticking to his sweat. Six mules bobbed their heads and snorted, nipping at each other in their traces. Tarpaulins covered dusty hills of goods behind the skinner, and he bristled with weapons: he held a shotgun across his lap, and she could see crossed bandoliers of bullets on his chest, and a scabbard held a rifle near the big wooden brake lever beside his leg.

He leaned over the side and spit tobacco.

"Is that it?" he said.

"What?"

"That desgraciado cattle drive. Is that all there is?"

"Sí, señor. I'm the last."

She sat on her donkey, peering up at him.

He drew a long knife from his belt and cut a chunk of tobacco off his plug and stuffed it in his mouth. Brown drool colored his lip and gray beard. He leaned over and spit: it barely missed Teresita. His right cheek was split by a red scar that went from his eyebrow to his chin. It vanished among the whiskers, and where it vanished, the whiskers were white.

He held the big knife up and said, "Boo!"

He laughed.

"I am not afraid," Teresita said.

He laughed some more.

He shook the knife at her.

"Uy!" he said. "Uy! Uy!"

She thought he was acting foolish.

He put the knife away.

"Where you going?" he asked.

"Cabora."

"Cabora? Never heard of no Cabora."

"It is our new ranch."

"You don't have no Goddamned ranch, you little pinche Indian girl. What are you, an Indian?" He took his knife back out, held it up to his scalp, cried, "Eeee!"

He laughed again.

"Indian!" he said. "You're an Indian, aren't you?"

"Good-bye, sir," she replied.

Adults should know how to behave.

"Hey," he said. "See this? See it?" He pointed to his face. "What are you, Apache? Yaqui? See this face? Yaquis did this to my face. How you like it?"

He moved his knife up and down his face, making squishy noises with his mouth.

"Yaquis!" he said. "Wanted my eye!" He spit — it flew over her head and splattered on the ground. "What are you, Yaqui?"

"Good-bye, sir," she repeated. She nudged little Panfilo in the ribs, and the donkey snorted to life and trotted away.

"Yaquis!" the skinner shouted after her. "They cut off men's feet and make them walk until they bleed to death! You little savage! Come back here! Yaquis hang men upside down from branches, put their heads in fire. I seen it! Burned their brains out! Come back here, I'm not done yet!"

She shook the reins and made the burro break into a run.

The last thing she heard from the mule skinner was his laughter. She was happy once she caught up with Huila.

※

Tomás cleared the summit long before Aguirre and Segundo could catch up to him. At first, he wasn't sure what he was seeing. But he slowly started to understand. His stallion spun in circles. Tomás had to wrestle him to a standstill.

He removed his hat and fanned it before his face, futilely trying to swipe some of the smoke stink away from him. He kicked his right leg over the pommel and slid off the saddle, then he went down on one knee and stared. He plucked a stalk of grass and put it in his mouth.

Segundo galloped up to him and dismounted in a cloud of dust.

"My God," he said.

Aguirre trotted up to them and let out a small cry.

"There must be some mistake!" he said. "Surely . . . this must be the wrong valley . . . ?"

Tomás stood, tossed the grass to the ground.

"There's no mistake," he said.

He pulled his revolver from his holster, checked the cylinder: fully loaded. He looked at Segundo. "Go get me the riflemen," he commanded.

Eighteen

THE RIDERS SPREAD OUT along the ridge, both vaqueros and hired guns, their Winchesters in their hands. One, a Frenchman, carried a huge Henry long-range gun, its octagonal barrel casting blue lights in the sun. He peered down into the valley with his hunting scope, but Segundo had already seen that it was too late.

Cabora was in a wide valley that opened onto a plain that stretched as far as any one of them could see. The patchwork of tilled fields and cattle pasture gave way to desert tans and yellows. Mountains to the east, hills to the west and north. Green creek beds crisscrossed the terrain. And toward the center, beneath its crown of writhing smoke, beside a dark chasm in the earth, lay the wreckage of the ranch compound.

The wagons from Sinaloa stalled on the backslope behind the riders, collected in the hollow like water. The People eddied among their animals, and no one knew what was above them, though they all watched the smoke columns writhe. They made the sign of the cross, clutched hatchets, butcher knives, old guns. Soon, word started to drain back down to them, falling from switchback to switchback, coming down the hill. "The ranch is gone," they said. "Cabora is gone."

Above them, Tomás remounted.

He and Segundo rode down into the valley with Aguirre taking up the rear. The riders fanned out behind him, all guns at the ready.

The main buildings still smoldered in the distance, their walls already gone in the fire, nothing but a charred chimney rising above the plain. The fences were down; some scattered livestock still grazed. The barns were burned, the workers' shacks smoking. Dogs, shot down and left beside the road, lay like mottled and softened rocks. A dead man bent over a fence post hung loose as laundry, blood thick and black and clotted all over him, his pants ripped away, an arrow inserted in his fundament. Flies sang like a wire in the wind, a high pitch, a terrible hymn.

Tomás snapped his fingers and pointed at him.

"Get him off there," he said.

A pig squirmed in the dirt, punctured by a fistful of arrows, transformed into a porcupine of agony, the arrows rustling and clacking as the pig groaned and dragged itself. Segundo drew his revolver and fired one shot into the pig's head. Aguirre jumped. "Por Dios," he said.

Segundo told one of the riders to take it back to the cook wagon.

They came upon a charred body in the ruins of the first burned shack. It was black and red and brown and yellow and white, but mostly black. Its mouth was open in a silent scream, or some thought a yawn, and others thought it was laughing, and its claws were hard as carvings and raised to the sky and its legs were dark bones and raised as if it could run up the columns of smoke and enter Heaven.

All the horses were gone.

The well was collapsed, the stones of its rim kicked down its throat. Intestines were hung like garlands from the cottonwood nearest the ruins of the main house, and none of them could tell if it was the inside of man or animal hung there and made crisp by the sun. And still, the windmill turned, its blades picturesque against the violet distance, its rhythmic squealing eerie in the great quiet of the valley. Hay bales smoldered. The hills were lilac in the late sun, the crops almost black in the distance. The men covered their mouths and noses with bandanas against the stench of death.

Tomás jumped off his horse and rushed into the triangular corner of the demolished barn. He came out with a child in his arms. The child was covered in blood. It was alive, though its head seemed to be made of some soft cloth, and it flopped on its shoulders and an old wound was dried into a hard scab.

"Take him to Huila," Tomás said, and a rider tenderly wrapped the child in his coat and spun and galloped back out of the long valley.

The cows were gone.

Aguirre pointed: an empty suit of clothing, spread across the ground as if someone had run out of his own clothes.

A woman's shoe with a broken glass of milk in it.

A dead man on a mattress floated in the stock pond like a sailor dreaming of home. They watched as the mattress slowly tipped and sank, the man's stiff hand waving once as he settled into the black water. They were startled to hear frogs. They were startled to hear anything. They had imagined the entire valley to be silent, but it was alive with sounds. Somewhere a dog barked. The flies raised their high cry. They suddenly heard chickens. The crackling of the many fires. Crickets. Doves. The many fat crows, gorging themselves on cooked flesh, laughing from the trees. Then, slowly, they heard the sound of human sobbing.

Survivors came forward, alone and in pairs. No Urreas lay among the few dead — the family had cleared out to make room for Tomás. No, they were comfortably waiting in the great house in the city, unaware of the destruction of their ranch. The only family members awaiting them at Cabora were old ghosts, tossed from their graves by the violence.

Tomás was stunned when a man with his left eye missing

stumbled out of the stock-pond reeds. Like the madman they had seen so many days ago on the road, this man was without pants, his white shirt stained with old blood. But it was a different face under the blood, the frank pockmark of the empty socket collecting sun: Tomás could see the inside of the man's head. He turned away and put his hand over his lips.

"Yaquis!" the man wailed. "They came out of the soil like devils!"

"Help this man," Tomás said.

A woman, inexplicably, came forth from the trunk of a cottonwood. Her arm appeared, then her torso, and her legs. Two children materialized before them, holding hands. The men who first saw them shook their heads, rubbed their eyes. Had this boy and girl been standing there the whole time? Had they been rendered invisible by the great destruction around them? More people came out of ruts in the ground, out of a small orchard, out from behind agave plants where they had hunched like rabbits or armadillos, the color of the sand, breathing shallowly and clutching the earth.

"Yaquis," they said.

"Llegaron con el amanecer, gritando como diablos. No montaban caballos. Vinieron corriendo, a pie, brincando como venados, volando como buitres."

The main house had been a large affair, built of wood and whitewashed adobe. The walls had cracked and fallen in, etched with terrible black shadows from the fires, the heat of the twisting red coals so fierce that none of the riders could go near it. Puddles of copper and brass on the fallen porch revealed where doorknobs had melted.

"Look here," Aguirre called.

The insides of the house had been ripped out and scattered, like the innards hung in the tree, broken and thrown with a kind of rage that was still frightening though the raiders were gone. Shattered glass, broken crockery, broken chairs and tables and gutted pillows coughing feathers into the breeze, hollow clothes like phantoms, massacred nightgowns. Murdered books flapped on the ground.

Aguirre stood beside a big overstuffed chair. Stacked carefully in it were all the crosses and crucifixes gathered from the main house. The family Bible and a statue of the Virgin of Guadalupe nestled there, along with a small statue of Saint Francis.

"They saved all the religious artifacts," Aguirre said.

"They're Catholics," Tomás replied.

"Are you serious?"

"I am."

He went to one of the survivors.

"Where are all my cowboys?" he asked.

"They ran away."

"Where are all my workers?"

"They have fled."

"Who was in charge?"

"No one was in charge."

"What can you tell me?"

"They came on foot. They took the cows, the horses. They took some women."

"Yaquis?"

"Yaquis, patrón. Yaquis." The man pointed to the west. "They live right over there, about ten miles."

"What? You knew them?"

"Oh yes. We knew them well."

Aguirre butted in. "But why?" he said. "Why would they do this?"

The man shrugged.

"They said they were hungry," he said.

Tomás patted him on the arm.

"The wagons are coming," he said. "They'll feed you."

"Sir?" the man said.

"Yes?"

"Would you be angry with me if I resigned my position?"

Tomás just walked away.

Segundo picked up a charred framed picture of unnamed Urreas.

"What next," he asked no one in particular.

The wagons and carts slowly creaked over the ridge and started down into the valley. Huila, kneeling in her wagon, had laid the soft-necked infant on folded blankets, but its eyes were already cloudy and blue, and it shuddered and let out a last breath, then collapsed. Huila thought of a sheet furled over a bed, swelling high, then collapsing as the air escaped. Flat. That was how the child left this world.

How many dead trailed behind her? She could not count. All the ones who died of fevers and pox, for lack of Yori pills. The sad mothers who died screaming and their babies, dead inside them. Dead cowboys with bullets in their hearts. She watched Teresita stare at the tiny body in the wagon, and she said a prayer, for the girl would learn the terrible truth now, that you could not save everyone — you could save only a few — and the rest were doomed, as you yourself were doomed, to lie in the dirt before you could ever be ready. She pulled a cloth over the infant's face.

The business of rebuilding had already begun. At the ranch, the men dug the graves and laid the charred and tormented dead into the ground. Across the dreadful plain, Huila had already organized the cooks, and Segundo had posted two guards to stand by the tent all night with weapons cocked and ready before riding back to be with Tomás, and Teresita had moved in near Huila in case the warriors returned. In iron pans balanced on flat rocks by the tall fires, the cooks melted lard, boiled water. For supper they ate caldo de ajo — garlic soup: all their stale bread that hadn't gone to the pigs or the goats floated in beef broth, salted and peppered, the garlic cloves soft in the broth like little fish. And they ate arroz con pollo, the fresh chicken mixed with prairie fowl the vaqueros had shot that day and the day before, boiled with rice and a pinch of saffron. In the morning, they would breakfast on peeled and diced beavertail-cactus pads, lard-fried beans, and their last eggs. It smelled like a festival.

Tomás, standing on the charred front steps of the ranch house, could see the campfires of his people far across the land. He stepped down and walked toward the impromptu graveyard they had scraped out of the soil beyond a stone wall that meandered toward the skeletal windmill that whined and screaked in the drying wind. Green water chugged out of the ground, spitting from an iron pipe and into rusted troughs, where the horses set their heads to drink, drifting across the sand and dust without escort by ones and twos, as if they were interested in the fate of the ranch house, curious about the battle.

The men around him cried for blood. Vengeance was in the air. They muttered and cursed, they called out their rage, spoke of filthy Indios, of savages. Yet Tomás wondered why there were not more bodies. Why had the Yaquis allowed so many to escape?

The Cabora plain was empty, dry. The Sinaloans were in their first desert, and the desert frightened them. There was no cover — few trees broke the sere waste, and beyond, the peaks were savage and violent, unsoftened by green. Elemental colors, vivid hues that shouted to them of copper and blood. This was a wicked place, they were certain, and this attack was only the first. "War," they were saying.

"Kill the women and children," Tomás heard one vaquero proclaim.

Aguirre joined him on the steps.

"Que en paz descansen," he said. May they rest in peace. It was a standard blessing.

Tomás nodded.

"A dark day, amigo," Aguirre said.

Tomás extended his hand before him.

"Four graves," he said.

"Yes."

"Four."

"Yes, four."

"Why not ten, Lauro? Why not a hundred?"

"I —" Aguirre started to say, then fell silent. "I don't know."

"This was a Yaqui war party," Tomás said. "They could have wiped out the whole llano, I'm certain."

"I couldn't say. You are the expert in this matter. Yaquis?" He shrugged. "Well."

They rolled cigarettes and smoked. When they were finished, Lauro spoke.

"What of these Yaquis? You almost had me convinced when you joked that they were Catholics."

"I wasn't joking." Tomás put his hand on his old friend's shoulder, and he told him a story as they walked.

When the Spaniards were finished with the Aztecs, they came, as you well know, north. They wanted to spread the Holy Faith, but they really wanted gold. And they were happy in Sinaloa, make no mistake. If not gold, then silver. They found oceans of silver down around Rosario and Escuinapa. But of course, they wanted to discover the Seven Cities of Gold they'd been looking for from the Andes all the way north. Cíbola.

Tomás moved a stone onto one of the graves with the toe of his boot. It was a gentle, absentminded gesture. Aguirre watched his friend with great tenderness.

Sooner or later, they would come this way. It was inevitable. It took them three hundred years to learn there were no cities of gold. But these Indians were sly. So the Guasaves, sad and poor to the south, told the Spaniards, "Oh yes! Great temples of gold! To the north! In the land of the Mayos!"

And of course *Mayo* sounded like *Maya,* so the Spaniards set out at a trot, imagining pyramids and sculptures. That's when they found the Mayos. When the Spaniards came, seven hundred of them, in armor, heavily armed, and wafting their stench after not bathing for a year, or two, or three, the Mayos were appalled. So they did the only reasonable thing — they lied the way the Guasaves lied. They pointed north, said, "Oh yes — great temples of gold! But these can only be found in the Yaqui lands. Go to the Yaquis, our brothers, farther up these valleys, along the

Río Yaqui, and they will share their gold with you! Tell them we sent you!"

And the Spaniards went.

The Yaquis were, of course, cousins to the Mayos. They spoke a variant of the same language. But these two tribes were like black ants and red ants. The black ants are peaceful and hardworking. The red ants are also hardworking, but if you should stand on their anthill, they will swarm out and do their best to kill you. So the Spaniards marched on to the Río Yaqui. They walked right up the valley, where the Yaquis were waiting. And the Spaniard leader said something along the time-honored lines of "In the name of the king of Spain, and the power of God Almighty, we have come to bring you the gospel of Jesus Christ our Lord. Oh, and where's the gold?" And the Yaquis ran out like red ants and killed all of them.

Tomás laughed.

Aguirre said, "This is not funny."

"It is if you're a Yaqui."

The sun was setting fast.

Aguirre looked around him. He held a cross in his left hand, and he laid his right hand on the butt of the gun he'd jammed in his belt. The crags and hills around them were, in his mind, alive with Yaquis. Comanches. The frightening Sioux might even be out there. He suddenly imagined a massive pan-Indian war party sweeping the continent, their cleansing of the land about to start with him.

"You like these people," he said.

"They're a great people."

"But they're killers."

"We're killers."

"But —"

"Nobody deadlier than a missionary, eh Aguirre?" He slapped his friend on the back. "Nothing more dangerous than the Church."

"You said they were Catholics," Aguirre muttered.

"Oh, they are. You see, for some reason, the Yaquis allowed some Jesuits to come into these regions. There were eight Yaqui centers, towns that the Jesuits made into missions. And — perhaps God, that old trickster, was really at work after all — the Jesuits allowed the tribe to exercise its own rituals along with the new Roman high jinks. Imagine, Lauro — deer dancers in the Mass. A native Easter!"

"Some might see that as heresy. Sin."

"Sin! Shit." Tomás walked quickly — Aguirre had to hurry to catch up. "Why was it not a sin to impose Roman rituals on a Hebrew religion? If there is a God, do you really believe he speaks Latin? No seas tonto. It was the genius of the Jesuits to handle these people in such a fashion. And when the Jesuits were expelled from Mexico, they left behind their religion. Now they're back."

They walked into the crowd of cowboys, bumping into the redolent horses as they shifted in the uneasy dark. The scent of gun oil hung between the flanks of the animals, and the sharp scent of leather, and the many kinds of sweat and fear came off the men like cigarette smoke. "Boss," the men said, some of them startled, as Tomás slipped past them. "Boys," he said, patting them on the leg, the knee, as they sat their horses. And when he'd made his way into the middle of the men, he stopped. They all stopped. They waited.

It was Segundo who finally spoke.

"So," he said, "what are we going to do?"

"I, for one," the patrón said, "am going to sleep."

Nineteen

THE FOLLOWING MORNING, as Don Tomás prepared to deliver his orders to them all, Teresita walked from camp to camp, watching the People ready their breakfasts. Huila had sent clay bowls full of beans and nopal cactus fried in eggs to the men at the ruined ranch house. Some of the locals had provided weird huge flour tortillas, and the men at the main-house ruins suspiciously wrapped their beans in these wads of what seemed to them to be wet laundry. Segundo found the tortillas de harina squishy and deeply improper, though by his third bean and cactus burrito, he started to enjoy them. Their rich taint of lard felt good and greasy in his mouth.

Tomás chose to remain loyal to his little corn tortillas. There was only so much he was willing to concede to el norte.

Most people ate beans. Fried beans or boiled with a gristly wad of fatback. Some ate bolillos that they dipped in their coffee. The two workers from Rosario's silver mines — Guerrero and Millán — fried the last of their little green bananas. Millán dangled one before his button fly and invited passersby to bite it. And eggs, hitting melted lard, spread their hiss through the wagons like water spilling over stones. The world smelled like food, and Teresita closed her eyes and went from delicious cloud to delicious cloud, her stomach singing and burbling, her jaws tingling with hunger.

At Huila's fire circle, she squatted down in the dirt with a tin plate balanced on her knees, and she scooped up slimy cactus and eggs with chunks of tortilla. The folded triangle of tortilla in her right hand served as a spoon, and the rough triangle in her left served as a scoop that moved choice bits around her plate. She had used spoons and forks before, but not often.

Huila set a mug of coffee before Teresita — the skin of boiled milk humped in the middle, raised by steam. Teresita lifted the cup with two hands and sipped. The old woman had already stirred in her traditional five spoonfuls of sugar. Teresita raked in the milk skin with her teeth and chewed it. After breakfast, she helped wash dishes. Then she set about beating blankets and shaking out dresses. She kept busy until lunchtime, but before she could examine the frying pans to see what they'd eat, riders approached.

Here came Segundo again, and with him, Don Tomás. The Engineer wore a checkered suit and his silliest top hat. Two vaqueros brought up the rear.

Tomás carried an empty bowl, balanced on the pommel of his saddle.

Huila stood.

"Buenos días," she said. "Did you like your breakfast?"

Tomás tossed his bowl to one of the workers beside her.

"Good," he said. "Gracias."

She tipped her head at him.

"What have you decided?" Huila asked.

Tomás combed his whiskers with his fingers.

"We stay," he said. "We rebuild."

There arose a murmur, though no one could tell if it was dread or assent.

"Some of us don't want to remain here. It is haunted," Huila said.

"Ay, María Sonora," Tomás sighed. "Don't you think all Sonora is haunted? Have we not seen strange things all the way from Sinaloa? Haunted!" He barked out a laugh. His riders also laughed; the People did not. "I have several ranches. Some of you may go work at Aquihuiquichi, and at Santa María. All right?"

Huila nodded.

More murmuring.

"And you will be rebuilding Cabora," Huila offered.

"Soon," he replied. "Soon. But Engineer Aguirre will be in charge of the ranch in my absence. He has my full authority — you will follow his orders without question, as if I myself had spoken."

"And you?" Huila called. "Where will you be?"

"I?" said Tomás. "I am going to go talk to the Yaquis."

Now, as Tomás rode alone into the hills, he remembered their cries of fear, their arguments and shouts. Huila argued with him, and the People begged him not to go. But he had already battled Aguirre and Segundo all night. He had overcome the will of his vaqueros and their endless rounds of debate that had ruined his sleep.

"For God's sake, you idiot — take armed riders with you!" Aguirre had cried.

"No."

"It's suicide, boss," Segundo argued. "Don't go alone. Let me ride with you, at least."

"No."

"They'll kill you," Aguirre shouted.

"I don't think so."

Tomás had a sense that the Yaquis would respect his boldness if he rode into their midst with no hired guns around him. And if they weren't impressed, he didn't want to see more of his men killed. Besides, Yaquis weren't horsemen like Apaches or Comanches — he knew he could outride any warrior that might come after him, and he wore two revolvers and carried a shotgun and a Winchester in scabbards on either side of his saddle. He'd shoot his way out if he had to. Or he'd go down shooting.

"I am a good Catholic," he joked. "They will join me in a rosary."

❧

His leaving had been nearly silent. Tomás took his firearms and a huge fighting knife on the back of his belt. He wore his silver concha black pants, a pair of rawhide chaps, and a big sombrero. In his saddlebags were two sacks of gold pesos to pay ransom for the stolen women. He had ridden out of the camp on the far edge of the red sunrise.

When he got to Alamos that afternoon, he was delighted to see cantinas and restaurants and trees. He fed a few peanuts to a great white parrot in a hibiscus tree. He ate chorizo and eggs, calabaza and papaya, a bowl of arroz cooked in tomato sauce with red onions sprinkled over it, coffee and boiled milk, and three sweet rolls. He went to the botica and bought some stomach powders in case the chorizo loosened his bowels, and he bought seven cigars and a tin of tobacco — he had read that Indian caciques liked tobacco. He turned his horse over to a stable and went to the hotel off the plazuela. There, he took a room and paid for a bath. He soaked himself in the steaming water, scrubbed the smell of cows off his body. The water, when he rose, looked like bean soup in a mug.

"I am a pig," he noted.

Pulling on clean trousers and a white shirt from his mochila, he looked in the mirror and slicked back his hair. Downstairs, he enjoyed a shot of tequila and a lime, then sat down to a game of poker. He paid the chanteuse for three songs. Then he made his way to his cousins' houses and sipped tea and dandled children. At midnight he rose to his room and fell in the feather bed and slept like a weary angel. At dawn, he dressed and sat down to a breakfast of fruit and bolillo rolls and ham steaks with green chiles and four eggs. He bought stout boots, had a haircut, and waited for the telegraph office to open. He sent Don Miguel a quick note: "Cabora burned! Rebuilding. I negotiate with renegades. Aguirre and Segundo in charge of rancho."

As he rode out of town, he stopped at La Capilla, the Urrea great house, and peeked inside at its finery. The maids were flustered. He winked at a cute little teenager from Nogales and said, "I will definitely be seeing you again! What is your name?"

"Yoloxochitl," she replied.

He found this marvelous, and he sprang into the saddle and trotted into the wasteland.

❋

The workers at Cabora had told him the warriors' village was ten miles away, but he realized he had failed to ask in which direction. His options formed an arc of almost seventy miles. He rode toward Bayoreca, the small mining town that was the only center of civilization outside Alamos. It would be a start, at least. He asked Indian-looking walkers on the roads. No one knew which band of Yaquis had attacked, nor what the name of their small pueblo might be. In Bayoreca, they told him, he might find informants. He might even find some of the raiders, for Yaquis often worked the mines, using their immense physical strength to pull ore carts up the shafts.

It was a day's ride away, and Tomás had his bedroll tied on behind him. His provisions were jerky steeped in chile peppers, a cork-plugged jug of beans, bolillos, a leather pouch full of boiled rice, a wax-papered slab of bacon, a few bottles of beer. He carried a burlap sack of crushed and burned coffee beans. Three canteens were slung over his pommel. Pans and plates and a coffeepot rattled behind him. Enough bullets. His beloved jujubes.

The world was silent around him. Silent and vast. Without the pulling weight of the cattle and the ranch workers behind him, he felt cut loose, light in the air as thistledown. He might fly, if the wind hit him right. He had never thought of how large the land was. The sky was even bigger. For all its hugeness, the earth was like the thin layer of caramel on a flan, and the sky rose in a rich dome high above, spreading forever.

Ravens were as small in the distance as the ashes scattering from his cigarettes. He could barely hear their squawks. Their voices hid behind the hiss of the wind, sounded as if they had been folded and tucked under the corner of the sky.

Then up: the dirt road climbed the foothills. Agave, ocotillo, creosote, mesquite. He saw tawdry huts leaning as if blown by stiff winds. Naked children with white bottoms covered in alkaline dust. Three graves beside the road; white crosses with no words upon them and stones also painted white, as if it had snowed in the heat. Flies worried his eyes, his nose. He pulled his bandana over his face, and the scrabbling poor men who saw him pass ducked in fear, certain this tall bandit had found them out in their sins and their indiscretions, the mala hora come at last, and they hunched their shoulders and awaited his bullets. But he was gone on his newest black stallion, El Cucuy, only the echoing clonk of its hooves marking his passing: no shooting, not a word.

Mountain schooners came down the road — lines of burros overloaded with machinery and tools, bundled loads under canvas. Driven by bored little men with sticks, men with no teeth, blackened skins, splayed bare feet that looked like fried leather, yellow and cracked in the dirt. They nodded to Tomás as they passed, glancing furtively at his weapons, turning their eyes away quickly.

"Is it far?" he asked.

"Not far," one answered.

He crested the ridge and beheld the jumbled tumble-down pueblo of Bayoreca. Town of smoke and powder. Mine tailings, drunken sots scattered like ripped clothes in the alleys, dead dogs, laundry. It was filthy. He could smell the place two miles down the road.

Twenty

TOMÁS HAD LEFT THE TENT intended for Doña Loreto behind, and Huila and the house staff moved into it, spreading their blankets over the cots. Don Lauro set up a bed frame under the cottonwood near the wrecked ranch house. He assembled the iron headboard and footboard and set a small table with an oil lamp beside the bed, set a rifle leaning against the table, and a gunbelt hanging off the headboard, which really looked like a black iron fence, all bars and crossbeams, and he slept there at peace in the night breeze. When he awoke in the morning, chickens were perched above him on the headboard, clucking softly and making purring sounds like rotund cats.

The workers of Cabora had fled after the Yaqui assault, and their small huts and rattling cabins stood empty beyond the corrals and the barns, and the workers from Sinaloa wandered to these houses and chose among them. This village was almost identical to the one they had come from — two ragged rows of shacks in a field with thin board and paper-wall latrines stinking in back, small pigpens behind these. The little street even held the same muddy puddle of donkey pee. People moved into these houses in the same order they had lived in the last village. Don Teófano, Huila's helper and mule driver, started on the left side of the street, farthest west. He saw himself as a sentinel and guardian of the village, though it would have taken a stick of dynamite exploding outside his door to wake him. Each family humbly bent to enter the low doorways and lay on the straw sleeping mats and took the former owners' fleas as their own. They soon named this neighborhood the same as their old neighborhood, El Potrero.

Those who overflowed this street — the cowboys and the ones who outnumbered the shacks — took shelter in the small unburned stables or slept under, in, and around the wagons. Teresita slept with Huila. Scorpions came down the walls at night, creeping out of the palm fronds and weeds the old workers had woven into roofs. Lizards also came down the walls, geckos and funny little multi-colored creatures that did push-ups at each other, then scampered across the wood and bricks in furious battles.

Engineer Aguirre had taken charge of Cabora. How could they remake the main house with no lumber? Adobe. They had clay, and dirt, and mud, and hay. Certain vigas and crossbeams, charred black, but still solid. Muscles and hands and feet.

They raked the charcoal and the ruin out of the main house, and Aguirre was delighted to find the foundation sound. The bricks had withstood the fire, and the hard-wood struts and supports were too dense to burn. The porch and the stairs were in good condition, and the fire-places and chimney still stood. While half of Aguirre's crew salvaged what they could from the burned house, the others used boards pried from the fences and the back of the near barn and a pair of dismantled work sheds to frame up long lines of adobe bricks. They lay on the ground like chocolate cakes. Teresita and the other children made games of stomping the clay and straw mixture in vats, the mud curling through their toes.

The Engineer found a load of copper pipe in the work sheds they took apart, and he immediately dedicated his afternoons to the design of a system that would bring the windmill's green water from the cattle's mossy trough to the center of El Potrero and the vicinity of the house. When finally laid out, the pipes on the ground created grids that the children made into a vast hopscotch game. Water drooled steadily into barrels at the near end of El

Potrero's dirt alley, and pattered into a vast clay jar near Aguirre's bed, creating a delightful and refreshing atmosphere for him when he lay reading, covered with Huila's coneflower salve to ward off mosquitoes. When he blew out his lamp, he watched the vivid skies, the immensities of the blue-white stars, the strange streaks of light when meteors unzipped the heavens. By match light, he consulted his small atlas of the stars, searching out the mysterious shapes of the zodiac. When the moon rose over the appalling black teeth of the sierra, Aguirre unbuckled a long leather case on his bedside table and pulled open a brass telescope to stare at La Luna's shadowed ravines and canyons, her craters and deep dead oceans. Europeans had always seen a man in the moon, something the Engineer had learned in El Paso. But his parents had always seen a rabbit on the moon's face, and this is what he saw every night, the hare on its hind legs, ears hanging back, seeming to nibble the edge of this ghostly satellite.

Sometimes, Teresita stood at the far edge of Aguirre's lamplight, watching him read.

The People thought him quite mad, sleeping outside like that in Urrea's big bed, with chickens perched above his head and toes, and camp dogs starting to congregate near him in greater numbers every night — with his white nightshirts and his spyglass, his books and his clay-pot fountain burbling noisily all night. When the barn cat decided he loved Aguirre above all men, and Aguirre let the little beast sleep on the end of his bed, they were scandalized. But Teresita found Aguirre fascinating.

The colored auras around some people had returned.

still faint but somehow clearer at the same time. She was starting to see things, as Huila had said she would. But mostly it wasn't anything magical — she was just old enough to notice what she had never noticed before. Recently, for example, she had noticed bulls pushing cows around the land from behind. Then she had seen horses pushing mares. And when she'd told Huila what she'd seen, Huila had pulled her behind the barn and told her what the animals were doing. And Teresita had shrieked in horrified delight, and they had laughed like two little girls.

And Huila had shown Teresita how to milk a cow, for she had only milked goats, and Huila had said, "You have no teats, but you will. Mine, ay mi hija, mine hang as loose as this cow's! They start out big, but they end up long. Bendito sea Dios." Teresita giggled at the old woman's rough talk.

Teresita had never noticed how many of the workers on the ranch had rotten teeth, or missing teeth, or twisted jaws and collapsed lips where their teeth had been. She had not seen the limps all around her — the injured feet and ankles, the legs twisted by injury or disease. Three different men in El Potrero had damaged arms — two crooked arms like twisted branches, and one hand missing half its fingers and bent into a dark claw. Missing eyes and white eyes and wandering eyes and crossed eyes. The vaqueros were scarred and some of them had lost thumbs or forefingers. She was astounded. The world was wounded in ways she had never seen.

Dogs ran on three legs.

What was this?

Dead chicks lay in the coops, being dismantled by insects.

No matter who she asked, no matter how many of the People, even Huila, even Aguirre and the seemingly omnipotent cowboys, nobody could explain why there was suffering, why there was pain or death or hurt in the world. It drove her mad with frustration to hear that suffering and disease were "God's will." Or the cowboys' philosophy that life was just hard, and you clenched your teeth when it hurt and didn't bitch and if it got too bad you rode out into the country and waited it out like a wounded coyote or a mountain lion. These answers frustrated her, too. Huila was the worst. Teresita was learning, to her undying shock, that the old one didn't have answers for everything. There were actually mysteries too deep for the old woman, and Teresita was not comforted by her serenity in the face of these unknowns. Teresita didn't dare say it aloud, but it was not enough to burn sage or sweetgrass or cedar, it was not enough to kneel, to dip holy water onto her forehead, to recite mysteries of the rosary or sing the old deer songs or raise an offering to the four directions. Didn't it drive Huila crazy to ask questions that were never answered? Oh, but she already knew Huila's reply, she didn't even have to speak — Huila would have told her *There are some questions you don't ask. There are some questions that are not given to you to be answered.*

Teresita wandered in a daze of seeing. Aguirre, in his big bed on the sand, in his small wobbly globe of light, his piles of books, may not have been the most puzzling thing about Cabora, nor of the great land of Sonora beyond the gates. But he was puzzling enough.

✺

One morning, Aguirre awoke at dawn. His chickens were standing watch above him; he had learned to turn them on the rail so their rears faced out and away from him, and the ground at the head of the bed was rich with their droppings. Five dogs crowded in near the foot of the bed, sleeping on their backs and piled against each other, their legs splayed drunkenly and their ears flapped akimbo like soft wings. Ticks hung off them like fat berries. And Teresita was sitting on the mattress, petting the cat.

For some reason, Aguirre blurted, "I beg your pardon?"

"Good morning," she said.

He held the sheet up to his chest.

"B-buenos días," he stammered.

"What do you read at night?" she asked.

"Of late, I have been revisiting the Quixote," he said. The chickens clucked. The dogs scratched. Aguirre thought: What a very peculiar scene.

"May I see it?" she asked.

"The book?" he said.

She nodded.

He sat up straighter and tried to pat his hair down with his hands. He fingered his whiskers. Then he took a clay cup and sipped water from it. He put the cup down and picked up the book, smiled at it once as if it were a well-known friend, and handed it to her.

The book was heavy in her hands. Its cover was soft leather. She liked the way it felt to her fingers. The letters were bright gold.

She touched the title with her finger.

"This?" she said.

"The title," he explained. *"Don Quixote de la Mancha."*

She touched the first, small word.

"This?"

"Don," he said.

"Don. Like Don Tomás?"

"Or Don Lauro," he said, hoping to remind her of his own standing. The child was strangely familiar with him. It barely seemed respectful.

"Don." She smiled. "Tell me the letters."

"D-o-n," he snapped, looking about to see if anyone was watching this absurd little school lesson.

"D!" she breathed. "O! N! Don."

She laughed. It was her first word. She had learned to read a word.

He took the book back and riffled the pages. He stopped. "There," he said. He showed her the page. "Look here," he said. He pointed to a line.

"What does it say?"

"Urrea."

"Where?"

He pointed out the letters to her.

"Is this Don Tomás?" she cried.

"No, no. This is hundreds of years ago. But it is Don Tomás Urrea's ancestor."

"There is an Urrea in this book?"

"Yes, there is. And Don Quixote notes that he is quite powerful."

"Is there an Urrea in every book?"

Aguirre laughed.

"Heavens no!" he said.

"Thank you," she said, hopping off the bed. "You should get up, Don Lauro. It's getting late."

She put the book down, waved once, and ran off in a whirl of yapping dogs.

Twenty-one

SEEMINGLY LOST on the red plain, his long shadow merging with the tormented wrenchings of the black cacti and ocotillo, came the lone rider. His sombrero formed a dense oval of shadow around his face, and his knife at the base of his spine threw sparks where it peeked from its deerskin scabbard. When he came upon pack trains, he tipped his hat, and when he approached other solitary wanderers or small lines of Indians, he unsheathed his rifle and held it across his lap.

Tomás had eaten rattlesnake in a small group of Apache hunters, hunched down with them around a small smoky scrub fire. They wore loose baggy pants and red bandanas around their heads. They had great handsome noses and crinkly eyes. The skins of the snakes were pegged out in the sun, and the pale violet and pink meat was skewered on sticks and turned in the flames. They ate off their knife blades, and they gestured at Tomás with their blades, and pointed to the fire and to him, and they all laughed. "You bastards," he said. They all knew, without sharing words, that it would be greatly entertaining to place him in a fire and watch his meat sizzle, too. The Apaches muttered to each other and laughed, rubbing their faces and shaking their heads at this foolish white man. They liked him. He made them coffee. They liked that, too. When it was time to part, they tied a fat rattle to a thong and put it around his neck. They stood around threatening him with their knives and giggling, and he pulled out his rifle and pointed it at them. Everybody thought this was hilarious.

He slept that night off the trail. He tied the stallion to a paloverde tree. He had heard of these trees, but had never seen them. They didn't seem to have much in the way of leaves. Their trunks were green and tender. He dug his initials into the wood with his thumbnail: T.U. He shook his rattle to scare away any javelinas or coyotes. Then he found a cutbank in the arroyo that formed a half cave, and he rolled out his blankets in the cool sand under this shelter. He dragged together brush and skeletons of dead chollas that looked like hollow logs with small windows in them. He built a little fire and pissed in a hole and cooked the haunches of a jackrabbit he'd shot, the great back legs looking like long turkey drumsticks. He rubbed salt onto the crackling meat and ate it, though the center was raw and vivid pink. Boiled coffee and poured a generous dose of rum in it. Jujubes for dessert.

Watching the sky, he tried to pray, but felt like a hypocrite.

Riding the trail the next day, he came upon the gates of a hacienda, La Paloma. DON WOLFGANG SIEBERMANN, PROP., the sign said. CATTLE, MAGUEY, HENEQUEN, COTTON. He ventured under the tall crosspiece over the road, upon which was nailed a cow skull. Horseshoes were arrayed down the vertical poles. Tomás had heard Don Miguel mention the Siebermanns — Don Wolf was known behind his back as El Alemán.

Tomás saw a group of vaqueros in the distance, gathered in a blinding patch of bare ground surrounded by dispirited horses.

He rode to them.

They turned and regarded him.

Ten men. Six of them held shovels. Between them, a mound of fresh dirt, and beside it, a second mound next to a deep hole.

"Buenos días," Tomás called. "I am Tomás Urrea, from the hacienda de Cabora."

The men looked at him and rested their arms on their shovels.

"Don Tomás," one of them said, and nodded.

Tomás thought them oddly surly.

"I was tracking renegade Yaquis," Tomás said.

They all looked at each other.

"Yaquis?" the leader said. "That's very bad business."

"They burned my ranch," Tomás said. "You might warn Don Wolf to be careful."

"Thank you for the warning, señor."

They stared.

"We haven't seen any Yaquis, though."

Tomás looked in the hole.

"Anything else?" the foreman said.

"No . . . no." Tomás squinted. Something moved in the hole. "Gracias. I will be on my way."

"Good day," the man replied.

The diggers took up their shovels again and bent to their tasks.

"May I ask what this project might be?" asked Tomás.

"Don Tomás," said the foreman. "We have been digging since dawn." He wiped his brow. "You're a patrón. You know how it is. If the patrón orders it, we all obey and don't ask questions."

"Commendable attitude," Tomás noted. "And what was your order, if you don't mind my asking?"

The foreman dropped his shovel and went to his horse.

He took a canteen from its saddle and took a sip of hot water.

"Well," he said, "it's a labor issue. These never cease."

"Ya lo sé." Tomás nodded. "No end to labor issues!"

"Sí, señor. Well, you see . . ." He wiped his mouth, took another sip, sighed, corked his canteen. "Don Wolf is strict, as one must be with these people. They are shiftless and untrustworthy. If your grip loosens, there is nothing but trouble."

"That's right," added one of the diggers. He threw in a shovel-load of sand: a great puff of dust rose out of the hole.

"Two workers fell in love," the foreman continued. He shrugged. "They rut like animals, these peones. But Don Wolf is caring for the herds — cows and horses and his workers, too. So when it's time to wed, Don Wolf is looking out for the healthiest pairings, you see. He has an infallible eye for selecting mates."

"Breeding!" the digger called.

Dirt fell in the hole.

"These two were denied permission to marry. But, ni modo, señor. They got married anyway."

Tomás felt cold slide down his spine.

The foreman gestured toward the far mound.

"That's her in there."

"Don Wolf," the digger said, "wanted him to see her buried first."

"Before we buried him."

Tomás saw it then: one foot kicking weakly as the dirt fell into the hole.

"You buried them alive?" he said.

The men all stopped working and looked up at him blandly.

"Sí, señor."

"She went in first. He fought like a dog," the foreman said. "But we were too many for him. It took a long time. By the time she was covered, he had collapsed. It was easier to get him in the hole once she was buried."

Tomás said, "Might I buy out this man's contract?"

"You want to save him?"

"I have money. I can pay."

The foreman shook his head.

"No," he said. "No. I don't think so."

"Besides," said the digger, looking into the hole. "He's stopped kicking. I think he's dead."

"You see?" said the foreman. "Too late, señor."

Tomás turned his back on them and rode slowly toward the gate.

"True love!" called the digger. "They're together forever now!"

The shovels made their silvery sounds as they let slip their pounds of gravel into the lonesome grave.

Tomás put his hands on his rifle, then thought better of it and took the reins in his fists and spurred his stallion and rode as fast as he could down the pale road and toward the wicked Yaqui hills.

Twenty-two

A FEW DAYS LATER, when Segundo rattled back onto the ranch with wagons of lumber and a dozen new men on horses and mules, no one had yet heard word of Tomás.

The bottom edges of the walls of the new house were already delineated by strings, and a few sun-hardened bricks were laid in. Aguirre had drawn up plans for a grand adobe house of two floors, with its porch transformed into a veranda. It was near an arroyo, where the wily Engineer was, as Segundo arrived, plotting spillways and sewage lines with a pencil and a sketchbook. Copper tubing, he was certain, was the answer!

Segundo set the new men to work — there were fences to repair, cows to attend to, holes to be dug. Tomás had requested a new stock pond be dug, and although there was no way in hell that Segundo was going to pick up a shovel, these boys from Alamos were ready to dig. Many of them were miners anyway. They were used to it.

Aguirre was summoned, and together they paced out beyond El Potrero, until they found a declivity that could handily be deepened and expanded — its natural walls would form the shores of a triangular pond. They agreed to create a berm at the south end of the dig to transform their little vale into a dam, a spillway linking it to the old stock pond. Aguirre immediately set to calculating the potential flow from the windmill. In the margins of his notebook, he spun out columns of numbers — what if he put bass, or the colorful truchas, in this pond? Would they not all delight in fresh fish every Friday?

"His head," Segundo said to Teresita, who now followed Aguirre like one of his dogs, "is very busy."

"D-o-n," said Teresita, "spells 'Don.'"

"Fíjate nomás," he said, which was his way of saying *You don't say.* He wandered off toward the barn. Even though the heat was already heavy, Segundo was planning to kick off his boots and fall into a mound of hay. He stopped. "Hey niña," he said.

"Yes?"

"Find out how to spell 'Segundo.'"

"I'll ask."

"Bueno," he said. He walked away.

Teresita ran back to Aguirre.

"Engineer," she called. "Teach me a new word."

"What new word do you desire to know?" he said, not looking up from his interminable calculations.

"My name."

He looked at her. Persistent little brat. Still, this seemed a reasonable enough request.

He waved her over to him. He took up a stick and squatted. "Look here," he said. He scratched a large T in the soil. "T," he said. She repeated it. "E." They went on through the letters of her name.

"Te-re-sa," she said. "It's like a song."

"I suppose it is."

"Don Teresita."

"No no no. *Doña* Teresita. Do you see?" He scratched the word into the dirt. "You are female. Not male. Doña."

This made them both laugh, for they both knew she was anything but a fine lady of high standing.

"Don Lauro," she said, extending her hand.

"Doña Teresita," he replied, taking her fingers in his and bowing.

Huila was standing behind them.

"What are you doing?" she asked.

Aguirre didn't know why, but this panicked him, and he jumped back a foot.

"I —!" he said.

"He's teaching me to read," Teresita said. "I wrote my name."

Huila stepped over to the scratches and looked.

"Looks like chickens came through here," she said. She wiped the name out with her foot. "You," she pointed at Aguirre. "You read."

"Yes."

"You can teach."

"I suppose. I have never given formal lessons —"

"Tomorrow's Sunday," Huila said. "You, Lauro Aguirre, give us church."

"Madame, I am no priest!" he protested.

"You can read — read the priest book."

She took Teresita's hand and led her away.

Thus did the Masonic Methodist Aguirre temporarily become the priest of Cabora. The People gathered on benches and rocks and they sat cross-legged in the dirt if they lacked a seat. Aguirre read to them from the twenty-third psalm, which comforted the People, though they asked him to put it in cattle terms, since so few of them knew sheep. Aguirre, abashed by the prospect of rewriting scripture, though he did not accept the scripture as a strictly infallible historical document, gamely bellowed, "The Lord is my buckaroo!"

Don Lauro, being Don Lauro, was quickly taken with his role as minister to the People. He instigated an afternoon salon, where he could lecture them on affairs historical or philosophical. Each day at three, they gathered near his bed under the great tree and heard talks on animal magnetism, the zodiac, the political machinations of the Díaz regime. In a lecture Aguirre had entitled "The Curious Yet True Adventures of Papantzín, Sister of Moctezuma, in the

Afterlife — Known to Us as Heaven — in Company of
the Great Architect Himself — Called by the Catholics by
the Name of Jesus Christ," Don Lauro told of the days
when the high Aztec priests had seen signs of the end of
the world. There were comets in the sky and wailing spirits
in the streets; indeed, he explained, the terrible Mexican
ghost, La Llorona, originally frightened the Aztecs when
she made her ghastly debut in their alleys. Their calendar
was coming to its cyclic end — the dreaded Nemontemi,
the era between eras, had begun. And messengers had
come from the coast with the terrible news that great white
seabirds lay on the ocean, and upon these white-winged
birds were the minions of Quetzalcoatl, bearded gods returned from the land of the sunrise. Today, all understood
that these birds were ships, and the gods upon them were
merely Spaniards. But the fear in Tenochtitlán, Center of
the One World, was great in those ancient days.

And Papantzín, sister of Moctezuma the king, lay abed,
sick with fevers and weak. So weak was she that she died.
And upon dying, she found herself in Heaven.

Teresita sat, as always, in the front of the crowd, chin
resting on both fists as she listened.

"Papantzín later told Moctezuma what she had seen, for
Papantzín did return from the dead! Oh yes, Papantzín was
sent back from Heaven with a warning — a warning to the
populace about the ravages of unjust rule!" Aguirre cleared
his throat and went on: "Papantzín was greeted in the land
of the dead by a fair man in a white robe." The People
crossed themselves. They knew a Jesus reference when
they heard it. "He took her through valleys and dales,
where she saw rivers and doves." Everybody nodded. "But
the Lord took her to a dark and terrible valley. And this

valley was filled with bones." They gasped. "Bones! Human bones! Skulls. And he said, 'Behold, your people.' For, the Lord warned Papantzín, her own people would be destroyed through their own ignorance. Their beliefs would destroy them. And Papantzín awoke in the tomb."

They bowed their heads.

"Can you imagine? Can you envision the deisidaimonia of the Aztecs upon her reawakening?"

They said, *What did he say?*

"At first, no one would come near the tomb, for fear that she was a ghost, some demon sent to harm them."

Teresita pressed her palms to her face.

"And then?" she blurted, but heard no answer, for the People were turning and rising, and there came the sound of snorting horses and hooves, and then they were all up and running to see the patrón.

Aguirre lowered his book and said, "Well, well."

He was relieved that his friend was back, apparently in one piece. But he was also a bit irritated that his talk was cut short. And he was alarmed to see that Tomás was followed onto the ranch by Indians.

Tomás sat astride his stallion and smiled down at them. Both he and the horse were yellow and gray with dust. Later, the People would say he was a different patrón from the one who had left. Something in him had shifted in those days riding alone.

The Indians behind him were grim and silent, and behind them, the women and children they had taken captive commenced wailing and caterwauling as the People danced and hopped up and down before them in joy. They jumped off their horses and flew through the crowds like scattered chickens, hands in the air, though nothing had happened to them, and they knew not a face in the gathering, and their shacks were now the homes of strangers. They were home, and that was all that mattered to them. They blended in and were absorbed. The vaqueros charged in from the plains and the dogs barked. Aguirre pushed through the revelers and reached up to Tomás and shook his hand.

"Welcome back," he said.

"Looks good." Tomás nodded, glancing around Cabora. "Nice work."

"Claro que sí," Aguirre acknowledged with a small nod.

He had already snapped an order: men were pulling a bed from a wagon and were assembling it near Aguirre's, under the big cottonwood. They set a clay jarrito full of cool windmill water beside the bed, and by the time Tomás finally lay upon it in the evening's lamplight, they would have a plate of candied yams and cactus jelly set on the small table with the water.

Tomás gazed out beyond them all, toward the Sierra. He shook his head and looked down.

"Huila," the patrón said.

"Señor." She nodded. "At your service."

"And you," he said to Teresita.

She wiggled her fingers at him.

Segundo wandered over, his horse-bowed legs making him look like a sailor on a rocking boat as he walked.

"Boss," he said.

Tomás smiled at him.

"I've been out there," he said.

"Yes, you have." Segundo nodded. He saw it in his face. "You liked it."

"Oh!" Tomás said.

He had intended to tell them all of his journey. Of the mad Indian who had led him into the warrior village. How the naked runner with deer antlers tied to his head trotted backward, yelling and jabbering and laughing at him. How the runner sped away and stopped and bent over, opening his ass at him and making the rudest of sounds. How the runner peed in the road, then held his hands over his belly and made exaggerated laughing gestures at Tomás. And how, when he tired of this laughter, he pantomimed crying, rubbing his eyes with his fists, then pointing at Tomás, clearly saying *Yori crybaby!*

How the runner led him to the village, and how the people came forth with their weapons and yelled at the runner, and the runner pranced and skipped and made his way straight through the village and out the other side, pausing only to waggle his bottom at Tomás before dancing out of sight.

He wanted to tell them of the fighters standing in amazement when he rode into their midst, some of them running to him, striking him with their clubs, threatening him with their machetes. How his stallion had stood still in the maelstrom, had then danced in place, had moved sideways and backward, cutting perfect squares in the center of the pueblo, the warriors falling back half-afraid and half-amused at this crazy Yori and his demonic horse. How the old man, the cacique of the people, had come forward, wearing a cross, speaking Spanish; and he wanted to tell of how they had spoken of many things.

He wanted to tell them of the stars. Of the lovers in their hellish graves. Of the Apaches and their snake barbecue.

Tomás knew suddenly that he would not tell. He had always fancied himself an untamed man, and now he had discovered he was half coyote. He had finally, over the last weeks, tasted what it truly meant to be untamed. And the coyote was doomed to live within the cage of his social standing. Tomás had no way of imagining how to set himself free.

These Yaquis didn't help. They had understood the coyote in him as soon as he dismounted his horse. They were part eagle, these men, part hummingbird and part snake. He never spoke to their women, for the Yaquis knew him for what he was, and they knew he was already in love with them, and they knew what his love would mean when the nights came and the girls walked to their homes. They liked him too much to kill him now, yet they liked their women too much to allow them to marry a Yori, even a rich one. So they had sat with him and told him of their lives. Of the destruction of their homelands, of the Yori invasions and the starvation that twisted their children and weakened their old ones, of the massacres and hangings, the tortures and assaults. Of whole villages emptied by Mexican troops, of families marched into the sea, of children pierced by tree branches and left to rot, fed to sharks, trampled by horses. Of scalps collected from lone wanderers and sold to the state for bounty. Of fear.

After he understood them, and after he had secured the release of his hostages, he decided to bring a few of them back to Cabora so they could make their case before the ranks of his People. But as for Tomás himself, he would not try to make his own case. Who would listen to him? Who among them would understand?

With a gesture, Tomás directed the Yaquis to dismount. They got down and stood, flat-footed in the dust. The old man stepped forward. Tomás slipped off his horse and stood with the old one.

The People fell silent. Teresita pushed forward, leaned against Huila's hip, and watched. The old leader of the village looked at the girl and said, "I know you" in the old tongue. "I saw you when the old woman was flying." She raised her eyebrows at him.

The old man cleared his throat, and said, in Spanish, "We're sorry we burned your ranch."

The People all looked at each other: Huila looked at Segundo, Segundo looked at Aguirre, Aguirre looked at Teresita, Teresita looked at Tomás. Then Huila looked at Don Teófano, and Teófano looked at someone else.

"We thought," the old man continued, "we were at war with you."

He shrugged.

"We are at war with everyone."

He crossed his arms. All this talk to half-breeds and mestizos and Yoris. Pah!

"We are at war with anyone who does not speak Cahita, you know. Some of you speak like real human beings, and we are not at war with you. We would not kill you if we came back to burn the ranch again."

"That's a relief, cabrones!" blurted Huila.

Everyone laughed, even the old Yaqui leader.

"We thought we were at war with the Sky Scratcher here," he said, gesturing toward Tomás. "We had not seen him, but we had seen him coming in dreams. All these Yoris. We thought they were the same."

Tomás offered him a cigar. He took it and lit it from Segundo's match. He nodded a gruff thanks.

"Why did you raid us?" Aguirre asked.

"We were hungry."

"Cows," said another.

"Cows!" said Segundo.

"Hungry," the old man repeated. They thought he was surly. Some of them thought he was stupid. But he just didn't feel like wasting too much breath apologizing to Yoribichis.

"Aguirre," said Tomás, "how much do priests demand from us in tithes?"

"They recommend you give ten percent of your earnings to the poor, my dear Urrea," Aguirre said.

"Ten percent," Tomás repeated. "From now on, Cabora will provide ten percent of its harvest and its livestock to the Yaquis. If we have one hundred cows, you take ten," he said.

The old man looked at his people. They nodded. He took his cigar out of his mouth and said, "Bueno."

"Your people will not go hungry as long as we are here," Tomás continued. "And the grounds of the Urrea ranches will always serve as refuge to you. Here at Cabora, at Aqui-huiquichi, at Santa María. You will protect us from Indian attacks, and we will protect you from soldiers."

The old man nodded. He and Tomás shook hands.

"I want to show you something," Tomás said to the People.

One of the Yaqui group was a woman. She was quite beautiful, in Tomás's opinion, but he thought almost every woman he saw was quite beautiful. She rode at the back of the group and had never said a word to him. She wore her hair long and straight, and it covered the sides of her face. And now, dismounted, she stood behind the Yaqui men,

silent. Tomás knew she would make his People understand.

"Chepa," he said, "por favor."

He gestured toward her with one hand, and she stepped
forward.

"This is Chepa," he said.

The old man of the village murmured something to her,
and she nodded, and he gently lifted the hair away from
her head. Both of her ears had been cut off. Under her hair
were ghastly stumps, ragged and white.

"White men," the old Yaqui leader said.

Then he lowered her hair and turned and started walking. Each of the Indians turned and followed him. Tomás
and the People stood and watched them as they walked
across the hot plain, leaving the stolen horses behind, wa-
vering in the light ripples, shrinking and seeming to break
into pieces, their heads and then their hearts dripping into
the quicksilver sky, until they were small pepper specks
and then they were gone.

Forever after, Aguirre would say that on that day, in that
place, no matter what anyone said, the Mexican revolution
was born.

Book III

THE HONEY
AND THE BLOOD

*With the threat of Indian raids ended, Don
Tomás turned his attentions to developing the
ranches, aided by large loans from his uncle.
He became a demon for work, spending day
after day in the saddle, supervising his
construction crew with astonishing energy. The
improvements at Cabora were made on the
south side of Arroyo Cocoraqui, overlooking a
steep bluff some twenty to twenty-five feet
high. . . . With low, diverting dams along the
bed of the arroyo, this tract of land could be
irrigated. . . . Don Tomás employed a sizable
crew of Indians to clear the land and then sent
for Lauro Aguirre. . . .*

— William Curry Holden,
Teresita

Twenty-three

THE BEES FLEW from thirty hives arranged in a wide arc along the southern boundaries of Cabora. Another ten hive boxes stood outside the main fence of Aquihuiquichi. These boxes were of pine, painted white and held above the ground on stout oak legs. Their slanted roofs were made of tin and were held firm against the wind by adobe bricks left over from the great reconstruction of the hacienda. The bottoms of the hives were a hard wood that would withstand rot. Each hive held nine panels a half inch apart, and these panels held walls of wax hexagons slowly filling with honey.

On cool days, the bees hung around the doorways to their homes in groggy gangs, only peeling away to fly to their jobs with great reluctance. At first, it would be difficult to see where they would go to find blossoms for their nectar and pollen. From above, Cabora might have seemed a desert. But the lowlands beyond the arroyo were green with irrigation water. Long rows of corn grew there, a small industry of maize and tassels and husks for tamales and dolls and cigarettes. The maize fed the three hundred workers their rations of tortillas, and the excess fed the pigs and cows, and the excess of that was sold to villages and ranchos nearby. During harvest, wagons would haul loads of corn to the Yaqui and Mayo villages in treaty with Tomás. The People fermented the corn and made the stinky mash they called tejuino, and they drank it and fought and knifed each other and vomited in the dirt and passed out facedown.

Beside the corn rows were long bright meadows of alfalfa and clover. Again, this crop fed the horses and livestock, the flowers feeding the restless bees. Beans and sweet peas on their poles and strings blossomed, as well. Guava trees. Jamaica.

All along the Río Yaqui, there were peach and apricot trees. Quince trees. Some apple trees. The mesquite bloomed. To the south of Cabora, Tomás had planted an acre of lavender. It made for a tasty honey, and Tomás experimented with its curious scent in a salve and a distilled oil. His newest project was five acres of strawberries. Old rusty food cans sprouted red, pink, and white geranium gardens before nearly every shack.

Tomás had read that asters appealed to bees, so he planted asters alongside sweet alyssum and nasturtiums and morning glories and, of course, great walls and fences covered in honeysuckle. He could tell when they were making aster honey because it smelled dark and earthy. Peach or clover honey was sweet. Lavender honey smelled like a spring wind. The honeysuckle made the People particularly happy, since it attracted holy hummingbirds, and as long as hummingbirds hovered nearby, things would be all right.

Still farther out, in the dry wastes beyond their arroyo and windmill, the desert gave up blooms. Even the small peyote cactus bloomed, as did the nopales and the few huge saguaros that were sentinels of the great north. Wildflowers erupted from the ground without any help at all from Tomás. In the summer, the rains came, and the magical event of toads bursting from the ground followed: toads started to shoot up from the soil, blinking their happy yellow eyes, excited by the first drumming of rain. Wildflowers were sure to follow. First toads, then flowers.

Desert marigold. Threadleaf groundsel. Paleface flower. Texas silverleaf. Sage. Desert calico. Purple mat.

If you knew where to look, it was a jungle in miniature. The bees knew where to look. And so did Huila.

Fagonia. Ratany. Filaree storksbill. Indian blanket. Daisies. Phacelia. Trumpet flowers. Purple groundberries. Burrobrush. Mormon tea.

The bee boxes stood about as tall as a short man. The beekeeper's hut was not far away, looking like the houses of El Potrero where the People lived, but painted white and with windows covered in screen to keep the bees away. Beekeepers' suits hung on pegs inside the door, and hats with veils stitched to the brims were stacked on the worktables. In the sheds outside, pry bars and slats and empty frames and sheets of wax and knives and gloves and the curious little bellows-pump smokers. And on three sides of the house, bright marijuana plants.

But Tomás knew his bees so well, and was known so well by his bees, that he didn't bother with veils. In the years since his epochal ride into the Yaqui villages, he had confided mostly in his bees. Loreto, delighted to be ensconced in the pretentious house in Alamos, had set about spending fortunes on lace tablecloths and lace-up boots and awful kneesocks his sons wore like little princes from an idiot's fairy-tale book. Loreto had not managed to come out to see Cabora. She did not care to be told excruciatingly crude and vicious tales of the ride or of the debased conditions in the demesnes of the savages.

Loreto had borne him a fifth child since the reconstruction. Now the Urrea children were all gathered in the city, learning to read and do factors. They had never branded a cow or castrated a horse. At times, Tomás was thankful for this. But they had also not slept on the ground, and his oldest boy, Juan Francisco II, had not yet learned to shoot. Leticia and Martita, the girls, helped around the house, though these duties were ably handled by the wash girls and the cooks and the maids. Leticia won a beauty pageant, and Martita had pale skin and huge lucid eyes. Alberto was a happy boy, dearly loved by Loreto. He was all muscle: Tomás liked to wrestle with him and feel his rocky torso strain to lift him off the floor. The baby, Tavito, was all smiles and laughter. Tomás liked to inform diners at Loreto's table that Tavito was born smiling.

Once a month, he rode to La Capilla, as the Alamos home was known. He bathed, slathered on unguents and eaux de toilette, suffered through delicate meals with fine little forks and thin little plates with oily businessmen and their powdered wives — every one of them holding out their pinkies as they ate. Nobody ate with a tortilla in Loreto's house. Nobody ate pork rinds or drank beer. After these interminable dinners, Tomás bid all his gathered children good night, then took Loreto's delicate hand and led her upstairs, where he climbed atop her and did his duties. For the first time in his life, he thought of other things as he served his bride. And when she gasped her "Oh! Oh! Eres tremendo, mi amor!" he often had to turn his head so as not to laugh. Everything felt rehearsed in Alamos. Everything felt as if the powdery ladies had given Loreto a rule book and schooled her in exquisiteness. And then, as if to pay for the sin of making love, she dragged him off to Mass on Sunday mornings, and he was more reluctant than his sons. It wasn't long until he concocted a plan —

Segundo would accompany him, and while he was being witty and courtly at La Capilla, Segundo would be whoring and drinking across town. The arrangement was that Segundo had to collect Tomás at dawn for "urgent" duties at the ranch. This, too, was an obvious contrivance, but Tomás was learning that fine society functioned by means of such pantomimes and dramas.

Bees were better companions than people.

When he came to their hives with great jugs of sugar water to fill their feeder trays, he told himself they recognized him and greeted him with affection. They boiled out excitedly, and they did seem to know him, fanning him with their wings, tenderly plucking at his face and hands with their hooked feet. He was never stung.

He took a pound of honey to each Indian village. In time, he dreamed of three hundred hives. Five hundred. One day, he would do away with horses and cows and only ride herd on vast tides of bees.

Gold poppies. Desert rose mallow. Chihuahua flax. Buffalo gourd. Menodora. Twinleaf. Desert gold. Ghostflower. Chuparosa.

Los vaqueros did not understand this flowery phase of Don Tomás's life, and they didn't trust the insects. Bees, to buckaroos, were evil little beasts that stung horses and cows on the rump and started mad dashes through cactus bottoms. To hell with bees, brother.

They just waited until he came back from the hives and stared, slightly nauseous, when he came to them with a dripping chunk of honeycomb in his mouth, honey drooling down his chin, dead bees and grubs stuck to his lips. He'd look up at them, chewing away like a skinny bear, and he'd say, "What?"

Between the beehives and the Arroyo de Cocoraqui, there were arrayed fields of hay, henequen, tomatoes. Beyond these were several alamos trees where the goats and pigs had pens. North of the pens began the great corrals and barn complexes. To the west was the vast plain where the cattle wandered. To the east of the corrals was El Potrero. Between the barns and the main house was the long bunkhouse where the vaqueros snored and played cards, their kitchen attached to the east. The new rendering plant was far to the east, where its stench could not overwhelm the main house. Tomás had created a factory of tallow and lard, candles and oil and glue. On the west side of the main house was the residence of the caballero de estribo, the top hand. There, Segundo lived — in his opinion, like a sultan. He had such astounding things as a couch and beds, and a cook and a girl to boil his britches and hang them out to dry in the air. In Segundo's palace, the orders were simple: coffee all day, at any hour. Coffee and cookies and lots of beans. No honey. Much beer. The inescapable Buenaventura often invited himself into Segundo's house and managed to end up in the guest bed without being given the least indication that he was welcome. Buenaventura amused him, like some stray dog stealing eggs. And he eyed the boy's Urrea face and thought his dark thoughts, until one night after they'd drunk many bottles of beer Buenaventura had confessed his secret and Segundo had gone off to sleep not at all surprised. This made him happy. A real man was never taken by surprise by anything.

On the brink of the arroyo stood the great main house. It was a full three miles from the hives, but the bees had no problem finding its walls. Rebuilt with adobe and pine planks from the Tarahumara Mountains of Chihuahua, the house spread two wings east and west from a tall center residence accessed through a flagstone courtyard that was shut off from the ranch by two swinging wooden gates. In the middle of the courtyard, Tomás had recently planted a plum tree. Around it, benches and a pair of small fountains made a sheltered sitting spot for Huila and any guests who might come to visit. Tomás had had the house painted white, like his beloved hives, and the roof was made of red Mexican tiles curved to channel rain to the gutters, and Aguirre had engineered the gutters to empty into great stone pilas at every corner, where a hundred gallons of water in each could easily gather in a few days of the rainy season. Atop the adobe wall that ran across the mouth of the courtyard, Huila had planted geraniums in pots. A great nopal stood fifteen feet tall on the west side of the gate. To the east, on the left side of the entrance, a series of trellises held up honeysuckle, morning glories, sweet peas, and trumpet vines. Three stone steps within led up to the great oak front doors with relief carvings of the Urrea oak tree and wolf escutcheon, and each door had a small window with iron bars over it so those inside could espy who was knocking or shoot raiding Indians through the portholes without exposing themselves. The great broad road from Alamos had been extended to sweep past the gate. Everywhere, chicken coops.

Huila had grown older. What else could she do? She grew more tired as her days seemed at once to be longer and shorter, interminable in the afternoon heat, and shaved down to only a few good hours by the time she went to bed. She felt the rust in her backbone, the painful catch in her hips, the dull ache in the dry knot of her womb. Her eyes felt forever dry, yet her vision was wet, as if tears had filled her eyes, or some film had fallen on them. Life shifting, as life does.

She had added sacred objects to her altar, as she studied this desert land. There was the troubling seedpod of what the local healers called the devil's claw. When she'd first seen it, she'd taken it to be the skull of some evil rat with long antlers. She had found a mummified baby rattlesnake that she kept beside her clear glass of bampo-water. It was too potent a talisman to let it stray far from a bit of clear soul-substance like that. Tomás had given her his Apache snake rattle, too. She knew these Yaqui bastards up here had some arrangement with rattlesnakes, so she was glad for the medicine. She had a pot of Tomás's honey beside her bed as well, but that was because she liked to eat it by the spoonful. Still, its clarity was worth meditation and prayer — Huila knew that any clear substance, especially one as sticky and sweet as honey, and one that came from bees, had to have some kind of hidden meaning and sacred use. She was just too tired to get around to it.

On the floor before her altar were desert skulls. She knew some crazy healers who kept human skulls in their homes, but this was a thing of demons. Let the devil come of a night and bugger them while they slept! Cabrones! That's what they got! No, she had two coyote skulls that seemed very sacred and wily and she had a javelina skull, with its wicked tusks rising orange from its bony jaw. These little stinkpigs were perhaps the true spirits of this land, so she studied the skull often and tried to orchestrate some agreement with it. One morning she had walked out into the desert, looking for a sacred spot where she could burn her herbs and talk to Itom Achai. As she had come around a hedionda bush, a javelina had snorted and burst from its shade in a storm of twigs and squeals and dust, and Huila had jumped two feet and fallen on her rump, spitting curses as the pig ran for its life, its tail whirling behind it like a propeller. And she had risen in time for the rest of the herd of pigs, forty-eight of them, to burst out of the bushes behind her with more uproar and she had fallen over again, heart slamming her old ribs. Perhaps she kept the javelina skull for a touch of revenge.

And the girl. Huila had seen the buds rise on her flat chest. More, she had seen the buckaroos see the buds rise. Teresita had ridden on their saddles, had bounced on their bunks, had sung their songs with their guitars. She had caught Teresita retching after one of them had given her a plug of tobacco to chew. And her face was more like pinche Tomás's every year. Huila had not known what to do with all these changes, so she'd sent Teresita to work at Aquihuiquichi, a half-morning's ride across the northern ranch. She had sent Teófano along to keep an eye on her. He reluctantly left his new shack, and he took along a niece who agreed to cook for him.

Huila's moon blood was long gone. But she could feel the blood coming on in the girl, the blood and all its power, coming down through the girl the way floods came down the arroyo. All the medicine people knew when the time of the moon was coming. The girls' lights grew brighter. Their breaths carried scents like distant flowers. Blue, copper, fire colors flew above their heads, and some of them bent the world around them as they walked. It was like looking through a curved glass. Butterflies and hummingbirds, even bees, knew when a girl was coming into her holy days.

Every morning, Huila prayed about Teresita.

Everything was in place. She rubbed her eyes, she picked up her snake mummy. Something was coming.

Twenty-four

CABORA WAS RUSTIC, compared to La Capilla and Alamos. But Aquihuiquichi was prehistoric compared to Cabora. There was no great house. The land was rocky and severe. Their one windmill creaked and moaned day and night, and it sucked a brownish trickle out of the earth, and horses, steers, and workers collected it from the rusty troughs dug into the sand under three gnarled mesquites. With no Segundo to keep the vaqueros working, nobody attended to the buildings or the rudimentary barns. Goats wandered in and out of the huts. Garbage piled up between the buildings, and pigs snorted there, adding their stink to the mess.

Teresita slept in the shack of Don Teófano and his niece. She considered it an exile. The shack was up a rise from the twelve other houses. It lay between two huge pale boulders, and these kept the house shielded from the sun for much of the day, and the one good thing about it, aside from the fact that Teófano kept his plot spotlessly clean, was that the structure retained the night's coolness long into the morning. In winter, when the desert turned cold, the rocks radiated sun heat into the night. They also diverted the wind. Teófano said they made the shack into a small fort, since he'd only have to shoot out the front and back walls in case of Indian or bandit raids. Of course, the boulders were also home to rattlesnakes, and Teresita learned to walk carefully when she exited the front door. It was common in the morning to find three or four snakes languidly taking in the sun on tall rocks at either side of the house.

Don Teófano hung an old blanket between his and his niece's side of the shack and Teresita's. When she disrobed, he was careful to step outside. He waited out in front at night until she had blown out her candles and gone to bed before entering and taking off his huaraches. He slept in his pants and shirt. When it was bath day, once a month or so, the niece boiled water and filled a laundry tub, and Teresita stayed outside, scandalized that Teófano was in there naked. This gave her fits of giggles.

Her arms were muscular from milking and working hoes in the bean rows and she had discovered an affinity for birth when a pregnant barn cat had sought her out in her hour of distress. Teófano wanted to drown the cat, but Teresita threw a tantrum and covered the animal with her body, then took the cat into her part of the shack. Teófano was so appalled that he immediately moved himself and his niece out to a storage shed at the foot of the slope that had once held beans. When his niece fell in with a buckaroo, the man moved in with them, and Teófano had to survive the indignity of hearing their amorous scuffling in the dark.

Teresita helped the cat bring five babies into the world. Within a few months, coyotes had eaten them all, and the mother had returned to the barn to kill mice and fight with the old tabby who ruled the hayloft. But Teresita had discovered a calling. She had wondered what her work would be. Huila had trained her in all these things, then sent her off to be a peasant in the dirt. Abandoned. But not now. Not alone. Not directionless.

She attended the births of foals. She reached into cows and adjusted the gangly legs of calves in the birth canal. She helped she-goats squeeze out slick bloody babies. By the time her own body was preparing itself to begin its childbearing years, the women of Aquihuiquichi began to ask for her to sit with the midwives as they suffered through labor. Las parteras knew they could not show her the Mystery that happened between the legs, not yet. Huila would have their heads. But they saw no harm in allowing her to witness the pain, to smell the odors of birth, or to hold the shiny babies freshly risen from the womb.

Teófano finally mounted his mule and rode to Cabora. He stood before the gates of the main house, afraid to enter. He stood outside the gates for two hours, hat in hand, watching the front door. It opened. A young woman with a pan of soapy water came out. She poured the water over the roots of the plum tree. "Señorita," he called. She shielded her eyes and looked out to him. "Huila, por favor." The young woman went back inside. In another twenty minutes, Huila came out. She saw Teófano and scowled. This, he knew, was a warm greeting from Huila.

"Come in," she said.

"Oh, no."

"Come on inside, man. Have some coffee."

"No, no," he said. "Not me."

She came down the steps.

She offered him a small black cigar from her apron pocket. He smiled. He put it in his mouth. She struck a red match on the wall and lit it for him.

"Gracias," he said.

After a while, she said, "So?"

"It is the girl," he replied. "She is attending births."

"Already?"

"Sí."

Huila sighed.

She said, "Shit."

Saturday morning seemed like a good time to sleep instead of taking yet another horse ride. Tomás was far too proud to ride a wagon like an old woman or a maize-delivery man. But he had skipped last week's visit with Loreto and the children, and were he to sleep in today he would miss another.

He stumbled through his predawn routines. A visit to the amazing Aguirre waterpot in its pleasant closet: Aguirre had arranged for water to drop from the ceiling and flush out the bowl. A call for hot water, and the blushing girl delivering a pitcher to him. Stropping the razor and shaving in the little round mirror. Down for breakfast. Coffee.

A knock at the door.

"I'll get it!" he yelled.

It was Segundo.

"Ready to go?" Tomás said.

"Boss," said Segundo.

"What?"

"Boss."

"*What?*"

"I don't know."

"What the devil is wrong with you today?"

Segundo looked around. Tomás looked out into the courtyard. That little street-dog kid Buenaventura was slouching out there.

"Boss, you once told me to report everything."

"Right. Y ese cabrón?" Tomás asked. "Qué trae?"

Segundo sighed.

"Everything, right?"

Tomás nodded to Buenaventura.

Buenaventura jerked his chin up once.

"Boss," Segundo said, "it's all a great mystery, right?"

Tomás looked long at him.

"Segundo?" he said. "Qué chingados dices!"

"Everything encompasses both good and bad. For the good of the ranch."

"Good-bye," said Tomás, tiring of this foofaraw and starting to shut the door in Segundo's face.

He stepped up on the veranda and whispered in Tomás's ear. "His name is Buenaventura . . . Urrea!"

"Mierda!"

"No, it's true."

"Goddamn it!"

"Ask him."

Tomás glared at Buenaventura.

"Who is your mother?" he snapped.

"Quelita."

"Quelita who?"

"Angelita the tortilla girl of Ocoroni."

Tomás blinked.

"Ah cabrón!" he said.

"You courted her sixteen years ago."

"Ay chingado," Tomás noted.

He knew perfectly well when he had dated Quelita.

"She lived in a blue house," Buenaventura said.

Tomás gave his most poisonous stare to Segundo as a memorable gift.

Then he said to Buenaventura: "I remember the blasted house."

Segundo said, "Sorry, boss."

They stood there staring off at the land, each one's eyes cast in a different direction.

After a few minutes, Tomás sighed, rubbed his face. "I suppose," he said, "you caballeros should come in for some coffee."

Twenty-five

"LOOK AT YOU," Huila said when she entered the shack.

Teresita jumped up from her table. A candle flickered there, and a sheet of paper and a fat pencil lay in its glow. Huila went to the paper and looked at it. Printed neatly, several times, were letters: TERESITA.

TERESITA.

"I am learning," Teresita said.

Huila touched the page and sat down.

"Do you have water?" she asked. "I am thirsty."

Teresita brought her a clay cup of water, and the old one sipped at it and looked for Teresita's altar. There was none.

There were no santos. Only a bare cross made of two iron-wood twigs.

Sage hung from the vigas of the roof. Other weeds.

"What is that?" Huila asked.

"Lavender."

"What does lavender accomplish?"

"It smells good."

Huila's eyebrows went up. She sipped more water.

"Stand," she said.

Teresita stood.

"You are big now."

"I am."

Teresita took up her pencil and bent back down over the paper. She put more Yori letters on the sheet. She turned the sheet around on the table and showed it to Huila. The old one bent down and squinted. It said: H U I L A.

"What is this?"

"It is your name," Teresita said.

At first, Huila wanted to snatch it up and crumple it. But she looked at it a moment longer. Put her finger on it.

"What is this one?" she asked, touching the H. "The one that looks like a ladder?"

"That is the H," Teresita explained.

"Get me a ladder," Huila muttered.

They laughed.

"Very interesting," Huila said. "May I keep it?"

Teresita nodded. The old one folded the page and put it in her apron, nestled among her buffalo teeth and small bones and bullets.

"You have visited births," Huila said.

"Sí."

"With the parteras."

"Sí."

"What did you think?"

Teresita closed her eyes and smiled.

"It is . . . wonderful, and it is terrible. I love the mothers, their terrible bellies, their strength. I love the infants."

"You don't fear it?"

"Oh sí, Huila. Claro que sí."

"Blood."

"Terrible."

"Suffering."

"Terrible."

Huila nodded.

"This is what you want to do, then," she said. "Bring young ones into the world?"

"No," Teresita said. "I don't think so."

"What, then?"

"I want to ease suffering."

Huila put her hands flat on the table.

They looked at each other for a long while, and they smiled for no reason. The candle burned low. Orange light filled part of the room, and brown shadows filled the corners.

"Very well," Huila finally said. "We must go to the teacher."

"You are my teacher."

"This is a different land, child. A different angel watches these deserts. We must find the teacher of these lands. We will go in the morning."

"Good," said Teresita.

"Do you have a bed for me?"

"Take mine."

"And you?"

"I was raised on the floor, Huila."

They knelt together and prayed as the candle quietly died, and Teresita helped Huila into her small bed.

※

Loreto slapped Tomás.

He had decided to bring Buenaventura along with him. He'd had some foolish idea that a clean slate was best for everyone. A reckoning. The scene of understanding and forgiveness in his mind was abruptly shattered.

"How *could* you!" she sobbed, then fled to her room. Juan Francisco II, his oldest boy, stared at him with a look of outraged betrayal. He turned his back on his father and strode from the room.

"Boy!" Tomás bellowed. "Come back here now!"

But, of course, Juan was out the door and stomping down the street.

Loreto came back out and threw ten of Tomás's books on the floor.

"Mi amor," Tomás said. "It was an indiscretion!"

"Bastard!"

"I don't know what came over me."

"Animal!"

"It meant nothing —"

"How dare you say *it meant nothing!* You betrayed me for *nothing?*"

"I suppose it meant something at the time, but —"

"Oh! So it *did* mean something to you? Did you love her? Did you love your little Indian whore?"

A teacup flew at great speed and hit the wall, distributing shards of china in a wide starburst.

"Don't think I didn't know!" she snarled.

"Know what?"

"*Don't. Think. I. Didn't. Know.* About your whores! About your endless adventures with every filthy peasant who opened her legs!"

"Loreto, really. Such talk!"

"Did you molest the cows and pigs, too, you cabrón?"

"Loreto — you must watch your tongue!"

"My tongue! Where was your tongue? In some peasant culo?"

"Loreto, Loreto, what has come over you?"

"Hypocrite!"

He put out his arms in a badly timed attempt to collect a hug.

She smacked him again.

"The shame!" she shrieked. "You shamed me every day of my life!"

"Shame!" he suddenly amazed himself by roaring. "Who bought you everything you ever wanted?"

"Uncle Miguel," she replied, archly. "Urrea," she added, as if he didn't know who she meant.

Stunned, he sat down.

"That was unfair," he said.

"Prove me wrong, Tomás."

She folded her arms and looked at him with the satisfaction of a hunter who has just shot a lion.

"I worked my fingers," he complained, "to the bone."

"Yes, and your knees got bloody from begging for loans all day, too."

"God."

He put his head in his hands.

"You used me," Loreto said. "And you used my womb, you failure."

"God, God."

"The big patrón! The master of the hacienda! What a pretty wife. What lovely children. By the way, did you hear he has been *fucking every lice-ridden whore on the ranch?*"

"That will be enough!" he announced.

"Oh no." She shook her head. "Oh no, my love. I am only beginning."

"What do you intend to do?" he cried.

"From now on," she replied, nostrils flaring magnificently as her cheeks burned a deep carmine, "you may sleep on the couch. Do you see my legs?" She lifted her skirt. "Do you see them?" He looked around to catch out anybody who might be spying on this dreadful scene. But the domestics were all gathered on the other side of the kitchen door, giggling into their fists. "These legs," Loreto whispered, "will never open for you again."

He hung his head.

"I could have lied," he said. "I could have kept the boy a secret."

Loreto bent down to him and looked in his eyes.

"Your mistake," she said.

The three riders headed out of town. Tomás was sullen. Buenaventura said, "Nice day, eh, Dad?" And Tomás whirled in his saddle and shouted: "Shut your hole, you little bastard!" Buenaventura turned to Segundo and made a hurt and baffled face. Segundo knew enough to keep silent. He only shook his head once and kept his eyes forward.

The horses soon sensed the glum mood, and their heads drooped and they shuffled along at a pathetic pace. They gave out long sorrowful sighs and only vaguely turned their heads toward roadside flowers. They were too depressed to bite off any tasty blooms.

"When you try to be good," Tomás said, "you are punished."

His horse sadly agreed with a long blubbery blowing of the lips.

"Women!" he said.

"Goddamned women!" Buenaventura offered.

Tomás pulled out his revolver and pointed it at him.

"Say one more thing," he said.

He stuck his gun back in its holster and kept going.

It took most of the morning to reach the Alamos turnoff. Tomás stared at the big cottonwoods that shaded Cantúa's restaurant.

"Let's eat," he said. "Life goes on."

Segundo, whose timing was always excellent, repeated this bit of wisdom: "Life goes on, boss."

"Yes . . . yes . . . I suppose it does."

Buenaventura rode up to them and smiled and Tomás held up one finger and said: "Shhh."

They tied off their horses and entered. The little restaurant was empty, except for the green flies. Señor Cantúa drowsed in a wooden chair, but when they walked in, he snorted awake and jumped to his feet.

"Don Tomás!" he exulted. "You grace us with your presence!"

"One cannot pass by Cantúa's," intoned Tomás, "without stopping to sample the wares."

"Very good, very good," Cantúa babbled, as he wiped off a table. "You are too kind."

They sat.

Tomás heard a sound behind him, and he turned to see

the kitchen door cracked open wide enough for one stunning eye to peek out. Those lashes! A strand of curling hair passed over the eye. It blinked. The lashes were like a garden! The door slammed.

Segundo nudged his foot under the table.

"Yes?" he said.

"The señor was saying something," Segundo said.

"Yes?"

"I was merely mentioning how curious it was to me that just this morning a wagon from your ranch stopped here for a quick meal."

"A wagon," said Tomás. "From my ranch? What wagon?"

Cantúa shrugged.

"A wagon. That crazy old woman. The witch."

"Huila? On a wagon?"

"Oh yes, that very one. Huila."

Tomás glanced at Segundo.

"How odd," he said.

"They took the Alamos turnoff," Cantúa said.

"You must be mistaken, maestro," said Tomás. "We came that way and saw no one."

"Oh, forgive me. I meant to say they went north."

"What!"

"Toward Arizona."

"Ah cabrón," said Segundo.

"Who was with Huila?"

"An old man driving."

"Teófano," Segundo guessed.

"No sé," said Cantúa. "I did not know him. And a girl. And two vaqueros."

"She took two vaqueros to Arizona?" said Tomás. He rubbed his face and threw his hands in the air. "Yes, well.

Who knows why Huila does what she does. I cannot worry about it right now."

Cantúa waited.

"What have you got?" Segundo said.

"We have a tasty cosido."

"Good," said Tomás. "And bring plenty of tortillas."

"Claro."

Cantúa gave them a small bow and hurried to the kitchen. Tomás craned around and caught a quick glimpse of the young woman's bottom before the door slammed.

"What's a cosido?" Buenaventura asked.

"Soup, buey," said Segundo.

"Don't call me buey!"

"Pinche buey!" Segundo said.

Tomás added, "Pinche buey pendejo."

Buenaventura fumed.

"I don't like soup," he said.

"It has meat and potatoes," said Tomás. "You'll like it."

"I don't like soup."

"Carrots! Onions! Corn on the cob!"

"I hate it."

"Oye, baboso," Segundo said. "Stop being ignorant."

"I like being ignorant!" Buenaventura proclaimed.

Tomás drummed his fingers.

"Huila took a wagon," he muttered.

"Women," said Segundo.

Cantúa came out with a clay pot of coffee.

"Say, Maestro," said Tomás. "Who is that in the kitchen?"

Cantúa smiled.

"In the kitchen, señor?" he said.

"Come now. You know who I mean."

"In my kitchen?"

"The girl, yes. In your kitchen."

"Oh . . ." A nervous smile.

"Ay, Señor Cantúa. I was only asking her name! I intend no disrespect."

"Old man," blurted Buenaventura, "you don't think Tomás Urrea knows how to talk to ladies?"

"Open your mouth again," Tomás said, "and I will horse-whip you."

Señor Cantúa wiped his brow with his little white towel.

"That girl in the kitchen would be my daughter, Gabriela."

"Gabriela!" Tomás enthused. Then he called her: "Gabriela! Could you come out for a moment?"

Señor Cantúa sighed. Don Tomás was very famous in love. He pasted a smile on his face. It was in the hands of God now.

She pushed open the door and said, "Papá?"

"It is all right, Gaby," Cantúa said. "Come out for a moment."

She stepped into the room, wiping her hands on a towel tied around her slim waist. Buenaventura whistled, and Segundo nudged him with an elbow and shook his head.

"You are Gabriela," Tomás said, rising and bowing slightly.

"I am."

"An angelic name," he cooed, "for an angelic young lady."

She regarded him and did not smile.

"I am Tomás Urrea," he said.

"Yes, I know."

"You do?"

"We all know you, Don Tomás."

"And why did I not know you?" He wagged a finger at Señor Cantúa. "You have kept this angel a secret, Maestro."

"I have been away," she said. "Studying."

"You went to school?" Tomás said.

"Yes, Don Tomás. These are modern days. Women attend college."

She smiled a little.

"Delightful," Tomás murmured.

"Excuse me," she said. "I have work to do."

Tomás bowed again. Buenaventura and Segundo rose as she left the room.

"Chingado, Cantúa," said Segundo. "Qué guapa!"

Señor Cantúa nodded, and he sighed again.

"I will bring your soup," he said.

And he did.

On the long ride home, Tomás would occasionally state: "Gabriela!".

Segundo and Buenaventura, wisely enough, only nodded.

Twenty-six

HUILA SAID: "Allí viene el hechicero."

She had led them north, into the Pinacate desert. The two armed riders were baffled the whole time, but they were happy to get away from hammering nails and building fences and hauling dead cows into the stinking rendering vats. They had almost forgotten what made them buckaroos in the first place. Don Teófano had steered the wagon where Huila had commanded him to go. They asked questions of peasants at stick-and-mud huts in the burning wasteland, and Huila seemed to follow an invisible map made of dreams and stories as they left the main road and followed narrow paths that threatened to break the wagon's axles. Don Teófano was worried about water, but Huila found a tanque by following butterflies and mockingbirds until she saw a dragonfly. So Huila's maps, Teresita realized, were drawn across the sky, as well.

Teresita enjoyed the ride, though she did not enjoy the sun, which burned her skin more easily than it did Huila's or Teófano's. She kept her yellow rebozo wrapped around her head and enjoyed the roadrunners and tarantulas and lizards on either side of the trail.

When they found the teacher's house — it looked to Teófano like another sad stick hut — Huila declared, "We are here." There was no one home. They made camp near the hut — the riflemen were ordered to camp on a hill removed from the holy man's home — and they waited two days. Huila watched the east. "He will come out of the sunrise," she told them.

On the third morning, the medicine man returned.

He sped toward them in the eye of a saffron storm of dust, his charging pony a small hard dot beneath him. The heat waves made him wobble, vanish, reappear. Sometimes his horse disappeared in a flutter of light, and all they could see was his figure, small in the distance, with a red shirt, seeming to hurtle through the air as if he were flying. His dust plume rose in a wedge behind him like the smoke of a prairie fire.

He reined to an abrupt halt and dismounted as his dust caught up to him and parted like curtains.

"His name is Manuelito," Huila said.

His hair fell below his shoulders. Teresita was surprised to see that he was tall, as tall as Don Tomás. She had expected a little bent man, like the tomato pickers among the People. His shirt was red, and the cloth wrapped around his forehead was red. His earring hung from his left ear, a dangling chain with a gold nugget at the end. Around his neck were thongs with teeth and beads and a chain with a silver cross. A deep blue cloth was wrapped around his waist. His boots were black and rose to his knees. He wore a long knife at his belly on a leather belt that vanished beneath the blue cloth of his other belt.

He pulled the red bandana from his head and shook out his hair.

"Manuelito," Huila said.

He stroked his horse. Wiped sweat from it with his head rag.

"I am Huila," she said. "From the rancho de Cabora."

He nodded.

"Huila," he said. "The Skinny Woman."

"Not so skinny anymore," she said.

He laughed.

"We have come," she said.

He nodded. Went around his horse, rubbing.

"For what?" he said.

"We require your teaching."

"For whom?"

"For the girl."

He looked at Teresita.

"She is white."

"I am Indian," she said.

"You're no Indian!"

He turned his back on her. Huila knew the routine. The medicine people always refused you. You usually had to ask three times.

Manuelito walked up to Teresita and stared at her. He lifted her hair and held it to the light. He took her hand in his — his gesture was brusque, but his touch was soft.

"White," he said. "What little Indian blood you have will fall out when your first month begins."

Teresita stamped her foot.

"I am many things," she said. "But if you need to know, I have already bled, and I am still Indian!" She had her finger in his face.

Manuelito nodded.

"I can teach you," he said. "Want to eat?"

Inside, the hut was decorated with colorful blankets on the walls. A great cross made of cholla skeletons and saguaro ribs hung among them. A hawk feather dangled from one arm, and a striped owl feather from the other. The floor, too, was covered in rugs. Wood carvings of birds lined the shelves. "I like birds," Manuelito said. In the center of the table, a carving of a blooming cactus, painted green, with small white slashes to indicate thorns. The single flower jutting from its crown had five petals and was red, with a yellow center. Rising from this flower was a blue hummingbird, attached to the flower by its delicate beak. It had six wings. Manuelito pointed to the wings and said, "I had to find a way to show motion in wood." He smiled. "It is a good carving," he said.

On his bed lay a guitar. Teresita picked it up and strummed it.

He served them a tasty stew made from goat and desert tubers and sage. Don Teófano gobbled his so fast he got a bellyache. Manuelito poured them cups of mint tea.

"What do you wish to learn?" Manuelito asked.

"Plants," said Huila. "She wishes to heal."

He sat back, rubbed his belly.

"Plants are a big responsibility. How many plants do you know?"

"I know thirty plants," Teresita boasted.

He sighed.

"A good herb doctor knows a hundred plants. An hechicero knows one thousand plants at the very least."

She was stunned.

"How long does that take?" she asked.

"Not long. One and a half lifetimes could prepare you."

"More stew?" Teófano asked.

"Help yourself."

"But I am smart," Teresita said.

"Being smart does not always mean anything in matters of spirit," Manuelito said.

"You are a strong girl," he added, "and you are also a wild boy."

A wild boy! She was so shocked by this that she just stared and blushed. What sort of insult was this?

"Are you insulted?" he asked.

"No," she lied.

"You are a boy. Did you not know?"

"How am I a boy?" she asked, her toes curling beneath her.

Manuelito said, "Why is my hair long?"

"I don't know."

"Guess."

"You're an Indian."

"I am also a woman." He took a great gulp of tea. "Why do you think we wear our hair long like this? Among my people, it is so the men might honor our sisters and the women within us. And you know we are the fiercest warriors in the world! My brothers will happily cut out an enemy's guts while he is alive and let him watch dogs eat them!"

"Dios mío!" said Don Teófano. These damned Indians!

"And then they'll set fire to him and laugh at his screams."

"I hope they don't come to visit while we're here," Teresita said.

Manuelito laughed.

"Still," he said. "Still. We are both man and woman. My brothers can be tender as mothers with their infants. Women can fight like tigers. Do you see? We are all a mix of each. Power starts when you strike the proper balance. Believe me when I tell you that the woman part of you is the better part. But you are also a man."

He put his hand on her face.

"It doesn't mean you are not very pretty."

Teresita loved Manuelito.

They stayed for two weeks. He told her what she could share with others, and what she couldn't share. He told her he had a wife and two sons at a ranchería not more than three days' ride from here, but the medicine was not to his wife's liking, so she lived near his mother and grandmother and their husbands beside a small pond at the foot of a ridge he called La Espina del Diablo.

"Is that where you rode in from?"

"It was."

"I thought you were off at war, or on a raiding party."

"I was eating chocolate cake and drinking buttermilk and trying to make a third child."

"Make a daughter."

"I would love to make a daughter! I can't wait to get back! I have work to do!"

"Manuelito," she warned, becoming his teacher for a moment, "don't let your wife hear you call that work."

They laughed.

He told her stories as they walked. Huila and Teófano, in the meantime, lounged and smoked and lied to each other and played cards. The two riflemen spent their days hunting rabbits and sleeping. They had hidden a few bottles of tequila in their bags, and these gave them reason to sleep.

He took her out to the shade of a scraggly tree with yellow flowers on it. They sat in the gravel, and tiny leaves and small yellow petals rained down on them. The tree was alive with bees. Manuelito said nothing. Neither did Teresita. He gestured up at the bees with his eyebrows. She listened. She could hear the bodies of the bees scraping around in the flowers. After a while Manuelito began to chuckle. So did Teresita. Soon, it seemed that the muttering of bees was the funniest thing they had ever heard. They sat there laughing out loud. They occasionally nudged each other and collapsed in hilarity. They wiped their eyes and laughed some more until they were crawling around gasping for air and weeping from how hard they laughed. Finally, lying on his back and clutching his aching ribs, Manuelito said, "You pass."

Teresita learned to walk slowly by pacing beside Manuelito. They spent their days strolling the desert, and he told her about each plant they met, and what it was like, and what it could do, and what other plants it liked and which it hated. Which plants were its relatives. Which plants could give you crazy dreams. He taught her which plants could kill as well as heal. He was often barefoot.

"I like to be in contact with my mother," he explained.

Teresita surprised Manuelito with a secret weapon of her own: pencils and a couple of Aguirre's notebooks. She sketched the plants in the notebooks, and she scratched their names and their details onto the pages. Manuelito was astounded by this. He made her teach him to write his name, and she showed him the letters. He held the pencil in his fist and made wobbly letters, then beamed at his name when he was through. They put the page on the wall of his house. When she was done with her studies, she had two hundred plants listed in her books.

"Why do I pierce my ear?"

"I know! I know that one! Huila told me!"

"Well?"

"You pierce your ear to show God you are no longer deaf! You are ready to listen!"

He was surprised.

"Very good," he said. "Now, here is another question. Why is it my left ear?"

"I do not remember."

"Because the left side is the side of the heart."

"If it is the side of the heart . . ."

"Then I show the Creator I am truly, deeply, listening."

Teresita nodded.

He continued: "Christians don't like the left side, but Indians do. Christians have forgotten their hearts. When a medicine woman hugs you, if she means it, she will move you to the side and put her heart on yours. Does Huila do this?"

Teresita laughed.

"Huila does not hug."

"Too bad for Huila," he said. "You should teach her."

They walked.

"Have you noticed," he asked, "how the Yoris hug?" He used the word from her own language. "They never put their hearts together. They lean in and barely touch the tops of their chests, and they hang their asses out in the wind so none of the good parts touch. Then they flutter their hands on each other's backs. Pat-pat-pat! One-two-three! Then they run away!"

From that day forward, Teresita always hugged people with the left side of her chest pressed to them, and she let the good parts touch if they had to.

When it came time for them to leave him, Manuelito sat cross-legged in the dirt before his house and painted blue flowers on the face of his guitar. He handed it to her. She took it in her arms and wept.

"I told you you would cry."

"You are a wicked man," she said.

"True."

He took his cross on a chain and put it around her neck.

"Remember me," he said.

She put the guitar down and threw her arms around him and sobbed.

"I will miss you," she cried.

He patted her hair with his great red hand. His fingers looked like big sticks to him as they moved down her hair. Her head rested in the center of his chest.

"Is this love?" she said into his shirt.

"Sí."

"How do I know?"

"Listen to my heart," he said.

She turned her head and put her ear against his great chest. She could hear his gut gurgling and whining. They had eaten fried beans for breakfast. She smiled.

"Thank you," she said.

He patted her head.

"Go now," he said.

As they got in the wagon, Huila said, "Gracias."

He waved.

"May we pay you?" she asked.

He shook his head.

"Pray for me when you think of it," he said.

Teófano turned the wagon away.

"And," Manuelito said, "be kind."

"Eh?" said Huila.

Teresita shouted, "Will I see you again?"

He did not answer.

Don Teófano said, "Andale!" and his mules surged ahead.

Twenty-seven

THE ENGINEER AGUIRRE had constructed a great white boiler-plate tank on the roof. A pipe led from a well beside the courtyard, and a brisk pumping session each morning on a long ax handle fitted to the pump-head worked a gurgling tide up to the roof. One of the kitchen girls started each day and ended each day working the handle. The only way to know the water had filled the tank was when it overflowed and ran down the roof tiles to Aguirre's gutters, which fed the overflow back into the previously installed tanks at each corner of the house. There, water for the herbs and flowers and dishes could be set free by the turning of a simple wooden spigot. The main house of Cabora was a marvel of engineering.

Three pipes extended from the rooftop water tank and snaked into the house. Two went to the fabulous scientific toilets, and one ran down to the sink in the kitchen. When one was going to use the toilet, a simple handle was spun counterclockwise until water fell into the tank above the toilet. Afterward, the old pull-chain unleashed an astonishing flood into the bowl and down the effluent pipe and into the arroyo, where it would delight frogs and salamanders and the snakes that ate them. No one knew how, but a catfish had managed to work its way into the toilet pond, and it grew huge eating the colonic offerings of the house. Every few weeks, one unlucky worker was sent to raise a floodgate and wash the sludge downstream. Somehow, the gargantuan catfish managed to hold its ground — it knew a good thing, and it wasn't about to let the occasional flood wash it downstream, away from such a constant and flavorful repast.

No matter how big it got, nobody ever considered eating it.

Buenaventura was caught trying to break the ax-pump handle one night, in a snit. Tomás had never forgiven him for ruining his marriage. The patrón never let him inside the big house. He was never even allowed within the gates to the courtyard, and that really made him mad, since he'd have loved to eat some of the fruit on Tomás's plum tree. Buenaventura knew Tomás was punishing him for being born.

When they caught Buenaventura, they dragged him to the front door by his ear. Tomás glared at him for a few moments, then suddenly announced he would be banished from Cabora for a month. He pronounced his sentence like an Old Testament king: "Banished to Aquihuiquichi!" The vaqueros immediately put Buenaventura on his horse and sent him galloping away.

Segundo missed all this drama. He was in his little house, wearing a golden silk bathrobe and soft leather slippers. If anyone had seen him, he would have had to get out his pistola and shoot. But nobody saw him. He sipped blackberry brandy. Nobody saw that, either. He tried it — and he liked it — he really liked it: he held up his little finger as he sipped. "Delightful, my dear," he said out loud. "The aperitif is perfectly lovely. May I offer you a pâté?" One of the barn cats sat on the small couch and watched him with bored yellow eyes.

Tomás, after the banishment of his bastard son, sat at the

table with Aguirre. Another country breakfast. Tomás was tired of eggs and steaks and beans and tortillas. He wondered what they ate for breakfast in France or that recent discovery, Japan.

"My dear Engineer," he said.

"My beloved brother, Tomás!"

"Me caes bien, pinche Lauro."

"And you, my friend, you too are all right by me!"

"Did you sleep well?" Tomás asked.

"Like the dead!" enthused Aguirre.

Tomás was vaguely aware that he was now as courtly with Aguirre as he had been with Loreto.

They spoke of engineering and of the political situation as the girls brought in squash blossoms fried in eggs. White goat cheese was crumbled over them, and chorizo leaked orange grease all over the plates. Frijoles smashed and fried in lard. The obligatory mounds of tortillas.

"Lovely!" Aguirre said.

"We eat well," Tomás agreed, taking a huge crunching bite out of a yellow chile. His eyes went red immediately, and then he started to sneeze. The chile made him sneeze over and over: *Yachú-yachú-yachú!* "Híjole!" *Yachússs!* "That's good." His brow was moist with chile sweat.

He crunched into the chile again.

Yaaa-chuuusss!

Huila shuffled out, looking like hell.

"Bless you," she muttered.

"Gracias."

Tomás noted that she had forgotten to brush her hair as he scrubbed his whiskers with his napkin.

"My nose is running!" he reported.

"Those chiles," Huila noted for the record, "they will do that."

This kind of absurdity passed for conversation most days in the main house. Tomás ached for the visits of Aguirre. Everyone else around him could only offer such brilliant insights as: coffee is hot — unless it's cold!

Somehow, after the miracle of Manuelito, Teresita had expected something better than to be exiled to her shack again. Huila had sent her away without blinking an eye. And here she was.

She wandered around the ranch, looking at weeds and comparing them to her sketches. When Teófano's niece came down with terrible menstrual cramps, she was able to consult her notes and concoct her first potion.

Menstruación difícil:
Abrótano
2% infusion
leaves and stems
steep for 15 minutes
3 cups daily

"Abrótano, abrótano," she repeated as she walked around, as if saying it would somehow conjure it. An old curandera in the village of Ojo del Chivo finally sold her a bag of it when Teresita rode a horse three miles through cactus forests to see her. The niece made faces when she drank it, but after the third dosage, the cramps eased. By the next morning, they were gone and her blood flowed out like water.

Teresita attended two more births. One girl had a navel sticking so far out of her belly that it looked like a brown finger. She had a dark brown line running straight up her middle, and her stomach was almost a pyramid, she bulged so terribly. The baby would not come. The poor girl writhed and cried for twenty hours, until the midwife fell asleep at her feet. Teresita moved the snoring partera aside and gazed into the painful maw of the birth canal. The girl was beyond this world in pain, making low noises. Teresita did not know what to do, so she put her hands between the girl's legs and opened her to see what was inside. She was astounded to see a tiny white foot. She knew this was wrong. She pushed her fingers inside and felt the little leg as it retreated back into the mother's darkness. All she could do was pray.

When the old partera awoke, the sun had come again. She found Teresita kneeling between the mother's legs, praying for a miracle that could not come. The mother had gone to sleep at last, and she would not wake up again.

They washed her and wrapped her and prayed over her. Teresita went to her husband, one of the People from Palo Cagado, a laborer who had come all this way from Ocoroni. She hugged him and whispered the terrible news, and he sobbed with his head on her shoulder. He was ten years older than Teresita. They all buried her together, and they put two wooden crosses on the mound.

After this terrible event, Teresita stayed home. She dried plants she had collected, and she looked into the eyes of the rattlesnakes on the boulders. She thought of her mother, in those days. It seemed odd to her that her mother would come to mind. But she wondered where Cayetana might be, what she might be doing. She thought of her until, at night, she dreamed of her. Cayetana wore a great straw hat with a wide brim. She carried a parasol. And she walked down a street in a great city. Streetcars clanged as she waited to cross. The buildings rose all around her, and flocks of pigeons flew in great clattering swirls.

These dreams were the sort that Huila had warned her about. She knew this because she awoke with tears on her face. And she also knew this because she had never seen a city, nor a streetcar, nor a tall building. But she knew what they were as soon as she dreamed them.

❊

When Buenaventura appeared, Teresita was delighted.

"Hey," he said, "you've grown."

"As have you." She smiled.

He sucked at his teeth.

"Can I sleep here?"

"Is that proper?" she asked.

"Why not?" he asked, hopping off his horse. "Pinche Urrea tossed me out. Thanks, Papá!" He strode into her house.

"People will talk."

"Why? You're my sister, ain't you?"

Teresita stuck her head in the door and said, "What did you say?"

"You didn't know?"

He was lying on her bed, one hand holding his hat up behind his head.

"How dumb are you, girl? Everybody knows who your father is!"

He put his hat over his eyes.

"Just look in a mirror."

It didn't take long for him to start snoring.

Teresita decided it was a good time to walk down to Teófano's shed.

He was waiting outside.

"Is there something about Cabora I don't know?" she asked.

"Like what?" he replied.

"Some secret nobody told me, perhaps."

Then he opened his mouth.

Then he closed it.

"Do you mean what I think you mean?" he asked.

Teresita crossed her arms.

"Ay Dios," he said.

Twenty-eight

A SNOT-NOSED BOY of about ten rode into Cabora from the big road, yelling: "The bees! The bees!"

Tomás was standing in the road, conversing with his neighbor, Segundo, when the boy reined to a snorting halt and shouted, "The bees!"

"What bees?"

"At Cantúa's!" the boy shouted. His horse, white-eyed and frantic, jittered in the road. "Muchas abejas!"

"What do they look like?" Tomás asked.

"Big black piles of bees! In a corner of the roof! He asks for you to come, please! Soon!"

Tomás clapped his hands.

"A swarm!" he cried. He grabbed Segundo's arms and said, "A wild swarm at Cantúa's!"

"Such miracles," Segundo intoned.

"Go!" Tomás yelled to the boy. "Tell them I am coming! Oh —" He fished in his pocket, came up with a gold coin. He tossed it to the boy. "There you go."

"Gracias!" the boy shouted as he spun his horse and tore away.

"Look at that little bastard go!" Tomás said.

He trotted into the house and changed his trousers, strapped on his double gunbelt (Gabriela might be impressed by this) and his smart Texan hat. A giant Mexican sombrero might lend a bit too much of a comic-opera aspect to the adventure.

"Aguirre!" he called. "Aguirre!"

"Eh?"

"Are you up?"

"Qué?"

"Bees!"

"What?"

"Bees! A wild swarm!"

He was out the door before Aguirre could answer. Nearby was only a burro that the gardener had loaded with trimmed branches from the plum tree and the vines. Tomás removed the load from the donkey's back and leapt aboard. He prodded the little beast to a slow canter, and he aimed it at the far beekeeper's hut. His long legs bounced madly in the air, held up near the donkey's chest to keep his feet from dragging in the dirt.

The Parangarícutirimícuaro beekeeper was still asleep, having finished off a sack of marijuana buds the night before. Without disturbing him, Tomás threw an empty hive box and a smoker into his bee wagon. He added gloves and a veil, just in case. He whistled for a couple of vaqueros at the corrals to bring a nag to hitch. They put a white draft horse in the traces, and Tomás stood in the box and flogged the horse until it started to trot. Aguirre was in front of the house, rubbing his eyes, and he had to jump back as Tomás sped by.

"Bees," Tomás called over his shoulder. "Bees!"

He rattled down the road and never slowed down until he got to Cantúa's. There, he was delighted to discover Gabriela standing well away from the restaurant, with white towels in her hands and her wild hair tied back. She spun the towels madly around her head every time a bee came near. She was in such a frenzy that she terrorized butterflies and dragonflies as well. Her hair was a great roiling cascade that reached the top of her round bottom.

Like a fresh peach, Tomás told himself.

Señor Cantúa was standing near the corner of his building, looking up at the roof, which was only about ten feet high. A nimbus of bees circled his head, and Tomás could hear the buzz even from the road. Cantúa was bent at a sharp angle, as if his worry had cracked him in half. He wrung his hands.

"Many bees," Gabriela said.

Tomás hopped down and, checking to see if Señor Cantúa was looking his way, quickly bowed and reached for her hand. She transferred the towel to her other hand. Elegance! he thought. He took her fingers and kissed them.

Caramel!

Cinnamon!

Dulce de leche!

"This lovely day," he said, "has suddenly become all the more lovely now that I have seen you."

This was what was known as a piropo. It was a specialty of the Sinaloans. Many affairs had been launched by the properly composed and delivered piropo.

She allowed her hand to linger in his grasp for a moment, then pulled it away slowly. Her fingers slid down his.

Aha!

He stood tall!

"You are," she said, "quite charming."

"I am a man without grace," he demurred. "Any elegance I display is only inspired by you."

She smiled and looked at the ground.

"I am only a cook," she said, automatically offering up a ritual response so he could show his mettle.

All right, all right — he could rise to this challenge.

"You are the essence of springtime in a woman's form," he said. "I have never seen anything as pure as your gaze. If I have grace, it is a reflection of your own."

She breathed in and blinked.

Cantúa was coming.

Time to risk it all:

"Gabriela, forgive me for being so forward. I hardly know you." The father was getting closer! "But when I see you, I honestly believe I might finally be permitted to believe in God!"

She put her hand over her heart.

"Bless me," he crooned.

"Don Tomás!" Señor Cantúa bellowed. "I have ten pounds of bees on my walls!"

He was frantic.

Tomás shook his hand and said, for Gabriela's benefit:

"My dear and noble Maestro Cantúa! This kind of problem is exactly why you should call on me. At any hour of the day or night, I count it as an honor to watch over you and your precious and saintly Gabriela." He tipped his head to the furiously blushing Gaby. "I have faced armed Yaqui camps alone, my dear Señor Cantúa. I have ridden hundreds of miles from Sinaloa, braving the dangers of the road. And I raise bees! I fear not. So allow me to rescue you."

He turned back to her.

"And you," he purred.

They followed him to the shady corner of the building, and there, like some strange lava flow, was a bustling wedge of bees piling up on one another and sticking to the wall. The very weight of the huge mass of insects was making it slide down the wood of the wall, and those bees on the bottom scrabbled furiously to keep hold. Those that fell off circled back and piled on again.

"This is a swarm," Tomás intoned. "At the center of this colony, we will find a queen. They are seeking a hollow tree or an empty barn to start a new hive. They have flown far, and they are thinking about bedding down on your wall for a good night's rest."

"He is so smart," Gabriela whispered to her father.

"However," Tomás continued, "they could very well choose the inside of your restaurant, and then you would have trouble. Now, the bees are your guests, and they will behave themselves. But once they go inside, then you are the bees' guests, and they can be terrible hosts."

"What would happen?" Señor Cantúa asked.

"You would have to burn the restaurant down, I'm afraid."

Cantúa let out a small cry.

"Don't despair, my good man," Tomás said. "I am here."

He fired up his trusty marijuana smoker, and then he opened the extra box. It had several waxed frames inside, ready for a new colony to establish itself. He threw a tarpaulin over the horse's back to protect it from stings. He moved the wagon over to the corner of the building, where he could easily reach the swarm. He gave them a few happy puffs of smoke. It smelled good. By God! It smelled very good. He took in a lungful. What a perfect day! He pumped out great curlicues of luscious smoke!

He smiled at the Cantúas.

Carefully, as if working the bloomers off a schoolmarm, Tomás inserted his hands into the swarm.

"Dios!" Gabriela cried.

Cantúa crossed himself.

"I have never seen such a thing!" he said.

Tomás moved a huge load of narcotized bees to the frame and slid them into the opening. He did it again, only this time he held out the double handful and offered it to Gaby, who yelped in delighted terror and skipped behind her father. Tomás smiled now, in charge of the world — that smoke was certainly pleasant! — and put the new bees in with the rest. He used his hat to brush stragglers off the wall and they dropped and lazily flew until they found their sisters in the maw of the open box.

"He is so competent," Gabriela said.

"They smell their queen," Tomás noted. "Now they will go to her."

He fit the lid on the top and slid open the entry door at the bottom so the confused bees still circling could enter.

"They should all be inside in an hour," he said.

Cantúa regarded him with a kind of awe.

"May I feed you?" he asked.

"Perhaps some coffee," Tomás said.

As they went in the door, Gaby said, "That is the bravest thing I have ever seen."

"I would do anything," he responded, "to keep you safe from harm."

"Ay, Don Tomás," she said. "You say the nicest things."

"Was that not test enough? You must believe me. Put me to any test, Gaby." He stood with hat in hand, so tall his head almost brushed the ceiling. "Anything," he said, "in honor of you."

Señor Cantúa brought out the coffee. It was too late to scowl. All he could do now was to sit there with them and keep them apart.

Tomás brushed his whiskers and smiled blandly. That marijuana, he thought, it adds something to the day!

"Say, do you know what?" he blurted. "I am hungry after all. Do you have any sweet rolls?"

Gaby jumped up.

"I'll go, Papá."

She flicked a look at Tomás as she went, and she managed to swirl her skirt as she passed through the door.

"My God, Cantúa," Tomás said.

Cantúa raised his hands.

"Please," he pleaded, "be a gentleman."

By the time Aguirre pulled up to the restaurant, Tomás had eaten all the sweet rolls, and was now tearing into a platter of machaca. Gaby had fried the shredded beef with eggs and beside the mound of machaca she had piled fried nopalitos.

When Aguirre rushed in, Tomás cried, "Engineer! Have a flour tortilla!"

"Didn't you eat breakfast?" Aguirre said.

"Suddenly, I was hungry."

Somehow, Tomás had found two violinists and a banjo player, and they plucked and fiddled folk songs as an old woman in the corner held up her skirt and danced barefoot. Señor Cantúa conducted the music with a blue and white serving spoon. Gaby shooed a chicken out the front door.

"Besides," Tomás said, "if my Gabriela's hand has prepared it, how could I not eat it?"

"Ay, Tomás," she said.

Aguirre thought: My Gabriela? And he thought: Ay, Tomás?

"What of the bees?" he asked.

Tomás waved his hand.

"The bees are safely in their hive, Aguirre! The bees are ancient history! Now we are having a party. My treat!"

The snot-nosed boy from that morning came out of the kitchen carrying a bowl of beans.

"Eat, cabrón," said Tomás. "Life is wonderful."

Aguirre sat.

Five travelers came in and immediately fell on the food that Tomás paid for in this burst of magnanimity.

Aguirre smiled at Gabriela.

"Water, please," he said.

She scrunched her nose at him and went to the kitchen.

"What a nose, eh, Engineer?" said Tomás.

"Her nose is," Aguirre replied, searching for the proper phrase, "eloquent."

The old woman asked Aguirre to dance. He waved his hands in a frenzy of dread, but Tomás pushed him to his feet. The hilarity that erupted in the room when Aguirre shuffled in a circle with his hands caught in the old woman's claws did not make him feel very happy at all. His obvious discomfort made all the travelers laugh even louder.

There was so much uproar inside Cantúa's that nobody heard the rumble of the wheels as Doña Loreto Urrea's buggies bearing all the children and the priest and herself rolled past on their way to Cabora.

Twenty-nine

THEY RODE BACK SLOWLY, and as always, carefully.

In Sinaloa, the tarantulas had been mournful and fat, with bright red legs. These norteño tarantulas were the color of coffee, and skinny, and seemed to be nervous. In Sonora, Tomás was witness to new breeds of vinegarroons and scorpions, horrible things with pincers and swollen fangs and dreadful scents. He was often amazed by their single-minded clanking progress across the Alamos road. The nasty little wind scorpions, all yellow and orange and black, like Jerusalem crickets — which he, like the People, called "niños de la tierra"— but with immense fangs and dyspeptic dispositions, actually lifted their front legs at him and displayed their dark fangs in sincere threats, and they spun in circles to track him as he moved around them to see what they'd do.

"I hope those blasted bees of yours don't sting me," said Aguirre.

From the back of the wagon came a contented murmuring.

"The bees are smoked down," Tomás assured him. "They are tamed."

"I don't trust bees."

"Bees are better than people."

Tomás looked over at his bearded friend bobbling along inelegantly on top of his horse as if he'd been stacked there, his parts badly tied to the saddle. Aguirre's hat even bounced, like a lid on a boiling pot.

"Bees," Tomás said, "are excellent engineers, better even than you. They are hard workers — they certainly work harder than these lazy bastards that work for me. They are brave as Indian warriors. And they make honey. Far better than humans, my friend."

Aguirre peered ahead.

"What's that?" he said, interrupting Tomás's entomological ponderings.

"Eh?"

Tomás looked down the road. There seemed to be two buggies parked before the main house.

"There is always something," Tomás sighed, "interesting in every day."

He accelerated his rattling wagon to a brisk trot, and he was worried to see Segundo in the road. Segundo looked chagrined. Tomás dropped the reins and stood in the box and shouted, "Qué pasa aquí?"

Segundo jerked his chin at the house.

"Her," he said.

"Which her?" called Aguirre.

"The big her," said Segundo.

"Loreto," announced Tomás, already hanging his head.

"And her," added Segundo.

"Who?"

"Her."

Tomás looked.

Huila was sitting near the plum tree with Teresita.

"Her, Huila?" he said. "Or her, the girl?"

"Her, both of them."

Buenaventura strolled up the road, whistling.

"Now," Tomás said, "my day is complete."

"What do you want?" Tomás asked the kid.

"Nada."

"Why are you here?"

"Mexico is a free country."

"It is my ranch."

"I will inherit it!" Buenaventura shrugged. "Why can't I take stock of my holdings?"

"Chingado," noted Tomás. "Stay out of the way."

Buenaventura started to reply, but Aguirre held up a finger as the two men dismounted and went through the gate.

In the courtyard, Huila said, "This girl needs to talk to you."

Teresita started to rise.

"Not now," said Tomás, heading for the door.

Teresita sat back down.

"Good day," said Aguirre.

Teresita rose again.

"Buenos días," she said.

She sat down again.

"Aguirre," said Huila, "tell Don Tomás we need to speak to him soon."

Aguirre tipped his hat as he went by, thinking Huila, too, was impudent.

Inside, Doña Loreto was walking through the parlor. She glanced up at Tomás and pointedly ran a gloved finger along one shelf. It came up black with dust. She shook her head and smacked her palms to clean her fingers. She pulled off her gloves. The children were storming up and down the stairs, yelling and hooting like Yaqui invaders.

"Please!" Tomás complained.

Juan Francisco slid down the banister, then stomped back upstairs. He sounded like thunder. Catastrophic poundings came from the upstairs bedrooms as the children launched themselves from the furniture and flew onto the beds.

"How rustic," Loreto sighed, "it all is."

She flipped through a few of the Engineer's magazines on a table.

"Tu casita silvestre."

This last elegance, this jape about the little country home, the little country cabin, was particularly pointed, and it drew blood like a paper cut.

Suddenly, Tomás's day grew immeasurably worse when a thin cleric came from the kitchen, munching on a stack of sweet rolls.

"My son," the priest said.

"Who are you?"

"Padre Gastélum," the priest said. "Vengo de Zaragoza!"

But he was speaking Castilian, and he lisped the word: *Tharagotha!*

A Spaniard priest, no less! Tomás pulled a bandana

from his pocket and wiped his brow. This was worse than any hostile Indian village.

"Why are you here now?" Tomás asked Loreto. "You have never shown the slightest interest in our ranch before!"

"I came to see if you had moved your whores into the house," she replied, sweetly.

This seemed an astounding thing to say in front of a priest, but Gastélum from Tharagotha stood placidly, chewing his way through three pesos' worth of pastry.

The engineer Aguirre tried one of his stratagems on Loreto: taking her hand, he exulted, "Loreto, as always, you are fresh as a spring morning." Then he brushed her knuckles with his lips.

"You are not Catholic," Gastélum noted, halting the Engineer's chivalric gestures.

"Excuse me?"

Loreto extracted her hand and drifted away like a malevolent fogbank.

"I was simply noting, for the record, that you are not Catholic," said the priest. "It is a point of reference. For my reports."

"Reports?"

"Oh yes," the priest said, "I am the Vatican's eyes and ears in Sonora. Did you not know? Unlike you Protestants, we have a Holy Father who is interested in the well-being of all his children. It is my duty to report. Name names and tell tales." He smiled. Chewed.

"Holy Father?" Aguirre said, just to say something.

"The pope, pendejo," said Tomás.

"I know that!" Aguirre snapped.

But Tomás had followed Loreto out of the room.

Father Gastélum added: "We have a second father,

perhaps not as holy — heh, heh, forgive me a slight jest — in Mexico City. Ahem."

The two men eyed each other.

Aguirre said, "And you make reports."

"I do."

"To Porfirio Díaz."

"Our leader."

"The dictator."

"Dangerous words."

"The truth."

"Do you have a clear view of truth, my son?"

"I do when it has to do with that murdering thief in Mexico City!"

"I will note it."

"Are you threatening me?"

"I serve only God . . . and the republic."

"I serve God and liberty!"

"Ah, liberty. Yes, Lucifer and his fallen angels said something quite similar."

"I'll be damned!"

"Perhaps," said the priest. "I shall watch the gates of Hell in the future and see if you pass through."

Aguirre flushed red.

"And does the great Don Tomás," the priest asked, "share your revolutionary views?"

Aguirre thought it was too dangerous to answer.

"I see," said the priest.

Aguirre could think of nothing to offer.

"I take your silence for a confession," Gastélum confided. "Very interesting."

Finally, Aguirre managed to say, "Have some more pastries."

"Ay, sí."

"Have some coffee."

"Gracias, mi hijo," intoned the priest. "I believe I shall."

Elsewhere in the house, the drama continued:

"Loreto!" Tomás cried.

She was standing inside the downstairs bathroom, regarding the amazing flush toilet. She pulled the chain and observed the water swirling in the bowl.

"Isn't this delightful?" she said.

The children were apparently breaking everything they could reach. A loud crashing and crunching came from upstairs.

"Goddamn it!" Tomás bellowed.

He stormed to the stairs.

"Juan! *Juan!* Juan Francisco!"

"Sí, Papá?"

"Come down here! And bring the others! Now!"

"Sí, Papá."

And here they came, a parade of chagrined children: Juan, Lety, Martita, Alberto, and Tavito.

Their father glared at them. What monsters.

"Out!" Tomás yelled.

The children trooped out the door. When Huila saw them, she told Teresita, "Wait here," and hurried into the house. The children eyed Teresita as they stood around the plum tree.

Suddenly, Buenaventura popped up like some demonic puppet and said, "Qué hubo, tú pinche puto?"

"Me?" said Juan Francisco.

"Me?" mocked Buenaventura.

"Watch your mouth," Juan said.

"Watch your mouth."

"Don't repeat me!"
"Don't repeat me!"
"Aguas, cabrón!"
Teresita rose, but it was already too late to stop them.

Padre Gastélum was in the kitchen, posing nobly for the cook staff while eating various delights they offered up to him. Mexicans had long understood that you could barter your way into Heaven, and they fed the skinny priest slivers of white crumbling wet cheese with green chiles drooping over them, fried little flauta tacos, orange slices with red-pepper powder, cactus candy, candied yams, jícama in lime juice. He was delighted to accept a small glass of cognac when the tray of French chocolates appeared. The girls were thrilled when he made the sign of the cross over each plate and over them. The Blessing of the Chocolates. The Blessing of the Goat Cheese. The Blessing of the Little Black Cigar.

In another room, Loreto slapped Tomás.

He spluttered an obscenity.

She slapped his other cheek.

He raised his hand.

Aguirre rose.

Huila, watching, clenched her hands — this was even better than she'd hoped!

Tomás dropped his hand.

Aguirre sat.

Loreto took up a coffee cup and hurled it.

Tomás snarled as the saucer sailed into the wall.

He took both her arms in his fists and shook her once.

Aguirre rose.

Huila sat down.

Loreto wrenched her arms out of his grasp, reached for a clay pitcher full of lemonade, and threw it in great swirling arcs of pink fluid into the glass-fronted hutch, where Urrea antique chinas exploded.

She laughed.

Aguirre sat.

Huila stood.

"I laugh!" Loreto taunted. "I laugh!"

"You think you laugh? *I* am the one who laughs!" Tomás roared. "Ha! Ha! *Ha!*" He put his hands on his belly. "Do you hear that? I laugh! Ha! Ha! Ha!"

"You beast!"

She sobbed.

Aguirre rose again.

Huila went to Loreto.

Aguirre chided Tomás.

"Really," he said.

"El amor," Tomás proclaimed, "es una guerra!"

"Animal!" Loreto sobbed into Huila's shoulder.

Huila cast dirty looks at Tomás.

"You too?" he said.

Great huzzahs erupted outside the house. Shrieks and thumps. Segundo appeared from somewhere and bellowed, "Hurry, boss!"

"Now what!" Tomás yelled.

He ran outside, and there found Juan Francisco and Buenaventura clutched in a fierce wrestling embrace, rolling up and down the road. They would free a hand and deliver a punch, then clench and roll again. Vaqueros and boys were lining the road, hooting and clapping. Dust everywhere. Somehow, Juan had managed to tear off Buenaventura's left pant leg. Buenaventura had tattered Juan's little jacket. Tomás didn't know which one he was prouder of, or which he was madder at. He waded into the fray and grabbed the boys by their collars and pulled them apart. They parted kicking and spitting and cursing, and the first time Tomás let them go, they flew at each other again and clawed themselves back to the dirt like fighting cats.

Tomás took a punch to the nose when he jumped back in. He noticed, out of the corner of his eye, that those good-for-nothing buckaroos were betting on the fight.

"Ya, pues, cabrones!" he snarled, yanking them apart. His nose bled all over his mustache.

"Don't curse at my son!" Loreto proclaimed.

"Stop fighting!"

"Don't you hurt my boy!" Loreto yelled. She rushed out to pummel Tomás's back.

"Segundo!" Tomás cried.

Segundo stepped up and grabbed Loreto, quite aware that he would never get the chance to touch the lady of the hacienda again, and he managed to get his hands on her breasts so he could tell the boys about it later. He pulled her back, cooing, "Miss, miss. Come now, miss."

The boys were gasping raggedly. They bent over, rested their bloody hands on their knees. Buenaventura spit a long pink load in the dirt. They were both crying from sheer rage.

Juan pointed at Buenaventura.

"He started it."

"Fuck you."

"Hey!" Tomás shouted.

Buenaventura spit again. "Fuck you, fucker!"

Tomás shook him by the neck.

"No más!" he warned.

Buenaventura jerked away.

Loreto got out of Segundo's grasp and rushed to her boy. Juan Francisco pulled free of his mother's smothering grip and pointed at Buenaventura again.

"He said he was your son!" he cried.

Stunned silence.

Loreto's eyes grew more slitted than they had been inside the house.

"Now everyone knows," she proclaimed. "My shame is complete!"

Tomás thought: Oh no.

Everybody from the hacienda seemed to have gathered. Huila stood to the side, and Tomás was even more worried when he saw her mouth hanging open.

Tomás offered the scoundrel's base response: he guffawed.

Aguirre hove into view with a look of deep mourning on his face.

"Father," said Juan Francisco, "how could you?"

Young Juan suddenly leapt to the nearest of the two buggies and charged away. Aguirre, gallant to the end, mounted his horse and pursued.

Buenaventura pointed at Teresita.

"I'm not the only one!" he cried. "Look at her!"

Loreto turned to Teresita.

If she could have, Teresita would have crawled into a hole.

Buenaventura was taunting them all: "That's his daughter! His daughter! His daughter! How do you like it?"

Loreto said: "I have always known!"

"Oh Christ," said Tomás.

"You," Loreto said. "You had no idea!"

Tomás wished he had a cigarette, that he was back at Cantúa's, watching Gabriela. He put his hands in his pockets.

"I don't even give a damn anymore," he said.

Loreto gathered her chicks and hurried to her buggy. Loyalty to womanhood suddenly overcame Huila's general delight in Yori misfortune, and she rushed to the buggy and climbed aboard as Loreto whipped her horse. Tomás watched them speed away in the wake of Juan Francisco and Aguirre. He was alone in the middle of the road.

Suddenly, Father Gastélum burst out the door crying, "What! What!" He glared at Tomás then scrambled onto the bee-wagon and lashed the tired nag and headed off after Loreto. "My bees!" Tomás shouted.

Segundo, suddenly grown respectful, led the vaqueros away.

Tomás stomped into the courtyard and kicked a flowerpot, which burst in a shower of dirt and geraniums. He flew into a rage of flying arms and legs, kicking pots and benches, cursing as he broke everything he could reach. He slapped plums off the tree and they splattered on the adobe walls of the house. When he had worn himself out, he stood there panting, head hanging down, hair in his face.

He noticed Teresita sitting primly on her bench.

"You're still here," he said.

"Sí, señor."

He said, "Only you remain."

"Apparently, sir."

He stood straight and pulled his hair out of his face.

"Are you really my daughter?" he asked.

"That is what they say."

He shuffled over to her bench and sat heavily beside her.

"Your mother?"

"Cayetana the Hummingbird."

He rubbed his face and groaned.

Tomás pointed at a lone bee investigating the slaughtered geraniums on the flagstones. "Better than people," he said.

"Oh," she replied.

They sat.

"Do you think they're coming back?" he asked.

"Not soon."

"No."

After a time, he said, "Daughter."

She turned to him.

"Yes?"

"May I call you daughter, or are you mad at me, too?"

"You may." Then: "I'm not mad."

"What a relief," he said. "Everyone is mad at me."

She patted his knee.

"Don't worry," she said. "These things pass, and life returns to normal."

He sighed.

"You're right," he said.

She folded her hands in her lap.

"I have been very bad," he said. "I didn't mean to be bad, but I have misbehaved."

"Yes," she said. "I saw."

They laughed.

"What do we do now?" he asked.

"I do not know . . . Father. May I call you Father?"

"Why not." He waved his hands over his head. "Why the hell not."

He stood.

Put out his hand.

"Since it's just you and me," he said, "why don't we go inside and enjoy my little country home?"

She took his hand and he helped her up, as any gentleman would for any lady. No one had ever offered Teresita a hand before. She took it in her cool fingers and rose.

"Gracias," she said.

"I still have your grandfather clock," he said as they went up the steps. "And weren't you fond of cookies?" he asked. "I seem to remember you had a fondness for cookies," he said as the big door swung closed behind them.

Thirty

TOMÁS HAD CERTAIN DEMANDS for his daughter. The course of study began on that first day.

Item A: Baths

Tomás immediately had a bath drawn for her in the big tin tub in the washroom. He pried open a couple of Loreto's trunks that had made the journey from Ocoroni. He delivered soaps and shampoos and lotions to Teresita as she went in the steamy room with the cook. Teresita had never taken a hot bath in a deep tub, and she was shocked, yet delighted, to feel the water cover her entire body. Bath salts and flowery pink oils went in the water and created the miracle of bubbles. She watched her own legs vanish beneath a rising mountain range of foam.

The cook poured a gourd of water over Teresita's head and worked French shampoo into her hair with long hard spidery fingers.

Outside the door, Tomás called, "A lady bathes every week!"

Item B: Grooming

The cook tortured Teresita with a hairbrush for a half hour. Her hair was tied back with red silk ribbons. The cook made her raise her arms, and she puffed great clouds of perfumed powder into her armpits, then she made Teresita do the same to her privates. A toothbrush was presented to her, and a small tin of gray tooth powder made in London. Teresita was used to washing her teeth with a little charcoal and honey and mint leaves. She scrubbed her teeth and spit and was embarrassed when the cook took her foamy tooth water out in its bowl to spill it into the arroyo.

Rouge made her cheeks look as if she had joined the circus. Creams and powders made her look like a white girl. Kohl around her eyes made her look like a mesmerist.

Item C: Undergarments

Teresita was irritated to be presented with Loreto's bloomers. She agreed to the ridiculous long panties, but she refused to wear a petticoat. Either one or the other. It was, after all, her own body.

Item D: Proper Attire

Loreto's steamer trunks delivered dresses. The house girls altered them. She chose a yellow skirt with a white blouse and light green shawl over her shoulders. She did not like the hats, however, and rejected out of hand the small pillbox-and-veil the cook set out for her.

"This looks like a spoiled cake covered in spiderwebs," she said.

The vast straw sun hat made her laugh out loud.

"That's a hat for a drunk mariachi!" she said.

Item E: Shoes

When he saw her, Tomás whistled. "Beautiful!" he enthused. But when he saw her rugged toes poking out from her filthy huaraches, he was offended.

"No, no!" he cried. "A young lady must never show her toes!"

"What's wrong with my toes?"

"No, no. No, I'm afraid it's not done. And those huaraches!"

"What's wrong with my huaraches?"

"Awful," he said. "Just awful."

She was marched back to the dressing room and subjected to the torment of hard shoes being hammered onto her feet.

"I do not like this," she announced.

The hard heels on the floor sounded to her like the hooves of a mule.

Whenever Tomás wasn't looking, Teresita kicked off her shoes and went barefoot.

Item F: Table Manners

She was no longer allowed to hold her fork and knife in her fists. She was not allowed to chew with her mouth open. She was dissuaded from slurping her drinks. She refused to stick out her pinkie when sipping, though.

Item G: Proper Sleeping Behavior

Teresita was shown to her bedroom in the west wing of the house. It was whitewashed. The walls had apparently been planned as they were being built, for they wobbled off plumb, and there were seven of them, a chamber of corners. Some of the walls were quite small, as if the builders had thrown up a bit of adobe to connect two planes that hadn't managed to meet in a corner. Her door and shutters were blue. She liked this.

The room had two windows, one in the south-facing wall and one in the west wall. A small table with two chairs. A freestanding cabinet would hold her new clothes; Tomás would not allow her to wear peasant garb in his house. In the corner, a washstand held a porcelain bowl with etchings of bucolic Swiss villages. A white pitcher with water. Soap.

Near the west window stood her bed. It had a wrought-iron headboard. Great piles of pillows. She had never had a good pillow before. She lay on the bed and was struck with a fit of giggles when she realized how soft the mattress was. She kicked off her shoes and slid her bare feet around on the smooth bedspread.

Cutting across the ceiling were two square vigas. Slightly lower, and at an angle, ran a charred third beam that had been rescued from the original fire. She stood on the bed and grabbed it and hung from it, swinging her legs.

She was given pink gowns and white gowns. Perhaps the Yoris were afraid they'd be naked in the dream time and the Indians would see their secrets.

Slippers!

Not even at night would Teresita be spared the torment of shoes! Yoris took off their shoes and boots, sighed and whined about their sore feet, even soaked their feet in salt water and made servants rub them. Then they put on more shoes to be "comfortable"!

Item H: Proper Conversation

Teresita was not to discuss midwifery, female problems, or medical details at the dinner table. These items, discussed with discretion, were permissible in Tomás's study, where he took her after dinner and sipped brandy or cognac as he read her stories and newspapers. He was, after all, deeply fascinated by what went on under skirts the world over. Any small detail of female biology put a sparkle in his eye.

She was also expected to ask questions about the bizarre imaginings of Edgar Allan Poe. And Tomás enjoyed hearing her opinions about problems of the day.

On her second night in the house, he offered her a sip of brandy. It made her cough and splutter. He slapped her on the back. She declined a puff of his cigar.

"The issue this evening," he told her, "is Buenaventura. I see him as a liability."

"Why, Father?"

"He's a rotten little bastard!"

"He has had a rough life."

"Is that supposed to be my fault? Don't answer that!"

"What would you do?"

"I'll cast him out!"

"Really?"

"I want him off Cabora!" Tomás announced. "Measures must be taken!"

"Try showing mercy," she suggested.

He puffed and regarded her.

"Mercy is your strongest feature, Father. Remember the Yaquis."

He smiled. The Yaquis.

"Hmm."

He took another sip. Puffed and blew smoke in the air. The grandfather clock started to chime.

"All right," Tomás said. "But he doesn't come in my house. To me, he is just another vaquero. He is nothing to me!"

Teresita knew this was bluster, but Huila had taught her to let men babble.

He picked up a leather volume and said, "Tonight, Poe's tale of Arthur Gordon Pym."

She crossed her legs under her, partly to hide her bare feet.

"Is it ghastly?" she asked.

"Oh yes! Quite."

Item I: Proper Horseback Riding

No more pulling up her skirts and straddling a horse! Tomás almost fainted in shock when she opened her legs and mounted. It was absolutely *indecent*. Teresita was instructed in the absurd and insulting method of sidesaddle riding, where her abysmal petticoats and velvet skirts and knee boots dangled like atrophied limbs off the side of a boring little striding horse.

When Tomás wasn't looking, she pulled up her skirts and raced Segundo all the way down the Alamos road to the Cantúa turnoff.

Item J: Absolutely no spitting or nose picking!

Item K: No mention, at any time, of her monthly female situation.

Item L: Pets

After she was discovered with a baby pig in her bedroom, followed by the barn cat and three dogs, she was prohibited from having pets in the house. The pig, loyal and in love, waited on the front steps for Teresita to come out every morning. Tomás started out by kicking at the little beast, but ended up feeling fond of him. He often took bits of his breakfast out to him. It was Tomás who named the pig General Urrea.

Item M: The People

Although Tomás recognized her deep connection to the workers and the vaqueros, she was urged to refrain from hanging out in the bunkhouse or in El Potrero, the workers' village. It was unseemly for the daughter of the patrón to be seen in these huts. This was an order she ignored.

Secretly, it pleased him.

Item N: Romance

Absolutely not!

Item O: Servants

No matter how much he cursed at her, Tomás could not break Teresita of the habit of making her own meals and even, shocking as it was to everyone, serving the maids and cooks. She even washed the dishes.

Item P: Herbs

She was allowed her collecting of noxious weeds as long as she hung them to dry in her own room and not in the kitchen.

Item Q: Church

"Mass?" Tomás cried. "Goddamn it!"

He arranged for one of Gastélum's troublesome circuit-riding priests to deliver Mass in his barn every Sunday. Teresita ordered him to attend, but Tomás spent every Sunday morning out with the bees. She wasn't going to make him kneel in a barn! Not to a celibate freak!

Still, he did concede to the occasional Bible reading to be added to their postsupper literary sessions. Aguirre came in quite handy on his visits, since he seemed to know the infernal volume the way he knew his engineering texts, and he and Teresita could spend boring hours debating Elijah and Elisha and any number of other Hebrew pendejos while Tomás guzzled brandy and thought about Gabriela.

Item R: Huila

If Huila ever came back from tending to Loreto, Teresita would be given exclusive access to her — and whatever Huila had on her agenda for the day would supersede any chores or plans Tomás had concocted.

Item S: Marriage

Someday. Not anytime soon. And Tomás would handle the arrangements. Including the identity of the groom.

"Have I no say?" Teresita demanded.

"Certainly," he said: "you may say 'I do' at the wedding."

Item T: Cahita

Tomás requested that Teresita speak Spanish at all times.
　　She could not comply.

Item U: Liquor

She could drink if she wanted to, as long as she was with her father.
　　She did not want to.

Item V: The Library

She petitioned for the right to read whatever Tomás had in his library. Una infamia! It was unheard of! He was appalled to learn that it was Aguirre himself, that snake, who had started teaching her to read and write. It took only three days of her angry silence to force him to acquiesce to her demands. The first book she read was Bernal Díaz del Castillo's chronicle of the Spanish conquest. She did not care for Tomás's beloved Jules Verne. Even in translation, it seemed boring and boyish to her. They began to order books by post. Juana Austen. Las Hermanas Brontë.

Item W: School

The only schools were in Alamos or Tucson. She did not want to go to school. He did not want her to go. Tomás and Aguirre created a course of study for her that she added to her field studies and dream work. Sometimes, while she was asleep, she read books in distant libraries. In dreams, French or German was easy to read.

Item X: About the Dream Time

Tomás preferred not to hear about any of her more peculiar enthusiasms or astral adventures.

Item Y: Friends

Teresita was allowed all the friends she wanted, as long as they were (1) female and (2) of her new social class.

Girls from El Potrero were not invited into the main house. But girls from the local haciendas and villages were. An Indian princess from some imagined Sioux or Cheyenne tribe would have been welcomed with ceremonial bowing and scraping, but an Indian girl from El Potrero would not be let in the door. Josefina Félix, her first friend, was a regular visitor. She slept in Teresita's bed with her three nights a week.

Tomás almost fell off his chair when Teresita returned from one of her horse rides with Gabriela Cantúa.

"Can she sleep over, Father?" Teresita asked.

"My God," he replied.

"How are your bees?" Gabriela asked.

Item Z: Loreto

Teresita was asked to remain cordial and respectful at all times, and this was no problem since she, like all the People, dearly loved Loreto and thought of her as a Great Mother along the lines of the Virgin of Guadalupe.

Thirty-one

TERESITA SLEPT IN HER HUGE BED between Josefina and Gabriela.

At nineteen, Gabriela was older than the other girls.

Josefina was a plump and giggly sixteen-year-old with dark skin and a small mole beside her nose. Teresita, fifteen now, was a year older than her mother had been when she'd been born.

"I am in love with your father," Gabriela confessed.

"Me too!" blurted Josefina.

"You and everybody else," said Teresita as they burrowed in the covers and whispered. "And Fina — you're in love with all vaqueros."

"Oh yes!" Josefina agreed.

"No, Teresa," Gabriela insisted. "I mean I *love* him."

"Yes. I know."

"Love him, as in love him?" said La Fina. "Or love him, as in have his babies LOVE him?"

"Babies!"

"Ay Dios!"

"Ay!" cried Teresita.

Laughter.

"What will I do?"

"Marry him!" La Fina said.

"He is married, tonta!"

"Oh. I forgot."

Teresita sighed, looked at Josefina, and made a face.

"Gaby will be my mother," she said.

The three girls burst out laughing.

Teresita turned to Gaby and put out her hand.

"Hello, Mother, how do you do?"

"Hello, Daughter! Clean your room!"

They laughed louder.

Beneath them, Tomás banged on the ceiling of the library to get them to quiet down. He would have to add a non-negotiable bedtime to Teresita's curriculum.

They put their hands over their mouths and gasped as they tried to silence their hilarity. They heard his voice coming up the stairs:

"Do I have to come up there?"

"Oh please do," crooned Gaby. "Papasito!"

This made them scream into their fists, and they heard a defeated Tomás slam his door in anger.

After a while, they grew still and all lay on their backs, feeling the house tick into silence. Moonlight washed over them, turning the covers silver in the darkness. A western breeze furled the curtains. Teresita had set some herbs on fire in a small pot to keep mosquitoes out of the room. They watched the small red flickers of the fire make patterns on the walls. Her dried herbs hung in aromatic bunches from the heavy square beams above them.

These were the best nights she would ever have, lying beside her two friends, blind still to what was coming.

"Take us on a trip," Josefina said.

"Do you want to?"

"Yes."

Gaby nodded her head.

"Yes," she said. "Take us."

"Are you sure?"

"Oh yes."

She had discovered a new talent in bed with these girls. It had come to her as a realization a few months before. She simply knew one night that she could capture their dreams and direct them. She could not explain how it happened, or why. But if she concentrated, she could take the girls on journeys as if they were flying in the wind.

"Where should we go?" she asked.

Josefina shuddered in expectation.

"I don't know!" she said.

"We went to the ocean last time," Gaby reminded her. "We saw ships all covered in lights."

"Oh yes!" sighed Josefina. "The people were dancing!"

"I have only seen the ocean on our travels at night," Teresita confessed.

"Me too," said Josefina. "Y tú, Gaby?"

"I have seen the sea," Gabriela said. "We go often to Guaymas. It was as it was in the dream. You can smell the salt in the air. The breeze never stops."

"We were really there," Teresita told them. "It was more than a dream."

"I believe you," said Josefina.

"Maybe," said Gabriela.

"I have never seen a city," Teresita said.

"Me neither," said Gaby.

"I have been to a city!" La Fina said.

"What city have you been to?" demanded Gaby.

"Alamos!"

Gaby laughed.

"Ay, cómo eres tonta, Fina! Alamos is not a city. Es un pueblo, but it is not a city! Cities are great things! Paris is a city!"

La Josefina sighed: Paris!

"New York, or Mexico City!"

Teresita smiled.

"Cities," she said, "are like a hundred towns all put together."

"One thousand towns!" Gaby whispered. "A city is like the ship we saw — all lights and avenues as far as you can see!"

"How do you know?" asked Fina.

"I just know."

"Hundreds of lights," murmured Teresita, as she closed her eyes.

She reached out to them under the covers. They put their hands in hers. La Fina wrapped her legs around Teresita's leg. She liked the contact, but she was also afraid to fly. No number of assurances from Teresita made her trust that she wasn't going to fall.

The three held hands.

Teresita said, "Feet — go to sleep. Go on, you've had a hard day. Now sleep."

She worked her way up their bodies, and they grew drowsy as she talked.

Slowly, her soft mattress felt as if it were surging, billowing beneath them. And they grew lighter. First, it strained against their backs. But soon, the sheet lifted from the bed as if it were being shaken out in the morning, and they rode the billows.

"We are rising, rising, can you feel it? We are light now as cottonwood fluff. Feel it. The earth falls away. We have been prisoners of the ground, and now it releases its grip on us. Yes. Yes. The air moves us freely. We are like water. The air is like water. We are water. We are clouds. We are air."

And then they were above the billows. They were in midair, held up by its freshness, its love. The air loved them — they could feel it.

"Is it angels?" Josefina whispered.

"Shhh," said Teresita.

The air moved through their hair like water. They were moving.

"Keep your eyes closed," she whispered. "Just a little longer. Don't look."

Sounds expanded all around them, and beneath them. The closeness of the room suddenly felt as if it were falling open into winds and echoes and river water shushing somewhere below. Dog voices were tiny as crickets.

"South," she said.

They felt themselves drift south, as if carried by a fresh spring in a grove of trees.

"Now look."

They opened their eyes.

❀

The library was rich with shades of red, gold, brown, flickering in the glow of oil lamps.

"I am in love," Tomás told Huila.

"Tell me something new," she said.

She took one of his cigars from its humidor and lit it without asking. He was beyond complaining about Huila's actions.

"No, I am serious."

"You were serious about the tortilla girl and the milk-maid before her."

"That, that was not love."

"Yes, I know," Huila said.

"What do I do now?"

"Be a man."

"Eh?"

"Be a man. If you love her, stand up for her. Face her father and face your wife. Stop whining like a pinche little girl and stand up like a man. If you want to claim the girl, claim the girl. Then learn to be a better man than you were before."

He nodded.

"Because, frankly," Huila continued, "you are a total failure as a man in my opinion."

She left the room.

He sat. The girls were quiet upstairs. The woman he wanted was lying in bed with his bastard daughter.

Tomás sighed and closed his eyes. If there was a God, he might just be going to Hell.

When their eyes opened, they were looking up into the giant tide of stars. Gaby turned her head and saw the edge of a small cloud as it drifted past her. The girls somersaulted slowly in the air until they were facing the earth.

The Sierra rose and fell in soft blue undulations of stone. Snow on its ridges burned pale violet in the moonlight.

"Look."

A scatter of silver coins to the west was the Pacific Ocean.

Clouds swallowed them. They passed through misty cold towers and burst back into clear air. Their eyelids glowed with moonlight.

They drifted south, south, so high they could see villages pass beneath them like small stains of light on the ground, as if a cup full of candle glow had spilled on a ruffled tablecloth. A wedge of migrating birds passed far from them, tiny as butterflies, gray against the deeper darkness of Mexico. Into more clouds and then, as the cloud banks parted, they saw a vastness of glitter. Dizzying expanses of light. A thousand, ten thousand small lights in lines and avenues stretching to the black mountains.

"Streets," Teresita said.

Yes, streets. They saw now the carriages clopping down

the boulevards. Buildings, houses, dark parks. Boats in canals.

Music rose from a far plaza. Cooking smoke. Song lifted to their ears. Voices. Trumpets. They fell to earth ensnared in the scents of the city: perfume, cigars, charcoal, steam, garbage, water, horses, carne asada.

Their feet touched wet cobbles.

"Mexico City," Teresita said.

My Friend, Cantúa . . .

No, that wouldn't do.

Cantúa, You Bastard!

No! No! Perhaps a letter to Aguirre! But not to Cantúa! He dipped his pen again and bent to the task.

My Esteemed and Gracious Friend, Honorable Señor Cantúa,

I sit here in my library, haunted and worried by the inexplicable directions in which life and the human heart often travel. Believe me when I tell you I never meant any disrespect to you or to your lovely daughter when I began to visit you with regularity. I did, I confess, have my eye on the girl. Forgive me! You would be a saint to forgive me! But my dear maestro, master of the green chile burrito and the carne adobada tacos! You, sir, are the father of an angel! And I, your humble servant, have fallen under her spell.

Oh, virginal untainted maidenhood! I will defend it

to my dying breath! I urge you to understand that I am a father, too!! I will never touch a strand of her hair, before God and the Virgin I vow it!!!!

Oh, how my head throbs and my heart grieves me. If it were only not so, but it is so. I love her, Sir. I love Gabriela! I do.

Forgive me this indiscretion.

But you are not only a father, Sir, you are a man!

May we meet at the soonest possible moment to settle this matter?

I will, of course, defer to your judgment, recognizing that you are her father. But of course! I, too, am a father! Do not forget! Blessed duty bestowed upon us by The Almighty!

Certainly, if we can make some familial arrangement between the Cantúas and the Urreas, the hacienda will be at your disposal, and all its riches will also be yours.

I await your speedy response with my breath held and my knees bent: one hand on my heart, and the other raised to God Himself in supplication!

> *Very Sincerely and Faithfully Yours,*
> *I Remain, Awaiting Your Kind Understanding*
> *And Merciful Judgment,*
> *Your Future Son,*
>
> *Don Tomás Urrea,*
> *La Hacienda de Cabora, Sonora*

He'd have Segundo deliver it in the morning.

❋

The girls gawked at trolley cars. They walked through the shadows of the great cathedral on the main square. Late in the night, they sat on a bank in Xochimilco and soaked their feet in the ancient waterways of the Aztecs.

Twenty years later, though neither Gabriela Cantúa nor Josefina Félix had ever been to Mexico City, they'd have no trouble pointing out their various wanderings on a map.

Thirty-two

SEÑOR CANTÚA WAS, like many restaurateurs, a philosopher. He was well aware of the fact that one could not stand in the way of destiny. Who knew the secrets of the heart, or the secrets of history, or the secrets of God's will? The truth was that Cantúa was tired of the Alamos road, tired of the stinking wanderers and the dreaded Rurales who ate his goat-meat tacos. He was tired of worrying about Gabriela. He had several other children back home, near the coast, and a wife he never saw because that seaside city was safer than these terrible haunted places where he had sought his fortune. And now Tomás Urrea was offering a kind of liberation. Gabriela was, after all, nearly an old maid!

Certainly, Cantúa figured, Señor Urrea would offer a fair bride price. Enough, perhaps, to open the restaurant in Guaymas that he really wanted to run. Open windows letting in a fresh sea breeze. Tuna, shrimp, oysters, and beer.

One daughter happy on a hacienda — a Cantúa running a hacienda! And five or six children and a wife, happy on the beach. Everybody rich!

Who was he to stand in the way of miracles when they came unbidden out of the sky?

He took up a pencil and sharpened it with a steak knife.

My Dear and Esteemed, Many Times Blessed by Our Merciful Lord, Noble and Courageous Leader and Shining Example to Our People, Don Tomás,

You at once honor and alarm me with your heartfelt testament of love.

We must meet like real men and discuss the fate of my daughter, Gabriela. No riches can ever equal her value to me! No price could ever meet her true worth!

However, we could speak of arrangements that, although never even reaching one small percentage of her eternal grace and Godly golden value, would have to be generous. Of course you agree! Anything less than a small fortune would be an insult to my Dear Angel! I only think of her suffering mother and her own peace of mind. Knowing of your kindness toward myself and my beloved bride and my dear, dear children, how can Gabriela feel anything less than truly loved? Loved and valued! By you, my dear Don Tomás! Gracias a Dios y Viva México!

Your humble servant and
Fellow Father,
Señor Cantúa (of the restaurant)
(Father of Gabriela)

P.S. One look in her luminescent eyes, my friend, and you will swoon as if you had tasted the ambrosial liquors of Heaven. You will forsake all other loves for my Gaby, Don Tomás. Of this I can assure you.

When Tomás finished reading this letter, he called Huila in and read it to her.

"What is he doing," Huila asked, "selling a horse?"

As a token of his respect, Tomás sent Segundo and the Parangarícutirimícuaro beekeeper in a wagon with a fresh side of beef, a barrel of soap, a crate of candles, tequila in clay jugs, and a bag of gold coins to cover any expenses Cantúa might meet in the celebratory weeks to follow.

"Ah cabrón!" Cantúa laughed, clapping his hands. "Ah cabrón!"

Gaby mounted the wagon to Cabora, never thinking she would stay. But one night with Teresita led to a second night, then a third, then Tomás offered her her own bedroom. And suddenly, there she was.

After a week, it seemed to Tomás as if Gabriela had always been there. They finally, secretly, made love. It seemed that her smell had always been on his fingers, her tart berry smell, and her long hairs had always been on his pillowcase, and her flavor on his lips.

They all knew something had to happen, but they didn't know what it would be. No one knew the hour, or the nature, of Loreto's wrath, though they all suspected that, sooner or later, she would explode. They had all felt it building over the months since her catastrophic raid on the ranch, and now, with this final outrage, Tomás had lit a fatal fuse.

Huila was first to see the buggy coming down the road.

The servants, not wanting to observe this development, rushed into the house. Aguirre was gone again, on some journey into the north, or he would have affixed his spectacles to his nose and studied the scene. Dogs slunk under the benches in the courtyard, though she was still a mile away.

They watched the black carriage come across the plain. It was speeding like a mad crow, coming at them in a wedge of dust. All of them knew, without knowing, that Loreto was holding the reins. Her rage flew high above the carriage like a great wind.

Tomás, with his arm around Gabriela's shoulders, stood before the great house and stared. Segundo moseyed away, back to the rendering plant. He preferred the stench of melting cattle to the wrath of Loreto. And Huila, older now than she had ever dreamed, leaning on a cane that would in a year become a crutch, sat in the shade of the plum tree on a yellow bench festooned with blue hummingbirds — a gift from Señor Cantúa.

"Ay, ay, ay," she mourned, digging in the dirt between flagstones with her cane. Though she couldn't keep a grin from her face, she lamented. "Mira qué cosas."

She shook her head.

She had always, of course, assumed that men were idiots. Tomás was chief among the pendejos. Their foolishness had amused her since the beginning of time. But suddenly she understood that women were idiots, too. That all people under the sun were fools. Wasting lives. Sniffing up each other's legs like dogs, scurrying around in circles while their days bled away. All life, she had been taught, was a dream — the flesh is the sleep of the soul. She liked Tomás, and she liked Loreto, and the new one, Gabriela, was sweet as honey on the tongue. But, if this was the dream, she couldn't wait to awaken.

Teresita, a little afraid of Loreto's coming, hung back, away from them all, and watched the small black vehicle bounce and shimmy as it came forward. She saw the dark rainbows in the air above it. She thought she caught Huila's eye from a distance. It looked as if Huila was laughing. It was a new laugh, bitter as burned coffee.

Gabriela was ashamed, but strong. She loved Tomás, and he loved her, and there was nothing one could do when love came. It was fast, and it was strong, and if it were not good, then surely God would not have allowed it such power. The power of her love made her giddy — Tomás spoke things to her that would make any woman swoon. "You talk so pretty," she had gasped one night, and for some reason, this had delighted him. He suckled at her like an infant, crooning poems, songs, speeches to her. Anything, anything, she would hear anything from his lips. Book chapters or newspaper reports, Bible passages — it was all music to her. His refined accent, his big words, words she did not even know. His awe when she dropped her dress — the way he studied her belly, the down near her navel, and the way he held her breasts to his lips, and the way he traced her spine, sighing as he did it, as if he had never been in the presence of something so holy. It made her laugh, and it made her weep. And the burning sensations he brought to her body, the clenching in her stomach and the explosion of lightning in her flesh, as if the darkness within her were laughing and screaming, her skin and organs yelling, this too made her weep. "Oh my love, my love," she cried into his shoulder, as if she could not contain a sorrow so deep it was joy instead, "I never thought I would feel these things. Es un milagro! Es tremendo este amor!"

And after loving, they slept entwined. He wrapped his long arms and legs around her, his fist clenched in her wild hair, his face buried there and smelling her as he dreamed. Before dawn, they awoke making love. He was already inside her, moving slowly, and neither of them even awake. And when he awoke, he too wept.

She had only been living at the ranch for a few weeks, but it was already hers. She had won it. She saw it in his face. In his smile. In his laughter. In the grimace of delight when he was atop her. Their love was destiny. She stood tall. She was ready to face whatever horror came. For her home. For her man.

Rattling, wheels spitting wedges of rock, the black carriage skidded sideways and rocked. The two horses foamed at the mouth, their lashed sides gleaming with sweat.

"Bastard!" Loreto cried, her voice echoing all across the startled landscape, cowboys and cows, mockingbirds and horses, children and dogs astounded by this outburst. Her hair was a tangle, an explosion around her head. Her skirts were hiked up, revealing her white legs.

Huila hit the ground three times with her cane, as if applauding.

Loreto's arm rose. The whip snapped.

"What have you done to me," she demanded.

Tomás held his hands out before him.

"What have you done to me!"

Her finger uncurled and pointed at Gabriela.

"Is this the one?" she said.

Tomás stood tall again and said, "Mi amor —"

"Don't you talk to me like that!" Loreto shouted. "Not in front of her!"

The cowboys were starting to laugh behind their hands. To the men, this was more amusing than shooting coyotes, or seeing a bareback rider bucked off. Millán, the former miner from Rosario, grabbed his crotch and squeezed it. "Bitch," he said to his companions. They moved away from him. Millán made them nervous.

Tomás knew he needed to take command of the scene, or he would be no man in the eyes of his cowboys.

"I am the patrón!" he bellowed. "I do what I please!"

He gestured wildly as he declaimed. "Yo soy el que manda aquí!"

"You give commands, do you?" she answered. "Did you order this tramp into your bed?"

He yelled. And she yelled back at him, and he yelled back at her: accusations and recriminations fouled the air. He was no man; she was less than a woman. And she was no wife; he was never a true husband. If she had been a wife — then there would have been no need for Gabriela. If he had been a husband, a man of any kind whatsoever, she wouldn't have turned away from him. They danced like this with everyone watching until the whip flew again and he caught it, wrenched it from her hands, and threw it to the ground.

The watchers were astonished.

"You," he said. "Get off my land."

"Tomás . . ."

"Get off my land now. Go away. Don't ever come back."

The People were aghast. They would tell this over and over, at supper, over their morning coffee, in the fields, in bed: the patrón ran Doña Loreto off the ranch. He banished her from Cabora. He didn't care what the Church said. If he saw her at Cabora ever again, he would divorce her. He was macho, after all. He was todo un hombre, they said, with a certain respect he had not earned before. It would have been better, the men said, if he had struck her. The women said nothing.

His face was a shade of red they had never seen.

Gabriela herself, humiliated and afraid, faded back into the house and hid in her room. Huila stood and muttered, "Tomás," but he could hear nothing. He dragged the horses back and forth by their mouthpieces, seeming to want to wrestle them to the ground, bite their throats as if he were a wolf. And he raised the whip to threaten Loreto, almost struck her with it, and ordered her to be gone, gone now, and never return.

He threw the whip into the carriage and slapped the horses and watched as she sped away.

No one went near him.

As the crowd drifted off, Millán said to Buenaventura: "I thought he had no balls until today."

Buenaventura walked away from him and headed for the rendering plant.

Millán turned around and walked backward and watched Teresita go into the house.

Thirty-three

WHERE THE OLD DESERT RIVERS struggled through the arid land, where the Gila steamed to nothing, where the Yaqui and the Mayo cut relentlessly toward Guaymas and the sea, and the old father Colorado surged toward its delta at the head of the Sea of Cortés, the desert turned green. For three years, crops wilted or sprang up, unfurled leaves or burned black and collapsed. The Yaqui lands, forever fertile and alive, swarmed with crows; ibis followed cows between the rows of green, spearing insects disturbed by the cattle's incessant grazing. And where a Yaqui plow sliced the earth, the white birds followed the farmer and plucked mole crickets, worms, beetles from the curling dark wave of the soil.

Some of the villages did as they had always done — communal fields of corn, beans, tomatoes or chiles, melons, squash, grew near the water. These milpas fluttered deep green in the dawn light, the land beneath them aware of its duty.

The army collected Yaquis from unprotected villages and herded them toward the sea. No one knew where they went — whole families vanished overnight. The devil, children said, was a gringo.

Tomás knew the stories were true. He had ridden out, deep into the north, deep into Indian territory, past Aquihuiquichi. There, he saw a patrol of soldiers leading a walking line of Yaquis into the desert. He spied Captain

Enríquez among the cavalry, and he spurred his horse toward his old friend.

"Oye!" Tomás called.

Enríquez turned in his saddle and smiled.

"Don Tomás!" he said.

The old friends shook hands.

"What is this?" Tomás asked.

"Bad business," Enríquez said. "Bad business."

"Where are you taking them?"

"It is better not to ask."

Tomás watched the tired Yaquis shuffle away.

"And their land?" he asked.

Enríquez repeated: "Bad business, my friend."

He didn't want to talk.

Then came a man atop a mottled horse. His buckskins were dark with filth and grease and blood and sweat. He rode near them, and Tomás smelled him. His long rifle rose high before him like a lance. His hat was tattered and drooping. The filthy rider wore a necklace of finger bones. Tufts of hair bobbed in the wind all over his saddle. He nodded once at Tomás.

"Enríquez," Tomás said. "Are those . . ."

"Scalps," Enríquez said.

"Por Dios!"

Enríquez squeezed his friend's arm.

"Go home," he said. "Go home, Tomás. This is a bad business, and you don't belong here."

Tomás gazed into his friend's eyes, and there he saw a parched dead landscape.

"Go home. Lock your gates."

Enríquez turned his horse away from Tomás and fell in behind the scalp hunter.

Tomás watched them until they were melted into the land and were no more.

❊

Huila had found another grove of cottonwoods, down the bluff and across the arroyo from the great house. Aguirre's men had planned to dam this portion of the arroyo, but Huila had pulled up his stakes and broken his strings, and when he'd come to complain, she had awaited him with her shotgun and her tobacco pouch, and she had called him a Yoribichi and a son of a bitch. Not being a fool, Aguirre had bowed to her and moved his staking project downstream, where the water would not drown Huila's trees.

When Teresita had first visited this place, Huila had pointed to the trumpet vines snaking up the bushes and tree trunks. "Hummingbirds love these," she'd said. "I see them every morning. God can reach me here."

The second time there, Teresita pulled her skirts aside and stared at her feet. All this time wearing socks and shoes had turned her feet white. They looked soft and somehow uncooked.

"Our power comes from the earth," Huila said. "Itom Achai sends us life through the ground. Look at the plants! Why do they have roots? Do they have roots in the air?"

Teresita smiled and shook her head. She could recite Huila-speak in her sleep.

"Look at the Yoris." Huila spit. "Shoes, boots, wagons, floors. They don't remember the earth."

She planted her feet wide, sagged on her knees a little.

"Stand inside the earth. Feel yourself standing inside it. Once you connect with the earth, nothing can move you. Not a hurricane, not a thousand cowboys."

She bobbed.

Teresita thought Huila looked as if she needed to go to the bathroom.

"Go on," said Huila.

Teresita clutched the ground with her toes, set her heels deep in the sand, then the balls of her feet, then the outside edges.

Huila had tried to teach her this most basic lesson of power before. Teresita had seen it work — Huila sometimes planted herself and dared the vaqueros to push her off her feet. Two, three at a time, laid their shoulders to her and shoved, but she could not be budged. This caused great hilarity among the children and the old people, watching the little dried-up woman withstand the assaults of strapping gunmen and wranglers.

"In the earth," Huila said. "Say it. I am in the earth."

"I am in the earth."

"And the earth is in me."

"And the earth is in me."

They breathed. They felt their lungs fill with sky, and they let the dark clouds inside them flow out. Then they connected to the earth.

"Lift the toes, and press with the balls of your feet."

"I feel silly."

"Part of being a medicine woman is feeling silly."

Teresita stood before her, digging into the ground with her feet.

"Now, push into the ground with the inside of your foot, all the way to the heel. You've got prongs in your heels, like a pitchfork. Two on the inside, two on the outside. Plug in the two on the inside of your heel. Push into the earth. Then you have roots, child. Do you see that?"

"Roots. In my heels."

"Yes. Plant them. Deep in the soil. Your roots."

Huila breathed out in a long swirl of nose whistling.

"Feel the earth, keep the integrity of the heart. Keep the spine in line. Let your heart shine. Relax, don't strain. The white man always has to strain. Has to flex his muscles. Be soft. Be like water. Water is soft, and it is the most powerful force on earth."

The Sonoran sun came through the tree branches and burned into Teresita's head. Crows laughed at them in the distance. A snowy egret cut across the sky, looking for some cattle to visit.

"Let your knees bob a little. There, connect. The earth's strength will spiral up your legs, to the inside. You'll feel it bring your knees together. Feel it? Now, feel those outer roots on your feet. Push your heels all the way in. Now the rest of your foot. You're standing in the earth now. Another flow of power is going up the outside of your legs. Feel it spiral. Soon, nothing will be able to overpower you."

"I can't be hurt?" Teresita said.

"I never said that. We'll all be hurt, child. We will all be hurt. What I said was: they shall not overpower you."

"I think I understand."

"I doubt it."

Crazy old woman.

Teresita shook her head.

"All right, I don't understand."

"People always want to *understand* everything," Huila sniffed. "Do you understand how the sun works? Yet it rises every day, whether you understand it or not. Do we understand how the vine makes a grape, and the grape makes wine? No. You don't need to *understand* any of it. What I want you to do is to remember it and believe it."

"I will remember."

"Do you believe?"

"I don't know."

"That is Faith," Huila said. "Faith, like Grace, is a gift, you see. It's one of those riddles nobody can *understand*. Niña — God gives you the gift of believing in God. If you cannot believe in God, then how can God punish you for your lack of Faith?"

"I don't know."

"Damned right, you don't know. It's a mystery."

Teresita thought for a moment.

"Faith," she finally said.

"Correct." The old one nodded. "Believe. You might never get explanations."

"And if I cannot believe, what then?"

"Then," said Huila, "God sends foolish old women like me to try to help you."

They held hands as they walked back toward the rancho.

Huila had once shown her the way the male's bone penetrated the female's cave. "Ugly old thing," she'd said. "Looks like a boiled turkey neck. But it feels good inside the fold." And now Huila knew Teresita was ready to work the births.

Huila and Manuelito had shown her all the herbs already — she knew the most basic of the plants. But Teresita knew the work was deeper, greater than brewing teas, binding with roots. Huila had insisted that she was too young for the work — until now.

Teresita knew why. Huila was tired. She needed help for the first time in her life. As Gabriela had mysteriously replaced Loreto in the main house, so did Teresita see that she herself was mysteriously taking over for Huila.

They trotted to a small cabin on the outskirts of El Potrero. The girl within screamed as if being flayed, and Teresita's hairs rose on the back of her neck. The girl lay, with her legs up and wide, and her belly heaving and quivering. Huila rubbed her between her legs with an ointment that turned her vagina yellow. The mattress beneath her was wet and stained, and heat rose from the liquid as if they had just brewed tea between the girl's legs. There was little hair until the baby's head parted her and its own black pelt filled the gap. Blood.

Teresita swallowed.

"Ay Dios!" the girl cried. "It hurts! It hurts!"

She reached down and clutched the dirt with both hands.

Huila said, "You see? We always reach for our mother."

She chanted, whispered, called the child forth. When the girl screamed, Huila slapped her hands together three times and rubbed her palms vigorously, heating her hands. She set her palms on the mother's belly and rubbed.

"Calm, calm, child," she cooed. "Feel my hands. Feel the warmth."

Huila gestured for her knife.

Teresita reached in Huila's mochila and pulled out a slender knife sharpened to a terrible cold gleam. Huila had her pull the girl's legs far apart and, with two flicks of her bony hands, sliced the birth passage open. Blood sprayed and the baby slid forth, facedown, in a spurting of awful fluids into the old one's hands. The baby swam, fell, climbed.

Teresita didn't know what it did — it simply was. There and writhing, red in the face, seemingly covered in wax, some pale salve from deep inside the mother's own wetness, its tiny fists already punching at the new world. The mother crying, Teresita crying, the baby crying, and Huila whispering, "Shhh. Shhh. Quiet now. Shhh."

Huila had Teresita press a poultice to the birth canal as she wiped the baby down.

"Look at the size of his balls!" said Huila.

She used her birth knife to slit the cord, and she tied off the end sticking out of the boy's belly and wrapped the remainder in a white cloth. The little one was on his mother's chest by the time the afterbirth oozed onto the ruined mattress.

The next day, they delivered twins.

Kneeling there behind Huila, Teresita learned all she needed to know of pain and wonder. Days and nights of shouting and terror, the dark awful joy when the skin ripped and the bowels released, and the meat stink of birthing came out of the girls. She pulled the pink-red envelopes out of the mothers, watched Huila slice apart the cords with her small knives, wrapped the cords into bundles and put them in small pouches for the mothers. She learned the truth about the Mystery. She learned that miracles are bloody and sometimes come with mud sticking to them. She learned that women were braver than men. Braver and stronger. She learned that she herself could one day stretch open as wide as a window, and it would not kill her.

At one point, after the cord had been tied with string and the slime wiped away with leaves and cloth, Huila nudged Teresita, and Teresita leaned forward and said her first birth prayer, whispering to the new one who still remembered the stars and the lights, "Your job is to survive."

Connected to the earth, she understood the words. They were terrible and true.

※

Huila had her own rituals, her own way of doing things. Strangely, she had become less and less interested in the workings of spirit, plants, medicine. Her body hurt, and her thoughts were quiet and melancholy. She grew less patient — she was capable of taking her cane and striking the maids when they behaved foolishly. She swung her cane at Tomás when he was rude to Gabriela. She knew that the deeper secrets were ready for Teresita, even if Teresita was not entirely ready for them. On some mornings, she was certain that the world was burning, until she had sipped her cup of coffee and eaten her bread and smelled her flowers. She dreamed her dead lover from those many years before. He came to her bearing six white flowers. The hummingbird hovered before her face, fanning her with its wings, and the smell the wings gave off was burning sage, the smoke of cedar. She watched her mother pass before her, walking on the far side of a river. Huila's time was coming. Her prayers changed in that season, and she asked to be forgiven her mistakes, to be made worthy of death.

"I never see Teresita anymore," Tomás complained.

He was most happy at breakfast. On certain days, he had an entire family gathered at the table. He sat at the head of the table, and Gaby sat on his right hand. At the far end, the engineer Aguirre often sat. Teresita and Huila sat on one side of the table, and Cantúa and Segundo sat on the other. Fina Félix was often in attendance, jammed into a corner and crinkling her nose at Teresita. Buenaventura was never invited.

Tomás was now, finally, the Great Hacendado — and he regaled his new family with boasts and tales, gesturing wildly with his coffee mugs and folded tortillas dripping beans and eggs. The ranch was a grand success, the mines were profitable. In spite of her rage and her disgrace, back in Alamos, Loreto was not ready to fully part from him. The good fathers had assured Loreto that the damnation was his, not hers. Gaby quietly plucked food off his plate and murmured "Ay Tomás" and "Ay mi amor" while making little faces, like Fina, at Teresita.

"We are busy," Huila said, soaking rolls in her coffee.

"Busy! Doing what!"

"Women things," Huila said.

The great house of the ranch reflected the good times — it was built and rebuilt in sections. The main room, Aguirre's first project after the Yaqui raid, was now a stone-walled fortress. Rising from the western corner was the new stone tower with Teresita's room high atop it and shooting slits in the shutters and battlements on the way up for sharpshooters to take aim. Aguirre had convinced him that a government attack could come at any time. Díaz had a long memory and a longer reach.

And now the second wing of the house was almost complete, and the third wing well begun.

Even in his joy, even while he smelled his beloved on his fingers and found himself delighted by his daughter's strange humors and graceful guitar strumming (they enjoyed duets on the veranda that set the cows lowing and the dogs howling), Tomás suffocated every day within its walls.

It was inconceivable to him that Teresita should go anywhere without him, much less out into the savage landscape around them to oversee anything as grotesque as childbirth. But the old one was tireless: she raged, cajoled, begged, suggested, demanded, explained until Tomás could no longer stand her voice. She refused any guards or riders — her only concession to safety was old Teófano.

"We rarely go off the ranch," she insisted. "And if we do, Teófano will guard us."

"If anything happens to her . . ."

"Nothing will happen to her."

Teresita stood beside her chair, looking at the floor. Segundo and Aguirre both thought: She certainly is getting attractive.

"And you?" Tomás said. "What do you wish?"

"I wish to go, Father," she replied.

"And you, mi amor?" he asked Gabriela. "What is your opinion?"

"Ay, Gordo," she said. She had taken to calling him Fat Boy, and he often called her Flaca — the skinny woman. "Let her go. It is her destiny."

"Destiny," he said.

He did not believe in such things as destiny. Superstition. Still, what had happened between Gabriela and him . . . it could be described as destiny. He rubbed his head. He sighed. He gestured for Teresita to step up to his chair. He kissed her on top of her head.

"Do your work."

"Bueno." Huila nodded. "It is done."

❋

They went, and as they worked, Huila taught Teresita all the secrets that could be taught. She taught of the blood and of the blood time, of the power of it, of the surge in strength that it brought. She taught her of the strangely twinned helplessness and immense powers of the gravid mother with life teeming in her belly. She taught Teresita secret words, and she taught her dangerous prayers. They knelt together in the gravel and prayed; they rose at dawn and prayed. Huila blessed her with smoke, anointed her with oils, bathed her naked in a desert pool green with algae and alive with tiny fish the color of coins. She fed Teresita secret foods, and she took her to speak to the rattlesnakes.

"You have power," Huila said.

Teresita, usually quiet about her secrets, confessed: "I make Fina and Gaby fly."

"Oh?"

"I take them to cities sometimes."

"Oh."

"At night."

"Be careful," Huila told her. "You are in danger, and those around you are in danger. You have chosen a way fraught with danger. Be careful."

Be careful of men, of dark spirits, of power, of love. Be careful of the plants, be careful with your own emotions, be careful with your pride. Devils, angels, lies, illusions, sex, God himself — be careful. Beware of your father. Beware of me. Beware of Gabriela, the People, Buenaventura, the buckaroos. Beware of yourself.

The first trembling came upon Teresita in those days.

It was a morning like any other morning. They had slept

late — Tomás made love so often with Gaby that on some nights they were devastated until ten or eleven in the morning. The hacienda ran itself — Segundo knew what to do, the workers knew what to do, Millán from Rosario knew what to do, even Buenaventura knew what to do. Some of the People were offended by Tomás's love, but most of them thought it was funny. The saying was: Love is the last thing to die. But the People changed it to: Love is the last thing to wake up in the morning.

Even Huila was asleep. She and Teresita had presided over a difficult birth that had lasted for three days. The mother was in such agony that nothing had helped. Herbs, teas, belly rubs, nothing. It was a terrible, long session with Huila and Teresita asleep on their feet. And a strange thing had occurred, so strange that it had Teresita awake early, even though Huila was still asleep. Awake in the courtyard, looking at the plum tree, and praying.

The night before, when she had thought surely that the mother would die on her back, if only from the pain, Teresita had felt the old nighttime glow in her hands. It was odd — she had not asked her hands to go to sleep. But they felt golden. Hot.

She suddenly sensed that she was intended to put her hands on the mother's belly.

She laid her palms on the mother, and the mother gasped. Teresita could feel the heat growing in her hands. The mother sighed.

"What are you doing?" Huila asked.

"Taking away her pain," said Teresita, but they did not seem to be her words — they seemed like words of another in her mouth.

The mother sighed again.

"Good," she said. "Yes, so good."

She moaned.

"Hot. Honey. It's hot honey pouring on me!"

And then the baby had come.

Now, Teresita wondered what had happened. She looked at her hands. They looked the same. They didn't feel strange, didn't tingle at all. She sniffed them, rubbed them slightly, flexed her fingers.

Then God spoke.

The Voice said:

"Do you believe in me?"

"I do!"

The Voice said:

"If you believe, stand."

She stood.

The Voice said:

"Walk around the house until I tell you to stop."

She went to the gate, turned east, and hurried around the house.

Huila came out an hour later. She scratched herself, looked for a ripe plum, then saw Teresita go by the gate. She was sweating, her hair pasted to her forehead.

A long moment later, she passed again.

"Child?" Huila called.

She went to the gate and yelled: "Child!"

Teresita vanished around the far corner. She was hurrying around the house. She must be cutting along the narrow lip of the arroyo in back. Huila stepped out into the road. It took several minutes, but Teresita appeared and came storming toward her.

"Child!" Huila shouted.

She grabbed Teresita. They struggled.

"Let me go!"

"What are you doing, child?"

"God told me to walk around the house!"

"What?"

"God told me to walk around the house. Now let me go."

"Are you insane?"

"Let me go!"

She tried to pull away from the old one, but Huila was too strong for her. She pulled Teresita in off the road and wrestled her to the bench in the courtyard.

"I must go, let me go!"

"Teresa! Stop!"

"God hasn't told me to stop yet!" Teresita shouted.

Then her eyelids fluttered closed and she became rigid. She leaned back against the wall and began to shiver, as if a cold wind had suddenly hit her.

"Tomás!" Huila shouted. "Please! Someone!"

Teresita trembled.

After ten days, Teresita reappeared in the big main doorway of Cabora's central house. She blinked in the light of the courtyard. She had been locked in her room, sleeping, and silent when awake. They thought she had gone mad, or fallen into some wicked witchery. Gabriela and Tomás ran to greet her, but it was as if she were blind and could not see them.

"God spoke to me," she said. "His voice is like the voice of a young man."

Huila kissed her cheek and sent her back inside.

Teresita climbed the steps to her room. Huila looked at Tomás and Gabriela and put her finger to her lips. They crept back inside, and they whispered to the maids and the cooks to stop working and leave. They silenced the great house, and when night fell, they crept to bed early and whispered to each other, careful to keep their laughter quiet.

When Teresita awoke, they fed her great plates of food. She drank milk and tamarind juice. She ate steak and fried cactus, beans and potatoes boiled in chicken broth. Tortillas and cheese and crisp lettuce with lemon juice. Then Huila joined her and they ate pudding and cake.

Tomás said, "So! What did God tell you?"

They stared at him until he looked away.

He didn't speak of her journey again.

Thirty-four

PERHAPS, DEEP IN HIS HEART, Tomás wanted no one to be wild if he himself could not run free. Even now, on many nights, he slept under the cottonwood, near a small fire, with his head on his saddle and nothing between his back and the hard Sonoran dirt but his thin blanket. When Gabriela called, of course, he was a fine gentleman, and he slept beside her in the soft ancient Urrea bed, smelling her delicate scents, her soapy hair. Listening to her soft little snores and sighs. He was particularly gentlemanly when he made his advances, which often began with a single flower plucked from Huila's vines outside their house. A small flower and a little grin, and she would say either "Ay, Tomás" or "Mi Chiquito"— my little one. She rightly suspected that "Gordo" was not a name for love play.

And when he went to Alamos, a place becoming delightful to him in spite of his conversion to more feral ways, he was finer still. He squired Loreto as if he were her loyal husband. He wore his dark suits and his golden vests, drooped watch chains across his flat belly, and waxed his mustaches until they swept out and up, bold and heavy as any bandido's. He traded his boots for gleaming flat shoes, which he always had polished on the corner near the church, and, on his sharpest days, he affected a cane with a silver nugget for a head.

There was no shortage of such ornaments, for Alamos was in the heart of silver country, and the Urrea mines were ripe with ore. Even after Tomás had sent Don Miguel his share of the profits, and after he had paid his miners, there were nuggets to spare. And gold. Santa María and Aquihuiquichi gave up crops of henequen and corn, and their cows formed considerable herds, which Segundo drove to Alamos and Guaymas and even to the American border, where Arizonans and Texans bid for them in Nogales and Tucson, even as far away as El Paso. Aguirre's projects employed workers from each of the arroyo's villages, and men from the Yaqui towns came to work. Logs were dragged from the hills; cut boards came from mills in Texas. Vast adobe works bristled near each of the small dams Aguirre designed.

Thus, in a few short years, Tomás had become powerful. Truly was he patrón, a man now, not a boy. He had his library. Thanks to Aguirre, he had water running in his white house. He had a fine life, and it would drone on exactly the way it was until he died. Little change. Few adventures. There would always be the dull excitements of a ranch, of course — storms and freezes, heat waves and droughts. Cattle would be rustled, coyotes would take baby goats. Men would be maimed and some would be killed, and difficult births would endanger fine mares, and the Indians in El Potrero would become restless or morose or demon haunted or ill. Loreto would have more babies. His Gaby, too, would have babies. Teresita, God forbid, would find a man and produce even more babies. But it would all seem, he already knew, as familiar as the face of his grandfather clock. Life would tick away, in circles, until he was kicked in the head by a mule, or lay back one last time in his feather bed, or was shot by a drunk vaquero in a dispute over his salary. It was all the same, always the same.

He often sighed, often sat and stared at the mysterious Sierra Madre to the east, wishing he could turn the whole operation back over to Aguirre. Wishing he could see the wild Tarahumara Indians, their fabled hundred-mile footraces — wishing for a bear, its raw pelt sour and stinking as it drooped over his pack mule — wishing for eagle feathers, lion attacks, a sighting of the red wolf, a gun battle. But Aguirre didn't understand these urges. He constantly called for political action, the "true adventure" of revolution. Tomás could not make Aguirre see the terrible truth: should a revolution begin in Mexico, the peasants would come for them first. Urrea's head and Aguirre's head would be mounted on spikes to turn black together in the sun. Their eyes would feed the first crows of the revolt.

In Alamos, there were sophisticates and even artists, but he had sworn to Loreto that he would not embarrass her in her newfound society. No freethinker debates. No drinking. No lovers. In Alamos, he played the swell, taking her arm and strolling the Spanish-looking streets. It was all he could do to keep himself from shooting out the street-lights. No one in Alamos, even his wife — especially his wife — understood him. Father Gastélum seemed to find his thoughts seditious, if not satanic.

At Cabora, Segundo had drifted into his own small world; Aguirre, ever more certain that Díaz was hunting him, spent more and more time hidden in Texas. And Gabriela did not want to listen to talk of wildness, or war, or wandering. Gabriela had come into a fine home and a true love — she would not hear any of this wild talk of his.

Teresita was his companion. Sometimes, he spent entire days talking to her about Díaz, or ranching, or horses, or history. He had been angered, at first, that Aguirre and she were teaching Gaby to read. He still didn't see what good it could do a female to enter the world in this fashion. Now, though, when he could argue with nobody about the latest poet or the latest newspaper scandal, he was growing more dependent on Teresita's responses. She spent hours working her way through his library, and late at night, when Huila had brought him his slippers, and he had sipped his brandy, he would light his oil lamp and offer her an opening gambit, as if it were a game of chess. (Chess! He would have to teach her chess, as well.) He might say, "Sor Juana Ines de la Cruz . . . unfair to men, don't you agree?" "Ay, Papá," she'd gasp, heaving a long and exasperated woman's sigh over the foolishness of her father. "How can you say that?" And they'd be off.

She scoffed at *Ivanhoe*. He turned to Marcus Aurelius and tried to best her when she championed the Psalms. Voltaire scandalized her, delighted him.

Now, if he could only get her to keep her Goddamned shoes on.

He hopped the rails of the corral, finding her in the stable, brushing her favorite roan stallion.

"Condenada!" he said.

For a man who did not believe in Hell, he condemned her to go there frequently.

Teresita giggled; she had realized by now that both Huila and Tomás showed affection for her by cussing.

"You stepped in horse shit," he said.

"It wipes off."

"Jesús," Tomás said. "What am I supposed to do with you?"

"Catch me if you can," she said, then grabbed the horse's mane and swung herself up. "Fat Boy!"

Her skirts were indecently flung up over her hips.

"No!" he shouted, though he was already smiling, for this was yet another battle between them.

Teresita still insisted on riding like a man, straddling the horse with her knees obscenely open and clutching the flanks of the horse as she galloped insanely across the llano. Teresita didn't even use a saddle, much less sit primly, sideways, with her knees held together.

Ladies didn't gallop.

Ladies didn't . . . *jump fences*, which is what she did every time she escaped him.

Leaning over the neck of the stallion, Teresita stormed through the madly wheeling horses in the corral. Her powerful mount exploded forward and she rode him into the air, seemingly ready to fly straight over the house like a hawk as they cleared the rails and sped away. Her petticoats were white in the sun.

Tomás ran out and stared down any of the cowboys who might be whistling their approval, or cheering her on.

"Imbeciles!" he snarled.

Then he snatched the reins of a horse away from the nearest vaquero and kicked open the gate and mounted the already trotting beast, one foot in the stirrup, one foot skipping, skipping, hopping in the dirt until he was aboard and racing after her, running so hard his hat left his head and circled in the wind before it fell in his wake.

The men watched and shook their heads, all of them in love with Teresita, and all of them knowing that no rider could catch her.

※

They blasted through the work crew in the arroyo. Aguirre fell on his rear in the dust, and a section of reed-and-stick frame fell over as the workers jumped out of the way of the raging horses.

"Cabrona!" Tomás bellowed at her. And on they charged, down the dry creek beds and up the arroyos, over small hills and into tattered and heat-wilted fruit trees. All around them, animals burst from the ground, fleeing from burrows or jumping for the brush or taking wing and exploding into the sun. Her skirt rose behind her like an indecent flag.

She slowed, then, until he caught up to her, but before he could admonish her, she surged ahead again, and he spurred his mount and tore down the serene valley beside her, their horses' great chests surging in rhythm, their horses' necks lying out straight before them, their mad eyes rolling white, and he began to laugh. Tomás laughed and laughed as they raced, Cabora now completely lost from sight, nothing before them but wild Sonora, and the bottomless sky above, father and daughter unleashed, growing smaller in the distance as their dust covered them, only the dirt smoke of their passing visible now, silent, vanishing, free upon the land.

Thirty-five

HER POWERS WERE GROWING NOW, like her body. No one knew where the strange things came from. Some said they sprang up in her after the desert sojourn with Huila. Some said they came from somewhere else, some deep inner landscape no one could touch. That they had been there all along.

Inside the shacks, Teresita and Huila always found the same scene: men outside, smoking and fretting, and women hunched inside, around the vivid centerpiece of the splayed mother, bulging huge and glistening in the firelight. Teresita prayed, she leaned forward and whispered. Teresita moved her hands in circles over the woman's belly, circling in toward each other, then out, away from each other, swirling as she whispered, swirling, as if stirring water, as if she had reached into a bath and were mixing hot water and cold, stirring, her fingers suddenly bending as if she were pointing into the womb as she whispered, around and around. "Yes," Teresita said. "Yes." And the mother gasped and drew a long breath. "Oh!" she said, and then she laid her hands on herself, on her straining stomach, on her ribs. "Oh." Teresita laid her hand over the mound of her belly and said, "The pain is gone?"

"Yes," the mother said.

The mothers loved her. She was the holy secret of the women, and many daughters were christened Teresa on the plain. Soon, Teresita was in greater demand than Huila, and the old one was astounded to find herself relegated to filling in for the child, attending to births that Teresita had no time for as her schedule grew busier.

One hundred children came through the honey in the womb.

Outside of the birthing rooms, too, the People saw that she had learned many of Huila's tricks. Teresita would stand still, connected to the earth, and she'd challenge the men to move her. "Come on, you weaklings!" she'd taunt them. The other girls of the ranch laughed and giggled around her, and the boys, getting big now and starting to want her, would sometimes join in the fray just so they could lay hands on her. Buenaventura would sneer at them all, scoff from a distance, unimpressed and angry that she got all the attention whenever she pleased.

"Move me if you can!" she challenged.

And Segundo would grab her around the waist and tug, and she wouldn't move. Little Antonio Cuarto, Segundo's nephew, grown up and stocky, but still shorter than she was, would join in and grab her around the hips, and together they'd shove and pull, but her feet would not even slide in the dirt. The watching children would laugh and clap and hoot and whistle until Segundo, red in the face, stepped away and offered his place to anyone who dared.

Millán pushed in and said, "I'll move you!"

"Big man," she taunted, laughing along with her girl-friends.

He moved close to her and put his hands on her breasts and shoved. She moved his hands away from her breasts. He put them on her ribs, then shoved again — she felt like a wooden beam. He bounced off her. Then he put his hands on her breasts again as he leaned in.

"Stop it," she said into his ear.

He laughed, stepped away, spit. And in turn, they laughed at him, the girls taunting, twisting their fingers at him like little knives, chanting "Lero-lero-le-ro!" He shrugged.

All the cowboys remembered these games and the tales of the women, so when mules kicked them, or they split their nails with hammers, or were shot or stabbed, they came to Teresita like little boys seeking their mothers. It was still Huila who set broken bones and packed bullet holes with herbs, but it was now Teresita who looked in their eyes and murmured to them, passed a hand over their foreheads or their hearts, and made them sleepy and calm.

"Poor boys." She'd smile. "They don't like pain."

"Boys!" Huila invariably spit. "What the devil do boys know of pain!"

The men clutched her hands and kissed them, so happy were they to be relieved of their aches. One day, she re-moved a terrible back pain from Señor Cantúa, and he went away happy, in a wagon, off to begin his shrimp stand beside the turquoise sea.

But there were people who were not amused. In confession, when Father Gastélum came and sat in the stables to greet them, some whispered of her heathen works, of her occult powers. One of her detractors was Buenaventura. Though no religious fanatic, he was appalled at her behavior. She romped with the Indian children, then sang filthy songs and common ballads to the slavering vaqueros. She rode her horses indecently, and she consorted with Gabriela, that intruder slut. If any woman should have lived in the main house of Cabora, it was his own mother. They should have sent for her, brought her from Ocoroni. Indeed, Teresita's specially built wing of the house should have been his. The library should have been his. The cook girls and the maids and the bed-maker girls and the wash girls should have been his.

The other was Tomás.

He had indulged her indigenous interests, and her explorations with Huila. He felt it was only fair to allow her an education in her Indian ways. It was a reasonable complement to her studies in the library. Aguirre had taught her well. She could discuss politics better than most men in the llano. Tomás was proud of her.

But this other business, this strange kind of reverence some of them were showing for her. This was simply not acceptable. Her spiritualist parlor games, her unseemly roughhousing with the men, these things alarmed him deeply. The damned natives were ready to charge off after messiahs and seers at the drop of a hat. The Indians in the United States were rising again, the Apache would not be tamed, and full-out war with the Yaquis here in Mexico was ticking ever closer. All he needed was for Gastélum or some other whore of President Díaz to send word that Teresita fancied herself some sort of female messiah. She refused to understand that spies watched them from all sides. And she failed to accept the burden of being an Urrea. Teresita was too special to be dirtying her hands with babies, with herbs and foolish spells. He had started to imagine the ranch run by a woman. He had begun to see Teresita in his mind as the great patrona. Teresa Urrea, riding her stallion among hundreds of peones, regal as a queen. The first woman to command the vast holdings of the family. He could *see* it.

It could be done, even if it seemed unspeakable.

Lately, Tomás no longer rode the herds or the fence lines, no longer wrangled wild horses or broke ponies. He didn't rule with a pistol or a whip or a stallion. Even Segundo had gone inside to work. No, Tomás ruled Cabora with a quill pen. He ran the herds and the cowboys and the grain harvest and the peones with ink — his pen, his ledger books, his abacus. Tomás tallied. And when numbers dictated a change in the work, he called in a hired hand and told him, and the needed change was accomplished. There were periods — days at a time — when Tomás did not feel the sun on his head. A woman, he thought, a woman could do this work. He smiled. A woman could probably do it better than he.

In his dreams, he could see himself set free. Riding home to his women from far journeys. Returning from a jaunt to San Francisco, in the company of Aguirre, perhaps even Segundo, and that gangly boy Buenaventura. His daughter the queen of Cabora awaiting him, his beloved little Gaby with an heir at her breast, and in the city, Loreto. He could smell it.

He did not believe the stories about Teresita, but he knew the People believed. She had somehow found a way to mesmerize them all. Now, if he could only turn her energies to ruling the ranch, instead of this Indian foolishness. He lay awake nights with the burden of his worry. He argued with Gabriela. He drank late into the night, staring into his glass.

Gabriela, as the new doña of the ranch, was not free to play with children or animals or young people. She was not free to ride wild with Teresita, or to swim in the stock ponds or the arroyo's dammed lagunas. She was compelled to behave like a mother, a fine creature of a more tender and valuable weave than the rest of them. Often, as on this day, she was left in the courtyard to fan herself and sew, while Huila snored and snuffled in the shade of the plum tree. She did not fear Huila the way the others did, but she knew Huila would never tell her any secrets. Huila would never even teach her how to make a simple healing tea. Gabriela wanted to learn something more than good manners, corsets, stockings, place settings. One of the girls came out of the house and asked, "Missus? Would you care for chicken and rice soup, or potato soup?"

She wanted to curse, the way Tomás cursed, but such things were not allowed.

"Chicken soup," she droned, "would be lovely."

Outside the garden walls, Teresita's voice rose — she was leading a group of children in some kind of chant.

Fina Félix and Teresita led a gang of kids in a race around the barn, then over one of the tumbledown fences. They jumped like horses, then galloped in circles. Buenaventura watched them, smirking. His back was to the barn wall, and his right knee was cocked, his boot heel jammed into a knothole behind him. He had learned to smoke. He hung a corn-shuck cigarette off his lip and blew smoke and said "Jesus Christ" to himself.

"Fucking savages," Buenaventura mumbled.

He was supposed to be working, but to hell with work. His *sister* never worked. All she did was run around like an idiot with the little Indios, then rub them on their heads and mutter mumbo jumbo in their ears. He shook his head.

Teresita was teaching them some sort of Yaqui bullshit. They chanted, and she led them.

"How cute," he said.

She glanced at him.

"Indians on the warpath."

She stopped singing with them.

"Hello, hermano," she said.

Teresita was stung by the change in him. He had grown distant, then angry, and she didn't know why. He frightened her sometimes.

He held two fingers up behind his head like feathers.

"Woo-woo!" he sang.

The children looked back and forth between them. Some of them laughed, but others looked down at the ground, unsure of what to do.

"Stop that," Teresita said, trying a small smile on him.

He hopped on one foot.

"Woo-woo-woo! Heya-heya!"

"Buenaventura . . ."

Fina Félix had stopped laughing. She stood up, brushed her skirt off. "You're just mean," she said. "Mean and stupid."

"And you're fat," he said.

"Stop it!" Teresita said.

He put his left hand over his head and made a fist with his right. He kicked up his feet as he mocked them, dancing in a circle, shouting, "I'm an Indian! I'm a Yaqui! Woo-woo! Woo-woo-woo!"

Teresita raised a hand toward him and shouted, "*Stop it!*"

And Buenaventura froze. His body locked in place. His left arm aimed at the sun, and the other clenched painfully before his heart, and his raised leg would not lower, and his other leg could not hold him. He fell over, caught in a horrible rictus, his face twisted in its hateful sneer. He squirmed on the ground, kicked, let out strangled cries. The children ran, shouting. Fina backed away from Teresita, her eyes wide and wild. Buenaventura, hard as a log, writhed on the ground in his seizure, spit foaming out of his open mouth. Teresita fell to her knees beside him.

"Oh my God!" she cried. "Oh my God! Buenaventura! What have I done?"

His eyes goggled at her, tears already falling from them as he tried to squirm away from her in terror. He rolled and kicked on the ground, his tongue lolling out. Grunting. Gargling.

"Get Huila!" Teresita screamed. "Get Huila now!"

Fina Félix ran to the house and stirred Huila from her sleep. Then she left the courtyard and kept running. She ran until she could slam shut the door of her own house and hide behind her bed.

※

They came running, Tomás first, with Gabriela close behind. Huila could not run now. She thumped after them as fast as she could, working her crutch in the uneven earth.

They came upon Teresita kneeling over Buenaventura, shouting, "I'm sorry! I'm sorry!"

He seemed to be dying of lockjaw, arching farther and farther back, forming a painful bow with his spine. His eyes, wild with terror, searched their faces, and his mouth had dirt in it, his tongue was muddy. Small sticks clung to his cheeks, his lips. Straw dangled in his hair. He moaned and whinnied.

Teresita looked up at them and said, "I can't fix him."

Tomás yelled, "What did you do? What did you do?"

"I don't know. I — nothing!"

Gabriela put her hand on her throat and backed away.

Huila pushed through them and dropped her crutch and groaned down to her knees. She shoved Teresita aside, saying, "Get out of my way."

Teresita scooted back, reached for Buenaventura's hand, but he jerked away from her, making piteous noises.

Huila turned to her with a scowl.

"I told you to be careful," she spit.

"What did I do?" Teresita begged her. "What did I do?"

Tomás grabbed the back of her dress, took a bunch of the collar in his fist, and ripped her up from the ground. Gabriela could hear the material tearing in his grip. He was talking through clenched teeth: *"What did you do to your brother?"* He raised a fist, as if to strike her, but Gabriela jumped on his arm and held his fist back.

"Gordo!" she shouted. "Gordo, no!"

Teresita closed her eyes to receive the blow, but wrestle as he might with Gaby, Tomás could not strike her. Instead, he flung her back to the ground.

"What is wrong with you?" he yelled.

She folded over, put her head against the ground, clutched the soil. Teresita knew how to grovel. She awaited the kicks with her eyes squeezed shut.

Huila snapped, "Get a plank. We have to get him inside."

Several ranch hands had wandered over to watch this scene, and Tomás pointed at them. Two of them trotted to the barn to find a plank that could hold the weight of Buenaventura's body.

They ran back carrying a six-foot length of wall board. They laid it in the dirt, and Huila and the men rolled Buenaventura's creaking stiff body onto it, tied him in place with a belt and Huila's apron. "Hurry," she said. "Run him to the house. The kitchen. Run — have the girls heat water. Go!" They lifted him and ran toward the house as he yipped and kicked one stiff leg. Huila struggled to her feet. Tomás gave her the crutch. She glared at Teresita for a moment, then hurried away.

Tomás pointed down at his daughter and said, "I've had enough of this! Do you hear me? Enough!"

She looked up at him, dirt on her face, her hair wild, and he was startled — she looked like an animal, just for an instant; she had a face like a coyote or a fox, her tears cutting strange colored lines through the dust on her cheeks.

"No more!" he said. "No more! No more tricks, no more magic, no more Indian garbage. Do you understand?"

She nodded, hid her face from his rage.

"I won't stand for it any longer! Are you out of your *mind*? Do you know what the government could do to us?

Do you know . . ." He turned away. "Pendeja!" he shouted at her, though he did not mean to be so harsh, did not mean to use such a crude term with her.

He pushed Gabriela aside and strode away, cursing, shaking his head.

Gaby stood staring at Teresita. She was afraid, suddenly. "Do you need help?" she asked.

Teresita shook her head.

She stood and dusted herself off. She wiped the tears and dirt from her face with her palms. Then she walked, silently, through the watchers and across the long yard, to the door of the house.

※

They worked on Buenaventura all night on the big table in the kitchen. He let out terrible cries as he spasmed and jerked. Huila poured cool water over him, tied his limbs down, forced herbs into his mouth. Tomás and Gaby worked beside her, stroking his brow, holding his legs. No one had ever seen such a thing, except for rabid dogs going mad down the arroyos before the vaqueros shot them.

Huila burned sage over him, rubbed oils on his head. She prayed the rosary and did a full limpia ceremony, driving ills from his gut. She undid his trousers and laid a stinking brown and yellow poultice between his legs. Gabriela covered her face.

Finally, as the sun was breaking out of the east, Buenaventura stilled. His clenched hand relaxed, and he sighed. The painful bow of his back straightened until he lay flat on the table. He started to snore.

"The boy will live," Huila said.

No one came for her all the next day. She did not eat break-fast or lunch or supper. She only drank water from her hand-washing pitcher, and she sweltered in the heat trapped behind her shutters.

It was an accident that she didn't even understand, and they all acted as if she'd planned it. She had been betrayed before, had been betrayed by her mother and by Tía and by her cousins. But this — to be betrayed by her brother, and by Huila, and by her father and Gaby. She felt her face — it was ugly. Ugly and lumpy. Her body was bony and pale and hideous. Her belly hung out, her ribs showed, and her bottom was wobbly and ugly as Huila's. They had all seen her for the freak she was. All along, they'd seen that she was a monster. The only one who had not seen it was she herself.

This was the day her worst fear was realized. No matter what she did, no matter who she helped or what pain she helped to ease, she would not be rewarded. No matter how much good she tried to do in the world, Teresita suddenly saw that she was always going to be alone.

She arose before dawn. She listened to everyone snoring, then walked down the hall. She was out on the plain before anyone awoke. She avoided Huila's sacred grove of cot-tonwoods, and found a small holy spot of her own. She prayed, though she was unworthy of God's ear. She waited until hummingbirds began their rounds, and she told them of her sorrows. They buzzed and rang around her head, hummed and sang their songs, songs too fast for any human ear to hear, songs that came to her like sharp kisses in the wind. Bees hovered at her eyes, her lips. Crickets clung to her rebozo and tinkled like small bells. Cicadas rose from the earth and cracked their shells and screamed around her as she walked. Coyotes followed her. Jackrabbits hid in the creosote bushes and watched her pass. Roadrunners trotted in front of her and behind, like an honor guard, waggling their tails, the leaders often looking back at her as they ran through the brush. The desert was alive at her feet. She crossed the shell-like prints of the javelinas' hooves, the long swirls of the sidewinder's passing. Rattlesnakes lifted their heads and flicked their tongues at her as she passed, but they did not rattle. Clover blossomed. And she walked on, walked alone, for hours — walked weeping over her brother, praying for forgiveness, praying to be found worthy. She walked until the sun burned her dizzy, and she had to lie beneath a mesquite tree or a paloverde, gulping hot air like water, sometimes falling into fretful sleep, jagged dreams.

Buenaventura mended slowly. Although his arm had come down from over his head, it was weak, and his hands shook. His left leg was painful, and he limped. He would limp for years to come.

He was quiet, polite. He addressed Tomás as "sir" and Gaby as "doña." He didn't speak at all to Huila. When he saw Teresita, he hung his head or left the room.

One day, Tomás sent for Teresita.

A kitchen girl knocked on her door and called, "Teresita? The patrón? He wants you in the library. Por favor?"

When Teresita opened her door, the girl flinched and hurried away.

She came down the stairs. Gaby smiled up at her. Reached out and touched Teresita's hand. Teresita drifted by as if in a dream. She no longer invited Gaby to her room. She had not seen Fina Félix since that bad day. They would never again sleep beside her. There would be no more flying trips.

She went down the cool stone hall and entered the library. Huila drowsed on the small leather couch, her crutch propped against her knee starting to slip. Tomás sat in his great chair, smoking a thin cigar. Standing before him was Buenaventura. He was dressed in his best brown suit, and he clutched his hat before him in both hands. The hat was shaking.

Tomás said, "Please repeat what you were saying."

Buenaventura cleared his throat.

"Sir," he said. "I would like permission to move to Aquihuiquichi. I . . . I would like to leave the ranch."

"Oh, Buenaventura," Teresita said. "Please don't leave."

He stepped away from her.

"My, my condition," he said, "makes it hard for me to ride or to do my, my work. And," he looked at the floor, "I think it would be better, sir, for me to be gone from here."

"I love you," Teresita said.

Her brother dropped his hat and held both shaking hands up before him.

"Please!" he said.

"All right, all right," Tomás said. "Enough."

He pointed at Teresita.

"Never again," he said.

He pointed at Buenaventura.

"Go," he said.

＊

She took her food to her room. Sometimes, she crept out at night, after they were asleep, and she ran through the moonlit fields. Coyotes paced her, ran invisible all around her, calling to her. And the dead, too, ran beside her. They cried out to her, the lost elders and the murdered children, the massacred grandmothers and the slaughtered warriors. They called to her, sang with the coyotes, raised hymns that sounded, in the forgiving dark, like far wind in leaves, like water rippling in a still cove, like the calls of some nearly forgotten migrating birds. When she thought God could hear her, she asked Him, "Why have you left me here alone?" The only answer she received was the parched midnight wind.

Book IV

THE CATASTROPHE
OF HOLINESS

An Indian woman was brought to me to be cured. One leg was paralyzed and she had not walked for a year. I placed my hands on the paralyzed part and told her to walk. Poor woman! She was afraid to try. She cowered and cried, but I insisted. She took one step tremblingly, then another and another. When she found she could walk, she ran back, raised her hands to heaven and cried "Santa Teresa!" It was thus that I was named.

— TERESITA,
New York Journal

Thirty-six

THE WORLD ROLLED FORWARD, for People and patrón, Indian and Yori, dizzy in the night and about to change forever.

The cavalry of Mexico chased a small army of Mayos loyal to Moroyoqui that had united with a larger group of Yaquis inspired by the teachings of Cajemé. The hunt took the mounted forces through the hills around Navojoa, and the plains around Cabora. Dark riders thundered through the ranch late in the night, and the army sent spies to see if Tomás was aiding the enemy. He was observed feeding bands of Indians, but it was never proven that Moroyoqui's raiders had visited Cabora.

The People passed on rumors. The cavalry had caught seven riders and had tortured them mercilessly on the llano. Buckaroos told terrible stories of the riders held down by soldiers, and the soldiers using their great knives to cut off the Indians' feet and then forcing them to walk for miles on the stumps until they fell. Mercifully, the soldiers shot them when they could walk no more.

In this cloud of dread and legends, Teresita recuperated. After Buenaventura left the ranch, she busied herself with her studies. After her prayers and offerings in Huila's sacred site, she spent mornings visiting the sick. She took a light lunch in the early afternoon, at which time she bantered with Tomás and Gaby. She did not seem morose or withdrawn. She did not always even seem particularly serious to them. Still, they noted that she no longer went on wild horse rides, and she never touched her guitar with blue flowers painted on it. After lunch, she retreated to her high room to take a siesta.

No one knew her thoughts in her white room. No one saw her stare in her mirror at her face — a face she regretted. At her hair — hair she wished she could trade for Gaby's waterfalls of curls. No one saw her pluck dried blossoms and leaves off her hanging herbs and crush them between her fingers, eyes closed, going into the scent.

She had never been kissed.

She lay on her bed in the crushing temperatures and tried to still her heart, her body, tried to let the roller of heat pass over her without flattening her. She locked her door and lay naked on the bed, with wet towels on her belly and chest. She fanned herself and tried to dream. But the afternoon naps didn't come. When her month blossomed, she felt deep knots of pain in her belly, and she folded cloths and hid lavender among the folds, but this did not help the pain. She looked away from herself during those days. Her eyes were sore and tired on many days. The light tormented her, and she took to placing a wet towel over them, too — folded to keep out the sun. When her headaches came, she could see strange webs of light. Sounds set off waves of color in her head. She sometimes smelled strange scents, and if she moved, the headache clamped over her skull and made her sick to her stomach and made her tired eyes feel as if they were going to pop out of her head and weep down her cheeks.

Teresita had never seen a train. But she had now delivered 107 children. She had never seen a city outside of her dreams, but she had buried five mothers and three stillborn infants. She had never seen a black man, or a Chinese man, though she heard that they existed, and she had once seen a photogravure of an African in one of Tomás's American magazines, the *Overland Monthly*. She had still never seen the sea.

Teresita had never stepped on a paved street. Even the streets of Ocoroni had been cobbles or dirt. She had never heard any music except for corridos and folk ballads and once, from a distance, a brass band playing in the old ranch house. She delighted Tomás one day by showing a little spark and proposing that a mariachi band play for the hacienda. He thought it was a joyous request, but for her it was a scientific exploration. El Mariachi Gavilán gathered in its finery on the veranda and commenced an unbelievably loud caterwaul that brought the People and mestizos from many acres away. The musicians' pants were embroidered down their legs, and their vast sombreros were the greatest hats anyone had ever seen. Teresita smiled and laughed and even lifted her skirt and clomped a two-step with her father.

Tomás muttered to Segundo, "See? She's all right."

Teresita had never tasted pancakes, blueberries, ice cream, chewing gum. She could not imagine root beer or spaghetti. She had never seen a hot-air balloon. She had never looked through a telescope. She had never heard of such things as zoos, museums, the North Pole. She had never seen a major bridge. She had never been in the mountains, though she had looked at them her whole life.

She had never seen a ship, except in her night flights that now seemed years ago and nearly forgotten. She had never met a doctor. Had never been cold. Had never seen a building taller than two stories.

If she knew so little, had seen next to nothing, then why, in her dreams, were the People calling her Queen of the World?

※

On Friday nights, no matter how sore or bent from work they were, the People and the vaqueros began to drink and fuss. Segundo set up a small cantina on the porch of the bunkhouse. Men bought bottles from Cantúa's old roadside inn (long forgotten as a beanery, it was now under the management of El Güero Astengo, and it was a cantina, La Pulquería Alma de Mi Gente) and the occasional hogshead barrel of beer. Segundo resold the beer at a small profit. The idea was the fiesta, not the money. But money didn't hurt, and it was better to lose an extra ten centavos on a drink than to lose your scalp to the head-hunting gringo demon mercenary on his blooded horse, or to be bushwhacked by bandits, or the Rurales. Who knew what could happen in the world? Cabora was big enough for them all, and even a dull workplace could look new by firelight, fresh when painted by tequila and beer.

Dances broke out on Friday nights behind the corrals. Tomás often took Gabriela's arm and strolled down to watch the People raise clouds of dust. When he was in a good mood, he paid for musicians to play. On many Fridays, he sent for a calf to be barbecued. Tortilla makers formed lines in the shadows, their incessantly patting hands seeming to keep the beat of the music.

These transplanted Sinaloans missed their green homeland. They missed tobacco fields and marijuana fields, tomato farms and hectares of vibrant red and yellow chiles on their fluttering green bushes. They missed rain. They missed romance — in Sonora there was nothing compared to the indelible dance of love one found in Sinaloa.

And Millán, the former miner from Rosario, perhaps the most romantic village in all of Mexico, missed these things most of all. Millán found that the women of Sonora smelled different. He often stole their clothes from shacks to smell, and they smelled bad, like cattle. Perhaps it was the food or the water that made them stink. Certainly, there was nothing as pure as the tides of the Baluarte River, river of his boyhood, green as it sped by the foot of the mighty mountain, El Yauco. Millán grew nostalgic when he drank. He filled a bag with round stones and hung it from his waist. When the others were dancing, he went out in the dark to kill dogs and cats with a rawhide sling. After he had cracked six or seven skulls, he felt calmer, more relaxed. If he drank enough after that, he could sleep.

It was Segundo who first approached Tomás with a proposition.

"Boss, we need a plazuela."

"You need a what?"

"We need a plazuela!"

"For what!"

"Love!"

He had to say no more to Tomás. In Sinaloa, each small town had a plazuela with a gazebo and some whitewashed trees. Each town square had a walkway around its perimeter, and along this were white benches. Old men often took to the benches to enjoy the gradual fall of night, the chiming of the church bells, and the appearance of the bats that gorged on the many flying insects that were drawn to the flickering gas lamps of the plazuelas. These plazuelas were what was sorely missing in the Sonoran desert. How could the grand ritual begin, if there was nowhere for it to go?

"Get to work!" Tomás barked.

Segundo, Teófano, three boys from Culiacán, and the limping Buenaventura (who had begun a cautious reconnoitering of his old homestead) pulled down the rails of the new burro and mule corral, the site where Lauro Aguirre had once slept. As soon as the People saw them whitewashing the trunks of the old trees, and setting out whitewashed rocks in a vast wobbly trapezoid, they knew immediately what was happening. "Una plazuela!" they cried. Tired men and women rushed to the corrals and swept, pulled weeds, shoveled sand over the ancient piss bogs in the ground. They raised planters using broken wheels from wagons and filled them with coffee grounds and eggshells and dirt and cow shit and they planted roses and geraniums there. It was soon clear that a gazebo of some sort was needed. Tomás pulled men off cow duty, pulled dormant woodworkers who had finished framing all the rooms and additions of the house. They immediately staked out a gazebo foundation, using strings the way Aguirre had taught them.

The Engineer could not enjoy their work. As the gazebo came together, two Rurales stopped at the gate of the courtyard in front of the main house and called for Don Tomás. Aguirre, in the middle of a delectable chorizo-egg-cheese burrito, rose and followed Tomás to see what they wanted. For a reason he would never determine, he paused just as Tomás threw open the door. He hid in the hallway, sensing something dire in the air.

The Rural in charge said, "Do you know a Lauro Aguirre, sir?"

Tomás stood in the morning sun and lied: "Lauro Aguirre? Let me think. I entertain so many guests!"

Aguirre flattened himself against the wall.

The rider cleared his throat and said, "We were simply curious if the engineer Aguirre might be here now."

Tomás cried, "Here? Now? This Aguirre? I don't think so, my dear officer!"

Aguirre peered out the small crack behind the door.

"Where might he be?" the Rural asked.

"I'm sure I don't know, sir," said Tomás. "I believe there is an Aguirre who frequents Alamos. An engineer. Hmm. I am sure you would find men of his ilk in a city, not here on a humble cattle ranch! If you need steaks, I have steaks! One thousand head of cattle, but not a single engineer."

They had sat on their mounts looking down at Tomás. They didn't believe him. But they couldn't merely raid his house, either.

"All right," the rider finally said. "Bueno. If you see him, please send out someone to inform the Rurales. We would like to . . . speak . . . with him."

The Rurales saluted loosely. They turned their horses.

"Good day."

Tomás exulted, "Good day! Y Viva México!"

Inside the house, he gripped Aguirre's arms in his fists and said, "Ya te chingaron, paisano!"

They packed Aguirre's bags and dressed him in an absurd buckaroo outfit with a great spangled sombrero, and Tomás gave him a clutch of outriders to cover him, and they set out after dark for the Arizona border. Once there, Don Lauro Aguirre changed into human clothes and boarded a stagecoach for the unfortunate journey to

El Paso, perhaps the most uncomfortable three days of his life.

He immediately began a newspaper.

❊

The gazebo was only a box with a sad little roof on it held up by four posts, but once it, too, was painted white, it was enough. Appearing like migrating flamingos in a tidewater slough, one afternoon the girls arrived, floating out of their huts at dusk. Girls from the Félix ranch a mile down the Alamos highway somehow joined them. The old men on the benches were delighted to see the end of their day enlivened by young ladies dressed in their finest clothes. Segundo's boys lit torches all around the plaza. The girls giggled and held hands and fanned themselves. They came in pale skirts, like dandelion tufts. They were accompanied by mothers and aunts, all of them, too, giddy with the stroll.

"Adios!" the men called to women they had seen fifteen minutes before, as if they had not seen each other in a week.

"Good evening." The aunties nodded. "Don Porfirio. Don Chentito. Don Teófano."

"Is that your niece?" the old-timers would squawk.

"It is, it is. My Alma!"

"She is my little Emilita!"

"Es mi sobrina, la bella Iris Violeta!"

"Wonders will never cease!" the old-timers bellowed.

It was so civilized!

"Adios!"

"Adios!

"And to you, adios, Iris Violeta!"

"And adios to you in return, Don Fulgencio Martinez!"
Everything was right in the world.

The girls and their escorts rotated in a counterclockwise
flow until the boys appeared, cowboys and gangly ranch
hands and tiny Indio chile pickers strolling forth in huaraches and boots and church shoes. All hair was slicked
back: their heads glistened like coal beds. "Allí vienen los
pendejos!" cried an old man, and they all laughed and
hooted and stamped their feet and pounded their canes.

Upon first sight of the boys, the aunties turned stern
and didn't smile again for the entire evening. This was
deep pleasure for them — watching the hands and eyes
of these young dogs lest they step beyond the bounds of
proper behavior and visit an outrage upon the persons
of their charges. The boys went to the outside, as if by
some genetic programming, and they started to stroll in a
clockwise direction, constantly facing their blushing sweethearts. Always walking toward, always walking away; in
passing glimpses, whole love affairs flared up, faded, and
died.

Yaquis, come from no one knew where, took up posi-
tions on the outside of the circle and began fiddling away
on their little violins. Doña María and Tía Cristina, two
hardworking women with no time for foolishness, set up a
taco stand at one end of the stroll and a torta stand at the
other. Segundo moved his stash of beer to the plazuela.

Teresita would not have joined in except that several of
the young girls — too young for the stroll — asked her to
help them make limonada. She made it in Tomás's kitchen
with her squadron of giggling kids. They set up a stand between two benchloads of old-timers. After an hour or so,
Fina Félix convinced her to step out and walk, and as soon

as she did, she began to smile and fan herself with Fina's paper fan. She flirted. She knew what to do as soon as she started walking.

Teresita was delighted and startled to hear her first romantic compliments on the stroll.

Carlos R. Hubbard, of El Real de las Minas, said: "I did not know that God allowed lilies to bloom at night!"

On the far side of the square, Antonio de la Cueva of Piedra Castillo said: "Muchachos, did you see if that angel had wings?"

César González, though he was a young Jesuit and bound for his matriculation, declaimed the following: "If I work my fingers to the bone, Teresita, I might one day write a poem as lovely as your walk."

Fina nudged her. On her other side, pretty Emilia Zazueta laughed out loud.

"Ay qué muchachos," she said.

"Tienes pegue," said Fina, which of course meant: you have struck them hard.

This was an astonishment to Teresita.

For a time, every Friday and Saturday night at Cabora became a small fiesta. Huila thought it was ridiculous, or so she said. Still, she was the first to get a seat on the benches when the sun started to move west in the afternoon.

Teresita looked forward to these Friday and Saturday nights. Sometimes, she walked with Gaby, but the piropos never flew in Gaby's direction — it would be suicide to be caught sailing a ripe piropo at the patrón's woman! So walks with La Fina were more fun.

The Arroyo boy, who sold shoes to the women of the ranch when he wasn't writing incendiary novels about farm boys startled by romantic feelings for each other, walked along, though he was watching the cowboys. Even he launched a semipiropo at Teresita: "If I liked girls, I would be yours!"

A young rustler visiting from Chihuahua (actually, he was hiding from the Rurales) named Doroteo Arango said: "I would trade nine horses, ten cows, and a bag of gold for one kiss of your lips!"

"Ay, tú!" chided La Fina.

Teresita called all these boys "Pancho," for she didn't know who some of them were, and "Pancho" seemed funny to Fina.

"Gracias, Pancho!" she called back to Doroteo Arango.

He tipped his hat.

Rudolfo Anaya the First, on a horse-buying trip from the far Llano Estacado, said: "The kachinas have blessed you, Teresa."

She turned and walked backward and watched him circulate into the gloom.

"Gracias, Pancho."

Fina laughed.

"What a cute boy," Teresita said.

"They're all cute boys!" Fina Félix enthused.

"Well, that is one Pancho I would like to see again!"

Teresita watched for Anaya as she came around the circle, but he seemed to have vanished. As she strained to find him, she came face to face with Millán. He stepped in her way so she had to stop.

"Your tits taste like sugar, don't they?" he asked.

"Excuse me," she replied.

She walked for a half circuit, trying to catch up to Fina, but she felt ill. She pulled out and went to Huila's bench and sat beside her and put her head on the old woman's shoulder.

"Piropos," she said, "are so stupid."

To maintain the plazuela's integrity during the work-week, Tomás had to create a new position at the ranch: Don Teófano was named Jefe in Charge of Plazuelas.

Thirty-seven

HUILA NO LONGER ROSE EARLY. For the first time in her life, she slept through the dawn. She no longer knelt to her prayers, nor did she go out to her grove to address the Creator and the Four Directions. When Huila awoke, she would lie, sometimes for an entire hour, as if her dreams had taken too firm a grip on her and refused to let her go. When she finally did rise, she did so slowly, and in a strange trance. She had always been grouchy, but this was different. She was unapproachable now.

One morning, when Teresita was nearly done with her breakfast, Huila appeared in the kitchen. She went to Tere-sita and touched her cheek.

"Girl," she said.

Then she went to the opposite end of the table and spooned three, four, five doses of sugar into her coffee, and she broke the bolillos and shoved them in the cup, and she slurped the dripping mess and let the coffee run down her chin. Teresita asked one of the kitchen girls to attend to Huila's face. The girl stood over the old one with a cloth, and she darted in like a bird and mopped the coffee and melted bread off the old woman's chin.

"You think I'm old," Huila said. "The wind is old," she huffed, "yet still it blows!"

"Yes, Huila," they replied.

"The sea is old," Huila said, "and it still makes waves!"

"I have not seen it yet," Teresita said.

"Ni yo," said Huila.

She looked as if she was falling asleep.

Teresita, still restless, decided to go outside for a walk.

Others rose early at Cabora. Tomás, though he no longer needed to greet the dawn, awoke by force of habit — now that his wildfire of lovemaking with Gaby had abated, as all fires must one day fade, just a bit, still bright, still warm, but now safer and not threatening to burn down the house. He lay in bed wondering what to do with himself. Books and ledgers were not like horses or cows. They did not need to be fed, or brushed, or watered, or milked. They did not need to be broken, or driven, or shot, or branded. The books just lay on desks and waited for his pen.

Often, he turned to the sweetness of Gabriela's arms. He could lose himself in her as if he were riding out across the hills. The smell of her lulled him, almost enough to put him back to sleep.

The vaqueros, too, rose early. Unless it was Sunday and they were in the bed of some young harvest girl in the shacks of El Potrero, the cowboys were pulling on their boots in the diminishing dark. Aside from their need to work, and their curiosity about the day, they had no desire to lie in the smoky gloom of the bunkhouse, listening to other men groan and belch and yawn and curse, smelling the cheese stench of their stiff socks. In wooden beds, stacked three deep, no windows to speak of, and the two shuttered openings they did have kept shut to lock out biting flies and mosquitoes, they awoke and swung their legs onto the floor or into the air and pulled on their cracked old boots and clomped to the wood floor and staggered into each other and slapped each other on the back or shoved each other away with a muttered deprecation. Matches scratched, sounding like the fingernails that dragged through their chin whiskers, and they tumbled out into the dawn, ready to eat, many of them pissing in the dirt at each side of the door, half of them already looping ropes in their fists or tying on chaps. The cookhouse was a fifty-yard stagger away from their bunk room, and they wrestled through its off-kilter doorway and swarmed the long rugged tables, heads drooping over blue tin mugs of fried coffee, blue plates of beans, eggs, pork, chilaquiles, cheese, fruit. After about three tortillas each, they were awake enough to begin boasting and lying.

Millán was out of bed earlier than the rest. He prided himself on a certain element of cleanliness. He was one of the few men who dabbed cologne on himself, and it was his habit to buy a bath at one of the shacks where the old woman filled her great tin laundry tub with warm water. He didn't mind showing his sex to the old one. He stood before her and smiled at her, watching her keep her eyes averted, but unable, finally, to avoid his dangling. It made him happy to watch her fumble. He would peel off his trousers before she had escaped the room, and he'd mildly ask her if she would launder them, holding them out to her while his member was half-hidden with one hand, though he knew and she knew he was showing her. She'd take his pants and hurry outside. On some days, her granddaughters peered at him from behind the blanket she'd hung in her shack, and he fingered himself in the water and pretended not to see them. It thrilled him to put on a show for the little ones. One of them looked to be about eleven. He had plans for her.

That morning, he had snuck out of the bunkhouse to kill cats, and he had crept near the main house to look at Gabriela Cantúa's underthings on the clothesline. The maids had hung her unmentionables near the house, behind a fluttering wall of bedsheets, but Millán just needed a short peek to fuel his desire. He smiled, pinched himself through his trousers.

He liked the patrón's bitch, all right. But the one he couldn't get out of his mind was Teresita. They all called her a blonde — she wasn't any pinche blonde. Her hair was almost as dark as his. Cabrona. Daughter of Urrea. Thought she was better than everyone. Daughter of a whore, he'd heard. His mother had always said, De tal mata tal flor.

From such a plant comes such a flower.

He tracked Teresita to the grove.

Out among the dirt and scrub and rattlers, Teresita decided to pray again. Huila had taught her many medicines. She lit her sage and smudged herself, and she lit her sweetgrass and offered the smoke to the sky, and she crumbled tobacco and other herbs and offered them as well. She prayed for Gabriela, her beloved friend who yearned for children with Tomás. She prayed for Loreto, who carried the family name alone in the city. She prayed for Tomás, that he might be cured of this terrible fever that drove him to try to cool himself with the bodies of strange women. She prayed for Huila, who was fast approaching her hour of rest. She prayed for the People, who fought for their lives and their land. She prayed for the land. She prayed for Buenaventura. She did not pray for herself. Huila had taught her: "Blessed are you when you pray for others. Shame on you when you pray out of selfishness and greed."

Besides, what could she ask for herself? She had already asked for forgiveness once, and Huila taught her that asking for forgiveness twice was an insult to the Creator. She did not know if praying to receive a boyfriend was bad or not, and she was afraid to ask Huila. Was loneliness merely selfishness? She feared Huila might say so. She decided to pray for any lonely boy who wished someone would love him — that the Creator might allow that boy, if he was a very nice boy, and a funny boy, and a boy who could play guitar and sing and could possibly ride horses, to find a nice girl to love him back.

When she was through, she sat on a flat stone and undid her hair. She kept it tightly braided when others could see her, but here, with only the crows and the mockingbirds and the mad squirrels watching her, she let her hair fall and blow. The breeze eased through the long tresses and crept over her scalp. She shivered and thrilled to it. She pulled up her skirt and her hated petticoats and let the sun burn her bare legs.

A snake-thin creek meandered through her grove, and she put her bare feet in the water. Watched the sun form wobbling lines and triangles of light on her skin. Watched tiny clouds of silt escape from between her toes and carry down the weak current, moving over the bright gravel like small rain clouds. She dreamed she was flying with brother crow, above a June storm as it passed over the land.

She wanted to strip off her hot clothes, lie naked and let the water run over her body. This was not allowed, of course. No woman would be forgiven an act as brazen as that. Girls might bathe together in the river, in a group, with angry aunties posted on the rocks and among the trees, ready to beat spies to death with their canes. But that nakedness would have been strictly for the bathing, not for joy. A woman naked, naked for the delight of her own flesh . . . even if no one could see her, Teresita knew such a thing would remain forever unforgiven.

Ah, well. Beetles swam in the water. Wasps and bees alighted on the small black banks of the creek and nipped up daubs of mud, sipped water. Butterflies touched down on the gravel and slowly opened and closed their wings, unreeling their coiled tongues into the wet. Teresita chewed clover stems, felt the wild tang of sour juices on her tongue.

Millán watched her. Watched her back, stared at her bottom as it was made wide by the ground pushing up against it, cupping it. Watched the way her bottom formed circles, oblongs, fruit shapes as she wiggled back and forth.

Millán liked to say: "Mexican women are dogs, but Indian women are cows."

Tomás sipped his coffee and watched Gabriela eat. She carefully sliced an orange half-moon out of her melon and took it between her lips. Her soft tongue darted out and took the cool flesh of the melon and pulled it into her mouth. He couldn't believe she was real. She was like some dream, some story old men told youngsters. She made a fool out of him with the slightest grin or pout. She slept in his bed, not beside him, but *around* him, her aromatic legs and arms wrapped around him, her mouth against his throat, her beautiful thundercloud hair over his face, his chest. He kissed her hair. Took it in his fist and kissed it, breathed it. He held her underwear to his face and kissed it, too. When she bathed, he smelled her clothes.

She looked up at him from her small chewing and crinkled her eyes at him. Oh my God! he thought. He didn't know what it was about her that made him more insane: her belly or the pale friction of her thighs; the small of her back or her armpits.

Huila staggered in from the garden and dragged a chair away from the table with a loud screaking.

"Good morning," Tomás said.

"Hnf," Huila grunted.

"Buenos días," Gabriela said. "Cómo amaneció usted?" she asked.

Huila shrugged.

"Café," she said.

The cooks hurried to bring her a cup. Tomás looked up at Gabriela and raised an eyebrow. Gabriela smiled.

"Feeling chatty, are we?" said Tomás.

"Ay, Gordo," Gabriela chided.

Huila slurped her coffee. Her hand shook.

"Where's my damned bread?" she said.

"You already had some," the cook said.

"I want more."

"Coming," called one of the girls.

"Huila," said Tomás, "I am in love."

Gabriela blushed.

"Love," Huila said, "and burial shrouds both come down from Heaven."

Tomás and Gabriela looked at each other.

"Well," he said. "Good point."

He sipped his coffee.

Huila said, "Every monkey to his own rope."

"I see," he responded.

Huila dipped her bread and sucked it into her mouth. She pointed at Gaby.

"You," she said. "Where is the girl?"

"Teresita?"

"Where is she?"

Gaby shook her head. "I haven't seen her," she said. "She must still be out at prayers."

Huila looked up from her cup. Her eyes were clouded, blue-white on their edges. She stared over Gaby's head. Looked once into her eyes. She said "Ay Dios," then slowly fell over. When she hit the floor, she made a dry sound, like empty burlap sacks thrown to the floor of a barn.

❋

Teresita cupped the water in her hands and ran it up her legs. It curled over her knees and ran down her calves in rivulets. She smoothed her cold hands up over the knobs of her knees, and the water was delicious on her thighs. She gasped and smiled and leaned her head back, letting the sun touch her throat. The dirt was already warm to the touch, and she dug her fingers into it. She curled her toes in the gravel bed of the creek, felt water bugs skim over her feet, ping into her ankles, then sweep away.

Huila, she thought.

"Get me a ladder," she whispered. It made her laugh.

She lay back slowly, laid her back on the good earth and felt it press her up toward the sky. The earth always offered you up to the sky. She lifted you, when all the time the People thought she pulled you down. Clover heads loomed above her face like trees.

Huila, she thought.

She closed her eyes. Hummingbirds somewhere were making their kissing sounds. Their thrum.

Huila.

And again: *Huila!*

Teresita opened her eyes.

"Huila!" she said.

She grabbed her shoes and leapt to her feet and turned to run back to the house.

Millán stood between her and the trees. He smiled at her. She half crouched, feeling like a wildcat, certain she could leap over him, leap into the trees, speed away from him. He was breathing hard. His eyes glittered with joy — he was giggling.

"Where are you going?" he said.

Thirty-eight

SHE WAS LIMP. He shook her — her head wobbled as if he'd broken her neck. He pulled her skirts down around her legs and looked over his shoulder.

No money.

Damn it.

Millán squatted on his heels and looked around. Not good, killing the boss's daughter. Well, hell. If he got back to the barn, he could slip out a good horse and be halfway to the Río Mayo before they even knew he was gone.

Too bad he didn't have enough time to hide her.

Huila's collapse sent a wave of dread through Cabora. The People hurried in from the fields when they heard. They collected their children and hid them inside their huts. They watched the sky to see if some dark rider did not come from the mountainous east, now that their protector was fallen.

When she dropped, Tomás kicked back his chair and dropped to his knees beside her, taking her old head in his hands and lifting her, as if he could gaze life into her rolling eyes. Gaby froze, hands over mouth, too afraid of the old one to touch her or even approach her. The cooks cried out and wailed, and some of them ran out the door before Tomás could stop them, raising the alarm —"Huila fell down!"

It felt as if an eclipse had begun, portions of the sun being bitten away, as if the devil's mouth could no longer contain its hunger for light.

"Huila's dead!" they shouted.

"She's not dead, damn you!" Tomás shouted. "Help me!"

But who could help him? Huila was the one he would have turned to in such a crisis, and now the great physician herself was limp on the floor, drooling, her hair slipping out of its braid.

"What do we do?" one of the girls said.

Tomás looked at Gabriela. She shook her head violently, put her hands up before her.

"I don't know!" she said.

"I don't know," he said.

"I don't know either," said the girl. "Should I splash water on her?"

He shrugged.

"Cover her," said Gaby.

"Good idea, mi amor!" Tomás cried. "Get me a blanket!"

The girls hustled out of the kitchen and came back in a moment dragging Huila's own rebozo. Tomás draped it over Huila's reedy chest.

"Put her in bed," said Gaby.

"Sí, mi amor!" he replied. "Bed!"

Tomás and two of the girls lifted her. He felt as if he could have pitched her to the ceiling — she weighed less than a bundle of sticks. Gaby led them as they shuffled sideways, trying to collect Huila's limp arms, which flopped open and caught on doorways and furniture. Gaby held open Huila's bedroom door. The group stalled there for an instant, since none of the house girls had ever passed through that portal. Tomás, too. But they forged forward, the girls dipping their heads as if they'd entered a church, and they laid her on her narrow cot. She opened her eyes once, when they lowered her head to the pillow, and gasped a terrible, phlegmy sound, bubbling and whistling in her throat.

Tomás took her hand in his.

"Don't worry," he said, feeling like a fool. He looked at Gaby. "I wish Aguirre were here," he said. "He would know what to do."

"Teresita," Huila whispered.

Gabriela said: "Teresita!"

Tomás, as if it had been his own idea, shouted: "Teresita!"

And the vaqueros were sent out on their horses to find Teresita, the only one who would know what to do to save Huila.

Segundo would never forget what he saw when he entered the grove.

The shadows were soft, rolling and tossing like waves. The clover had some blossoms, and the bees moved across the ground like sparks from a campfire. Spiderwebs billowed in the tree branches, looking like the sails of those ships he had seen in Los Mochis so many years before. Iguanas the size of dogs frowned at him from the shade. The little creek was green as it meandered along the fold in the earth that was the floor of the grove. And there, lying on her back, was Teresita.

It took only a moment to see it all, but it felt later as if he had stared at her for an hour.

Her head lay in the water. It was only as deep as her ears. He could see her small gold earrings in the water, the fuzz of dark hair at the hinges of her jawline. Her long hair was pulled downstream by the current, fanned out like a great flow of blood. Her eyes were slightly open, her lips were parted. Blood ran from the corner of her mouth and from her nose. Her legs were bare, and the front of her dress was torn. Her palms were upturned, and her fingers were curled. She was twitching slightly, her feet kicking like the feet of a sleeping dog that dreams of running after rabbits. Her mouth opened and closed. But what frightened him were the butterflies.

Blue and white and red-yellow butterflies had settled on her. Butterflies stood on her open arms, slowly flapping their wings as if trying to lift her into the trees. Butterflies perched on her belly in a rough circle. Butterflies stood over her eyes, opened their wings, and covered her brow. A single hummingbird hovered near her left hand, then flew up and out of sight through the trees, gone in a flash of burning green and metal blue.

Segundo knelt beside her and collected her in his arms. The water ran off her body and soaked his pants. "Don't die," he whispered. "Segundo is here." He carried her to his horse and laid her facedown over the saddle so he could mount. Her hair hung down the far side, and the horse turned its head and stared at it. Segundo rose into the saddle and worked her back up into his arms. "Come on, you bastard," he said to the horse, and he steered with his knees as he tried to cradle her the way he would have held a foal just fallen from its mother's womb.

He rode back to the house with Teresita in his arms. He could feel her breathing, but she never made a sound. Her body vibrated: he thought of guitar strings. When he walked his horse through the front gate and into the little plum-tree courtyard, the People let out a terrible cry that rose and rose and brought Tomás running.

He gently took his daughter from Segundo's arms and carried her inside.

The People felt night coming fast now. They ran to light candles. The cowboys were breaking open casks of mezcal and getting mournfully drunk.

Huila was already forgotten.

Thirty-nine

THUNDERING, MILLÁN RODE SOUTH, his horse covered in foamy sweat. He did not sleep that first night. He stepped into a cantina on the old road back toward the Río Mayo, and the thin Indians there turned as one and glared at him, thinking him a hangman, perhaps, or a bandit there to burn their hovels. He bought pulque, awful and milky, but the cheapest liquor he could find. It burned his mouth, seared his throat. Could they tell what he'd done? What the hell did they care what he'd done? As he counted out more coins, his hands shook. Oh, Christ — Don Tomás was going to kill him as sure as the sun rose. "Otro," he ordered. The surly barkeep poured a bit into a clay cup. He held his breath and swallowed it. Coughed. If he could only get as far as Rosario! He'd skirt Ocoroni, of course. He'd be needing a new horse soon; this one was going to drop from its punishing charge. He didn't think to steal money from the bunkhouse, and the girl didn't have any money in the pockets of her skirt. He dipped his head. He'd steal a horse. It couldn't be any worse for him if they caught him than it already was. Culiacán? Could he go to Culiacán? Probably not. Rosario. Sweet Rosario. If he stayed far away from Tomás's cousin Don Seferino Urrea, then the Millanes de Rosario would help him. All he had to do was get south of town, to Escuinapa, and across the bridge into Nayarit. Nayarit, if he could only get to Nayarit! Tecuala or Acaponeta! The Indians stared at him. "What!" he bellowed. They put their hands on their machetes. He bolted for the door. Lightning ripped the silent sky and the west went red as open meat and the coyotes yipped and frolicked and he whipped and whipped his horse as he tried for home.

Segundo moved his bedroll out of his house and went to sleep at his sister Juliana's house. He refused to eat for the first two days, then slurped at coffee cups full of chicken broth. Several of the vaqueros saw him sitting outside her door on a crooked wooden bench, holding yellow baby ducks to his lips, disconsolately hiding their heads under his whiskers.

In Segundo's absence, Tomás was forced to send lesser hands to Alamos to fetch a doctor. Buenaventura came back to Cabora and went to Segundo's abandoned house. Doña Loreto had telegrams sent to Tucson, requesting the services of a gringo doctor. Then she sent a telegram to El Paso, so Aguirre would know of the tragedies on the ranch. She went to church and arranged for a novena to be said for Teresita. Gabriela drifted back and forth between Teresita's room and Huila's room, helpless and panicked, reduced to putting cool wet cloths on each of their foreheads. Tomás sat by his plum tree and drank. Fina Félix said her chickens laid black eggs.

Teresita lay on her back, lost in her coma, alabaster white and unmoving. The only signs of life were her shallow breathing, and her left hand, which slowly curled and lifted to her mouth and formed a fist there. They called to her, shook her, spoke sweetly to her in her sleep, but she did not wake, did not smile. Bruises spread under her skin — bruises on her face, on her throat, across her ribs, and down the small of her back. Tomás sat beside her and took her unclenched hand and read to her from her favorite books, but she did not smile or give any sign she heard his voice. Gabriela kissed her cheeks, her forehead, her hot dry lips. Nothing stirred. Morning and night, Gaby took a silver brush to Teresita's hair, and when more blood trickled out of Teresita's nose, she wiped it with soft paper that looked, pinked and crumpled, like rosebuds in the wastebasket.

Her lids cracked open and hung halfway up her eyes. They could see the iris and pupil of each eye, rolling back and forth, as if they were untethered from her body, sliding helplessly in her skull.

"What does she see?" Gaby whispered.

"Nothing," Tomás responded. "She sees nothing."

And the doctor, when he arrived from Alamos with a nurse and Buenaventura, repeated it: "She sees nothing. She is as one dead."

Buenaventura almost touched her.

Huila awoke and asked to see her.

Tomás and the doctor formed a litter for her of brooms and blankets and carried her into the room. She was too weak to rise, but she lifted her head from her pillow and looked on Teresita and released a small chuff of sorrow — her desiccated voice puffing into the air like dust from the harvest. She sobbed and raised a hand toward Teresita. Then she put her head down and seemed to sleep. They carted her back to her own bed and laid her down again.

She ordered the house girls to soak cloths in water and herbs and place them on Teresita's face.

The doctor from Tucson arrived after five days. He was a great blond American with thinning hair, and he conferred with his Mexican counterpart, both of them bent like cranes over Teresita's body. Her hair had grown so long that it reached her feet. No one knew when this had happened. Gaby laid it out along the sides of her body. The doctors often had to lift her hair and move it out of the way when they tried to examine her.

They could not force liquids into her. Her lips would not part, and when they tried to pour water in her mouth, it ran out the sides in rivulets. Her skin dried; her lips chapped. Her heart, drying in the desert within her, became weaker each day, almost mute. Both doctors swarmed over her pale stone chest with their stethoscopes, trying to find a beat. When they held a mirror to her lips, she could barely make a fog on the glass.

Her body grew hard, stiff as a plank of shaved pine, all her bones sharp and unforgiving in her shrinking flesh.

※

One of the buckaroos mentioned to Segundo that Millán had taken a stallion and not come back.

"When?"

"Almost a week ago."

Segundo rounded up two Apaches. He never spoke a word of it to Tomás or anyone else. They rode fast and hard, because Segundo knew Millán would try to get home to Sinaloa. And when Segundo returned, his eyes were black with some awful secret, and the People said he carried two ears in a bandana, and he laid those ears on the table of the patrón and walked back to his sister's house, where he slept for two days.

He had returned on a different horse from the one on which he'd left. They said he rode three horses to death chasing Millán. The Apaches never stopped when he returned — they rode past Cabora without a glance. The People saw them and whispered terrible theories.

Segundo was quiet after his long journey. Only once did he say anything, and those who heard him did not know if he was talking about the manhunt, or if he was just drunk. They were drinking, waiting for a pig to barbecue in a rocky pit in the ground, and he had squatted among them, drinking from an American whiskey bottle. And, in the middle of the party, he had said: "If you hang a man upside down over a small fire, his brains boil in his head until his head bursts." Greeted with silence, he had drunk more whiskey and said, "Good night." The People had watched him go back to his small house and slam the door.

For twelve days, Cabora slept like Teresita.

Maguey cutters left their machetes hung on nails and stayed in their huts. The cowboys let their cattle wander the llano, hungry and thirsty and dusty. The only things moving were Tomás and the doctors, and when the doctors took him aside and told him there was no hope for his daughter, Tomás mounted his stallion and rode wild toward the village of Bayoreca, then out to the foothills, toward Navojoa, then back. He wept and cursed where no one could see him.

When he returned, he called for Segundo.

"I want a coffin made," he said. "I want the best wood and the smoothest silk."

Segundo hung his head and said, "Sí, patrón."

When he left through the front door, he had to push through a crowd of field hands and workers, of vaqueros and wash girls. All the children from the workers' village shoved into the courtyard. Buenaventura stood in a corner, back pressed into the seam between two walls. He held a cigarette in his fist, in the manner of the outriders, cupping the glowing coal with his palm as if sheltering it from a great wind. He raised his eyebrows at Segundo in a silent question. Segundo shook his head.

The American doctor, unable to do more, packed his bags and left.

On the thirteenth day, Tomás awoke from a terrible dream of fire and shouting. He pressed his fists to his temples, then turned to Gaby. She slept in white, her thick hair pulled back and tied with red ribbon. He pulled the bow free and she opened her eyes. His eyes were wet with grief. She smiled and put her hand on his face. "It will be all right," she said. And, "Come here, let me show you." He rolled on top of her — her strong body held him up. They made love.

Huila awoke and felt as if she might eat.

Segundo paid three times the usual amount to a carpenter in Bayoreca. The old man had agreed to work around the clock and to deliver a coffin of oak and fragrant pine, lined in pale silver silk, in two days. Segundo rode back to the ranch and collected Buenaventura and they went to the hills.

Tomás, like Huila, thought he could finally eat something. He sat at his breakfast table and ate boiled mango with a spoon. Then he drank a cup of coffee, and ate three eggs fried with beans and chorizo. He ate tortillas. He ate white goat cheese. A slice of melon. A second and third cup of coffee with milky Mexican pralines and a slice of cactus candy. Someone brought him last week's paper from Alamos, and he sat reading as his delightful Gabriela picked at one poached egg and some toasted bolillo. Té de canela, her favorite cinnamon tea.

One of the housekeepers approached the table shyly and stood there.

It took Tomás a moment to notice her. He glanced over his paper and said, "Yes — you may clear my plates now. Thank you."

He went back to his paper.

She stood there.

He looked at her again.

"Sir?" she said.

"Yes?"

"Teresita, sir?"

"Yes?"

"She's soft."

He put down the paper.

"I beg your pardon," he said.

"Señorita Teresita," she repeated. "She's gone all soft."

"Soft."

"All soft in her bed. All floppy."

He jumped to his feet and ran upstairs.

The room was still murky and dark. She lay on her back, her arms now loose and falling over the edges of the bed. He was afraid to approach her.

"Teresita?" he whispered.

The room was so silent, it could have been filled with cotton.

"Hija?" he said.

He crossed to her, sat in the chair, and took her wrist. It was soft. Cold. Her hand flopped loosely at the end of her wrist.

He squeezed it, seeking a pulse, but the river of blood within her body had stilled.

He laid his head on her chest, but her heart was silent.

He went into the hall and called for the Mexican doctor, who came upstairs with his bag and knelt beside the bed and listened and prodded and held the mirror to her lips. Her mouth was turning pale blue. He tapped her eyelid with the edge of a metal tool: it remained still.

"Doctor?" said Tomás.

Gaby stood in the door with her hands over her mouth.

The doctor sighed, then lifted Teresita's hands and crossed them over her chest. He stepped over to Tomás and put his hand on his shoulder.

"Teresita," he said, "is dead."

Forty

HOW QUIET IT IS.

She could have guessed that death would be quiet, but this is a stillness that feels like early morning, perhaps after a snowstorm, though she had never seen a snowstorm when she was alive.

She is sure she knows what snow is now.

"Oh! Deer!"

The deer leaps in a green land that was not there before. Flowers. She follows. The deer is gone, and water stands before her: golden fish.

Coyote drinks from the pool and looks at her with happy yellow eyes. She watches his fur ripple. He looks to his left, and she follows his gaze and beholds the Mother standing in the shade of a tree.

"Did you bring me a ladder?" she asks.

They laugh.

They embrace.

No mother has ever held her in her arms.

Trees she has never seen twirl silver, purple, golden leaves that fall and take flight as butterflies.

She sees the three old Yaquis from her dreams walking in the distance.

"They are so nosy!" says the Mother.

The walk to Itom Achai's humble home is short.

He has a small garden. His door is open. Light pours

from his windows. He steps out — he has painted a blue line down one cheek.

"Do you know me?" he asks.

"God," she says, kneeling.

"I am."

He puts out His hand and lifts her to her feet.

His hair is a long braid of waterfalls, honeysuckle, comets. She sees eagles in His eye. When He speaks, she hears music and laughter.

"Take this cup, Daughter," he says in Cahita.

"You speak the mother tongue?" she asks.

"I speak in every tongue," He says. "I am everyone's Father."

She smiles.

The cup He hands her has reflections of stars in it.

"Drink. You thirst."

She drinks.

"I have a gift for you," He says.

God brushes back her hair and hands her a rose.

Forty-one

DEATH WAS SOMETHING the People understood. It's not that they were happy Teresita had died. It's that they were relieved that someone, anyone, had died. Their spell of dread was broken. They could finally weep with real feeling, and while weeping, they could plan their wakes and their prayers and sew their dresses and arrange their gatherings. They could dream of the beauty of the funeral, for surely the patrón would throw a funeral to rival their best weddings. All could agree that weddings were the best entertainment on the ranch, followed by first Communions and confirmations (presided over by the somber Father Gastélum), followed by the fabulous quinceañera coming-of-age parties where fifteen-year-old girls got to dress in virginal white gowns and dance with older men who would slip them pesos and gifts. Secretly, however, funerals were far and away the favorite Cabora pastime. Shows of grief, like piropos, were an art. Secretly, in the dark corners of their huts, the People were already practicing faints, contortions, and taciturn sighs. Already — at the well, at the supply shed, at the corrals — people were saying: "I knew her best."

Inside the main house, it was chaos. Tomás felt as if he had lost his footing, as if his home had tipped on its side, and his boots could not find purchase on the boards or the tiles. He walked from wall to wall, from doorway to doorway, steadying himself, clutching the corners to keep himself upright. His insomnia returned in these days. The bed seemed too hot, too narrow, and he would move through the gloom of the house in his white nightshirt like a ghost, move out into the front courtyard and filch plums from the tree and stare at stars and stretch out on the rough wooden benches.

Gabriela was silent in her grief, remembering the nights she had lain beside Teresita and whispered her secrets, had closed her eyes and flown. Her body now thirsted for that flight again. It was as if she had always lived in a desert, and she had tasted water once. Now, there was no way to taste that water again.

Huila sank back into silence.

Teresita's body spent the first night in her bed, the white sheet tucked up under her chin, the shutters latched shut, with a solitary candle burning in the corner.

In the morning, the women came for the body. They collected it and carried it gently down to the kitchen. They laid it out on the big metal table.

Gabriela had already sent one of her own dresses to the seamstresses, who came first to the body, to measure it and drape it to ensure their work fit Teresita for the funeral. Then the women took Teresita's old clothes off the body, stripping it naked. They brought tubs of warm water to the table, and they washed her body with folded cloths and ragged orange sponges. They made sure her face was clean, and they prayed as they washed the body itself, chanting holy words over it, ritually purifying it for the long journey ahead, calling on God and the saints to have mercy on her soul. When the bath was done, they pressed white towels to the body's skin, to mop up the water. Then they covered its nakedness with undergarments and a shawl.

Gabriela came to it next, with her brushes and combs. She stroked Teresita's hair until it glowed in the kitchen light. She used her best combs to hold the hair back from the body's face, anchored it with hairpins, and asked one of the girls to help her make a thick braid, which they laid out beside the body.

The seamstresses returned and worked their dress onto the body, struggling somewhat with its stiffening limbs.

After they were gone, Gabriela returned with face creams, powder, lip color. She made the face pale, covered the bruises. She drew in thin black lines around the eyes, painted the lips pale pink, brushed rouge onto the icy cheeks.

When it was painted, powdered, combed, and dressed, they carried the body into the parlor. Vaqueros had hauled most of the furniture out of the room, and they had set up a wooden table in the center, with a white crocheted cloth covering it. A small satin pillow was at one end, to hold up her head. Candles lit the room. In the morning, they would open the double doors to the outside, so mourners could shuffle through for the viewing. That night, the wake would begin with teams of people sitting watch over the body, praying rosaries. Tomás and Gaby would sit first watch.

Teresita's body was set out on the table. They wrestled its hands into a prayerful clench and rested them on its chest. They wrapped the hands in a rosary, so Teresita looked as if she were praying in death. The rosary held her hands together. Gaby laid the braid over her shoulder so it rested beside her praying hands.

Teresita's body spent the second night on the table in the parlor, in the company of murmuring mourners until three in the morning, when it was left alone and the candles were blown out.

The two best shovelers were dispatched to the small graveyard where the victims of the Yaqui raid and three vaqueros and five infants were buried. They dug a perfect hole for Teresita, making sure the edges and corners were straight as if cut with a knife. The pile of dirt beside the hole was shaped as well, its flanks pyramidal in the morning light.

Segundo's coffin arrived after breakfast. It came on the back of a small wagon, covered in cloth to keep the dust off its shiny sides. Tomás and Segundo helped the carpenter carry the coffin into the room where the body lay on the table. Old women traded shifts watching over it, praying, lighting candles. The carpenter faltered when he saw Teresita's white face. After he put down his end of the coffin, he crossed himself.

They pulled the cloth from the wooden box, and they admired the craftsmanship. Not a nail could be seen. The wood glowed with many layers of wax. The silk within was tacked in so it formed soft-looking puffs of material. Tomás nodded his approval, stroking the wood.

The carpenter asked for a moment to pray over the body. Tomás ushered the old women out of the room and quietly shut the doors.

Teresita's body spent the third night in the company of friends and family. Gaby sat with her, then Fina Félix. Juliana Alvarado came late, and then Gaby's father, Mr. Cantúa, came all the way from Guaymas. Old Teófano, Jefe de Plazuelas, muttered a rosary over her deep in the night. At three o'clock, Buenaventura stood in the corner farthest from her, and stared at her face. And in the morning, the women of the rancho returned to pray her through her last day.

Forty-two

THAT LAST DAY found Teresita in the company of five praying women. The sun was already moving down the western sky, and four old ones knelt around the table, and Fina Félix sat in a chair near the door. All of the women prayed as one, calling to the Virgin to bless Teresita. None of them saw her eyes open.

They prayed on for another minute, dogged and blind to anything but their folded hands, offering up the pain in their knees to Jesus, as a gift, as an offering to trade against Teresita's safe passage to Heaven.

"Mother of God," an old voice piped.

And all answered: "Pray for her."

Teresita sat up.

"What are you doing?" she asked.

A screaming eruption of women fled the room, a howling explosion of rosaries and candles, a stampede.

"God save us!"

"She lives!"

"The dead are walking!"

Fina Félix, for the second time in her life, ran all the way to her father's ranch.

Animals bolted.

Donkeys kicked.

The women burst out the doors and fell over each other as they ran and shrieked.

Buckaroos fell from their horses.

Chickens, driven to a feather-dropping panic by the screaming women, blew through Cabora in a frenzy of wings and squawking.

"The dead!" the women cried.

Vaqueros tumbled out of their siestas and drew their weapons and commenced firing on the little graveyard, shouting, "Kill the dead! Kill the dead!"

Women fainted.

Tomás ran outside, his pistol in his hand.

He saw his men shooting at the graveyard and he started firing, too.

"Where are they!" he bellowed. "Where are the bastards!"

Segundo stepped lively and let loose with two barrels of a shotgun.

"Apaches!" he yelled.

"Rurales!" hollered Teófano, and he popped off a round with his old revolver.

"The dead! The dead!" the old women sobbed.

"Jesus and Mary, the dead!"

"What?" Tomás yelled as he reloaded. "What!"

"Ave María Santísima, Purísima!" Tía Cristina the torta lady testified.

Buenaventura ran up to Tomás and shouted, "Who are we shooting at!"

"I don't know!"

"Teresita!" one of the women was blubbering, kneeling in the dirt and striking herself in the chest, flinging dust in the air.

Tomás stepped to her, holding his pistol up and away from her face.

He shook her, stared into her eyes.

"What is it?" he demanded.

"She's awake!" the woman bellowed.

"Who is?"

"She is."

The woman pointed to the doors of the parlor.

"No."

"No chingues," Buenaventura cursed.

Tomás staggered into the parlor, and his pistol dropped from his hand and thudded on the floor.

Teresita sat in the middle of the table, unblinking, her face showing a vague, reptilian curiosity as she scanned the room. She looked at the candles, and the coffin, at him.

Gaby shoved in behind him. Segundo, children, Teófano, Buenaventura.

"What is happening?" Teresita asked.

Tomás sputtered.

"Oh no. No," he said. "No, you must be kidding."

Teresita yawned.

"Why am I on this table?" she asked.

Buenaventura whistled, and Gabriela felt faint and leaned on the doorframe.

"This is your wake," Tomás managed to say.

"My wake?"

"You're dead!"

"I am?"

"Oh Christ," said Segundo.

She turned to stare at the coffin.

"And this? What is this, Father?"

"This is your coffin," he said.

"No."

She shook her head.

"I will not sleep there," she said.

She looked at him with a mild expression.

She said: "Someone will soon die, though. You can use it then. Expect a funeral in five days."

She lay back down and closed her eyes.

"It was a long trip," she said.

Even Tomás, then, made the sign of the cross.

They led her to her room.

She was terribly cold. Her passing chilled the air as if they were taking a block from the ice wagon into the house. She never blinked. Her head turned on her neck like a machine as her eyes took in the alien details of her home. The family didn't know she could see through them. Their flesh to her was a shadow, and their bones danced within, visible to her as legs seen through a dress when the sun is bright. And deeper, still: the marrow in their bones glowed like thin wires of fire. Their skulls each held a clot of light, a charcoal ember. The burning marrow caused their bones to gleam within their flesh like narrow pink lamps.

She said, "I am tired. I have come a long way. Have you been there yet?"

Tomás coughed. How was one to be a father to a dead girl? Did one scold her? Correct her?

In her room, she lay back on her bed. She stared at the ceiling and disregarded her weeping father, the trembling Gaby, and the terrified house girls.

She said, "I am thirsty."

They brought her water. She gulped it. They brought another glass. She took it in both hands and gulped it, too. Then she closed her eyes.

She looked dead again, save for her breathing.

They backed out of her room, fled silently down the

stairs, hid in different parts of the house alone, drawing the curtains and pulling down the blinds, unable to speak of this moment, afraid somehow to face the day.

The next day, they found her sitting in the chair in the corner of her room. She still wore the burial dress. When Gaby tried to help her remove it, Teresita languidly slapped her hands away. When they brought her food, she left the plates on the floor. She drank more water. She never spoke.

"Really," Tomás said. "This is too much."

She said, "I will see Huila now."

Tomás had been standing on the other side of the room, watching her stare into space. When she spoke, he jumped. "She is not well," he replied.

"I know."

"Are you strong enough?" he asked.

"Strong?" she said, never looking at him.

He stepped across to her and took her hand in his. She slowly turned her eyes to his hand and regarded it coolly, as if it were a lizard crossing her path.

"I can see your bones," she noted.

He let go of her icy fingers.

"Daughter," he said.

She said, "Am I?"

He was stung. He backed away from her. Put his hands in his pockets.

"You frighten me," he said.

"I will see Huila now."

❊

Gabriela took one arm, and Tomás the other. They maneuvered her downstairs and along the hallway.

"Your womb is ripe," Teresita told Gaby.

They opened the door for her, and Teresita walked through as if struck blind. She held her hands before her chest, palms out, fingers slightly curled, as if she were feeling the air that encapsulated things, as if she were seeing the color of the world through her skin.

The room smelled old. Musk and dust and death were in the air. The others held back at the open doorway, as if they were afraid to breathe that cloud of stink. But Teresita did not seem to take notice of it at all. She stepped in and closed the door behind her.

Huila, dry as a skeleton in the bed, stirred when the door latched shut. She was asleep, her old chin sprouting thin white whiskers. Teresita laid her hand on the old one's head, then she sat in the corner. Huila jumped and snorted. She opened her eyes, craned her head on the pillow. Her eyes squinted, then popped wide.

"Where are the chickens!"

"There are no chickens, old woman."

"Who is cooking supper, then!"

"Supper has been taken care of."

"Nobody cuts off a chicken head like me."

"You are the best at handling chickens."

Huila snorted. Jerked. Looked over.

"You," she said.

"It is I."

"Have I died?"

"No."

"Is this Heaven?"

"Hardly."

"Are you a spirit?"

"We are all spirits."

"Have you come back to take me to Heaven?"

"No."

"Hell?"

"No. Wherever you are going, you must go alone. No one takes you."

"I don't like that!"

"You and I do not make the rules."

"Things would have been different, let me tell you."

Teresita said: "I am alive. They did not keep me."

Huila laid her head back down. Sighed.

"Well," she said. "That's good."

"They told me I had work to do."

Huila nodded.

"They like to keep busy," she said.

Huila seemed to sleep for a minute.

"Get me a ladder," she said.

Neither of them laughed.

They were quiet for a time.

"I've seen people come back before," Huila said. "Once when I was a girl."

Teresita nodded.

"Will I come back like you?"

"I don't think so," Teresita said.

Huila coughed.

"Can you help me?" she asked. "Spare me from death?"

Teresita scooted her chair across the floor, leaned forward in her seat, and passed her hand up and down the old woman's body.

"No," she said.

"Will I die now?"

"Yes."

They were silent again.

"I don't want to die."

Teresita closed her eyes.

"I know," she said.

"Does it hurt?"

"No."

"Will I be afraid?"

"Oh no."

Teresita could hear her father whispering to the people outside the door. All around the house, they were still shouting. She could hear that silly Fina Félix crying and carrying on.

Teresita said, "Do you know how it is when a child needs to go to sleep? How a child fights and bargains. Asks for a story, or cries, or suddenly needs water to drink because she won't go to sleep?"

"Yes."

"But you know it is time. For whatever reason — it is time for the child to sleep. It's late, or she needs to get up early in the morning, or she is ill. You have to make her go to sleep, sometimes against her will."

"Yes."

"This is how it is with God and us. God has to put us to bed, and we don't want to sleep yet."

Huila swallowed. It made her feel terribly sad. "Will I like being dead?" she asked.

Teresita opened her eyes.

"Did you enjoy being alive?"

Huila thought about it.

"Yes," she said.

"Then," Teresita said, "you will enjoy your death."

Huila smiled. Closed her eyes. "This isn't so bad," she said.

She gestured for Teresita to come closer. Teresita touched the edge of Huila's bed with her knees. She took Huila's hand in hers.

"I wish you could stay," Teresita said. "I will miss you."

She could feel the faint pulse of Huila's old heart through the bones and thin leather of her hand. Huila's blood was cool and slow, almost blue in her veins. She squeezed Teresita's hand.

"They'll bury you in my coffin," Teresita said.

Huila smiled.

"I like that," she said.

Teresita prayed. Huila must have fallen asleep, for she snored a little, mumbled in her sleep. Her dreams were full, Teresita knew, of her dead parents, her dead brothers and sister, her dead lover. All the doorways unlocking before her, all the hallways swept clean, the lamps being lit. The gate to Huila's garden coming unlatched. The old woman jumped.

"Girl?" she said.

"Aquí estoy," Teresita whispered.

"Do you want my shotgun?"

"No."

"Do you want my tobacco pouch?"

"No, thank you."

"You know where my herbs are."

"Yes."

"Use them."

"I will."

Huila sighed, long and dry.

She reached out her hand. Put three cracked hard objects in Teresita's hand.

"What are these?"

"Buffalo teeth! From long ago!"

Huila closed her eyes.

"I am tired," she said.

"I know."

"May I go now?"

Teresita leaned forward and kissed the old woman on the cheek.

"Go," she said. "Everything is all right."

She patted Huila's hair.

"Relax, old woman. Your work is done."

A tear rolled down Teresita's cheek.

"You brought goodness to this world."

"Did I?"

"You lived with honor."

"Do you really think so?"

"Don't worry. Go to sleep. When you wake up, you will see deer."

Huila's eyelids fluttered.

"Fall asleep. I love you. Fall asleep."

Huila stiffened. Her eyes opened once. Then she was gone.

Forty-three

ALREADY, THEY WERE COMING. You wouldn't have noticed them at first, and you wouldn't have noticed them at all if you didn't know where to look. The word had already carried far across the llano and into the hills. They came in small groups to see the living dead girl. In among the workers' shacks, you would spot a few new bodies huddled in the shadows. There would be a strange woman among the girls washing laundry. Alien children stood at the edges of the crowds, watching the house.

When Tomás rode his horse out to some business in the fields, he didn't look down, didn't give any hint that he was aware of the new ones on his land. But he watched carefully, while not watching, looking out of the corners of his eyes, studying motions and faces, gaits and strides, like a madman accumulating data for some fabulous new theory of the world, maniac proof of forces and plots swirling around his head, infiltrating his ranch. He didn't want them to know he was watching them, though he could feel them watching him back. He didn't know what they wanted, what harm they might have brought with them, what dark designs.

For all he knew, they had come to kill her, come to attempt to set some aberrant cosmic scale aright. Or they had come to marry her, to pet her, to follow her. No one knew she was insane, sitting in her room like a mannequin, staring into the infinite depths of the corner of two white

walls, seeing devils and angels and babbling horrible foolishness about bones and dreams. These superstitious
types, they were starving for miracles.

He could not scientifically explain Teresita's resurrec-
tion, but he knew there was a reason for it, a *reasonable*
reason. But these people, who saw the faces of Jesus Christ
and the Virgin of Guadalupe in burned tortillas, were a rabble frantic for something, anything, to make their shopworn
world a little more special. They wanted to believe there
was something more, some heaven awaiting them after
their lives of idiotic toil. And they seemed to think his
daughter could somehow bring them closer to this myth.
He knew the price would be dear when they discovered
that she was simply human, after all.

He shoved his heavy Colt revolver into his pants, and it
rose across his belly at an angle, dark blue and cold, rose-
wood handgrip like a spurt of blood on his stomach, pirati-
cal and ready to hand. And in a scabbard, dangling at his
left hipbone, a great knife with a buckhorn handle,
stropped bright and sharp, close to his hand and ready.

Days had passed since they'd buried Huila. Teresita had
stayed in the courtyard near the plum tree, showing no interest in the burial of the old woman. Lauro Aguirre would
have been the perfect man to speak some final words over
the grave, but he was in El Paso, trying to incite the Mexican revolution from the safe confines of the United States.
He published broadsides and wrote incendiary tracts de-
nouncing President Díaz, and if he had come to the funeral, he himself might have been a candidate for interment
beside the old woman. So Tomás had muttered a few
vaguely remembered religious platitudes, then had tossed
in a rude handful of rocks and dirt. It clattered on the wood

like a fist knocking on a door, and several of the People stepped back, lest Huila rise like Teresita and scold them all. But that day it was fated that the dead remain dead.

When the Urreas returned from the funeral, they found Teresita lying facedown on the flagstones. They thought she had died again, and a great wailing started to ascend, but when they hurried to her side, they found her merely asleep. Her hands were tucked under her body, and her face was turned away from the sun.

"This," Tomás said, "I cannot bear."

Gaby wiped his sweaty brow with a bandana.

Teresita opened her eyes.

"You are awake when you sleep," she said. "To awaken is to slumber."

They shook their heads, took her under the arms and lifted her. She did not resist.

"The world is cold," she said. "Everything is ice." She patted the stone wall. "See how it is all melting?"

"Get her out of here," Tomás said. "I can't hear any more of this!"

They hustled her up to her room, laid her on her bed. She rose immediately and went to her chair and sat, staring. Tomás came into the room and leaned against the wall.

"She's gone mad," he said.

Gabriela said nothing.

"Life is death," Teresita announced.

They backed away from her.

"The flesh is the dream."

"Go," Tomás whispered.

"Father?" she said. "I am friends with God."

They quietly closed her door and latched it so she could not roam outside and come to further harm.

Tomás sat at the breakfast table. He couldn't eat. He sipped a glass of thick tamarind juice and spooned chunks out of a fat raft of papaya. Gabriela drank coffee and cut the top off a boiled egg in a small silver holder. He nibbled the pale fruit.

"Is she locked in her room?"

"Sí, mi amor," Gaby replied.

"Good."

"This can't go on," she said.

"No."

"Not much longer."

"No."

And Teresita appeared beside him, leaning on his left shoulder.

"Father," she said.

He jumped, spilling his juice. He watched the heavy glass float to the floor and strike, divide in six even sections and bloom, throwing the shards in all directions, the brown-orange essence of tamarind gouting in thick ropes of fluid, spattering, each spatter forming new blossoms on the floor, the entire spill a bouquet blooming within a bouquet. He could hear nothing.

"Father?" she said.

Gaby threw herself from her chair and left the kitchen as Tomás nodded, watching the juice spread between the clay tiles of the floor.

"Prepare yourself, Father," Teresita said.

"For?" he murmured, looking at her bare feet: toes filthy, nails black with dirt.

"Riders approach."

The cooks listened to everything, ready to report to the pilgrims what the dead girl said.

"Yes?"

He looked at her sad thin face. Black eyebrows. He thought: Gaby must teach her to pluck them before they grow together.

"Teresa," he said, "there are no riders."

"Riders," she replied. "A wounded man."

"Is this a prophecy?" he said.

"It is."

"I see."

He took her elbow in his hand: he could have cracked the bones like walnuts in his fist.

"How did you escape from your room?" he asked.

"I am no prisoner."

He tried to lead her away from the table. He could not move her.

"Why don't you rest awhile?" he said.

"Riders. Tomorrow morning," she said. "You will not have time to eat."

She pulled her arm from his grasp and went down the hall. He followed. She opened the front door and went to the plum tree. She lay down in its shadow and seemed to fall asleep. He moved to the garden wall and peered over it, one hand on the butt of his gun. No one was visible. The ranch looked empty, as if a plague had swept in from the llano and killed them all. The edges of the buildings already flaking, adobe coming apart in the wind, walls smoking away to powder in the endless cycle of the days.

✳

The next morning, Tomás ordered eggs fried with beans. As soon as the platter was placed before him, the thunder of riders rumbled through the house. He threw his napkin aside and hurried down the hall as the voices rose in alarm outside the door. He pulled his revolver and followed it out the door. Two riders on panting horses circled before the gate of the courtyard until one called, "Two more coming! With the wagon!"

A Yaqui worker had been kicked in the head by a mule. The wagon came rattling, and the men pulled the convulsing worker out and laid him on the ground. He writhed and foamed and they stood about him staring at his agony. Blood dropped from the crack in his head. They shrugged, spat. What could they do? He was doomed.

Teresita came forth, unbidden.

She walked between the men, pushing them out of the way. She said nothing. She knelt and took dirt in her hands. She spit into the dirt, rubbed it in her palms, making a red mud. She bent to the man and rubbed the mud across his brow, whispered a prayer over him. His feet, then his hands stopped jerking. He rolled onto his side, clutched his head, opened his eyes. He shook his head, smiled, rose. He shook her hand.

"What did I tell you?" she said to Tomás.

She walked back into the house.

One of the riders adjourned to the cookhouse and ate some cold beans. He got drunk that night and bought a whore. He didn't think about the miracle, nor did he mention it to his friends or his women and when asked about it later, had no memory of it. The other rider lived off the ranch, and he lay beside his wife that night and told her of the strange doings at Cabora: they had brought a man without a brain to the ranch, and Teresita had poured mud in the empty skull and he had risen and danced a jig. Fire could be seen in her eyes.

The next day, his woman spoke to others at the laundry basin. Her husband had taken the corpse of a man who had been beheaded to the grave of the dead Teresita, at Cabora. A mysterious Yaqui elder had told them to bury the man beside the body of the young witch, and three hours later, she had risen from the grave with the man in her arms — he had a new head, and it was made of red mud!

Ten women listened to this tale. From these ten, thirty retellings radiated. From these thirty, three hundred versions of the story emanated, dribbling down the grand arroyo, sliding along the banks of the Río Mayo, the Río Yaqui.

The medicine men started out for Cabora, where they hoped to see Teresita, the risen dead girl. On the road, they met a band of Lipans heading to the sierras. Among them were two boys twisted and pale with fever. Over a meeting fire in the lee of a crumbling cinder cone, the elders told the Lipans about the girl in Yaqui lands who had risen from the dead and who filled the skull of a scalped warrior with mud, thus bringing him to life and at the same time teaching him the secrets of the earth. This warrior could now speak to the deer, could understand the words of the rockslides and the sandstorms.

The Lipan leader ordered his people to follow the old men to Cabora.

※

Teresita did not dream of them coming toward her. She did not see the villagers and the Lipans. She did not see Don Antonio Cienfuegos steering his wagon toward her from the hills, bearing his dying wife. She did not see Pancho Arteaga, the border bandit, coming to see her about the bullet lodged in his left buttock. She did not dream of the whores, Petra and Paloma, coming from Guaymas in a cart with their pox sores, or the García family from the silver mines with their father in a travois, or the nameless mother walking out of the wasteland with her dead baby wrapped in a tatter of blanket and slumped on her shoulder.

She straightened a lame man's arm.

Unless they fed fluids to her, she would not remember to take in water or juice. She still had not eaten solid food.

"You do not believe in God," she told her father. "Then you do not believe in love."

"Love!" he shouted. "What then of death? What of hunger, disease? What of your beloved Yaquis being slaughtered in the hills!"

"Love is hard, not soft," she said.

She wandered into the vaqueros' bunkhouse and laid her hands on a man who had sores on his legs. He sighed.

She told Gabriela: "The Virgin is as tall as I am. She warned me that love caused more pain than war."

That day, Gaby noticed the smell of roses coming from Teresita. She took her to her room, filled the bathing tub, and washed her. After she had toweled Teresita off, the smell was stronger than before.

"The Virgin," she said, "still laughs about the ladder."

But no one understood her; there was no one left who knew the story.

Forty-four

IT WAS LIKE A SUNRISE. She awoke one day and turned her head and looked in the corner of her room. There, her workbench held jars and leather pouches. Above, from the beams, hung her old dried herbs. And, as if it were any other morning, she tested herself.

Centaurea: boiled into a tonic to break fevers.

Jojoba: eases inflammation.

Verbena: sedates patients, stops blood from spilling.

Adormida: halts spasms.

Ruda: the uncivil little cousin that insults tapeworms out of the gut.

She smiled, enjoying the test. Early mornings were always hers alone. She lay there and worked her memory.

Estramío: the "Herb of Satan." Terrible odor, oval fruit, breaks into ten capsules. Ten ounces of leaves can make a tea strong enough to kill the largest man. Cured in the sun, rolled into cigarettes, these same leaves ease asthma, eye pains, epilepsy, and consumption.

She could smell herself, but it was a strange odor. It was . . . roses! How odd. She never wore perfumes.

She sniffed her armpits: rose scent. How sweet. The house girls, maybe even Gaby herself, had washed her.

They must have put some rose cream on her. Or perhaps they daubed her with rose cologne from Gaby's bedroom. But when?

She sat up, leaned forward over her knees to wait out a sudden attack of dizziness. When it passed, she stood and walked to the pitcher on the washstand in the corner. She poured water into the blue-edged bowl, tied her hair back, and washed her teeth. Then she washed her face. Goose bumps rose on her flesh.

She stepped to her closed window shutters and grabbed the handles, made hot as the sun burned into their outer surfaces. It was a small ritual she had, a small way to hold back the day — keeping her eyes shut and waiting before flinging the shutters wide. And she did it now, waiting one extra beat.

She was already throwing the shutters to the window open when she sensed it, and it was too late, and the full blast of sun hit her eyelids.

Her eyelids rose slowly, and she gasped. Before her, the land was full of bodies.

Below her, people milled on the ground of Cabora, and the mass of bodies extended from the front-porch gates to the far bee pastures. Faces turned to her. All movement stopped. Fingers rose to point her out. Pilgrims knelt. Old ones lay on pallets in the dirt. Children ran and shrieked. Soldiers sat their cavalry mounts. The clatter of cooking stilled. It became so quiet she could not believe she had not heard the noise before.

"There she is!" someone shouted.

"There! In the window!"

A woman cried, "Teresita!"

And another, "Heal me!"

And a third, "Santa Teresa!"

She flung herself back from the window and pressed herself to the wall, the scent of roses billowing up out of her nightgown. She suddenly knew, to her horror, that her own flesh was exuding the smell. Her own sweat had turned somehow to rose water. And Huila was dead! It was coming back. It was there, behind her eyes, starting to form.

Huila was dead.

And she herself was dead.

Now alive.

Dizziness took her again. She braced her hands on the hot wall.

She remembered the Mother's voice, before they sent her back, saying, "This gift we give, you must take back to the children. You may never profit from it, but give it freely."

And she had cried, "Don't make me go!"

"Your work is not done."

"Let me stay with you!"

"You must go back."

And she fell into her hot heavy stinking body. Not dreaming, returning. The lilt of wings in her veins melted back into meat and the slowness of blood. Her fingers slipped down her own fingers, as if they were empty gloves. She saw the blows that felled her. She saw the box and the cold face of Huila.

"No," she said.

And the vision expanded. She saw herself, inert and leaking a sweet pink scent. And the house girls bathed her in the tin tub, and the water came off her smelling too of roses. Everything she touched smelled like a fresh bloom. And the girls, after she was back in her bed, took the rose bathwater and put it in bottles and sold it to the pilgrims. And now the pilgrims smelled her. They drank her dirty water, blessed themselves on their foreheads with her smell. Hundreds of strangers passed her odor among themselves and used it to make signs of the cross as the little bottles went from hand to hand.

"I did not ask for this," she whispered. "Please do not do this to me."

But she knew it was already done.

She pushed away from the wall and looked back out the window.

"Teresa!" a crooked man shouted. "Help me! Have pity!"

And she did have pity. Perhaps pity was all she had.

"I will come to you," she said. "I have brought you a gift."

The pilgrims who sipped her essence from their little bottles were moved in strange unwelcome ways, tasting her though they'd never seen her. Hoping they might be blessed while thinking of the naked flesh the water had touched, while rolling her dirt and perfume on their tongues. Those who had smelled her, tasted her, poured her water over themselves, felt they owned her. She was now their lover, their saint, their mother, their friend. It was already too late to return to her old life.

And these pilgrims had continued to pour into Cabora, the thieves, the gypsies, the curious, the insane. Revolutionaries and spies circled the paddocks. Apaches lurked in the arroyo. Prostitutes came to be absolved and start life anew, or to open their legs in the barns and the bunkhouse and the shacks. Yaquis scattered rose petals saved from their Easter ceremonies. Highway bandits mingled among the believers and the fanatics, come at first to steal from the pilgrims, some of them converting and throwing their guns into the arroyo, where the Apaches promptly collected them. Drunks slept in the shade of the kitchen. They sniffed the air for the scent of roses. They fought with fists and knives out among the cattle. They stabbed a bull to death and left it to rot. Some preparatory students from Alamos drank their first mezcal and stoned a burro to death for fun. The cottonwood tree under which Aguirre had once slept was somehow knocked down, and once down, it was hacked with machetes and hatchets into firewood, its branches stripped to build ramadas in the dirt. The chickens that had slept on Aguirre's bed frame were slaughtered and eaten. The fence around the corn milpa fell. Horses, children, drunk old men trampled the maize plants. The hungry stripped ears of corn off the stalks and boiled them in fires fueled by the dead cottonwood and tumbled fence posts. Huila's extensive herb garden withered under a constant spray of urine from the wanderers. Her cilantro was gone in two days, sprinkled into salsa and over fetid beans to rescue their flavor. Her sage was not used for smudging or praise, but smeared on goat meat, stolen chickens, lizard meat.

"Don't worry," Teresita called to them. "I am coming to you now."

She wrapped her rebozo around her head, to respect the sun as Huila had taught her years before.

"Where is Lauro Aguirre?" Teresita asked, eating her third plate of eggs and nopal cactus.

She gulped black coffee, orange juice, tamarind juice. She had eaten yellow cheese and mango, papaya, and guayaba paste. She ripped tortillas apart and devoured the eggs with them.

"This is delicious!" she cried. "I could eat all day!"

Tomás stood away from the table, his hand on the butt of his pistol, watching her. He had forgotten to comb his hair. The vaqueros had awakened him with a report of pilgrims from Chihuahua killing a draft horse and butchering it beyond the eastern gates. Gaby sat at the end of the table and stared.

"Aguirre," he said, "is in Texas."

"Doing what, Father?"

"Fomenting revolution, no doubt," said Tomás.

Teresita scooped up a wad of beans and stuffed it in her mouth. She patted her lips with her napkin. Licked her fingers.

"How so?" she said.

"Aguirre has started a newspaper," Tomás said. "He publishes political stories."

"Politics," she cried.

Tomás glanced at Gabriela.

"Yes," he said.

"I love politics, Father," Teresita exclaimed. "I will write for Uncle Lauro."

"But," he sputtered, "what do you know of politics?"

"God gave this land to these people," she replied. "Other people want this land and are stealing it."

She drained her coffee cup and put it in the middle of her empty plate.

"Politics," she said.

❈

The pilgrims destroyed the little plazuela. Don Teófano could not keep them from kicking over the painted stones, from stealing the benches, from breaking apart the gazebo for firewood. They overran and crushed the small gardens in the cracked wheel rings. The lowest branches of the whitewashed alamos trees were stripped in three days and burned. Within a week, the entire space was full of tents and lean-tos.

Segundo and his men discovered two government snipers in the cottonwood grove where Teresita had been attacked by Millán. They roped the men, confiscated their Hawken rifles, and dragged them to the main house, where Segundo and Tomás sat in judgment over them in a hasty trial held in the kitchen. Tomás voted to allow the men to go free.

"Tell your masters," he said, "that we spared you."

"We won't be so easy on the next sons of whores that come around here," Segundo added.

They rode the two halfway to Alamos, then tossed them off their horses and cut them free.

"Don't come back," Segundo warned.

That day, Tomás ordered the building of a small chapel beside the main house. He couldn't have Teresita wandering the ranch without protection, and she didn't want guards, and she would not stop her morning prayers or whatever the hell it was she did in Huila's damned old cottonwood grove. He ordered cases of brandy and tequila. He smoked. He screamed at the builders to hurry, hurry, get the no-good church finished. Now.

And the word spread, no matter what fences Tomás mended, what walls he ordered built, what chapels he grew out of the cracked earth. They walked from the shores of the sea. They rode the new rail lines from Arizona to Guaymas, then rented wagons and came east. They

filtered down from the high peaks and the darkened
canyons of the sierra. They ate cactus, snake meat, crows.
They ate dogs and stale bread and they ate nothing. They
carried sacred cornmeal, or they carried sacred pollen, or
they carried sacred tobacco, or they carried rosaries and
Bibles, holy water, rattles, deer skulls, medicine bundles.
They bore weapons and they came naked. They carried
their dying and their dead, pulled travois with withered old
women thrusting their bone-knob knees at the sky. They
dragged sacks with bloated infants caught in the burlap
like wounded seals. They bound their green stinking limbs
in banana leaves, in foul bandages, in hemp ropes, tied
their crushed arms to their sides, made slings of old clothing and aprons. They bound their split feet together and
hobbled. They packed herbs in dank eyeholes where they
had been shot or stabbed, where wire had sliced their eye-
balls and infection and worms had destroyed their sight.
Their brown and red gums dripped blood when they spoke
her name. They left blood and bandages, pus and teeth,
abandoned dead and feces all along the trails and roads
that led to Cabora, snaky lines in the dirt, where a thousand feet hurried and crept, marching tirelessly to be near
Teresita. Soldiers bivouacked near the ranch abandoned
their posts and hid among the pilgrims.

Two thousand pilgrims gathered at Cabora to form the
first camp. In two weeks, the camp swelled to 5,000. One
month later, the count was 7,500 pilgrims — and 1,250
vendors, gawkers, fugitives, soldiers, and whores.

Reporters found the ranch infested with 10,000 campers.

El Monitor reported with some alarm that Teresita was
preaching "extremely liberal views." She was quoted as saying, "Everything the government does is morally wrong."

A colonel in the army, Antonio Rincón, took two hundred Yaquis, men, women, and children, prisoners, and carried them in the gunboat *El Demócrata* and dropped them in the ocean between the mouth of the Yaqui River and the seaport of Guaymas, all of them perishing. In the presidential palace in Mexico City, President Díaz first read of the atrocity in Lauro Aguirre's El Paso newspaper. The article was written by Teresa Urrea.

When the group of Mexican reporters arrived at Cabora, they were astounded to see the stinking, heaving, smoking mass of bodies. They had been sent by Díaz, increasingly alarmed by the Yaqui troubles in the north, and hearing more and more disturbing accounts of the "Girl Saint," this female *writer of propaganda*. On his orders, they had traveled north to write a satirical series of stories about the fanatic hick Joan of Arc and her tattered minions in their sandy kingdom. They had been told to expect a tumbledown peasant's hovel with naked savages prancing about, shaking spears. But Cabora was a vast estate, and the main house rose white behind adobe walls. A veranda ran the length of the house, and to the west, a round chapel rose to a red-tiled roof that stood above the roofline of the main house. Atop it, a small wooden cross. It looked like a lighthouse positioned on an island in a sea of human flesh.

The leader of the expedition, a political writer of some renown in Mexico City, was completely bald. When Buenaventura led him to Don Tomás, he found a frantic man who dashed across the ranch with no seeming sense of direction.

"What do you want?" barked Tomás.

"We have come to see the saint," the reporter replied.

Tomás glared at him for a moment. "There is no fucking saint on this ranch!"

He was later quoted by the reporter in *El Imparcial:*

"The day I believe my daughter to be a saint is the day she causes hair to grow on your —— head!"

Thus welcomed to Cabora, the reporters threaded their way through the crowds and found themselves standing before the porch where Teresita attended to the pilgrims. She greeted them and invited them in. They remained in her company behind closed doors for the next several hours. When they wrote their articles, they alarmed President Díaz further by extolling her virtues, reporting several miracles performed in their presence, and suggesting that the government attend to native rights in the issue of the land thievery and genocide currently taking place along the Río Mayo and Río Yaqui valleys. But the part of the story the People most delighted in was the part about the bald reporter. Before he left the ranch, he sought out Tomás. He didn't say a word to him. He only bent toward the patrón and rubbed the peach fuzz that had appeared on his head and laughed.

Forty-five

SHE ROSE IN THE COOLNESS of the earliest morning. Teresita could no longer go out to the sacred spot to pray or burn sage. Instead, she stared out her window at the heaving shadow of the masses, as if hills had slunk toward her home in the dark and lay without, breathing. She would wash her teeth because it felt wrong to pray with a dirty mouth. She knelt in the dark and lit candles and prayed. Her altar was bare — no santos. She knelt before a bare wooden cross. Huila's glass of water was to the right of the cross. A small picture of the old one stood in a silver frame to the left, not as a saint, but as a reminder of all she had learned. Far to the right of the cross, beyond the few candles in their small cups, stood a figure of Guadalupe, standing on her moon, roses in her cape. Teresita did not pray to her, though she did like to say good morning.

It was half past four in the morning.

After her prayers, which were painful because her knees protested being pressed to the tiles of her floor, she pushed herself up and went to her basin and washed. She did not like to take long baths anymore, for fear that the maids would still take her water away and sell it.

She carried an oil lamp and made her way to the kitchen, where she ate a light breakfast with the cooks. Lately, she had gotten weary of meats of all kinds. Even fish made her feel poisoned. She sometimes ate eggs — it was hard not to like eggs scrambled with cactus and salsa. But she mostly ate bananas and chicken fideo soup — broth and noodles, no meat. She liked rolls dipped in coffee, perhaps a few slices of goat cheese and some boiled mango in a bowl. Guayaba, prunes, papaya when it came, prickly pears, tortillas with butter.

At six she greeted Tomás and Gabriela and often helped serve them their breakfasts. Then she retreated to Tomás's library and attended to letters, hoping for some from her dear "uncle" Aguirre. Since her awakening, she had not found time to read literature. She had wanted to read the Spanish versions of Mark Twain — picaresque boys! That would be so amusing! But the time never seemed to offer itself to her. She often opened the scriptures at random, to see what God's message to her that day might be. His random directions to her were occasionally baffling — Leviticus 14, for example, and its orders to kill a lamb and put its blood on somebody's earlobe and on somebody else's thumb. What, Lord? She kept these arcane passages from Tomás.

After God had spoken to her through the Book, she went outside, offering greetings to those gathered at the door. Usually, the day began with well-wishers and pilgrims who had come to shake her hand or offer an endearment. They brought her gifts — a chicken, a basket of cookies, a small stone idol of a heathen god, a nugget of gold, a knit shawl, a writhing pink piglet (she was always partial to pigs), a donkey, five pesos wrapped in dirty cloth, locks of hair tied in ribbon and offered to her as a manda to bargain for God's blessings, the wrapping cloth from a dead infant brought as the most valuable thing the mother owned. Teresita accepted all gifts, even the ones that were too dear. She knew that the giving was the important thing. If she turned away their presents, she would really be turning the giver away. So Segundo ate the cookies. The coins and gold went to Tomás — she did not know what he did with them. She didn't want to know.

Father Gastélum sometimes appeared on their porch on these early mornings. She knew he was watching her for irregularities and heresies. She did not disappoint him —

when she began to preach against priests, he turned crimson and scribbled in his notebooks.

"For God," she preached from her porch, "religions are nothing, signify nothing. Because positive religions are generally nothing more than words — words without feeling. Religions are practices that focus on the surface of things, that affect only the senses, but that fail to touch the soul, and fail to come from the soul. For that reason, these words and practices fail to reach our Father. What our Father wants from us is our emotions, our feelings. He demands pure love, and that love, that sentiment, is found only in the selfless practice of love, of good, of service.

"We are nothing compared to our Father. Without doubt, the honeyed words pronounced by our lips don't even reach our hearts. How could they reach God's ears? How can we hope to love God if we can't even love our neighbors? We don't even see God! A black cloud hides Him from us!"

Like the Protestants they called "Los Aleluyas," the People shouted, "Amen!"

"Let us do good," she preached. "Let us love. This is the only religion. Let us put aside our hatred and take up love. Yes, brothers and sisters — the doing of good is the only prayer that God requires. Work!"

Gastélum cried, "What of clergy? What of the Mass?"

"Priests love because they are ordered to love."

"How dare you!"

"I don't need Rome to tell me how to love."

Tomás, on that morning, invited the good father into the house for some coffee and the latest magazines.

"Ay, hija," he hissed at her as the affronted priest huffed into the parlor.

Teresita extended her hand toward the crowd.

"This, Father," she said, "is the true church."

He looked out at the beggars, filthy rabble, dying, crippled, insane; he looked upon the horse thieves and bandits, the whores and the idiot children tied to posts, at the malformed and the criminals; he saw Indians and peasants and fat bastards from Arizona desperately herding their sick children. Beyond, soldiers and Rurales watched from their horses. Drunks fell among the bushes.

"Wonderful," he said.

He slammed the door.

⁂

By 9:00 a.m. the healings and advising sessions had begun.

A girl from Guaymas with an issue of blood. Teresita saw a dull glow in her womb the size of an apple. She rubbed the girl's belly and whispered the Lord's Prayer in her ear. They laughed.

Blindness.

"But your eyes are gone," she told the man.

"I thought you could grow me new eyes."

"You left your eyes on a barbed-wire fence!" she said.

He hung his head.

"I was drunk and riding in the dark."

"I'm sorry."

"Oh well."

A man with a twisted arm, lame from a mule kick.

Old bullet wounds to the back.

Tuberculosis.

Sadness.

Pregnancy needing a blessing.

The crowds had grown so large that Tomás had hired

assistants to manage the flow. Teresita sat on a kitchen chair on the porch, and the helpers brought the thirsty forward all morning. Bloody cough. Diarrhea. Festering leg wounds. Pain. More pain. Unfocused pain in the belly. Lumps in the breast. Nipples drooling clear fluid. Rotten teeth. Blood coming from the rectum.

"Do you need to see my *fundillo?*" the man asked.

"No, thank you," she replied. "Your description was adequate."

A child who could not stand or speak.

A dead infant wrapped in burlap.

"Mother," Teresita said, "I cannot raise her."

"Can you bless her?"

"Let us bless her together."

She called for Segundo and his boys to take the mother and the infant to the cemetery and help her bury her child.

By lunchtime, her hips and knees and back hurt from bending to all the pilgrims in her hard chair. She rose painfully and stretched. Raised her hands over the crowd and blessed them.

"I will be back soon," she said.

They applauded. They called her name. Someone threw flowers at her feet. A few hours later, she returned for more.

※

Teresita was so sore on some evenings that she limped. Her throat was parched. Strawberry juice always made her happy — especially if there were pieces of strawberry floating in it.

They talked or sang or read to each other until supper at nine. Teresita often sat and listened to the day's news as her father rattled the paper and declaimed. She ate fruit for supper, and she ate quickly. She was in bed by nine-thirty. She was often startled to remember she had gotten in bed without praying, but was too tired to get back up.

On Sundays, she sat in the courtyard and enjoyed the flowers. Then she went up to her room and opened her inkwell and took up her pen. Otherwise, she only had time before she went to bed, squinting in the light of a candle, and she would often fall asleep with her head on the page. On Mondays, a buckaroo would carry her articles to Alamos and post them to Texas.

Forty-six

THE TIGERS OF THE SIERRA had left their village of Tomóchic and followed the River of Spiders as it flowed west and down, falling in rapids and cataracts until it bent away from their path, as if the desert below were too extreme, too hot for water, and the river shied away to hide in less volatile light. A rear guard of nine riflemen waited in the foothills for their return. When the waters left the men, they began to trot. They were sons of the Papigochic, partly descended from the great Tarahumara, and like the Tarahumara, the Tigers could run for hundreds of miles when they were hunting or at war, their dark carbines across their backs, muzzle down, tied on with string and rope. Machetes and long knives rode their hips, and leather water bottles and, for those who required comfort, a blanket to sleep in when they finally stopped beneath the stars. Their sandals had soles of leather, softened and dyed by immersion in human feces, tied to their feet by knotted rope. Like the Yaquis, they were Catholic, and they wore rough crosses around their necks. None of them had ever seen a tiger and no one knew where the name Tigre came from. But there it was.

Like their namesakes, they were silent, relentless, and deadly. Catholics who rejected Rome, they maintained an uneasy truce with the nomad Mexican priests who brought their endless circuit ride of masses and ceremonies through el norte. The Tigers still owed allegiance to a long-dead Jesuit who was said to fly over mountain passes, who could walk through a mile-high fin of pure stone and appear, an hour hence, in the next village down the mountains, a man who was reported in Navojoa and Tomóchic at the same time, on the same day. These stories the Tigers took as gospel, the medicine of Christ. If they had seen the messiah Niño Chepito in his Sal Si Puedes valley, they would have shot him.

The Tigers rejected the ways of the lowlanders. These Tomochitecos were farmers and silver miners and hunters and traders who answered to one man only — a fighter selected by the village, who was also their pastor and warrior chief. This man, part medicine man and part priest, interpreted scriptures for them, led the daily church services, and counseled the people in all matters great and small. He was the lawgiver and the judge, the religious leader and the war maker. He commanded the militia.

Cruz Chávez.

He could read, and he started every day with a scripture

reading for all gathered. The women covered their heads, and the men carried rifles. Each man was expected to defend his family, his church, his village, and his crops, in that order. Each citizen of Tomóchic was free to offer an insight or opinion about that day's Bible verse.

Cruz carried his Bible in a small backpack woven of wool. He was a righteous man, whose only vice was smoking hand-rolled cigarettes, though in that place tobacco was not known as a vice. He was a mighty guerrilla fighter, and he was told by the angels that he was the godliest man in Mexico. This led him to announce — it only made sense — that he was the acting Pope of the Mexican Republic, and as such, he was the final authority on all matters Mexican.

He was a tall man with a barrel chest. He wore a thick black beard, carried a Winchester repeater rifle everywhere he went. He had learned to read and write in his time away from the mountains, a time he considered wasted, except for the learning. He maintained a small milpa of corn, and he hunted deer for the village. He had three children. He was descended from Spaniards, but the people of Tomóchic did not hold that against him.

Cruz Chávez put up with Padre Gastélum, even though he found him rude. Not wishing to entirely alienate Gastélum, and loath to bring overmuch government attention down on their own heads, the Tigers invited him to give guest sermons. He leapt at the opportunity — and he bullied and lashed them when he took the pulpit, sometimes for over an hour. They were children; they must follow the orders of their fathers in Mexico City; they must come under the control of the Mother Church. Not surprisingly, it was his impassioned denunciation of Teresita — a heretical Indian half-breed, he exclaimed, fanatical enemy of the great General Díaz, consort of the warlike Yaquis — that first caught the Tigers' interest.

❊

When they came out of the trees, and then out of the foothills, onto the terrible plain of Sonora, they decided to trot to Cabora. Cruz took the lead, then his rifleman, Rubén. And following, not slowed at all by his affliction, came old José Ramírez, his neck twisted and purple with a tumor. It had been growing at the base of his skull for years, and although nobody stared at him in his village, they all said that one day it would grow big enough to snap his neck bone and kill him.

War parties had parleyed with Cruz in his fortified home west of the town church. They came quietly and squatted in the dark, smoking clay pipes and reed pipes, holding their guns and their bows. Rarámuri runners came, Yaqui spies, some Chiricahua and Mescalero. Pima traders passed through Tomóchic and accepted his invitations to eat with him, to speak of this new saint of the lowlands.

She had healed the sick, they said. And she preached revival. Dangerous revival — even war. *War,* he said, *what saint preaches war?* They had heard her with their own ears, this half-Yori girl, sweet in her face, but strong and sturdy in her spine, telling them that God himself had given them their lands.

"Do you believe in God? Do you believe in justice?" she had asked them. And they murmured *Yes, yes — God, justice.* "Do you? For the governors and the soldiers, the priests and the presidents, they are spiders, falling upon you, drinking the blood of your children! Do you believe?

"Do you believe God put your feet on this land? God

gave land to every man and woman! And this is your land! This land is holy! *Do you believe?*"

Yes! We believe!

"These octopi strangle you with their sinful arms. Greed! Greed is a sin! No man, whether he is white or brown, can take the land from you! It came from God! Only God may take it away from you!

"Tell me now! DO YOU BELIEVE?"

They had yelled her name. They had danced. They had lifted their hands and fallen to the ground.

She had smiled.

"This is not a call to war," the Pope of Mexico said.

"It is to us," his men said.

It took them two days of running. At night, they slept close together on the hard ground, their feet overlapping, each body heating the other. Traditionally, the one in the middle changed each night so all members of a party could have one night's warmth, though Cruz and Rubén had voted to keep José in the center on this mission.

Cruz would give this saint a simple test. She could heal José, or she could fail to heal him. And if she failed, Tomóchic would renounce her as another imposter.

They squatted in the morning and ate jerked venison and berries from pouches on their belts. A swallow of water each. A pebble in the mouth to make refreshing spit. Cruz pointed to the west and set out at a brisk pace. The others fell in behind.

Cruz found the arroyo before noon, and they ran along its edge. They found the first of Lauro Aguirre's dams, and they stopped to look at the green water. They'd been running for only three hours — they didn't need a drink yet, but it was refreshing to look. Already, little willows and alamos trees were sprouting on the banks.

Cruz ran until the main house was in sight, then he slowed to a walk.

All three of them pulled their rifles around in front of them and walked with their weapons across their chests, ready to fade into the brush and shoot anyone who threatened them.

They stopped at a small camp to stare at a twisted child writhing on a pallet. Her knees were terrible balls of bone, and her hands formed claws that scraped the air. She strained her head to look at them, and she seemed to laugh, though it could have been a scream.

Cruz spoke to the mother:

"Sister, what is wrong with your child?"

"No one knows, señor," she said. "She was always like this. It is the will of God."

Cruz looked at his companions.

It was a good answer.

They approved.

."God," he said. "If it is His will, then why have you come here to try to change it?"

"It may be His will to heal her now," the mother said. "Glory be to God."

Cruz leaned on his rifle.

"Do you believe God changes His mind?"

"God does what God does." She blessed herself. "It is not for me to question. I come to God as a child, asking favors of her father."

He nodded. The girl on the pallet strained her arm toward him. He reached out with one finger and touched her hand. She clutched his finger.

"You are very pretty," he said to her. "Will you marry me?"

She grimaced and shouted.

It sounded like *Yot!*

The mother laughed.

"She says no. You are very old and hairy for her. She is laughing."

Cruz tipped his hat to the girl. He smiled down at her.

"What is her name?" he asked.

"Conchita."

Conchita pulled at his finger and made her sounds. He gently pried his finger out of her grasp. He winked at her. She flung her hands over her mouth.

"Has she seen the saint?"

"No, señor. Not yet."

"Why not."

The woman extended her hand.

"Many pilgrims," she said. "Many pilgrims."

A screen of mesquite trees obscured his view of the house.

"If this saint is real," he said, "we will carry Conchita to her."

"Gracias, señor," she said.

"Adios, beloved," he said to Conchita. "We could have been happy together. I leave with a broken heart."

Yot! She laughed.

Feo!

He nodded to her mother and walked on. Stopped. Came back.

"Do you know who I am?" he asked.

She shook her head.

"We're from Tomóchic," José said.

It meant nothing to her.

"In the Sierra Madre."

"Ah!"

She was afraid of the Sierra Madre. It was a place of crags, ice, Apaches, wolves. She shuddered. Surely, these men were warriors.

"I am the leader of Tomóchic," Cruz said. "I am Cruz Chávez. I am the Pope of Mexico."

Conchita drew a squealing breath and laughed again.

"Benditos sean," her mother whispered.

Cruz made the sign of the cross over them. He hefted his rifle onto his shoulder and walked away. His warriors followed, blessed by the Lord, reconciled, holy in this day He had made, and ready to shoot.

They came in sight of the great house, and it shimmered in the light.

The pilgrims were arrayed before the home, spread far. Smoke and dust. The Tigers wandered through the camps, looking down at the sick and twisted, the merely old and the truly lame. Blind children. Limp babies. Some of the small camps had corpses wrapped in cloth from head to foot and being loaded onto wagons. And hucksters — men selling Teresita scapulars — wandered the yards. Men sold tin pictures of the Saint and her small angels. Women sold tacos, small woven crosses made of black string, ears of corn, fermented-maize beer. A soldier stumbled into Cruz.

He laid the barrel of his rifle against the man's shoulder and said, "Leave this place."

The man swallowed once and hurried away.

"This," Cruz said to a salesman. "This picture?"

"It is the Saint. One peso."

"One peso! For a picture?"

"Yes, yes, but this picture will stop a bullet."

They walked on.

Cruz led them through the throng. He pushed his way ahead of the many who waited before her door, and when they started to protest, he looked down at them and they fell silent. When he took his place at the front of the crowd, they scooted back, made room for him. He took off his hat. He squatted on his haunches and laid his rifle across his knees. With the rest of them, the sick and the curious, the crooks and the mothers, the blind and the dying, he waited for her to appear.

Forty-seven

TERESITA CAME OUT THE DOOR, wiping her hands on a cloth.

Cruz watched her move — she was light on her feet. She flowed out the door almost before he saw it was open, her dark dress seeming to materialize from the darker space within. Yet when she stopped, her roots seemed to plunge deep into the earth, as if she were drawing water up through the crust, as if she were a slender alamo glittering in the wind. He approved.

"Pretty," José said.

Cruz nodded. He didn't feel it was right to show too much enthusiasm for her looks, but he noticed them. Still, he warned José: "That's enough of that."

Her hair was pinned up, and her face was clear. She was slender, and he could see a light fuzz of hair along the hinge of her jaw.

She smiled at the crowd and said, "Where should we begin?"

They cried her name and reached for her, they wept and sang and made the same mewling little noises beggars made to get a passerby's attention. A woman to Cruz's right produced a baby. It was wrapped in a rough length of cloth, and it coughed wetly and kicked its feet. The woman held the baby out toward Teresita — like a chicken, Cruz thought.

"Let me see him," Teresita said.

She took the infant in her arms and lifted the cloth off his face. He coughed again, ragged and bloody.

"Consumption," Cruz said to his men.

"He's an angel, señora," Teresita said. "Poor boy."

"Sí, mi santa. Sí, Santa Teresa."

"He has consumption."

Cruz nodded at his men.

"What did I say? What did I say?" he demanded.

They patted him on the back.

Teresita passed her hand over the boy. Cruz watched her fingers, as they struck strange poses in the air over the child's body. Then she laid her hand upon the boy's chest. The baby stopped coughing, but what did that prove?

Teresita gestured to an assistant, and she whispered in the girl's ear. She ran inside, and after a few moments, came out with a bundle.

"Make a cigar with these leaves," Teresita said. "Blow the smoke in his face."

"How often?"

"Morning and night."

The woman kissed her hand.

"He will be well," she said, handing the baby back to the mother.

"Gracias, Santa," the woman cried, falling to one knee. "Gracias!"

Teresita blushed. She pulled the woman back up to her feet.

"No, no," she said. "You mustn't thank me. It comes from above."

Later, Cruz would hear her explain repeatedly that she was not a saint. Her favorite line seemed to be: *I am only a woman.*

This also met with his approval.

A bustling group of nuns pushed forward. She smiled at them, took all their small hands in hers, and said to the oldest, "Bless me, Mother."

She went down on one knee as the old nun laid a hand on her head. Then she rose, and they whispered and laughed and then the nuns went on their way.

After a few hours of watching her, Cruz stood. His knees cracked.

"You, Saint," he called.

"Did that hurt?" she asked, glancing at his legs. His men giggled. He shot them a look.

"You," he repeated, for he did not know what else to say. "Saint."

She looked him up and down. She looked at his rifle, at his dusty huaraches.

"You, Warrior," she said.

"We have come from Tomóchic to see you," he said.

She smiled.

"Tomóchic? Really? All this way?"

"You know of us?" he said.

"Everyone knows of Tomóchic," she replied.

This made him stand taller.

"I did not know that," he said.

She came close and looked at them.

"The Tigers of the Sierra have come to see me."

She grinned. She made a muscle. "Great fighters. Great lovers of God." Teresita laughed as she flexed her arm.

Cruz was tongue-tied. She burned into his eyes with her own. Was she making fun of him?

"I have come to test you," he managed to say.

She put her fists on her hips and stared at him quite frankly. He did not appreciate the boldness of her stare. "How will you test me, Tiger? Shall we shoot at cans? Race horses?" She put up her dukes. "Fistfight?"

Cruz opened his mouth and said, "Uh."

"If you try to wrestle me," she warned, "I can beat you."

"Wrestle?"

José stepped forward. He clutched his soft straw hat off his head.

"What he means to say, Miss Saint, Miss Teresita, señorita, is that our village hopes to make you our saint, our *patron saint,* you see, and he must see if you are real . . . miss." His nerves were getting the better of him. He suddenly shouted, "I am José!"

She put her hand out to him. He took it. She squeezed his hand slightly. He squeezed back and blushed.

"Look at that, Don José," she said. "My hand is flesh and bone. I am real."

"Sí, señorita," he said.

"But I am not a saint."

"No, señorita," he said.

She let go of his hand.

"They say I am a saint. But you see, dear José . . . like you, I am only a servant."

"A servant, yes."

He was suddenly scared out of his wits. The Saint of Cabora was talking to him!

"Of the Creator," she said.

This stirred up a babble of religious chatter from the crowd.

"And the People," she said.

Teresita stepped up on the porch.

"But I am tired. You will have to test me tomorrow, señores."

"José," cried José. "Please. Just call me José."

Cruz was watching this exchange with raised eyebrows. Teresita smiled.

"Joseph, like the father of Jesus," she said.

José hung his head and blushed some more.

"Why," she exclaimed, "you look exactly like Saint Joseph."

"I do?"

"Without a doubt."

She gestured for him to come closer.

"We must fix that growth on your neck."

He covered it with his hand.

"Tomorrow," she promised.

She turned away, but before she went in the door, she looked back at Cruz.

"And you, Tiger? What is your name?"

"Cruz Chávez!" he bellowed, a little too loud. Caught himself snapping to attention. He cleared his throat and slouched a little. Then he informed her: "I am the Pope of Mexico."

"Oh my!" she said.

She glanced at José.

"He is a little crazy, no?" she said.

José laughed, though Cruz glared at him.

"That's all right," she said. "People say I am crazy, too."

She stretched and sighed and opened the door, and before she slipped inside, she said, "I am glad to meet you, Cruz Chávez. It's about time we had a Mexican pope!"

The door slammed.

The three warriors stood there.

"Is she laughing at me?" Cruz said.

Both of his men replied, "Yes."

The next morning, they were waiting for her. She came forth at eight o'clock, eating an apple.

"Saint Joseph," she said, holding her free hand out to José.

He hurried up to the porch, and she gestured toward the door. He took his hat off and peeked inside. He hung his head, glanced back at Cruz and Rubén, giggled, and stepped in.

"Your Holiness," she said to Cruz. "You may sit here."

She gestured to a swing, hung from the porch rafters on chains.

"I —" he said, but before he could finish she had gone through the door and closed it.

Pulling himself up as tall as possible, Cruz stepped onto the porch and sat on the swing. It rocked back, and he leapt to his feet. He had never seen a swing. He ordered Rubén onto it, and he watched Rubén sway. Cruz stopped it with his foot and he joined his rifleman. He used the butt of his rifle to push them back and forth. Rubén turned to him and smiled. Cruz remained stoic. He had slept little. His mind jumped and sparked with Teresita. Her eyes, her voice. Those roving hands. When he finally fell asleep, he dreamed that they fished trout in the rivers of Tomóchic. He caught very big fish, and she admired him.

Presently, Tomás appeared on the porch. He stared out at the mob and shook his head. He turned to the two on his swing and said, "Who are you?"

Cruz stood and gripped his upright rifle in two fists.

"I am the Pope of Mexico," he said.

Tomás gawked at him.

"Jesus Christ!" he said. "Another maniac!"

He jumped off the porch and stormed away, pushing pilgrims aside as he went.

Cruz sat back down, resumed swinging.

"What's his problem?" he said.

The door regularly opened, and her assistants came forth to gather a child or two, but she did not reappear.

Cruz opened his Bible and read silently, while Rubén snored. Flies came, wandered their faces, then flew away. It was another day. Hot. Dry. Full of invisible motion. The windmill barely stirred, and it squealed, squealed, squealed. The pilgrims slumbered. Squeal. Squeal. A horse shifted, its hoof clopping once. Bees moved above them all, sniffing their breath as it rose.

Cruz drifted into sleep. In his dream, Teresita was covered in blood. "Help me!" she cried. When he awoke, he jerked to his feet. José stood before him, clutching his rifle.

"What happened?" Cruz asked.

"She touched me." José looked down at him kindly — now that he was to be the new Saint Joseph, he was sure his countenance must reflect a certain holy glow. "After she touched me, she healed a deaf boy. It was the most remarkable scene, Hermano Cruz. She took him in her arms and whispered to him. It seemed odd, I admit, to whisper into a closed ear. But the boy suddenly smiled, and they laughed at some small joke." He shrugged. "I don't know what she said. But the boy's father fell to his knees and praised God. He knew right away that the boy could hear."

"Amen," said Rubén, just to add something.

"And then?" Cruz demanded.

"Cookies."

"Cookies!"

"Cookies and coffee."

José smiled in a saintly fashion.

"The boy had milk. We had coffee — with honey!"

Cruz pondered this report for a moment.

José had a blue bandana tied around his neck.

"Show me your tumor," Cruz said.

But before the cloth could be removed, Teresita was standing before them. She curtsied to Cruz.

"Your Holiness," she said.

Rubén snickered.

Cruz spun on him and fixed him with a stormy glare.

Teresita looked at Rubén and said, "You. What is your name?"

"Rubén."

"You are a warrior."

"Sí."

"Are you a killer?"

"Perdón?" he said.

"Do you kill, Rubén? Do you kill men?"

Rubén grabbed his rifle and hopped off the porch and ran away.

"You are unnerving my men," Cruz told her.

Teresita sat on the swing.

"Cruz Chávez," she said. "I am ready for my test now. Shall I fetch a pencil and paper?"

José grinned at him.

"José," he said. "Go away."

"I will find Rubén," Saint Joseph said.

They were alone, if being watched through the windows by family and servants could be considered alone, if ten thousand eyes in front of them watching their every move were a form of privacy.

He looked at her out of the corner of his eye. The way the light caught Teresita illuminated her hair like small lightning bolts. She smelled like roses. She patted the seat beside her, and he sat down. They swayed slightly. The tumult of the beggars and lame had faded into a steady rumble, almost beyond his hearing. He cleared his throat, but he had nothing to say. A small boy ran up to her and gave her a bouquet of clover blossoms. She embraced him. The boy ran back into the crowd.

"Do you fish?" he blurted.

"Excuse me?"

"Nothing."

They rocked. The noise around them was muffled, as if by cotton. Bits of metal flared in the light. Everything seemed as if it was across a wide valley. Bees inspecting the madreselva vines on the wall were louder than the voices of the People.

She said, "I do believe, señor, that this is the easiest test I have ever taken."

He cleared his throat.

"Don't worry," he reassured her, "you are doing well so far."

She accepted a mango from a drunkard who patted her head.

"How do you stand it?" Cruz asked.

"What?"

"This," lifting his hand to the wall of faces before them.

"It is my work," she said. "Do they make you nervous?"

"Many," he said. "Son muchos."

"Not so many pilgrims in Tomóchic, I imagine."

He blew air out through his lips.

"Four hundred," he said. "Five hundred live there. Pilgrims? Perhaps ten, twenty at a time."

"And do many come to seek counsel with you?" she asked.

"A few." He looked away. "Not many." He tapped on the floorboards with his rifle butt. "Not like this."

"Ah. Well, this."

She sighed.

"These are nine, ten thousand. I never thought of it, Cruz Chávez, but I had never before seen this many people in one place." She stared out at them. "It's really quite interesting."

"I saw this many," he said. "In Guaymas. Didn't like it. Went back to the mountains."

He looked at her. Grinned. She smiled.

"I don't like it much, either," she noted.

They rocked.

"Lemonade, Señor Chávez?" she offered.

"No."

"Bueno."

"But," he said, "how can you stand this, this crowd? How can you sleep? Eat? All these sick people calling to you."

"Those who presume to save, señor, win a cross."

He'd heard that one before.

"You are not here to save?"

"I am here to serve. But I am also here to live. I offer my work to God, and I stop when I am finished for the day."

"Some could die," he protested.

"I have been dead. I will die again."

He looked at her for a moment.

"What if one dies while you sleep?"

"Then they were supposed to die. I can only do what I can do. To try to do more would be a lie. A lie is worse than doing nothing."

"Is this God's will?" he said.

"God?" Teresita sighed. "For you, God is a notion. Not for me. You must remember, great Tiger, that unlike you, I have met God."

He pushed the swing with his rifle.

"And what is God like?" he asked.

She turned to him and smiled.

"He's not as serious as you."

He nodded.

"Ah," he said.

"God doesn't carry a gun," she said.

They laughed.

"Cruz Chávez."

She nudged him. He didn't feel any kind of electrical charge or miraculous energies.

"A hundred years from now, when they remember you, they will all say, *He was so serious*."

He frowned.

"Is this a word of prophecy?" he asked.

She shook her head, then punched him on the arm.

"I'm getting some lemonade," she said. "I will bring you some. Don't worry, you don't have to drink it."

She jumped up and went back to the door, and when she rose, their voices rose with her, and her name floated higher into the air, and they cried, they pleaded, they begged. Softly, as if hoping not to insult them, she closed the door behind her.

Cruz set the sweating glass down on the boards of the porch.

"What do you think our work is here on earth?" he asked.

"Love for God, love for each other. Reconciliation. Service." She poked him with a finger. "Joy!"

"Joy," he said. He squinted into the distance and said, "See those armed riders out there? Do you know what gives them joy? Killing the People, taking scalps. That is what makes them happy. Did you know that when they burn a village, or shoot the men and take the women, they always laugh? You never heard so much laughter as when those men are killing the People."

She crossed her arms.

"I have heard that laughter."

"No you haven't."

You don't know me, she thought. But Huila had taught her well: men postured and wise women let them.

"They pierce infants," he said, "and they laugh. They cut off the heads of women, and they laugh. That is joy to them."

"I see," she said.

She sipped her lemonade, turned to him.

"I will consider adopting a theology of misery, then," she said. "In honor of you."

He hadn't meant to sound so harsh. He felt like an idiot talking to this willow of a girl. He wondered if she knew he was smelling her.

"So," he said. "You are finished for the day." He waved at the pilgrims.

"For the day, yes. Even Jesus ate supper. Even Jesus slept. Jesus probably — I don't mean to upset you, Tiger — took baths and went to the bathroom."

Cruz did, in fact, draw breath. An unwelcome picture of Jesus and the apostles urinating on roadside bushes invaded his mind. He had never, not once, imagined the Lord pissing. This girl was bold, he was sure of that. Possibly a heretic.

"I will eat supper," she said, "and I will go to bed. I'm tired. I cannot do the impossible."

"God can do the impossible," he proclaimed.

"Really?" she said. "Then why does He not cure all of these suffering people, right now?"

"I don't know."

"Tell me which is worse, Pope Chávez — is it that God *cannot* cure them all, or that He *will not* cure them?"

Cruz was silent. He had no answer. He resented the question.

"This," she said, "is what I live with."

He shrugged.

"You should know the answer," she said. "You should know what it is you really think of God."

She got up from the seat.

"Then," she continued, "you should decide why the president of Mexico does not help these people."

She drained her glass with a long swallow, set the glass on the plank floor, and held out her hand.

"Decide where you stand on the matter."

He took her hand. Her grip was dry and firm, but soft. He resisted the urge to feel her knuckles with his thumb.

"God likes tools," she said. "You and I, we are the tools of God. We cannot afford to rust or break. Do you see?"

She leaned in quickly and kissed his grizzled cheek.

"Good night," she whispered. "Pope."

Forty-eight

Cabora, Sonora
This Pinche Madhouse

Aguirre, You Cowardly Son of a Whore!
Aguirre, Quaking in Fear in Tejas!
Pinche Aguirre, My Dear Friend and Mentor!

Ay, cabrón, if you could see this madness! This insanity. Somehow, I have used my substantial and legendary loins to sire the Female Christ. By Christ! And oh, Christ. . . .

Have you ever noticed, you nearsighted visionary, how many words we have for "fool"? Idiota, simple, tonto, baboso, pendejo, mamón, buey, retrasado, imbécil, bobo, sonso, bruto, menso! A million phrases. But what words are there to describe religious fanaticism? I shan't say "holiness," cabrón, because I cannot claim my daughter is "holy." But these mensos, etc., can only think of one word for this insane behavior of Teresa's, and that is in the epithet "Saint"!

Saint!

Oh how rich! My bastard daughter a saint. What next? Will they see me as Moses, perhaps? Will I part the Sea of Cortés and walk to Baja California? Say, that wouldn't be so bad, come to think of it. We could open a gold mine!

Oye! Pay attention to what I say!

*Saint Teresa is now preaching bizarre antigovern-
ment and antichurch sermons. If it weren't so alarming, it would be pathetic. Circumspection dictates that
I leave her mute on the page. You can infer what you
wish.*

*And allow me this moment to thank you, you imbe-
cilic piece of shit, for starting this new wave of mania
with your little Texan fish-wrap newspaper! Who ever
told you it would be smart to allow Teresa to endanger us all with written screeds about the Yaquis! Eh?
CHINGADO, Aguirre.*

Well, I must go soon.

*The "pilgrims" (ha ha ha) have now destroyed two
cornfields, have killed seven cows, and have overflowed the old outhouses. We have holy shit flooding
the camps!*

Perhaps it is one of your biblical plagues?

A rain of turds on Egypt.

*We all miss you here, and I hope this finds you well.
(Note, please, that I did not say "I pray . . . ," eh!)*

> *Tu Amigo Cansado y Casi Loco,*
> *Tomás*

El Paso, Tejas
Later That Same Year

My Dear Saint Tomás, also known as the Doubter:

*You heretic dog, you low rancher, you rural clod,
I greet thee from the metropolitan grandness that is*

El Paso. Thou dost not imagine the sophisticated delights of this fine city — the stink of cows, the turds of noble steeds that pass gaseous blasts as the horses totter down these dirty streets about to keel over in a swoon of hunger and neglect, the bowlegged Texan with his squinty eye and his globs of tobacco drool staining every post, corner, tree trunk, and stray dog. My great friend, pistoleros clump along the wooden sidewalks of this city, and sheriffs with six-guns upon their skinny hips eye the wanderer, and ladies with parasols turn their faces away from Mexicans! El Paso! Yesterday, some wicked fools fell upon an illegally employed Chinaman with rocks. The Americans are deeply offended by Chinamen crossing into their country uninvited. Ah, but the railroads must go on. Industry will foment the next Americano revolution, just as land reform and indigenous rights will fuel our own.

I beseech thee, my dear amigo de mi corazón, survive the dreary desert wastes! Give succor to the revolt! For surely the forces of the regime must topple! The noble Apache! The fierce Yaqui! The angry Papago and the pacific Pima and the yoked masses of the mestizo campesinos will rise! Down with Díaz. You must agree.

Teresita, the phenomenon of Teresita, is something we attend to from afar. In her lies hope, my brother. In her lies the flaming ember of liberation for all Mexicans. Revolt!

By the way, I tried a most interesting lime ice from Italy today. When you come, I will buy you one.

Loyally,
In Revolt,
Lauro A.

Aguirre:

Are you out of your Goddamned mind? Have you considered what would happen here if the government intercepted your letter? A censor? You revolutionaries have no sense at all. No seas pendejo, buey! Show some restraint. Things are bad enough already. How would you like to sing the praises of your saint if she were hanging from a tree? Or is that what you desire? All of us killed for YOUR cause? Calm down, Lauro. Please.

Angrily,
T

Mi Querido Tomás:

All kidding aside. The tide is turning, do you not feel it? All over the world, the People unite and fight. No fear, no doubt, no cowardice can hold it back. Do not fear the changes, my friend. And should we all be sacrificed, then it is for a greater, better day. I know you. I know your torments. When you fall into your fears and doubts like this, you become mesmerized. You see nothing outside yourself, my brother. It is as if you walked down a road forever gazing into a mirror, walking toward yourself and blind to the world. Have faith.

L.A.

FAITH. STOP. AGUIRRE YOU FOOL. STOP. THE ONLY FRUIT
DANGLING FROM THE TREES WILL BE NAMED URREA. STOP.
YOU WILL EAT ITALIAN ICE IN TEXAS AND SLAUGHTER US
ALL. STOP. HYPOCRITE. STOP.

Forty-nine

NIGHT LAID ITSELF OVER THE PLAIN, and groups
of bodies seemed to be dancing as the red-yellow glow of
their fires leapt and wobbled. Cruz could not find Rubén or
Saint Joseph. They were not at the various guitar-and-
tequila parties on the outskirts of the camp. They were not
at the evangelist's tent where the mad Protestants called
"Hallelujah!" They were not near the soldiers, or the taco
carts, or the huddled muttering family groups. He looked
for them for an hour or more, and when the dark finally
clamped down over him, he made his way back to the
camp of the twisted child, Conchita. She was asleep and
snoring.

He bowed to her mother and said, "Doña, may I sleep
here?"

"Claro que sí," she said. "Make your home with us."

By the time he had spread out his blanket, she had
scooped him a plateful of beans and shredded beef. She
put three tortillas on top of the food and pushed the plate to

him. He dug for a coin to repay her, but she shook her head. In the glow of the coals of her fire ring, she looked young again. He ate his food with wedges of tortillas, and he looked at sleeping Conchita, and he felt he might almost cry, but it was only a feeling, and after a while it passed, and he stretched out and sighed.

Teresita couldn't sleep. She rolled from side to side in her bed. She sighed. Sat up. Lay back down.

She got up, paced her room. Reached up to the crisp branches of herbs hanging head down from the rafters, crushed them in her fists, breathed in their sharp scents. She went to the corner and poured water into the basin. She plunged her face into the water. Scrubbed her cheeks. Tossed her head and sprayed water all over her room.

Cruz couldn't sleep. He sat up, swept pebbles out from under his blanket, lay down again. Turned over and tried to sleep belly down. Jumped up, shook out the blanket, lay on it again.

He rose and eased himself into the bushes and made his water there. Stepped back into the small camp and stoked the dying fire. Conchita had kicked off her thin blanket in her sleep. He pulled it back over her.

He dug a five-peso coin out of his pocket and left it on a flat stone beside the fire, collected his things, and walked away.

Guards paced around the main house. Two men, each carrying a Winchester. Cruz watched them make their rounds. They crossed before the porch and walked to the far ends of the house, where they passed out of sight to pace around the back.

He laid down his rifle and rushed to the porch steps with a fistful of pebbles. He threw one at her shutter. Threw another. Pitched about twenty in a bunch.

A gruff voice said: "What are you doing?"

Cruz spun around. Segundo was pointing his rifle at him.

"I was pitching pebbles," he said.

"Why?"

"We need to speak."

"You might need to speak," Segundo said. "She needs to sleep."

"I am the Pope of Mexico."

"I'm the King of France."

Teresita's shutters banged open above them.

"Quién es?" she called down.

"It's me, Segundo. Some idiot was trying to wake you. Go back to bed."

"What idiot?" she called back.

"Me. Cruz," Cruz said.

"Oh, that idiot!" she said.

Cruz scowled.

"Hold him, Segundo!" she cried. "I'm coming down."

Segundo jacked a round into the chamber. He smiled at Cruz.

"If I had my rifle," Cruz said, "you would not be smiling."

"But you don't have it," Segundo replied.

"I could fry you like a catfish," Cruz said.

"I could poach your eggs."

"I could shit in your boot."

"I could whip you like a dog."

Teresita came out the door.

"What did you say?" she asked.

"Nothing," mumbled Cruz.

"Nothing," Segundo muttered.

She crossed her arms.

"Boys," she said.

"Shall I wake your father?" Segundo asked.

"I'll handle it," she said.

She pushed his rifle barrel away.

"I have custody of the prisoner," she intoned.

Segundo stared at her. So did Cruz. Segundo shook his head. He knew better than to argue with one of these mule-headed Urreas. Especially this one.

"I'll stay close," he said.

"Yes," she replied. "He might be dangerous." She grinned.

"Next time," Segundo said.

"Bring your friends."

"Bring yours."

"You'll need them."

"My mother could kick you in the ass."

"Boys," she repeated.

"Bring your mother," Segundo said, "if you can get her out of the barn."

"Now *boys!*"

The two men looked at each other. Segundo put a finger against his eye. *I'll be watching.* He backed off to the far end of the porch, and Cruz recovered his rifle.

"I could shoot him," Cruz said.

"Cruz Chávez," she snapped, "you behave!"

"Sorry."

He scuffed the floorboards of the veranda with his toe. Crickets, cicadas, cows, coyotes, boot heels, snoring.

"Why are you bothering me at this late hour?"

"I couldn't sleep," he said.

"And you thought I should suffer because you are awake?"

"Sorry."

She took his arm. He jumped.

"Come with me," she said, "into the chapel."

"Alone?" he blurted, but she was already pulling him down the steps and around the corner of the house.

The chapel was round, made of white adobe. Its doorway was trimmed in blue. Its walls were thick, rough. No matter how hot the day could get, the chapel would remain relatively cool.

She pushed open the door and gestured for him to go first. He pulled off his hat and stepped through. The room was small — it held about nine benches. The floor was red-clay tile. The walls were curved, so there were no corners to speak of.

Directly across from the doorway, a dark wooden cross hung above a small altar. He recognized the pagan glass of water on the altar. It was very Mexican, he thought. Incense, candles. Oil lamps mounted on the walls guttered. Peaceful.

"I like it," he said.

"Thank you."

She sat on the first bench and folded her hands in her lap.

"You aren't going to cover your head?" he said.

"No."

"But this is God's house," he said.

"The entire earth is God's house," she responded. "This is my house. God comes here to visit me."

He put down his rifle and sat at the far end of the bench.

"Your life is difficult," he said.

"Oh?"

"You are lonely."

"Lonely . . ." she murmured.

"Everybody here to see you," he said. "But nobody *with* you."

"Yes," she said, cautiously. "I have thought of this."

He rubbed his hands on his knees.

"I did not choose this fate," she said. "But I won't turn from it." She laughed. "Though I wouldn't mind going to a dance once."

"I don't dance," he said.

"Because you're the Pope?" she asked.

"Because I dance like a donkey!"

They laughed.

Outside, Segundo listened through the door and frowned.

"How do you do it?" he asked.

"Healing?"

"Sí."

"I don't do it. It . . . it comes through me." She looked up, opened her hands before her. "It feels like water. Or something . . . golden. It comes, I can feel it, it comes to me from above. It passes through me, in through my head and my heart, and out through my hands." Her fingers curled into loose fists, her hands fell to her sides. "God is the healer," she said. "Not I."

"Always?" he said. "Is it always like this?"

She shifted in her seat. She cleared her throat.

"Not always."

"It is not always from God?" he asked, alarmed.

"It is always from God," she replied. "Everything is from God. But, sometimes . . . I don't know."

She turned away from him.

"Tell me, Teresita. Please."

"Sometimes, I can talk to them." She searched for the words. "I can use my voice to calm them. Sometimes . . . it *is* me."

He nodded.

"What is it like?" he asked.

She smiled.

"It's like falling in love."

He blushed, looked at his hands. She patted her hair — a few strands had escaped the bun in back, and they framed her face in the orange candlelight.

"You love them," she said. "You feel a tenderness toward them, an unbearable softness in your heart. You feel a tingle in your belly, you feel like crying. You want to kiss them, but you know you cannot."

"Why not?"

"Oh, Cruz! My father would never allow that!" She put her hands over her mouth and laughed. "Can you imagine Tomás Urrea allowing me to kiss pilgrims? Ay, Dios!"

Cruz smiled.

"Or dance with them," he said.

She laughed again.

"Can you imagine?" she cried. "Can you imagine me waltzing with a pilgrim?"

He shook his head.

"Sometimes," she said, "I don't actually touch them. I can see the colors around them, the light that comes from the body. Sometimes the light breaks. Do you understand? No? Let me see. It is as if the body were a candle."

She took his hand and led him to the votive candles.

"The flame might be the soul. But see the way the wax glows? The burning flame casts light through the candle. See?"

He watched the candles; their waxen bodies glowed below the flames, reddening as if blood were in them.

"I see," he said.

"Soot on the candle"— she wiped black ash on the side of one of them —"blocks the light. So too does illness. Do you see? The sickness makes . . . a shadow. I see the shadow."

She went back to her seat.

His hand, where she'd held it, felt warm. He rubbed it on his pants.

"I can sometimes touch the shadow," she said.

He went to the bench and sat behind her.

They were close enough to smell each other.

"May I touch you?" he asked.

She was quiet a long time.

"To bless you."

"Usually it's me doing the blessing."

"But I am here now. May I?"

"Yes."

He put his hand on her back. His other hand on her head.

"Bless you, Teresa."

Then he laid his forehead against her spine. He closed his eyes.

"Sometimes," she murmured, "I take their pain into my body. I pull their affliction into me, and then God cures *me*.

It is very hard. It leaves me very tired. It is the ultimate test of faith."

He rested his face on her back and smelled her.

❊

When Cruz awoke on the pew, she was gone.

It was morning, and the jangle and smash of the cooking, feeding throng filled the air. This was the day the Tigers were to return to Tomóchic. Cruz rose, genuflected and made the sign of the cross, retrieved his hat and rifle, and stepped into the day. He blinked in the harsh light and pushed through the bodies.

Teresita was already speaking to a small group on her porch. Cruz spied Rubén and Saint Joseph standing near the steps. Segundo stared at him, leaned over the railing, and spit.

"Where were you?" Cruz asked his men.

"Sleeping," said Rubén.

Saint Joseph smiled at him.

"I had a miracle," he said.

"Oh?"

Cruz had already forgotten the tumor on José's neck.

"Show him," said Rubén.

José pulled the bandana away from his neck and said, "Look."

Cruz turned his eyes away from Teresita and stared at his neck. The oblong purple growth was gone. A long pucker of flesh remained on the back of José's neck where the tumor had been. José laughed. Cruz gasped, laid his finger on the old man's neck. It was hot, scaly as a lizard's, but there was no tumor.

"Gone!" Saint Joseph laughed.

Cruz stared at Teresita. She looked up and smiled at him. "Daughter of God," he said.

Fifty

THE NOTE WAS LEFT on the porch swing, held down by one of the recently dislodged white rocks from the plazuela.

From: I, the Pope of México Libre, Pastor Cruz Chávez, Leader of Tomóchic, Captain of the Tigers of the Sierra

To: You, Daughter of God, Teresa Urrea, also known as Saint of Cabora, But I prefer Teresita

My dear Saint. No, you do not care to be called Saint, and God bless you for that! Does it not state in the Good Book that we who believe are all Saints in Christ! Amen!

Dear Teresa.
May I call you Teresa? Honestly, I would like to call you Teresita. All right?

Teresita! It is me, Cruz.
The Lord has directed me to inform you that you have passed the test we brought to you. Did I say that right? Forgive me my failures of orthography (I thought you might like this big word) but I do my best. Amen.

José was healed by your touch. By the Holy Spirit! Glorious is the Spirit! Amen. We must go back now. Amen.

You do not like the name, but we place you among our pantheon of saints and guardian angels. Tomóchic will be forever in your personal congregation. We await the day you come to our mountains and preach your gospel.

Until that day, we pray for you. We light candles in your honor.

And in the name of all that is Holy, we will kill anyone who comes against you. Amen and amen.

In God,
Cruz Chávez

Write to me!

I SEND THIS BY COURIER!

My Dear Pope, Your Holiness:

Today, I was forced to let a man die. It was very sad. (Perhaps you recall our conversations. I do!) His sons had brought him on a pallet. He was old and frail. His insides were all hollowed out from cancer.

They cried for me to save their father. I knelt beside the old man and held his hand. "I cannot save you," I told him. "Must I die?" he asked. "You must." The sons started yelling, saying I was a fake, a devil. Saying I had no power. I tried to silence them. I told them, "I never had power. The only power I have is the power you yourselves have. God has the power. We are here to serve." But they were angry at me.

Cruz! So many people are angry at me! I never liked being yelled at, you know. My auntie used to yell terrible things at me. Ay! It would be nicer if everybody liked me. Do you feel this way? Oh, you big Tiger — you don't care if people like you or not, do you? So fierce!

I whispered to the old man. I told him what we both know. (Heaven and God.) It was he who silenced the sons. Can you believe it? He called them to him and said, "Don't yell, boys. Don't be angry. She has given me the best gift — better than healing. She has given me peace. She has given me a good death. I am not afraid."

They carried him away.

My head hurts after a day like that.

I was sad to see you Tigers were gone. But I cherish your letter.

> *Your Friend,*
> *Teresita*
> Not *the "Saint"*
> *of Cabora*

P.S. Do no violence. Kill no one.

Fifty-one

TOMÁS COULDN'T SLEEP. Even on the nights when his delightful Gabriela took him into the tender fragrance of her sexuality and they made love late, he lay awake afterward. He could feel the press of the bodies through the walls. The weird gurgle of the crowd. Coughs and scuffles and cries and hiccups. Bellies and noses made endless ugly noises, but they were so faint, especially as the crowds slept, that it almost became a lulling chant, like the sound of the river on that long-distant day that they had begun their journey from Ocoroni and had ridden the leaky ferry raft. One thought led to another. The sound of the wind somehow took him back to the apocalyptic graves of the two Indian lovers in the desert, and he imagined them writhing there still, trying to dig through the unyielding earth with the crowns of their heads.

Gabriela was asleep beside him in her usual cloud of deliciousness. He put his face to her hair and smelled her. Then he put his mouth on her bare belly and lipped the edges of her navel. He pulled the sheet up over her, kicked his legs over the edge of the bed, and leaned his elbows on his knees.

"Oh hell," he muttered.

He rose, pulled on his trousers and let the suspenders hang down in back. He wore a white undershirt. He washed his face and ran his fingers through his still-thick hair. Not going bald yet! He fixed his mustache.

Might as well go down to the kitchen and see if there was anything to eat.

Tomás snuck out barefoot and made his way down the stairs. He checked the front door, to make sure it was locked. Went down the hall by touch, running his left hand along the wall. He turned the corner into the kitchen and found Teresita sitting at the table.

"Ay!" he said.

"Ay!" she cried.

She had lit a pair of candles. She had a plate before her with a large slice of calabaza. A glass of milk she had strained through a cheesecloth clotted with curds and cow hair.

"Father," she said. "You startled me."

"I couldn't sleep."

She nodded.

"I thought a snack," he added, "might help."

She gestured at her calabaza.

"Me too."

He stood for a moment, unsure of how to proceed. He finally stepped to her and put his hand on the back of her head. He caught a whiff of roses. Yes, that. The legendary scent. He was almost surprised to feel her hair was sleek, and her skull hard beneath it and curving. He almost blurted: *You're real!*

"Well!" he said. "Let's see what we have!"

He marched to the pantry with great manly strides.

"A can of peaches," he called.

"Sounds good."

"What is this?" he said, holding up a can.

"Plum pudding."

"What's that?"

"I don't know. It's from England."

He studied the can.

"It says here there's rum in it."

"You like rum," she said.

"I certainly do!"

He took the can to the big metal table and went after it with a can opener. The rich aroma of plum-and-rum pudding filled the kitchen.

"Do you think the coffee is still warm?" he asked.

"I doubt it. Besides, Father, you don't want to drink coffee at midnight."

"Perhaps not."

"Have milk."

"Gack!"

"Milk is good for you!"

"Milk," he informed her, "is disgusting!"

The milk in her glass was watery and nearly blue in the candlelight. "I don't see anything wrong with it," she said.

"It *squirts*," he said, "out of a *cow*."

She laughed. He plopped the pudding into a glass bowl and sniffed it. He took a canister of cream and poured some of it on the pudding. He sat.

"That squirted out of a cow, too," Teresita pointed out.

"I'm not drinking it, I'm eating it. And the rum improves it. Look"— he held a spoon up to point at her —"drinking milk is like drinking blood."

She took a big gulp of milk to wash down a sweet wad of chewed calabaza.

"You have gone insane," she noted.

"You should know."

They laughed.

He took a small spoonful of the pudding and worked it in his mouth.

"Oh yes," he said. "Tasty."

"Father," she said, "I didn't know you had things that bothered you."

He waved his spoon.

"A million things!"

"Like?"

He shrugged.

"Like, let me see. If I am eating a fish, and I bite a bone, it makes me ill."

"Really!"

"Or a pebble in my beans. In fact, any unexpected thing in my food makes me want to vomit!"

She laughed.

"You are so delicate!"

"Oh really! And I suppose you have nothing that you hate to eat?"

"I don't like beer."

"Beer! Beer is life itself."

"Spoken like a true drunkard."

"Show some respect, you."

The rum was making his nose run.

"I always thought," Teresita continued, "that beer would taste sweet. But it was bitter. I thought tobacco would taste like chocolate."

He scraped the last of the pudding out of the bowl with his spoon. "It seems to me your problem lies with your expectations."

She ate some more calabaza.

"I was never realistic."

"Idealism will kill you," he said. "I'm still hungry."

"There is ham in the wall."

Aguirre's last act at Cabora had been to create a cooler deep in the wall farthest from the fireplace. A water cistern sunk in the adobe enclosed the cooler slot and kept the clay from getting warm. Tomás dug out the ham and found some crusty bread and a big knife.

"Wine?" he said.

"I don't really like wine, thank you."

"Another revelation."

He poured himself a stout glass of burgundy.

"All right," he said. "I have something bothering me."

"What?"

"Why must you smell like roses?"

Teresa looked at him blankly.

"I smell the roses," he said. "On you."

She sniffed herself.

"I can't smell it anymore. Is it strong?"

"No."

"That's a relief."

"I have always wondered — why roses?" he insisted.

She smiled at him as he sat.

"I suppose," she said, "all saints smell that way."

"I have looked in my books," he said. "A few have smelled like you."

"The Holy Mother likes roses."

"Ah! Well! That explains everything. The Holy Mother."

"The Virgin of Guadalupe brought roses to Juan Diego."

"Yes, yes," he said. "I know who the Holy Mother is."

"But, of course, you don't believe."

He spread his palms at her.

"Read history, my dear. That hill where she appeared, Tepeyac. Aztecs had been 'seeing' their own goddess there for years. Tonántzin, wasn't it? A virgin? The priests just laid one fairy tale over another, and they used the same spot for the same kind of fairy."

She squinted at him.

"The world of reason must be a lonely place," she said.

This startled him.

"Father," she said, leaning forward, "do you not think the Mother of God is older than the Aztecs? Do you not think that, if she were to appear right here, right now, the People would think her a Yaqui or a mestiza? That the Aztecs could only understand her as an Aztec figure? How would they know anything other than Aztec religion?"

"Touché," he said.

Each of them felt a warm glow in their chests. They secretly loved arguing with each other. They were both grinning.

"But these roses," he continued, as if she hadn't spoken at all.

"Roses denote grace," she said.

"To whom?"

"To God. To Our Lady."

"What did I tell you? Fairy tales!"

"Is this smell a fairy tale?" she said, raising her arm. "Explain it."

"Why not honeysuckle? Lavender?"

She shrugged.

"I thought you liked the smell of roses."

"Who told you that?"

"I don't know," she said. "I thought everybody did."

"Not me."

"You never liked the smell of roses?"

"No."

"Not even now?"

"Hell no!"

She clapped her hands. Laughed.

"This is marvelous!" she cried.

"Sorry," he said.

She put her hands on her cheeks.

"Wonderful."

They laughed and ate.

"Did you see the Apaches?" she asked.

"Today?"

She nodded. "Apaches come to see me sometimes."

"How do you tell them from all the other Indians?"

"They say, 'We are Apaches.'"

He smiled.

"Very funny."

"They wanted to ask me why the Yaquis and the People at Cabora were interested in Jesus."

"And what did you tell them?"

"I told them that Jesus rose from the dead and walked again."

"And what did they say?"

"They said, 'That's all? Medicine men do that all the time!'"

"The sinners did not accept your savior, eh?"

"My error, I'm afraid."

"You will have to go to confession," he said.

"Yes, I seem to have lost a chance to evangelize."

"Dangerous doctrines!" he bellowed. "Indigenous heresies!"

"Shhh! Not everybody is awake, you know."

He shrugged. Sipped more wine.

"Aren't you tired of it?" he asked.

"What?"

"You know what."

"All this?" She gestured with her spoon.

"Sí. Esto. Todo esto. Este desmadre de santos y pecadores. Todo esto, hija."

She was quiet for a moment. Toyed with her spoon. Dabbed at her lips with her napkin.

"Every day," she said.

"What would you do if you could?" he asked. He patted the table loud enough to get her attention. "And don't tell me 'Nothing'!"

She thought, looked at her hands.

"I don't know. . . ."

"Come, come. Tell me. I am your poor old Papá."

"Oh," she looked at him. "I would be quiet."

"Quiet? That's not exactly clear to me, Teresita. Quiet how?"

"Quiet. I would live in a small cool house under trees. Where no one would look at me. I would grow mint and corn and some tomatoes. I would grow cilantro and find a little humble man and have a baby and I . . . I would be forgotten."

They stared at each other for a long time. Her eyes became wet. He reached across the table and took her hand.

"Teresita," he whispered.

She shook her head.

"We could send them all home."

"No."

"We could stop all this," he said. "We could start again. We could move to Alamos, and you could have a little house there. Or —"

"It is not my destiny."

"You make your own destiny."

"God makes our destinies."

"God is a fairy tale!"

She shook her head.

"You forget," she replied. "I have seen God. His hand touched my palm."

Tomás let go of her hand, just in case there was some kind of jolt, some mysterious tingle. He wasn't ready for heavenly gestures at the moment.

"It was a hallucination," he said, not unkindly.

She turned pitying eyes to him.

"You cannot win your argument with God," she said. "You are angry — you were orphaned. Your parents died when you were just a boy. You shake your fist at God, and you cry and curse Him every night in your bed. But you cannot win. In the morning, He is still there, waiting for you. All unbelievers are the same."

He rested his chin on his fist.

"And?" he prodded.

"And you always thought it made you different. You always felt unique. Above all the fools who followed God. But everyone who stops believing thinks he is the smartest one. You all compete with each other, not with God. Do you know how a child says 'I'm not afraid' when she's afraid? How a child will tell you how innocent he is, no matter if there is a broken window and he stands before you holding rocks? You unbelievers are like that. Sad little boys."

"How do you think you know these things?"

"It is obvious if you only look," she replied. "I can see more than you think."

"Like?"

"Like your aura — it wants to be gold and white, but your rages make it turn red —"

"Hija, hija, hija," he interrupted. "Stop that." He shook his head. "Daughter, you worry me."

She sat back in her chair.

"I know." She rubbed her face. "I worry myself."

"Who are you?" he said.

"I am the same girl I was."

"No! No. Don't tell me that. Whatever you have become, you are not the same girl. Not now. Not anymore."

She took her plate to the sink.

"Perhaps not," she said. "I don't know."

"It is obvious," he said, only slightly mocking her, "if you only look. Does that make me a saint, too? My seeing the obvious?"

"I never said I was a saint."

"But they do."

"I try to stop them."

"You've wanted to be a saint from the day you could talk," he said.

She turned and stared at him.

"Tell me I'm wrong."

He went to a shelf and found a small black cheroot and struck a match and took a puff.

"Sí, o no?" he said.

She sighed. If she were a vaquero, she would have taken that moment to spit.

"Perhaps," she said. "I never thought about it."

"Yes you did."

"Is it a crime to want to be good?" she cried.

He took the little wicked cigar out of his mouth.

"Easy," he said. "Easy. Don't get excited."

She put her hand on her head.

"Oh," she said. "I don't know." She sat down. "I wanted a boyfriend. A puppy. A pink dress."

She looked up at him and grinned.

That was when they heard the tapping on the back door. It must have been going like that for a while, but they hadn't noticed it.

"What is that, a mouse?" he said.

She shrugged.

He got up and went to the door and threw the latch, yanked it open.

There, on the back step, was a stinking and filthy urchin. His scent of sickness and garbage wafted into the kitchen.

"Ah cabrón!" Tomás said.

He was an Indian boy. His bare feet were black, his toenails split and bloody. He wore ruined trousers and a beaten and burned jacket, no shirt. His eyes were runny, and his upper lip was caked in crystallized snot. His hair was hard and vertical, coming off his scalp in spikes.

"I saw lights," he said.

Tomás reeled from his stench.

"Of course you saw lights," he snapped. "We live here."

"I waited," the boy said. "People say I stink too bad. They won't let me come in the day. They won't let me come close to her. I waited for everybody to go to sleep so I could come."

Teresita reached out for him.

"Come in," she said.

She took his hand.

Tomás tried to block him with one knee, but Teresita nimbly steered him clear of her father.

He stepped in shyly, his cloud of odor filling the room.

"Boy," said Tomás, "you smell like shit."

The boy burst into hoarse sobs.

He covered his face with his hands and wailed.

Teresita put her arms around him and held her head away from his head, where the main stink seemed to be centered. His hair was hard and shiny. The back of his neck was wet.

"What's wrong, boy?" she said.

"I'm sorry!"

"Now, now," said Tomás. He cleared his throat. "Crying's for girls. We are big strong men! Somós machos!"

The boy's collar was stiff. His reek was of rotten meat and old blood. Teresita looked at his head — it was full of infected sores. Pus formed peso-sized pools on his scalp, and the pus had drooled down his back and coagulated in his hair. Dirt stuck to the mess and made the hard spikes on his head.

Tomás bent down and wrinkled his nose.

"Damn!" he said. "What is that?"

"Sores," she said.

Tomás suddenly remembered the old man with the infected lash marks on his back. When was that? Years ago. He could not remember the day, or the year. He wanted to tell Teresita about it, but there was no time.

She gently pulled apart the boy's hair, and she revealed dark little creatures drowning in the pus. They wiggled their legs in the swampy wounds.

"Good God," said Tomás. "What is *that?*"

"Lice."

"Lice!"

"You've never seen lice?"

"No, Teresa, I have never seen lice! What do you think I am, a peasant?"

"Hardly, Father," she said. "I had lice."

"You did?"

"Everybody outside of the big house has lice."

"No!"

She looked up at him and wondered what it felt like to be so ignorant of the world.

"Look," she said. "They bit him so much he scratched until he tore his scalp. It got bad. All rotten."

Tomás went to the table and took a gulp of wine. Poured himself some more.

"Poor boy!" he finally said.

The boy sniffled. Teresita sat him in a chair and pulled away his pus-shellacked jacket. She put cookies on a plate and poured him some of her clotty milk.

"When did you eat?" she asked.

"I don't know."

"Where are your parents?"

"Dead."

"Who takes care of you?"

"Dogs," he said.

Tomás made a sound in his throat.

Dogs!

He went to a drawer and brought out a piece of chocolate. He handed it to the boy.

"My own parents are dead," he offered.

"Really?" the boy replied, looking up at him. One eye was wobbly. A louse appeared in the boy's eyebrow. Teresita plucked it off and popped it between her thumbnails.

"Get scissors," she instructed.

Tomás searched through the house until he found some

big scissors in Huila's old bedroom. They had left it untouched all this time. No one had the heart to clear it out.

"Good," she said. "Now, put some water on the fire. Get some of the purple flowers from Huila's room. They're hanging in the middle of the room. Break off a fistful and put them in the water while I cut his hair."

He rushed back into Huila's room and looked through the bundles of herbs hanging there. He found the purple ones.

"Leaves too?" he called.

"Just the flowers, please."

"Right."

She bent to the boy's hair and carefully snipped away the stiff locks.

"You will look a little funny," she said, "without hair. But we will take away your lice."

"As long as I don't stink."

"We will take away your stink," she promised.

Tomás tossed the dried flowers in the water.

"Now what?" he asked.

"Come."

He went to the chair. Teresita had snipped away most of the boy's hair, leaving gooey bristles among which the sluggish lice could be seen.

"Pluck," she told her father.

"Pluck what?"

"Lice."

"You're kidding."

"No, I'm not kidding. Pluck them and pop them."

"But I'll get pus on my fingers!"

"You can wash your hands."

"But it's disgusting!"

"No, Father. Letting an orphan suffer is disgusting."

"Chingado," he said.

He gingerly pinched one of the awful little beasts and popped it between his nails. It was oddly satisfying.

"Got the bastard," he noted.

"Good work."

He caught another one. It was funny, but if you smelled the stink of the boy's rotten head long enough, you stopped noticing it.

They plucked lice for so long that the boy fell asleep under their fingers. Tomás wiped so much pus on the front of his pants that they had two ugly stains. For the first time in his life, he felt — well, saintly.

Unexpectedly, Teresita disrupted his thoughts by saying: "Jesus washed dirty feet, you know."

She went to the pot of purple water and set it on the table to cool. The boy was snoring. When the water was cool enough, Teresita soaked white cloths in the tea and began to gently dab at his wounds. He jumped, but kept snoring.

"We don't even know his name," Tomás said.

"Let's hope he's not another Urrea," she said.

She was grinning.

"That's not funny," Tomás muttered.

They washed the pus off his head. She smeared a pale yellow ointment on the wounds, and she wrapped a white bandage around his head.

"What shall we do with him?" she asked.

"Why are you asking me?"

"You are the patrón," she pointed out.

"I am not in charge here," he said. "I have lost control of everything."

She picked the boy up in her arms and carried him to the

parlor. She laid him down on the couch and sat beside him, patting his skinny chest.

"Get me a blanket," she said.

Tomás ran upstairs and pulled a blanket from the cedar chest in his bedroom. When he came back downstairs, Teresita had fallen asleep with her head on the boy's chest. Tomás watched her sleep for a moment. He then took her feet and lifted them, turning her slowly so her head rested on the far end of the couch. Her feet lay next to the boy's face, and the boy's feet were at her armpit. Oh well, it was the best he could do. He covered them both with the blanket.

When he sat on the floor for a moment to think about his night, he fell asleep beside them, and that's where Gabriela found them all in the morning, dreaming together in the cool orange light of dawn.

Book V

THE OUTER DARK

Was she an illusion, this young nervous girl, vibrant and sweet, sweet and tenacious, who carried in her eyes a turbulent flame, as stimulating as a ration of gunpowder and liquor, yet as benign, placid and lulling as the smoke of opium . . .

The Saint of Cabora!

Had those eloquent eyes — whose radiance bathed her face in a nimbus that ignited miraculous enthusiasms in the poor pilgrims who came to her from distant mountains — had these eyes suggested to the villages of Sonora, Sinaloa and Chihuahua that they should begin revolts that could only be stopped by drowning them in fire and blood?

— HERIBERTO FRÍAS
Tomóchic

Fifty-two

THE FIRST SIGNS OF REVOLT seemed mild. Excited Mexicans mixing their religion and their tequila. A rock flew through the presidente municipal of Navojoa's window. A lone Rural was chased out of a nasty little village by a gaggle of angry grandmothers with sticks. The old bodies of two Indians that had hung in an alamo beside the road to Sal Si Puedes for two years were cut down and buried.

Soon, however, things got more interesting.

Soldiers on patrol were often greeted with cries of "Viva La Santa de Cabora!" The commanding general of the Fort Huachuca garrison outside Tucson noted the wearing of Teresita scapulars among the natives, and he put it in his report to Washington. A Prussian land-grabber not far from Cabora was burned out one night. The local People said his house had been hit by lightning, and by "the great power of God." Rurales thought they saw charred torches in the ruins.

Father Gastélum had been riding the Chihuahua circuit now for months, having escaped the heat of Sonora and the idiocy of the "Girl Saint" and her rabble. His difficult transit carried him up the Sal Si Puedes ravine into the sierras, and over into the Papigochic region, home of the Tarahumara and the recalcitrant Tomochitecos. He preached at the Tomóchic church once every two months. He had been appalled to find a wooden carving of Teresita in their chapel.

The imbeciles had lit candles to her. They had pinned silver milagros to her pathetic rebozo, some scrap they had wound around the statue. Heresy!

In Chihuahua City, he made his reports to Governor Carrillo, and he sent a telegram to Mexico City and an incendiary report of heresy to the Vatican. Father Gastélum promised himself he would stop this blasphemous movement if he had to set fire to Cabora himself.

Lauro Aguirre wanted to go home, and he wanted to see Tomás again, and he wanted to observe the transformation of Teresita firsthand. But at this point, he knew he would be stood before the first available Mexican wall, or worse, hung from the first tree a cavalryman happened to lead him to. From the relative safety of El Paso, Texas, he wrote an endless series of articles, pamphlets, editorials, and broadsheets extolling the virtues of Yaquis, of revolt, of the Saint of Cabora. He castigated and reviled Díaz, and he occasionally ducked down alleys to escape Mexican assassins and goons sent up from Ciudad Juárez to try to silence him. But he would not be silenced. He published his newspaper, *El Independiente,* in a small shop in the heart of downtown. Most of his workers were fellow refugees who had fled from the Díaz regime.

Aguirre clipped articles from gringo newspapers and magazines, most of them mad and inaccurate, steeped in bigotry and cynicism. Friends mailed him bits from the San Francisco and New York press. He regularly bought the Arizona papers and the New Mexico papers, watching for any mention of the Girl Saint. Tucson, Tombstone, Silver City. Teresita was a flame waiting to be fanned. Aguirre translated American articles and mailed them straightaway to Tomás. Perhaps the American press could convince his old comrade that the time for revolt was at hand.

Weekly, Aguirre published astounding testimonials to Teresita's miracles. Aguirre did not believe in miracles, of course, at least not miracles that happened outside of scripture. Even those miracles, he suspected, were mythologized folktales and tall tales. Some of his own people believed the grave of Benito Juárez, or the portrait of General Santa Anna, could heal the sick or grant them fortunes and romantic conquests. Mexico was rife with "miracles" and "saints."

But the Mexicans of the borderlands believed and that was exciting to Aguirre. Yaquis were ready to fight. The populace of the northlands of Mexico, however, would much sooner march off to revolutionary war if the Virgen de Guadalupe appeared to them. Aguirre could call for revolt until he was out of breath, and the most they would do would be to nod and say, "Yes, yes, amigo — somebody should do something about it." But a saint! By God! A saint! Teresita was the goddess of war.

"The 'Saint' Calls for Freedom and Land!" he wrote.

"Yaqui Girl Saint's Theology of Liberation!" was the headline of a Sunday column.

"God Gave Your Land to You, Cries the Sainted Girl of Cabora! — and Politicians and Oligarchs Have Stolen Your Patrimony — Insists the 'Holy One' of Sonora!"

✳

His hope was never dimmed. He wrote endlessly, tirelessly, madly, spewing tract after tract, hoping to transform the very fabric of the world with his noble screeds. He wrote:

> *In mankind the sentiment of Justice is innate:*
> *That sentiment that occults itself not in himself*
> *But rather manifests itself with major intent*
> *In his actions, meanwhile the less illumined*
> *The less educated the individual because of a law*
> *Unwritten of Compensation, natural and necessary*
> *To the Law of Human Responsibility, in that the*
> *Reason finds illustration and the Ideas and*
> *Sentiments become educated and sentiments then*
> *Lose their instinctive urge to be, as ideas and*
> *Sentiments, guided by Reason!*

Even Tomás, when he received these broadsides, stared at them for long minutes before saying, "What the devil is he talking about?"

✳

Tomás called Teresita in one afternoon. He said, "Sit down."

She sat across from him in his study, kicked off her shoes, and wiggled her toes in the carpet. He glanced at her feet and frowned.

"Bare feet," he said.

"You should try it," she said.

His smile was pained and false.

She said, "Let's have chocolates."

He grumbled and opened a tin of French chocolates and slid it to her across the low table between them.

"Who invented chocolate?" he said.

"Mexicans, Father dear."

"Damned right. The noble Aztec invented chocolate."

"We gave the world chocolatl. And cacahuatl."

"The great peanut!" he intoned.

"And aguacatl and guajolotl!"

"Avocados and turkeys!"

"Corn!"

He sat back and smiled.

"Truly," he said, "we are the chosen people."

She bit into her bonbon and closed her eyes. Then she gobbled another one and groaned.

"That's not very saintly behavior," he said.

"I'm no saint."

She licked her fingers.

"Oh," he responded, "I know that. Look," he said, "Lauro has sent us another article about you."

"What does it say?"

"Madness," he said. "Just crazy things. He wrote this one."

He read the column to her.

"What did he say?" she asked.

"I'm not sure," he replied.

"Ay, Don Lauro," she said. "He's so complicated."

He put his reading glasses on the end of his nose and squinted. "Let's see . . . in this other newspaper, you're the Queen of the Yaquis. And your father is a poor old drunkard. Fat."

"What's wrong with that?" she said.

"Oh, you're so funny."

"Yaquis don't have a queen."

"They apparently have you."

She bit another chocolate, but was already feeling nauseous.

"Anything else?"

"Yes. You are the Mexican Joan of Arc."

This left her speechless.

She picked up her dark cherry bonbon and decided to eat it anyway.

Pilgrims came to Aguirre to offer him eyewitness accounts of Teresita's miracles.

One day, a wagon bound for San Antonio reined in before his house. He stepped outside with a pistol tucked in the back of his pants and a cup of coffee in his hand. A skinny Mexican, almost black from the sun, sat on the bench. In the back of the wagon, his flea-bitten family peered at Aguirre. An old woman reclined on a pile of blankets and scratched the sad ears of a mongrel dog.

"Señor Lauro Aguirre?" asked the skeletal mule skinner from on high.

"Yes?" said Aguirre.

"We have come from Cabora," the man said.

"Who was sick?" Aguirre asked.

"My mother," the man said, gesturing with his chin at the old woman in the back.

"You were healed?" Aguirre asked.

"Sí."

"May I ask what ailed you?"

"An issue of blood," she said. "Out of my insides."

He nodded.

"Down here," she added, touching herself between the legs.

"Yes, I understand."

The driver said, "That tall one, the man at Cabora."

"Don Tomás."

"That one. He said you might pay us for our story."

"Did he."

"We asked for money to get home on, but he said we could sell you our story for your periodical."

"That rascal."

The people in the wagon said nothing.

"Well," said Aguirre. "You might as well come in."

They came off the wagon with great rattlings and noise.

"I suppose," Aguirre sighed, "Tomás said I would feed you, as well."

"Oh yes. We haven't eaten," the old woman said. "And we're thirsty."

"I hope your story's good," he said.

"It is," she replied. "I hope your money's good."

He laughed.

"It is, old woman," he said. "It is."

The house was small and yellow. Behind a cement-block wall, two fat dogs danced and yipped. Geraniums bloomed in old cans. One rosebush. The screen door was crooked, the wire mesh rusted dark. The stucco walls were faded, though the white trim was still bright. The gate in the block wall was hung on springs, and they made *yoiiiing* sounds as Aguirre pushed the gate open for them. His fingers were black with ink. The dogs nipped at the woman's ankles. She kicked them away.

In the house, the smell of old cooking and burned coffee.

Cigarettes. Coughing. Their voices were old, dry as the desert around them.

The old woman was nearly blind. She sat in an orange chair, and even though it was hot, she asked for a blanket to tuck around her knees. Her thin hair was white, pulled back tight over her skull. Her cheeks were sunken, and her teeth were gone, causing her lips to flap. Aguirre thought of the wonderful Mexican word for being toothless: molacha.

Her eyes were cataract blue, clouded and rolling. She held a rosary in her lap, and beside her, on a small tray, Aguirre had placed a cup of coffee that sat in a puddle collected in a saucer. Her family crowded into the corners like anxious sheep.

"Teresita," the old one said.

"Yes," said Aguirre.

The old one closed her eyes. A clock ticked. Two of the old woman's family looked at each other and rolled their eyes.

She reached out her hand.

"Señor," she said. "Come closer."

He stepped forward.

"Five pesos," she said.

Her family sucked in air, as if they'd burned their tongues.

"Tell me first."

"Ten pesos."

"First, your story."

Aguirre opened his notebook.

"You were there," he said.

"Claro. Claro que sí. I was there."

She coughed, took a sip of coffee, set the cup down at an angle, spilling more into her saucer.

"La Santa touched me once, and I was healed."

She smiled.

"I bled for thirteen years, señor, and she touched me, and the blood stopped. Glory to God."

Her family muttered *Gracias a Dios* in their corners. *Bendito sea Dios.*

"She was friendly, La Santa. She touched everybody. She was walking through our camp. We all camped there. It was like a holiday. We slept under our wagon. And she came walking along, and I saw her and I went up to her and she put her hand on my face and said, 'Hello.'"

"That's all?"

"That is all, señor. What more do you want?" She drained her cup.

"Mother," said the blackened Mexican, "tell him about the caballero."

"Caballero?" said Aguirre.

"Don Antonio," the old woman said. "He was a bad one, that boy. Handsome. A Yori, son of a landowner. He lived in Alamos, he said.

"Pues, Don Antonio had been visiting Hermosillo on business. Who knows what — Yoris are always throwing pesos on counters and making demands." They laughed.

"Now, Don Antonio had a wife — I'll call her Meche because I can't remember what the señor said her name was. Meche was younger than Don Antonio, and sly as a cat. Muy viva, esa muchacha. Eh? She married Antonio's money instead of Antonio. Do you understand?"

Aguirre nodded.

"Good," she said. "Antonio was no angel, either. Men." She blew her slack lips out in disgust. "Antonio had women all along the road." She shrugged. "That's the way it always was. And I am sure he had women in Hermosillo. That is what everybody at Cabora said. Where was I?"

"Antonio and his wife."

"Pah! Wife! So Antonio came riding through the countryside, on his way to Alamos. He pulled up at the ranch and said, 'What is this?'

" 'A pilgrimage,' we told him.

" 'What kind of pilgrimage?' he demanded.

" 'A pilgrimage to see Teresa Urrea, the Saint of Cabora!'

"Now, Don Antonio knew Don Tomás — all of those hacendados were cut of the same cloth, you see. As the old men always said, 'The same cactuses bring forth similar flowers.' " She adjusted her blanket over her knees. "They were alike, those boys. Muchas mujeres. Mil mujeres!"

The woman clicked her tongue and shook her head.

"And Don Antonio, hearing the daughter of Urrea was a saint all of a sudden, laughed in our faces. 'What!' he yelled. 'The daughter of Tomás Urrea, a saint?' He had been drinking, of course. All those men drink. He was bold. He insulted the pilgrims. He said, 'Any woman who eats food like me then sits on a toilet like me is no saint!'

"Then the gentleman took his blankets and went to sleep."

"And then?" said Aguirre.

"Well, then everybody woke up. It was morning."

"And what did Teresita do?"

"Ay, ay, ay — that was rich, what she did!"

"What was that?"

"Oh well. She came out like every day. First, she prayed in her little chapel. Then she went in the house to eat. Then she came out to us. Like every day.

"On this day, she stood on the porch, and she called out,

'Don Antonio!' Everyone turned, looking around. He was saddling his horse. 'Don Antonio!' she cried out. He said, 'Me?' His face went white. 'Me?' he asked."

The old woman smiled at the memory.

"He went forward. He looked like a little boy in trouble with his teacher, dragging his feet. Everyone was silent, watching him. When he got to her porch, he said, 'I am Antonio.'

"Teresita said, 'Señor, I wanted you to know that I eat only fruit and vegetables.'

"They say he flinched as if slapped.

"Then she said, 'As for the other matter — the bathroom. I have no control over that process.' He backed away from her, but she said, 'Another thing, Don Antonio. Your wife is sleeping with your best friend in Alamos. She lies in his arms as we speak. And they plan to surprise you when you return home. Look behind the door, for he will be there with a machete, and he will kill you as you enter.'

"That Don Antonio tore out of there as if devils were pinching his ass!"

The hermanita laughed so hard she started to cough. Her son stepped forward and patted her back.

"You know," the old woman said, "they say he got home early and caught his friend in the bedroom, and the machete was right beside the bed!"

Aguirre paid them fifteen pesos.

He ran the cautionary tale of Don Antonio on the second page of the Sunday edition. It appeared under a headline he had plagiarized from his own letters to Cabora: DOUBTING THOMAS!

Fifty-three

THE GOVERNOR OF CHIHUAHUA, the *licensiado* Don Lauro Carrillo, was encamped not three miles from Tomóchic in his Papigochic demesne. His pack mules formed a bucolic remuda downslope, stoically nose-tied to a drooping rope among the ponderosa pines. Six tents yellow as tallow formed a fine square, and the pickets assigned to guard duty sat upon folding chairs imported from Bavaria. At the eastern edge of this canvas plaza, a well-stocked fire burned at all hours. Here, Carrillo sat and read his reports, he sipped his fine liquors, and he debated and boasted endlessly with his honored guest, Don Silviano González, jefe político del distrito de Guerrero.

Señor Carrillo was on his yearly tour of the great state of Chihuahua, his personal fact-finding mission. It was the only way for a dedicated governor to really see for himself what the state of his state was. But it was also a grand opportunity to escape the Municipal Palace, to brush off the minor functionaries that buzzed around him like gnats, and to escape his wife and children. May God bless them and keep them!

El Señor Carrillo rode his horses and drank as much as he wanted. He ate what he wanted. He went where he wanted. He carried English rifles in cherrywood cases and killed what he wanted. When he wanted women, his assistants found him fine whores from the towns he passed through. Don Lauro would have liked to tour all year long.

Don Lauro Carrillo dragged el Señor González from natural wonder to vast astonishment like a mad tour guide: Behold, my dear colleague, our red canyons, our violet vistas, our terrifying chasms, our velvet expanses! Our eagles soar, our bears roar, our lions vanish like golden smoke, our red wolves wail at the moon. And only the Chihuahuan moon is so big in the sky, is it not so? Only the Chihuahuan moon is orange and close. The Sierra Madre! Burning desert at her feet, and snow upon her crown. Surely, she is the queen of the continent!

They rose through the terrible levels of the Sierra Madre on trails yellow with dust upon the crimson and violet and gray faces of the mountains. Mule trains thinned down to single file as they descended, their fat packs brushing the knees of Carrillo's ascending riders as they minced along the narrowest parts of the precipice. Don Silviano often leaned out and frightened himself by looking down into dizzying abysses where thin white-silver ribbons revealed themselves — ribbons that were rivers surely a mile below.

Now, they rested.

Don Lauro poked at the fire with a whittled branch. On a small folding table imported from Paris by the last governing body to have vacated Chihuahua City, they had decanters of brandy and tequila. Don Silviano jotted notes in his journal and the sparks whirled above them.

"Gastélum," he said.

"Nasty priest!" replied Don Lauro.

"Will he be able to enact your plan, my friend?"

"He must, my dear Don Silviano!"

"He has no choice."

"Claro que no."

They sat back, extended their feet to the fire. A brisk

toc-toc-toc-toc came from behind them. Don Lauro lifted a finger.

"A woodpecker!" he announced.

Don Silviano bent to his journal and entered in it: *A festive woodpecker sounded in the trees behind us, its industrious hammering representative of Nature herself bending toward the construction of a New Mexican Republic — God Himself putting Nature on the Díaz plan!*

Don Lauro poured them each a copa of amber liquor.

"To Gastélum," he said, raising a toast.

"To Tomóchic," replied Don Silviano.

They had met Gastélum two days before. He had been directed by post to come into the camp above Tomóchic. There, he had dined on wild turkey and roast potatoes. The governor had preserved his finest bottles of champagne for his illustrious guests, and he had prepared a cot in a solo tent for the good father. It was the most comfort the priest had enjoyed in many weeks.

As they had sat in front of the fire, enjoying Cuban cigars and warming their feet after supper, sipping coffee-and-rum, Gastélum had worked off his redolent boots. His stockings were filthy and worn to the consistency of a particularly clotted cheesecloth. One of his toes had gone bad on him, and he hoped the fire would dry out its endless seeping. The governor and the jefe político tried to combat the scent of Gastélum's rancid toe with well-aimed puffs of their cigar smoke. Soon, they each found subtle ways to move their seats away from the padre. Don Lauro called for fresh socks. An assistant appeared quickly with white cotton stockings from the governor's own trunk.

"Lord bless you," said Gastélum.

He peeled his own decomposing socks from his feet and then, to the horror of his companions, threw them in the fire.

"Good God!" Carrillo let slip. As Don Silviano noted in his journal: *The noxious plume of Father Gastélum's richly spoiled flesh wafted downwind to, no doubt, drive bears and coyotes into a panic — great fleeing migrations could probably have been heard if we had listened!*

Freshly socked, well fed, smoked, half-drunk, and warmed by good coffee, Padre Gastélum felt the Holy Spirit near to him. When Governor Carrillo told him of the plan, it seemed providential. Surely, the hand of God moves in bold strokes.

And, truly, the plan was simple. The church in Tomóchic was known to hold artworks of great interest. A series of twelve oil paintings had been arrayed around the interior of the chapel. No one knew whence these canvases had come, nor whose hand had painted them. The heretics of Tomóchic believed angels themselves had painted these icons, since Tomóchic was the seat of "true religion" in opposition to Rome. The gall!

It was Governor Carrillo's rare genius to recognize that the recent miraculous enthusiasms gripping the tribes of the desert and the mountains had come to Mexico City's attentions. And it had also occurred to him that the Indian wars festered and refused to die. And it had further occurred to him that the great leader himself, General Porfirio Díaz, God grant him long life, was a Christian man. His proposal was, then, succinct and breathtaking: would it not serve the Lord and the great state of Chihuahua if they conspired to steal these religious canvases from the rebels of Tomóchic and present them as a gift to the great leader?

"With this gift," Carrillo told his guests, "presented to the great leader's bride as a gift from me, I can be assured of procuring her support and affections. And with these, I can retain the governorship in perpetuity!"

"Why," said González, "you will win every election."

It had been so clear, so audacious, that the three men had laughed out loud and drunk toasts late into the night.

Now, in Tomóchic, Gastélum prepared for his most important sermon. Upon reviewing the state of the chapel the night before, he had been appalled to discover the carved wooden statue of Teresita, the girl-witch, still there; its painted blue eyes as vacant as a devil's. Painted! He had heard that such an abomination was in the offing, but he had not expected to actually see it in its obscene niche. He had gone about blowing out the candles at the statue's feet.

Raging, he had called on the jefe político of the village, Don Gregorio — as if one of these peasants could be called a Don! Gastélum knew that Don Gregorio was a drunk and an adulterer, perhaps the only real sinner in town. It was God's unique wit to use such a man to do His divine will.

Don Gregorio handled civic duties while Cruz Chávez was busy being Pope. He had balked when Gastélum had first told him of the plot, but Carrillo had sent a bag of Mexican coins, and when Gregorio's puffy eyes saw so many golden eagles, he blinked and blinked and nodded sadly.

Now the church bell rang, and Father Gastélum went into the church and waited for the flock.

⁂

July 1891 — Tomóchic

My Dear Teresita:

I greet thee as Pope of the Sierras and as Your Representative to Mexico and the Tribes of the North. (It is me, Cruz!)

Bad situations have befallen us in Tomóchic, your mountain home should you ever choose to come. Forgive me the length of this letter. It is going to be more of a newspaper than a letter! But by God's will you will be able to read it all and forgive my orthography and grammar!

The heretic priest Gastélum came to our village and preached a sermon full of viper's poison directed at you! I will ask your forgiveness for reporting such unpleasant things, but you must know what the Enemy says about you now. We arose in defiance of the Roman papist! But first, I will relate as best I can the sermon he preached:

— Today's sermon (he began), The Satanic Practices of Miss Teresa Urrea.

We stirred in our seats, and some of the men tried to rise, but I gestured them down. — Sit, brothers, I told them. — Let us hear what the papist says.

— This young woman is an infernal abortion. She is Satan incarnate, for who is better to portray Satan than a rebellious woman? Her practices are diabolical. Her healings are an empty work of the devil! Nothing more! Proof that this young woman is Satan

in the flesh? She preaches against the teachings of Jesus Christ and his apostles!

We cried out. We shouted. But he continued.

Terrible things. I don't even recall what he said. He spit his poison for an hour or more, and the warriors grew still. For they had resolved in their hearts to allow me to confront and rebuke this despot.

I stood as he tried to leave the pulpit. My first shout froze him in his steps, and I addressed him firmly:

— Señor Priest (I said) from what we have heard thee say (I used the Usted form to show what scant respect I had left for him) we have seen that thou dost not know what thou is saying! (He gasped. It was resounding, like a slap!) If thou knew what thou wast saying, thou wouldst see that the Saint of Cabora does not preach against the teaching of Jesus Christ, but she herself commands us to go forth and live the preachings of Jesus Christ! (The people gathered around me cried "Amen" to this, I promise you!) The Lord God Himself has put before us a great example, a great teacher, and that is Jesus Christ! If we follow His teachings, if we live His words, then we will be in the footsteps of the Master and in this way we might too be as obedient as Jesus.

Gastélum put his hand over his heart as if I were stabbing him.

— Idiots! he cried. — She only says that to trick you! She has ensnared you with words! You have been seduced by a harlot! (Forgive me, Teresa, but that is what he said.) You will all fall into Hell in the hands of demons.

— *Perhaps we will, sir, I replied* — *I knew then he could do nothing to me or my people: Gastélum had no power of God on him at all.* — *Perhaps. But if she is evil, why are her actions purely generous, acts of charity and pity? Love. And thou and the rest of thine priests only preach hatred. Why is this? You hate all who are not Romans, and all you conspire to do is to take our money!*

— *Tithes! he cried.*

— *She has never asked a tithe of us! yelled Rubén.* — *She has only given succor!*

I interrupted him: — *Can you tell us why Satan would advise people to love God and their neighbors while you, who are representatives of God, advise us to hate anyone who does not follow your religion?*

I began to preach!

— *We, sir Father, are very ignorant, it is true. And perhaps we cannot tell the difference between those who have reason and those who do not. We are simple people. Do you speak the truth, or does the Girl of Cabora? I can tell you that our hearts tell us it is she, sir. She speaks the truth to us. She is the one who tells us to love all men, regardless of their failings or beliefs, because we are only men under God, and as such we are all brothers. While the priests tell us those who are not Romans are removed from God and not loved by Him. And she tells us that the farther a man has wandered from the path of God, the more we must practice goodness and love toward him so he might be enticed to return.*

— *So, you see, sir, our hearts dictate that Teresita tells us the truth. Our reason, then, tells us that if she speaks the truth, she cannot be sent by Satan. She has been sent as a daughter of God to put us on the road to goodness.*

The priest cried: — Blasphemy! How do you dare contradict and defy the rules and orders I have given you! Generation of vipers! Fools! Heretics! You and your devil should be excommunicated for all time from the Christian Church!

And so on. We followed him outside and there commenced a spirited session of yelling and cursing until the good father finally mounted his horse and sped out of town, calling curses down on our heads.

It was not until today that we discovered that someone had entered our church and cut our angelic cuadros from their frames and spirited them away! Devils? Romans? The government.

Someone is in league with Gastélum, and I do not know if he hates you or me more than the other.

I pray for you in the trust that you pray for me.

How is your porch swing?

Tu amigo i sirviente,
Cruz Chávez

❋

The response arrived in Tomóchic by mule train. It had been taken as far as the foothills by a vaquero on his way to hunt bear. He had paid a Rarámuri runner to carry it for him into the Papigochic wilderness. There, a mountain train of pack mules passed across the runner's path, and he handed off the letter to the second mule driver, who was a cousin of Cruz Chávez. It was now April of 1892.

Everybody was eager to see the mail. When Cruz opened the letter, he read it quietly.

December 1891

My Dear Pope Chávez,

Forgive me the tardiness of this letter. Your own only just arrived here, and I despair of this response returning to you by the New Year or even the Day of San Valentín! Oh! For the wings to fly! Then I could be with you in Tomóchic, my friend, away from these spies and dangers and troubles that encircle us every day!

Harm no man! That is God's iron rule, Cruz! You have been done a great harm! But together, we shall resolve to have your artworks returned, and your land blessed and inviolate forever! This is our holy battle. Justice for Tomóchic!

I await your next message . . .

With hope . . .

Your Friend Always,
Teresita

"What does she say? What does she say?" they cried.

He read it again, then folded the letter and put it in his pocket.

He cleared his throat.

"Teresita," he announced, "says she is in danger! She is surrounded by spies and evildoers!"

They stirred around him.

"And she says we must begin a holy war to save Tomóchic!"

Rubén started the shouting:

"Viva la Santa de Cabora!"

Fifty-four

SEGUNDO HAD AWAKENED one morning in May to find himself old. It took him by surprise. He looked in the mirror and realized his mustache had gone white, and his sideburns were silver, and gray wires seemed to be threaded through his hair. Oddly, his eyebrows were still black.

He had given up his home to Teresita. The crowds had made the forecourt of the main house into a bottleneck, and the back was too difficult to defend. So Tomás had asked him to build a stout fence around his small home and then move out. Oh well, a burro was never intended for a prince's bed, he decided. He had moved into Teresita's old bedroom in the house.

For the fence, his men had sunk tree trunks as uprights at a distance of fifty feet from the walls and doors of his house. There was a new guardhouse at the far corner so a buckaroo could keep an eye on the rear while Teresita slept or ministered in the front. The front of the fence had a wide gate with a swinging barricade that two men could handle to control the flow of bodies to the porch. The crossbeams of the fence itself were stout half trunks from pine trees in the hills.

It was Segundo who first noticed that Cabora itself seemed to mirror Teresita's moods. If she was happy, the crowd was joyful and full of laughter and song. If she was ill, the crowd was sullen and listless. She ate at the main house. When he went to eat breakfast, he saw that her hands were jittery. Teresita had these moments of sheer nervousness, almost manic. Noises made her jump, and small frustrations set her off. This morning, she suddenly jumped to her feet and snapped that she could not stand eggs ever again, then dropped her plate. It broke on the floor. She slapped her hands to her face and cried, then ran upstairs.

Tomás, numb now to almost anything, stirred his coffee and stared at the cooks.

Segundo picked up the pieces of the plate.

"She is having a difficult morning," he noted.

"Why should she be any different from the rest of us?" Tomás said.

When Segundo stepped out on the porch, he saw that the crowd, too, was nervous. They stirred and shoved. He heard shouts.

"It is going to be a bad day," he predicted.

Shortly, a contingent of cavalry and Rurales appeared at the far end of the crowd. Their brasswork gleamed in the sun. Plumes, flags. This seemed like no normal patrol. He opened the door and called inside: "Boss!"

Tomás joined him.

"What is this?" he asked.

"Trouble."

The people in the crowd shied away from the horses of the soldiers, like cattle trying to evade ropers. Suddenly, five soldiers waded into the crowd and pummeled a man to the ground. Tomás could see their rifles rise and fall as they butted him where he lay. The crowd jumped, surged. A man on the other side broke and ran. Tomás watched the mounted officer gesture once. His riders raised their rifles and fired as one. The sound was small and blunt in the heat, like a thin piece of wood being broken in half. A cloud of dust exploded from the runner's shirt, and he somersaulted over the edge of the arroyo.

The officer's horse started toward the house. The crowd parted. They fell far back, trying to make a wide path for the rider. He came ahead, leading a horse with a slumped prisoner tied to its back.

It was Juan Francisco, Tomás's eldest son.

And the officer was their old friend, Capitán Enríquez.

Tomás stepped forward.

"What is this?" he demanded.

"Don Tomás," said Enríquez, tipping his hat.

Juan Francisco had a black eye.

"We found this bandit on the road to Alamos," said Enríquez. "He claims to know you."

"You know very well he is my son!" sputtered Tomás.

"Do I?"

Enríquez gestured for his men to cut Juan free.

Segundo helped him down and took him inside.

Enríquez said, "Will you offer a representative of your government a drink of water?"

"Of course," Tomás replied.

Enríquez dismounted. He removed his hat. Tomás called for the house girls to bring a glass of water. Enríquez drank it down when it came and wiped his lips on his sleeve. He handed the glass back to the girl, who ran to the safety of the house.

"Gracias," he said to Tomás.

He looked at the restless crowd.

"We hear much of this rancho in Guaymas."

"What do you hear?"

"Nothing good."

Tomás said, "There is nothing bad here. Perhaps some fanaticism. But it will pass."

"Will it?"

Enríquez patted his horse.

"We found two rebels in your yard, Don Tomás. Do you doubt there are more?"

Tomás raised his hands.

"Surely, you can't expect me to know who is in this throng."

"Why not? Is this not your ranch? Are you not in charge? If you are not in charge, then who is?" Captain Enríquez turned to him. "The cavalry would be happy to control this situation for you if you are not able to attend to your own duties."

"Captain!" Tomás said, grabbing his arms. The riders behind drew their weapons. A Rural was off his horse in a second, holding a rifle in Tomás's face.

Enríquez raised one hand.

"Calma," he said.

The crowd was slipping back farther as they spoke.

"There has been talk of this place," Enríquez said. "And I have been charged with warning you. The talk will cease. This," he gestured at the pilgrims, "will stop."

"How?"

"My old friend," said Enríquez, "I will honor you by

offering you the chance to repair this damage on your own terms. Find a way to end it, or we will end it for you. Comprendes?"

Tomás hung his head.

"Sí."

"Now."

"I understand."

"Your son," Enríquez said, "could have died today. We could have hung him. You are very lucky. You should count yourself blessed and get on with your life."

He mounted. He tossed Tomás a crisp salute.

"Make sure, Don Tomás," he said, "that you go back to your old harvests." He turned his horse. Then, over his shoulder, he added: "Or I can assure you that Cabora will reap a harvest of lead." Enríquez spurred his horse and trotted away. His riders jumped aboard their nags and followed him.

The beaten man was already tied at hands and feet, and he was tossed over the back of Juan Francisco's horse while a small group of women wailed and tore at their hair and their dresses.

"Harvest of lead!" said Segundo. "What a poet."

Tomás went inside. He was red in the face. He had never been so humiliated. Or so frightened.

He hugged Juan Francisco.

"Where is she?" Tomás called.

Gaby said, "She is upstairs, mi amor."

"Where?"

"In our room."

Segundo stepped forward.

"Don't be angry at her," he said.

Tomás reached out and pulled Segundo's revolver from

his holster. This was the final proof to Segundo that he was too old to do anyone any good — the boss was able to steal his pistola!

"Wait!" Segundo said.

Tomás stomped up the stairs. He pounded on his own bedroom door.

"Go away!" Teresita yelled.

He threw the door open and stepped inside. "You and your idiotic dramas!" he shouted. "Get out of the bed and face me!"

"Father?"

"No more ridiculous little-girl scenes!" he roared. "The real world is here, now! The real world! Do you understand me?"

"What? What? I don't understand!"

"It ends now."

"What?"

"They came, do you know that? Did you even know that? They were here!"

"Who?"

"You mean angels didn't tell you? They killed one of your followers! They beat one of your pilgrims and took him away to hang him! *Who?* You ask me who?" he shouted.

He was insane with panic and rage. He grabbed her hair. *"Stop. This. Now!"*

"I cannot!"

"You will. You will. By God you will, or we will all die."

She sobbed. "Father! You're hurting me!"

Teresita sank to the floor.

Tomás suddenly realized the gun was in his hand, as if it were put there in a dream. And, as if in a dream, he raised it slowly and looked at it. He pulled back the hammer and listened to it cock.

"The army," he said, almost whispering now. "The army. They almost killed Juan. They drew guns on me. On my own front steps! They gave us fair warning, Teresita. They will kill us all. Kill your followers."

He bent down to her.

"They shot a man in the back. And do you know what? I think they did it to make a point. I don't think he was a rebel or a bandit. They just picked anyone to die so I would understand. These are the enemies we are facing."

"Father, father!" She wept.

"I am so sick of it," he spit. "The Saint of Cabora!"

"We need to pray."

"Prayers are bullshit."

"We have to rely on the Lord."

"The Lord doesn't care."

"Pray with me!"

"Prayers do not stop bullets. Prayers are nothing."

He put the gun to her head.

"What are you doing?" she cried.

"I am stopping this now."

"No!"

"If I do not stop you, everything is lost. You've pushed me to this! You and your insane pride!"

She covered her eyes. He yanked her hair with his free hand.

"I have to do this," he said, his voice shivering in his throat.

Suddenly, he let go of her hair, spun, and shot a hole in the wall. Below, all was screaming and terror in the house. Tomás threw the gun against the wall and fell to his knees before her. He put his arms around his daughter. She clutched him. Together, they sobbed.

"Please," Tomás cried, "please, please, help me. Stop this. Please, Teresa, please . . ."

Segundo cautiously stepped into the room.

"Oh Jesus!" he said. "I thought you'd killed her."

He backed out of the room and closed the door.

He stood guard outside it until they were done crying, and when Tomás came back out, he remained silent.

"Watch her, would you?" Tomás said.

"I always have."

Tomás looked in his eyes — his own eyes were red and tormented as if coals had been placed inside them. He reached out and laid his hand on Segundo's arm.

"What now, boss?" Segundo asked.

"The end," Tomás replied. He buttoned his jacket and squared his shoulders. "The end of everything," he said. And slowly went downstairs.

Supper was almost ready when the first bullet came through the window.

They all fell to the floor, hiding under the table. Segundo was already running for the door, his revolver in his hand. Tomás, alone, sat upright at the table, lit by a silver candelabra squirming with candle flame as he smoked. The second shot exploded through the wood of the window frame, showering the room with splinters. The family yelped. The cooks screamed as they crawled on the floor.

Tomás drained his glass of vino. He poured himself another. A third round came through the shattered window and blew adobe out of the far wall. "Buffalo gun," he said. "Fifty caliber. Sniper sons of whores."

Teresita rose slowly and peered around.

Tomás looked at her for a moment.

"I love you," he said.

They could hear distant tumult: great hootings and cursing.

Tomás took another sip of wine and looked under the table at Gabriela and Juan Francisco.

"Where do you suppose my supper is?" he asked.

He looked at his daughter again. She pulled out a chair in defiance of the bullets and sat beside him. He nodded, then. He knew what he would do.

Fifty-five

THE END BEGAN QUIETLY. Enríquez, in his command tent beyond Cantúa's old restaurant, took out his fountain pen and parchment. The pilgrim his men had arrested swung in the alamos trees, already attracting crows eager to eat his eyes. Enríquez had eaten a platter of beans and broiled pork. He drank milk with the meal. Then he sat at his small folding table and composed his report of the policing action at Cabora, the estimated number of hostiles — he put the number of indigenous rebels conservatively at twenty-five hundred out of an occupying force of eleven thousand supporters. He recommended immediate action — though, if possible, leniency for Tomás Urrea and his household in the ensuing unfortunate campaign.

Enríquez sealed the letter with wax and delivered it to a courier, who rode fast and delivered it to a mounted patrol that took it on to Navojoa. There, the letter was given to a telegraph operator, and Presidente Díaz was reading its contents by suppertime on the fourth day.

That was not all that he read. Padre Gastélum had written a blistering letter to Rome demanding the excommunication of the heretic Teresa Urrea, of her father, and of Cruz Chávez and all his apostate flock in Tomóchic. He had followed this with a telegram to Mexico City reporting on the brewing uprising in Tomóchic.

At Gastélum's urging, Governor Carrillo had included a report with the stolen canvases. In this report, he warned of the revolt now starting to sweep the Indian of the Papigochic. Valuable mining and timber lands were at risk should yet another Indian war be allowed to ignite. Worse yet because it was a war of fanatics, inflamed by the witch, Teresa Urrea of Sonora. These reports had arrived within days of the Enríquez telegram. Díaz was swift to respond. A force of one hundred riders from Chihuahua and Sonora assembled. They united in the desert and began their ride to Cabora to put an end to the insurrection.

At dawn, Cruz Chávez and a light militia party began to trot down the banks of the River of Spiders, and by eight o'clock they were dropping out of the sierra. The men were indistinguishable from the land that held them. They stretched their bodies between the boulders of the slopes, lay in the pathways of snakes without moving, allowed lizards to slink along the lengths of their weapons, felt the small claws pluck at their knuckles as the reptiles of the valley took the sun on the stocks of their Winchesters.

And they inserted themselves into the bushes and stands of nopales, settled into languid crouches that became comfortable as they configured themselves to match the twists of the branches and trunks, as they let the cool squares and triangles of shade soothe their backs, the creases and ripples in their clothes matching the shifting patches of shadow until they vanished.

And they settled themselves along the trunks of alamos and willows, along the crooked pillars of the pines and the wilder, more passionate extremities of the mesquites. Their rifles, wrapped in tattered cloth, tied with flowers and weeds, grasses and leaves, lay along their quiet bodies like branches and deadfall. They sucked pebbles and chewed grass.

Indians on the road had warned them that this was the spot. Those riders of the government who sought to silence the power of God — and the daughter of God — with bullets would pass by here. All armies ultimately crossed this nearly dry streambed.

They were the Tigers, and they waited like tigers, still. Some closed their eyes. Some watched. All of them periodically glanced at Cruz Chávez, settled near the road, in a triangle of boulders not ten paces from the brook that tossed green and yellow worms of sunlight into the low branches of the trees. The men dreamed as they waited.

"I sent her a letter," Cruz said. "She knows our troubles."

The men made assenting sounds, grunts, clicks of their mouths.

"We will stop the cavalry before it can do harm to her or

to our village," he said. "Then we will go to her, and she will bless us. She will get our paintings back. She will give us our blessing back, you'll see. And we will carry her back to Tomóchic! No one would dare enter our valley then!"

"Viva Teresa," they murmured. "Bless us, Teresita."

When Cruz rose, they would all rise with him, and they would be shooting.

❀

They had been told the cavalry was coming. Riders had sped to Cabora and warned Tomás. He rushed to Teresita's chapel and took her by the arms and hurried her upstairs to her old room in the tower. It smelled like Segundo now.

"They're coming," he said. "It has begun."

"What do I do?" she asked.

"Stay in your room. Promise me," he said. "Do not come out of your room until I come for you."

He looked out through her shutters.

"I don't know what the army wants. If they come to take you away, your fanatics . . ." He looked at her and shrugged. "I'm sorry," he said. "Your followers might revolt. You can imagine the bloodbath . . ."

He looked back outside.

"I don't want anyone hurt," she said.

"I know."

"Not even the army."

"I know."

He slammed the shutters closed, latched them.

❀

The twenty-eight Tigers lay in the landscape for many hours. They whispered prayers of thanksgiving. They whispered

Christmas hymns, and they dreamed of roast goose, ham, fresh soup, dried corn. They dreamed of their wives. They dreamed of the toys they would carve for their children, looked ahead to the Day of the Three Kings, when all children received gifts along with Jesus himself, back behind them so far in time. They promised themselves to kill quickly, cleanly, so they could return to their homes, their beds, their families, their church.

Buenaventura appeared on the porch. He had his old .44 pistola in his belt. A new repeater rifle.

"You!" said Tomás.

"Me."

"Where have you been?"

"Around."

"Thank you for coming."

"They won't be taking my ranch away from me!" Buenaventura boasted. His father cocked an eyebrow.

Tomás's security force was complete. Ancient Don Teófano wore a scowl and held his shotgun across his knees on a bench on Teresita's new house's porch. His niece sat on the step with a machete, a pistol, and a hunting rifle. Her husband manned the guard hut in the corner. Two vaqueros lay on the roof with rifles. Juan Francisco was behind a wagon parked to the east of the main gate of the big house. Segundo hid behind the wall on the west side. Shooters crouched on the main house's roof. Tomás stood on the porch, and Buenaventura stood beneath him. He looked for plums on the little tree, but couldn't find any. Inside, Gaby and the maids and cooks all had revolvers. They passed them among themselves, trying to figure out how to use them.

Tomás looked at his pocket watch.

"Wait for it," he called.

They didn't wait long at all.

The cavalry appeared in the shimmering distance — a double column of horses, standards flying above in a ripple of violent color. They appeared and faded inside their own cloud of yellow dust, like ghosts riding out of fire. Their trumpets warbled across the llano, steely insectile sounds, piercing and drifting away with the relentless hot wind. As the column neared, the ground began to reverberate with their coming, the four hundred hooves of the big steeds shaking the pebbles, feeling like a heartbeat through the feet of the People.

Rurales galloped out to join their comrades. Pilgrims slunk away from the house. Hundreds of them dropped into the arroyo and crouched in fear. Many more simply moved outside the fences and took up a position of curiosity, looking innocent and blank as the soldiers passed, as if they had bought tickets to a bullfight. Those most loyal to the Saint of Cabora took up their arms and faced the horde. Old rifles, rusted pistols, bows and arrows, lances. Old men held hoes and pitchforks.

Buenaventura said, "Papá? I don't mind dying!"

"Who are you calling Papá, cabrón?" shouted Juan.

"No one is dying today," Tomás grunted as he mounted his stallion.

"I am not afraid!" Buenaventura cried.

"I am," his father replied.

He rode among the pilgrims, saying, "Calma, calma." Segundo watched the far edge of the crowd. At least his eyes were still good. His men rode among the pilgrims. They talked to them as they would have talked to spooked horses or jittery cattle. Soothing them. Calming them.

"Stay cool," Segundo said. "Don't get excited."

"I'm not excited," said Buenaventura.

"Liar."

And Tomás continued crooning to them all until the cavalry leader rode through the main gate.

"Calma, señores, por favor. Calma."

❋

Emilio Enríquez rode at the head of the column. His men drew their rifles from their scabbards as one and rode with their fingers on their triggers. Tomás turned his stallion sideways in their path and sat with his hand on the butt of his revolver.

"Welcome back, Captain Enríquez!" he called.

Enríquez smiled at him. "Major," he said.

"No!"

Major Enríquez dipped his head.

"At your service, Don Tomás."

"A promotion," Tomás said. "In honor of this precarious duty, no doubt?"

Enríquez dipped his head again.

Tomás reached over and shook his hand.

"Muy bien!" he said.

"Word of my promotion arrived last night with the courier, Señor Ponce de León."

"Oh?"

"He bore many documents. Some troubling. But some pleasing to me."

"Ah!"

"Don Tomás." The major nodded. "It is a fine morning, is it not?"

"It is!"

"Though there are seditious rumblings in the hills."

Tomás watched the cavalry and the Rurales spread out.

"However," the major sighed, "in spite of the rebellious spirit afoot in the land, this fine ranch is a bastion of loyalty to the president. Am I right?"

Tomás said nothing.

"Is this a social visit?" said Urrea. "Would you like to come in?"

The major removed his hat. Wiped his brow with a white handkerchief.

"If only I could, sir," he said. "However, Señor Ponce de León has delivered to me a series of documents that link your daughter to the rebels hereabouts."

"Rebels? Where?"

"Quite a party you have here," said the major, gesturing at the pilgrims. "I see no one has chosen to go home."

"I believe," said Tomás, "they are as eager as I am to see what your disposition is today. After they see how the great army is feeling, then they will go home. I am certain."

"A political rally, eh?" said the major.

"It is . . . religious in nature."

"Religion," Enríquez repeated. "Worse than politics."

"Indeed."

"I hear tell there's a heresy here. Word came of that last night as well. Oh! Señor Ponce de León had quite a portfolio! Not simply revolt, you see."

Tomás snorted. "As if the church itself isn't so much horse manure."

Enríquez looked away. "That's debatable, my friend."

He gestured around him. "And these Indians? Are they here for religion, or war?"

"It's their country," said Tomás.

"*Really?*" the major replied. "I thought this was the Mexican Republic."

"Where your horses are standing now, it is the Urrea Republic."

"Ah! That clarifies things for me."

The major's horse shook its head, rattling the bit in its mouth.

"Sedition, you know, is even more dangerous than heresy."

He turned his horse away.

"For now," he said, "you and your daughter are under house arrest. My men will keep watch. Feel free to have your assistants do their work as usual, but all preaching stops. No contact between Miss Urrea and the . . . *pilgrims.*"

"Until?" Tomás asked.

"Until new orders arrive," the major replied. He saluted. "I must oversee the hunt for the rebels," he said. "An officer's work is never done."

"Good day!" Tomás shouted as he retreated, but the major never looked back.

❈

Enríquez returned the next morning.

"Major!" Tomás cried with false goodwill. "Will you dismount today and have a coffee with us?"

Enríquez shook his head.

"Not today," he replied.

"Have a smoke," Tomás said, offering the major a thin black cigar.

The major spurred ahead and stood his horse beside Tomás. He bent down. They shared a match. He had dust on his whiskers.

He said, "I apologize, Don Tomás. We have been sent to stop the turmoil here, as you know. Your daughter has preached liberal doctrines. Anti-Díaz in nature, no? And now she has been charged with consorting with armed rebels."

"Una pendejada!" Tomás scoffed.

"I had hoped you would have left last night."

"No! We were under house arrest."

"True, but then you would have been someone else's problem."

The major gestured at the scarred Rurales glaring at Tomás. He felt as if he was seeing them for the first time. Ugly brutes, dark men, eyes like flat buttons, thin Chinese whiskers at the corners of their mouths, horrid ancient knife wounds running their cheeks and chins.

"We have troops with us come from Huatabampo to interdict the Tigers of the Sierra. Men are riding from Cocorit, from Hermosillo, from Guaymas, and Guerrero in Chihuahua."

"Tigers?" asked Tomás.

"Come now." The major puffed his cigar. "We have reports of their being here, armed. Talking strategies with your daughter. We know you spoke to their leader on your porch."

"I speak to many people." Tomás shrugged.

"We received a report that they're coming back to confer with her."

"Why?"

"Armed revolt, Don Tomás. Armed revolt. They have

recognized your daughter as a saint. Only she can express God's plan to them, you see. They're coming to seek her counsel."

"Don't be ridiculous," Tomás said. "Teresita doesn't care about politics."

"Orders are orders," said the major.

"And what are your orders?"

"We are to stop the Tigers," the major replied. "And Miss Urrea."

"Stop her how?"

Enríquez looked at him sadly.

"I suppose that is your choice," he said. "Either she dies, or she goes to prison."

Tomás stared at him.

He looked at each of the military riders.

"Not acceptable," he said.

"Oh? Do you believe you have a choice?"

Tomás smiled.

"A free man," he said, "always has a choice, my dear Major Enríquez!"

Enríquez blew air through his lips.

"How do you like that cigar?" Tomás said.

"Very rich."

"One takes small pleasures where one can."

Tomás raised his right hand.

"For example, I," he said, "dearly love to shoot my guns when given the opportunity."

Juan Francisco stepped out from behind the wagon, levering a round into the firing chamber. Segundo and his men pulled their rifles and ratcheted their rounds. Don Teófano pumped a round into his shotgun. His niece raised her gun. The soldiers raised their rifles. Pilgrims scattered.

Buenaventura worked the lever on his rifle. It was a small symphony of metallic snicks and clacks.

The cavalrymen jumped at their weapons.

The major raised his hand.

"Hold your fire," he yelled.

The apocalypse was deferred.

"You are making me raise my voice," Enríquez said. "This is bad form."

"Leave," Tomás said.

Enríquez looked down at him. "You are hurting my feelings," he said.

Tomás offered Enríquez one of the sayings of the People: "If one doesn't feel like it, two can't fight."

Enríquez looked at him.

Tomás dug in his vest pocket, produced a key ring.

"My dear Major," he said. "My daughter is sitting in her bedroom, as any chaste Mexican lady would. Her room is there, on the second floor."

He gestured to the main house.

The major glanced at the shuttered windows.

"Her door is, of course, locked. There are rough elements here who would not honor or respect the safety of a young lady. I am sure you understand."

Tomás offered the keys to him.

"Our front door is also locked. One never knows these days. But here, take the keys. Do enter my home, and do open her door and take her from us."

The major looked at the keys.

"But kill me first," Tomás said. "I would become very emotional if you invaded my home, so I suggest you try to shoot my right-hand man over there —" He waved toward Segundo. "He is very protective of Teresa. Shoot him first.

I recommend you then kill my son by the wagon. Then, on the porch, you might see my stepson." Buenaventura beamed. What was a stepson? It sounded fancy to him. Tomás continued: "Be sure to shoot this crazy old man with the shotgun. I don't know what my cowboys will say, and I cannot speak for these damned pilgrims. They're all insane, if you ask me. But once you've cleaned them out, do me a favor. Shoot my wife. She is armed and, frankly, at the point where she might kill anyone who comes in the door."

"She is very tense," Segundo offered.

The major smiled. He barked out a laugh. "Pinche Urrea!" he said. "Qué cabrón eres." He laughed again. "You are sly, I'll give you that."

Tomás puffed his cigar and squinted. "I love my daughter."

The major scratched his chin. "I have two daughters," he said.

"What, no boys?"

"God hasn't graced me yet with boys."

Tomás made a sound like *Uf!*

"You should live longer," he said. "Have sons."

The major took the cigar from his mouth, studied the coal at the end. "We had fun in Los Mochis, didn't we," he said.

"We drank beer," Tomás reminded him.

The major turned in his saddle and gestured to his men. They put their arms down. "All right?" he said.

Tomás waved at his people, and they lowered their rifles.

Enríquez spun his arm around once, over his head, and pointed at the gate. The men slid their rifles back in their scabbards and turned their horses and trotted back toward the exit of Cabora.

"For the children," he said.

Tomás flicked his little cigar away.

"Gracias."

"I understand your . . . situation," said the major. He glanced at the house. "It will probably cost me my head. But I will give you some time to, ah, speak to your daughter. We will camp outside the ranch, near the creek there. I will call a meeting of my officers. We need to discuss our plans. And you . . . you can do what you must. I can give you two, possibly three hours."

Tomás put his hand out. The major took it. They shook.

"You are a gentleman, my friend," Tomás said.

"I am a soldier," the major replied. "Nothing more."

He backed his horse away, but before he turned to ride out alone, he said, "Be careful."

"We will."

"Be fast," the major said. And, "Happy Easter."

"We missed Easter this year," Tomás said.

"Pity."

Then Enríquez rode out of the ranch, nodding to the pilgrims and the vaqueros as he went.

Fifty-six

THEY TOOK LITTLE WITH THEM. Tomás wrapped some food in a blanket, and he took his weapons. Gaby cried as he embraced her.

"Don't weep, my love," he said. "No one can catch us — we're the fastest riders on the plains."

He kissed her feverishly, hard enough to hurt their mouths.

"I'll have her in Aquihuiquichi tonight," he said. "By morning, we'll be rested enough to get things ready for you. A few weeks in the country, and we can all return home."

"And if there is trouble?" Gabriela said.

"Listen, Enríquez is a good man. You saw that here today! We'll slip away to the mountains. I'll take Teresita to Bayoreca, or into Chihuahua. We'll seek asylum there! Then I'll get her to Texas, and Aguirre will shelter her. Don't cry! I will be back here with you all in a month at the latest."

Gaby hugged Teresita.

Segundo already had two strong horses saddled and waiting.

Teresita took nothing. She left her rosary behind. She left her herbs and her wooden crosses. She was beyond religious symbols now. What she had of God, she carried within her, and there was no totem that could give her comfort or strength anymore.

She held Gaby in her arms.

"I'm sorry," she whispered.

"I will come to you," Gaby said.

"I love you."

"And I love you."

Segundo offered Teresita a small silver pistol. She shook her head.

"Please," he begged.

"I cannot."

She put her face against his chest. It was hard. The wool of his chest hair scratched against the cotton of his shirt.

"I wish I could go with you," he said.

"You must defend the ranch."

He put his hand on her hair.

"Bless me, then," he said.

She kissed him and held him and whispered, in the old tongue, "Lios emak weye."

Segundo was startled to find he was shedding tears.

They hurried through the house.

Buenaventura stood on the front steps.

Tomás stood beside him.

"Son," he said.

Buenaventura turned to him.

"You did well today," said Tomás. "I was proud of you."

Buenaventura smiled.

"You are a man now."

Tomás put his hand on his son's back.

Juan Francisco joined them.

"Teresita and I must flee the ranch," Tomás explained. "We can't take anyone with us — they'll only slow us. You know your sister rides like a hurricane. I think I can keep up with her."

"And the ranch?" Buenaventura asked. "Will Segundo run things here?"

"Segundo!" said Tomás. "This is our ranch. He's the second in command. Always has been. He'll follow orders."

"Whose orders?"

Tomás leaned away and pretended to stare at them both in shock.

"Can you two get along?"

The boys nodded.

"My other children are all in Alamos. I need men here. It's *our* ranch," Tomás said. "It's *your* ranch, boys!"

"What?"

"You run the ranch. You're the men here."

"Me? Run the ranch?" cried Buenaventura.

"The two of you. I'm leaving you in charge! Segundo and the vaqueros will do what you say, so be smart. And you protect my Gaby, you hear?"

"Father?" Buenaventura said.

"Take care of things for me." Tomás embraced his boys, and kissed them each on the cheek.

When he left, Buenaventura sat down on the step and stared at the ground. Juan Francisco stood taller and stared at the confused pilgrims staring back at him.

Tomás rode his immense black stallion. Segundo had chosen a fast palomino for Teresita. She slit her skirts with his knife and drew up her petticoats. They moved out, slowly at first, keeping the bulk of the main house between themselves and the front of the property. They slunk away from the kitchen, down between the outhouses and the ravaged herb garden. They cut around a long chicken coop, where the chickens had mostly been poached and all the eggs stolen and eaten by pilgrims, then behind Segundo's house. They eased down the bank of the arroyo, moved around the turbid green water of last winter, their horses' hooves pressing deep crescents in the black mud, a glitter of tiny flies fleeing their shadows. The cottonwoods were soft with new green, just starting to fill out in their May finery; still, the ends of their branches were bare, and they clawed the sky like skeletal hands ripping chunks of sun out of the storm clouds. Heat lightning skittering around the crowns of the hills. A heavy darkness rising from the far sea, coming toward them, tattering into white streamers and evaporating above the llano's heat. Horseflies stinging blood out of the flanks of their mounts. Pilgrims already calling to her as she passed.

"Bless you, Teresa!"

Hands extended, she touched their fingertips as they reached for her.

"Come back to us, angel!" they said.

She touched their heads.

"Viva Teresa!"

They climbed the far bank.

"Viva la Santa de Cabora!"

Tomás looked back at his home one last time and put his silver spur to his horse. The horses exploded over the banks and screamed across the burning plain.

And the People began to slip away. With their saint gone, they went to the four directions. Some hurried. Some tarried. But the camps began to break down within the hour. Fires kicked asunder.

The Yaquis went north and the Mayos went south. The few Tarahumara ran back toward their sierras, and the

Apaches galloped to Arizona. The Pimas moved west of Tucson, and the Seris walked toward the sea.

Mestizos hurried toward Sinaloa, their dream of salvation shattered. The Arizonans and New Mexicans and Texans hove their wagons onto the dusty roads and made less haste — the Mexican army would not dare attack gringo caravans. But all along the way, people stopped them and asked, *Is it true?* And *Have they taken the Saint?* And they spread the word — they said, *Yes, she is gone.* They said, *Yes, she is dead.* They said the army was set to massacre them all.

In the hills, the fighters gathered. They whispered of fire. They spoke late into the night of rifles, machetes, ambush, and slaughter.

As the People fled, the warriors drew closer to Cabora and watched.

Fifty-seven

THE SHADOW OF THE MESQUITE that extended onto the road a few feet beyond the shadow tucked between the three boulders spoke:

"Do you remember the crippled girl at Cabora?"

The shadow between the boulders raised its head.

"Rubén," Cruz said. "You know better than to talk."

"I was just thinking."

Cruz lay back down.

His twenty-eight gunmen remained invisible. He could

have spotted many of them from the road. But even knowing where to look, he could not have seen them all.

"So?" said Rubén. "Do you remember her?"

"I remember."

"We never saw her again."

"Yes."

"Do you think Teresita healed her?"

"Of course." After a while: "I know it by faith. She healed
José, didn't she?"

"That old goat."

They chuckled.

"She will bless us. We must do this out of loyalty to her.
She will care for us, but we must protect her the way we
would protect our own wives."

"Amen!"

"Now be quiet," Cruz said.

"I was just thinking," Rubén repeated. "Just thinking
about that girl at Cabora."

"Think about soldiers," Cruz said. "Think about soldiers
arresting Teresita. Think about soldiers entering our church,
taking down our saints."

"I am."

"Think about soldiers in Tomóchic."

"I am."

"Think about them shooting Teresa. Shooting your
mother. Your wife. They will do it if we allow them the
chance. That girl in Cabora? Think of your daughter
instead!"

"I'm thinking about Indios in the trees, Cruz."

"Yes."

"We have all seen Indios hanging."

"Yes."

"Bastards."

"Yes."

Cruz heard the cold sound of Rubén's hammer being pulled back.

※

From far above, where the buzzards and the turkey vultures now gathered, turning slow circles, the entire landscape seemed alive with movement. The tides of pilgrims aimlessly wandered around Cabora, around and around. Waves of brown bodies broke away this way and that — trailing toward Alamos, toward Hermosillo, toward the sierras, toward the far American border, down the arroyo and the Río Yaqui toward Guaymas and the sea. The cavalrymen and the Rurales cut through this human flood, surrounding the main house and dismounting. And a column of horsemen set out at a fast trot on their way to the mountain road, planning to climb into the sierra and police the insurgents at Tomóchic. Dust like smoke and smoke like clouds of dust carried in all directions with the whipping wind. Yaqui warriors flitted through the dry hills, attracted by the doings at Cabora, ready to fight the cavalry, and the thieves along the roads made ready to attack the fleeing pilgrims. The empty land was full: wagon trains, herds, neighboring ranches alive with cattle, the mining mule trains, American outlaws raiding a string of horses, vaqueros. And two small figures racing between foothills, small and lonely on the vast land — and behind them, coming from the bosques beyond Cabora, a wedge of horses, fast riders bent low over their necks, tattered standards snapping behind them, the quickest attack squad of the cavalry — racers and killers — cutting the trail of the fugitives, reading the signs as they sped, not yet in sight of Teresita or her father, but running full out, gaining, gaining.

※

The cavalry moved smartly up the foothills road. The riders maintained order, riding in two tight columns, their bright metalwork flaring in the sun, their uniforms clean and their hats shining. Their saddles, rifles, saddlebags, swords, lances, flagpoles, spurs, reins, bits, trumpets, iron horseshoes all rattled and clanged, raised a musical jangle that could be heard for a half mile. The soldiers' brass buttons were nearly blinding, throwing sparks.

Ahead, a group of old women appeared. The women seemed to rise from the soil itself, materializing, the way Indians always seemed to, out of nowhere. They were dressed in black — long dresses, and shawls over their heads.

The lieutenant riding at the head of the column had been put there by Major Enríquez personally. He saw the old ladies and said, "Are they going to Mass?" to his assistant. He was laughing. His hands had just risen off his pommel, palms out, fingers splayed and down, in a gesture any Mexican — even the Tigers — would recognize as a sign of bafflement, surrender to some greater mystery. His shoulders rose in the exaggerated shrug that completed the gesture. The corners of his lips bent down sharply.

He turned back to the hags and shouted his challenge: "Viva quién?"

Rebels would shout *Viva Tomóchic!* Or *Viva la Santa de Cabora!* A wise traveler would simply cry *Viva Porfirio Díaz!* and live. But the old women said nothing.

"Viva quién!" the lieutenant repeated.

The women stood, mute.

"I said, Long live who!"

And a male voice shouted: "Long live Holy Mary, Saint Joseph, and the Saint of Cabora!" The old women whipped back their skirts. And in an instant it became clear they were not women at all. Cruz Chávez, at the center, pulled his rifle out from his petticoats and fired.

The lieutenant was still shrugging when his heart exploded. A four-foot geyser of blood, bits of heart and bone sprayed the faces of the riders behind him. Then the other Tigers opened fire. Three riders had fallen by the time the cavalrymen drew their rifles and shot back. The valley filled with smoke and clouds of dust kicked up by the horses. One of the army's volleys went through the upper left chest of José Chávez, Cruz Chávez's elder brother.

The Tigers ran as fast as they could while holding José between them. He cried and gurgled. Blood made his shirt greasy and cold as it gushed from his chest. When they were sure the army could not see them, Cruz himself clamped his hand over José's mouth to still his yells of pain. They tore their shirts, made wadding that they packed into the gaping holes in José's back and chest. They used the women's dresses in which they had hidden for black bandages.

Cruz laid hands on his brother's head. He prayed over him. The men wept to hear José's ghastly cries. He was insane with pain and blood loss.

"What do we do? What do we do?" they asked Cruz.

They had never seen him afraid, but this was his big brother. His hands shook as he held José to his breast. His own shirt became sticky with blood.

"Cabora," he gasped. "We must carry him to Cabora, my brothers! Teresita can save him!"

"Amen!"

"Viva la Santa!"

They took his right arm and his two legs and they held him between them. They made a sling of the remaining skirts of the old women and used them to hold up José's sagging midsection. And they ran.

Fifty-eight

BY THE TIME Tomás and Teresita got to Aquihuiquichi, they were too tired to do much more than sit. They had ridden like creatures fleeing a fire. They leapt fences and logs, leapt over creeks, scattered cattle and deer in panics, drove crows and coveys of quail into the sky in explosive terror.

The horses were stumbling by the time they reached the smaller ranch. Teresita's legs shook, and she retched when she dropped from the horse. Tomás fetched her a cup of water and held her as she shook.

"Rest," he said. "Rest an hour."

"Just a few minutes," she said, but once inside, she fell into a bed. By the time he had secured the door and come back to check on her, she was asleep.

Still, the cavalry came. And by the time they entered Aquihuiquichi, scattered riders from the ambuscade had joined them, inflaming them with stories of the rocks coming alive, of Indians dressed as women stepping out of tree trunks and murdering their comrades. They rode on the house firing their weapons in the air, yelling curses, coming in a chaos of noise and murder.

"Teresa Urrea!" they shouted.

Tomás stepped out the door, waving off his few cowboys, who were outgunned by the soldiers.

"Bring her out!" the officer in charge shouted.

"I will not."

"She will die in the house, then," the cavalryman responded. He signaled and a rider came forth with a tree branch wrapped in torn cloth. "Light it."

The rider struck a match and lit the torch.

"She burns," the officer said. "To kill the lice, burn the bed."

"For the love of God, man!" Tomás shouted.

"God? We don't worry about God here!"

"In the name of all that is holy!"

"I am all that is holy," the officer said. "I am your religion now."

Tomás held up his hands, as if he could stop the horses by himself.

"She dies here," the rider said, "or she dies in prison."

The door behind Tomás opened. He smelled her before she stepped out.

"Teresita, no," he hissed.

"Do not burn this house," she said.

"Teresa Urrea?" said the rider.

"Sí."

"The one they call the Saint of Cabora?"

"It is I."

The cavalryman looked at her. He sneered, shook his head.

"You? You're nothing!"

He laughed. His men laughed.

"She's not even pretty," a rider shouted.

"Age?" the officer demanded.

"Nineteen."

"All this trouble, and you are a stinking *little girl?*" He was disgusted with this whole thing — with Indians and fanatics, with messiahs and criminals, with this niña and her hysterical father. "Shoot her," ordered the officer.

Rifles rose.

"No!" Tomás shouted.

He stepped in front of her and opened his arms even wider.

"No!"

"Move aside."

"Shoot me first."

"I'm telling you to move aside, señor."

"If you shoot my daughter, let the bullets pass through me first."

"You have no charges against you."

"Kill me first."

"Sir."

"Kill me."

"Chingado!"

They moved in, began kicking him, trying to break Tomás away from Teresita. But he gritted his teeth and took their boots to his ribs and his head.

"Suéltala, pendejo!"

"Vas a ver, buey!"

They rained curses down on father and daughter.

"Te vamos a dar una madriza, cabrón!"

"Mátenlos a patadas!" they started to yell. They wanted to see the two of them kicked to death. But one of the riders came to his senses and said to the officer, "He's a friend of Major Enríquez."

"Eh?"

"The major has slept in his house," the rider warned.

"Shit!"

The officer called off his men, using his reins to flog the nearest soldier's back.

Tomás had a line of blood running down his lip. He and Teresita were breathing like winded animals. And still he did not let go of her.

"You will not step aside?" the officer asked.

"Never."

"Damn you."

Tomás took handfuls of Teresita's clothes in a tight grasp and pulled her against his back.

The cavalrymen looked at each other. They shrugged. Tomás heard one say, "Let's kill him and the bitch and go home."

The horses moved together. The riders conferred. "She's just a witch. Kill her." The officer shook his head, muttered.

He turned his horse back to Tomás.

"You are making my life difficult," he said. "To take your daughter to prison, we'd have to ride to Guaymas. Look how tired we are. And she'll only die on the gallows there. Or she'll die on the road. You would save us all a lot of trouble."

Tomás stood his ground.

"I will accompany her to prison!" he announced.

"For what reason?"

"I am directly impeding the doing of your duties. Am I not? Do you think I'm an idiot? Do you think I'll let you take my daughter off alone?"

The cavalryman sighed. "A bullet would be kinder than the rope," he said. "And I will have to requisition a wagon for her. And another for you! Come now!"

"We will go to the prison," Tomás said. "And if they hang her, I will dangle on the rope beside her."

The officer shook his head, laughed.

"Have it your way," he said. "But if I get bored with you on the ride to Guaymas . . ." He held up his finger, aimed at them, and made a pistol-shot noise with his lips.

They waited out the night inside the ranch house. Tomás berated himself. He should have ridden on. He should have vanished in the hills. He thought he could preserve something of his life, something of Cabora. Teresita shushed him. But he was beyond consolation.

By midmorning, two crude wooden wagons had appeared. They looked like lion cages from some abandoned desert zoo. Tomás was thrown roughly into his. Teresita was lifted by two soldiers. She briefly thought of making herself too heavy to lift, but did not, for fear that they would harm her father.

Next came the days on the open roads. Hands tied. Kicked and cursed at, sunburned, infernally thirsty. When she went to relieve herself, the soldiers followed her and laughed at her, shouted obscenities. Once, Tomás tried to defend her, and they clubbed him over the head with a rifle butt.

"Kill them," he whispered to her through the bars of his cage. "You can do it."

"Father, please."

"Remember what you did to Buenaventura! Do it again."

"I must not."

"All right. Don't kill them. Just . . . just paralyze the bastards. Do it! Blind them!"

She turned from him.

"If you love me, you will kill these pigs. Kill them."

"No," she cried. "No, no, no!"

"Shut up," her guard snapped, kicking her cage.

The soldiers parked Teresita's wagon near a small stand of trees. They rolled Tomás down the road. "Teresa!" he called. "Teresa!" He called to her until he was out of sight.

She heard a faint trumpet bleat.

"Here he comes," said her guard.

"Who?" she asked. She was on her knees in the cage, turning to keep her eyes on him as he circled. He pulled his horse back.

"The general," he said. "General Bandála."

They all laughed.

"He will want a look at you," the rider said.

"That's not all he'll want," called another.

They laughed again, and she watched them slap each other on the back and the arm.

For the second time, Cabora had been destroyed. Passion had torn apart the fences, had trampled all the crops. The gardens were moldering dung heaps. Windows on Segundo's house were broken by angry youths fleeing the cavalry. Dead dogs lay in the distance, dead burros. A lame bull limped near the tumbled beehives, a bullet hole visible in his haunch. The People, those of them left, hurried to El

Potrero and hid in their shacks. The vaqueros stood around, seemingly stunned by blows to the head. It was a dead place of inaction. Even the few chicks that walked across the Alamos road seemed dirty, covered in dust. The gates to the main-house courtyard were open. One of them was pulled off its hinges and hung at an angle.

The men from Tomóchic put José down outside the gates. The little plum tree had been uprooted. As Cruz stepped up to the door, a young girl hurried out, carrying a silver platter. She saw Cruz and gasped and dropped her tray and ran back in the house.

Segundo came out. He put his pistol in Cruz's face. He said: "You."

"What has happened here?" asked Cruz.

Segundo pulled back the hammer. Cruz watched the cylinder rotate.

"The end of the world," Segundo said.

Cruz stared at the pistol.

"Do not think," Segundo continued, "that you can come here to take anything."

"Take?" said Cruz.

Juan Francisco came out behind Segundo.

"Who is this?" he said. Then, seeing the silver platter, he said, "What is this?"

"I am Cruz Chávez," Cruz announced. "I am a friend of Teresita."

Juan Francisco shook his head.

"Spare us any more friends," he said.

He stepped out, picked up the platter, and walked back inside.

Cruz sat on the step and put his head in his hands.

Segundo saw he had dried blood on his shoulders and down his back.

"Are you shot?" he asked.

Cruz shook his head.

"My brother."

Segundo heard the groaning coming from beyond the wall.

He lowered his pistol.

He went to the wall and peeked over.

"That cabrón is in a grave state," he said.

"Sí. Mi hermano está grave."

Segundo holstered his pistol.

"It is all ruined," Cruz was saying. "All ruined."

Segundo put his hands in his pockets.

"Those damned pilgrims," he said. "They destroyed everything."

"And Teresa?" asked Cruz.

Segundo shook his head.

"Gone."

Cruz put his head down.

"All ruined. All ruined."

After a few moments, he rose. He went out the gate. Segundo watched him. He stood in the road and faced his men. "Teresita," he told them, "has left. Things here," he gestured with his left hand, "have ended."

Segundo was amazed to see the men fall to their knees and weep like children. They rested until dusk, then they trotted away. Cruz, as ever in the lead, cried all the way into the mountains. José, left behind, moaned as Segundo had him put on the porch.

❈

General Bandála came forward in the midst of a troop of heavily armed men. He rode directly to Teresita's cage and peered in at her.

"So this is the great saint," he said.

He drank from a canteen, offered it to Teresa through the bars of her cage. She turned her face from it. He corked the canteen and hung it on his pommel.

"That's all right, that's all right," he said. "You will be thirsty soon enough. You will ask for water, and we will see if I feel like giving it to you."

His men laughed.

He dismounted.

Teresita saw that as soon as he was off his horse, he looked like a toad. His legs were bandy from spending his life in the saddle. His torso was short, and he was tubby and neckless. Rubber lips.

"Ride on," he ordered.

The men saluted and galloped away.

Two guards took up posts on high ground.

The general smacked the bars of the cage and smiled in at her.

"Now we'll see," he said. "Now we'll see."

He unlatched the gate at the back of the wagon.

"What are you doing?" she said.

"You will find out soon enough," he said. He was smiling. He threw the latch and let the gate swing open a handbreadth.

"Do you wish to escape?" he said, laying his hand on the shiny flap of his black holster. "You would like to run," he said. "Verdad? Eh?"

"I will stay with my father," she said.

General Bandála looked around.

"Your father?" He laughed.

He heaved himself into the cage with her. The wagon tipped up with his weight. The wood creaked. The wooden tree attached to the two mules in front jerked up and caused them to shift backward. The metalwork on their leads and in their mouths clinked like small bells.

"What are you doing?" she repeated.

She could smell him.

"I am going to enjoy you," he said.

She moved to the end of the cage.

"No thank you," she said.

"You whore," he breathed. "You have no choice."

He undid his belt with one hand and grabbed her ankle with the other.

She kicked him in the chin.

"Ah, cabrón!" he yelped, clutching his chin. "Bitch!"

"I will remind you that you are an officer of the army," she said.

He undid the top button of his pants.

She stared in his eyes.

"Look at it," he said.

"No."

"I am going to put it in you!" he said.

"Put it in yourself," she replied.

"What kind of talk is that?" he cried, deeply offended by this sort of discourse from a young lady. "Have you no manners?"

"Sir," she said, "a bandit on the highway would not dare abuse my situation. But you, who claim to be a gentleman and a general of the Mexican army, are more miserable and cowardly than a bandit."

He got up on his knees.

"You should know," he fumed, "that it is up to me to decide whether you should live or die. My displeasure could lead to your being put before the firing squad. It is you who can choose between life and death."

"Kill me, then," she said. "Kill me, but do not insult me, General."

He fastened his trousers and backed out of the wagon.

"Do what you want with my corpse," she said, "if you need relief so badly."

He made a face as if he had smelled something rank.

"You are too foul to touch," he sniffed.

He yelled to his distant men:

"You! Get over here now! Get this dirty creature to Guaymas! Double time!"

They rushed to the wagon and climbed aboard and shook the reins. General Bandála mounted his horse and stared at her as the wagon lurched down the road. Slowly, he nudged his horse into motion, and he followed her, but tried to stay well out of her line of sight.

Within an hour, a cavalry patrol was on the ranch. Segundo had no reason to protect these idiots. He turned José over to the colonel in charge. They dragged him to the same arroyo where he had helped ambush the cavalry, and in the morning, they tied him to a tree trunk by his neck. He was so near death anyway that he couldn't stand. They watched him choke for a while, and when they got bored with that, they took turns shooting him.

Fifty-nine

GUAYMAS. She had never seen the sea, and in spite of her exhaustion and pain, Teresita was stunned to see a deep blue sliver of ocean curling along the coast in the distance. She closed her eyes. She could smell the salt.

She had swooned in the heat in a courtyard, cramped inside her cage. It seemed as if she had been there for hours. She could smell the stink of slops coming from the cell windows. Men screamed. Once, there was the startling crack of a firing squad, and an uproar from the cells: cursing, cups banging against the bars. Flies found her and dug in her eyes and nose. She was frantic from brushing them away, slapping herself because they came first in pairs, then dozens, then in hundreds until her face and arms were nearly black. Her wagon jiggled, and the latch snapped and the gate creaked open.

"Get out."

The guard was dirty and looked as if he might be a prisoner himself. He carried a short whip, and he had a pistol in his belt. His cheeks were covered in wiry stubble. A fly alighted on his lip: he blew it away.

She crawled to the back of the wagon and fell out. Her legs were too cramped for her to stand or walk.

"Help me, please," she said, putting out her hand.

He kicked her on the haunch.

"Does that help?" he asked.

Two jailers standing well behind him burst out laughing.

"Aren't you a witch?" he said. "Can't you turn into a bat and fly?"

"Watch out, Pepe!" yelled one of his friends. "She might turn *you* into a bat!"

"No mames, buey!" Pepe cursed.

Teresita grabbed the edge of the cart and pulled herself upright. Her knees shook.

"Do you have water?" she asked.

Pepe patted his groin.

"I have water here!" he said.

His friends laughed again.

"Let's go," he said. He shoved her away from the wagon. He prodded her with the handle of the whip.

"Be a good witch," he said, "and I won't whip you."

She staggered forward.

Faces peered down at her from the cell windows.

"Chula!" somebody called.

"Oye, vieja! Give us a kiss!"

Pepe shoved her again.

"Hurry up," he said.

One of the prisoners called: "Leave her alone!"

"Shut your mouth," Pepe yelled back.

He hurried her through a stone courtyard and to a heavy set of double doors.

"We can't stick you with the men," Pepe said. "So you can sleep where the oxen and pigs used to sleep." He laughed when he opened the doors and the stink hit her. She reeled for a moment.

"I have slept with pigs before," she said. "Thank you for your help."

She walked in.

He stood at the doors for a moment, unsure of what to say to that.

Teresita sat on the small cot shoved against the wall. "You have been very kind," she said. "I will pray for you." Her gaze unnerved him.

"Por nada," he said, just to say something. Then: "There is water in the bucket."

He slammed the doors and padlocked them. He stood there for a moment and listened. When he walked away, he walked fast.

※

Now, in her cell, she shivered. It was hot, but she shook. Coughed. She had eaten only dry crusts of bread on the journey, drunk a gulp of water a day. Her eyes blurred.

She took up the bucket and drank clouded water.

The guards the night before had tied her hands. When they had untied her this morning, her wrists were chafed raw and bleeding. One of them had put his hands on her bottom and squeezed when he shoved her inside her wagon.

"Take your hands off my daughter!" Tomás had shouted. He was answered by another blow to the head.

"Don't cry for this witch," the guard had spit. "You'll both be dead in a few days. All your troubles will be over." He had laughed. Everyone around her had been laughing. Teresita thought back to Millán. She wondered why the wicked were so happy.

She got up and pressed her face to the window slit.

White birds. White birds with vast wings formed great V shapes in the sky. Like angels, she thought.

She turned to her cell. It was a stone box, dank and steamy. The straw and dirt on the floor were clotted with mud and the old dung of the animals. Across the back, a stone shelf with one thin blanket heaped at its foot. She pulled off the blanket and wrapped it around her shoulders and sat on the cot.

Time slithered.

She tried to pray for her father, but she could not. She was asleep as fast as her head touched the canvas of the cot. All around her, vermin stirred.

Mosquitoes and biting flies, gnats and midges, came in the open windows. Fleas came from the blanket, sprang from between the paving stones. Lice sought out her hair, began to climb it. Spiders fell on her from the ceiling. Ticks made their way under her skirt and sank their heads into her thighs. She didn't stir. Even when a great roach climbed her face, pressed its head in between her eyelashes and drank her tears, she did not wake.

How many days did she wait for the noose?

She lost track.

The guards brought tin plates of beans to her at seemingly random hours. The first breakfast was alive with small worms. She picked them out of the soupy beans with her nails and flicked them into the corners, then ate the sour beans. Sometimes, Pepe threw her an old chunk of sweet bread, or gave her a cup of watery coffee. He often laughed at her, especially when he insulted her, or touched her body when she was within reach, or stood at the door fondling his crotch. She ignored him.

Her body prickled and burned at all hours. The bites

were everywhere. From her navel to her pubic hair was a wide, bat-shaped redness that stung and itched at the same time, but if she rubbed it or scratched it, ribbons of wet flesh peeled off and clogged her nails. She could pry the scabs off her hips, feel the heavy orange water leak out of her skin.

She shivered all day, coughed and retched — some fever brought to her by the night, some wickedness fuming up from the floor, perhaps, or injected into her by the thousand biting mouths that hunted her no matter where she crawled. Her prayers were not answered, or perhaps she did not pray anymore. She had nothing left to pray for. Was her father alive? Was he dead? Was it he who cried out so terribly when the torturers took another man to the screaming rooms? Had Cabora burned? Was Gaby alive? Buenaventura? Segundo? Had Cruz escaped? Not even Huila, in the afterworld, responded when she called.

When Pepe opened her door for breakfast as her fifteenth day in the hole began, he said, "Where is your water?"

"I poured it on myself," she said.

She was pale white, and thin as a skeleton. It looked to Pepe as if her fevers had already killed her. The witch was already famous for coming back from the dead — perhaps she was dead now. He shivered, looking in at her. He could smell her. She smelled bloody and rotten.

"You are a big mess, girl," he said. "You are disgusting."

She could barely get whole words out, but she struggled to speak. "Why, thank you for that kindness, Don Pepe. Surely, God has graced you with the ability to speak to women. You are a prince among commoners."

Though she wasn't sure she had said any of it. She might have only made a weird groaning noise. Just this morning, she had watched Indians dance in the sky. Her face pressed to the window slit, staring up at the slice of blue above the stable yards, she had seen Yaquis with deer heads tied to their own heads, Apaches with fearsome crosses on their heads, strange feathered and naked men, women as well, twirling in the sky, whirling above her. And among them, she had seen Cruz Chávez in his white shirt and billowing trousers, and she had called to him: "Cruz! Cruz! I am here! Aquí estoy!" But he had danced on, following the skyborne warriors toward the sea.

"Want more water?" Pepe asked.

"More."

He took her bucket outside and worked a pump handle. She heard the water spurt into the bucket. She crawled to the open door and looked out into the sun. It hurt her eyes. She covered them with one hand. She extended her other arm to let the sun hit her skin. Pepe saw the scratch marks and the hundred red welts on her wrist.

"Jesus Christ!" he said.

He put the bucket back inside and stood looking down at her.

"You must go back inside," he said.

"Please."

She lay facedown on the warm stone. He watched her skinny back shiver. Her hands quaked, but she reached for the sun.

"Please," she said, "just a minute of sun."

Pepe scratched his chin.

"Chingado," he said. He looked around. "What the hell."

He went over to a wooden stool and hooked his boot toe behind one leg and dragged it over to her and sat. He lit a cigarette.

"Smoke?" he said.

"N-no. Gracias."

He watched the lice move across the top of her head.

"Are you really holy?" he asked.

"Do I look holy?"

He leaned back, stretched out one booted leg.

"Not today," he said.

When his cigarette was done, he pushed her backward with his boot and closed the door.

Kill them, she heard her father whisper.

And when the guards came with their rotten food and their obscenities, she knew she could kill them. She could open her mouth and speak the words, and they would, all of them, fall to the floor and squirm until they were dead.

"What?" said Pepe on her twenty-first day in the prison.

She shook her head, strings of wet hair hanging wild before her face.

She smiled.

"God bless you," she said. "Lios emak weye."

He dropped her plate and backed out of the cell.

She was laughing.

Night.

A cool wind had finally sought out the prison, coming in from the sea with its smells of waves and fish, distance and salt. But she did not feel it, so hot was her fever. She slept on the floor, curled like a dog, the way she had slept a million years ago under Tía's table. She shook with the heat of the fever, clutched herself. The floor rolled, heaved, a carpet on water, tossing in waves. She woke ten times a night. Awoke now, afraid. She pulled her feet closer to her body, as if something could grab them.

She pushed herself up, pressed her back into the stones.

"Quién es?" she rasped.

She pulled her torn skirts tight over her knees. She no longer smelled of roses — she had only the scent of meat and sweat, animal fear.

"Who's there?"

A knot of deeper shadow stirred at the end of the cell.

She squinted in the dark.

"What do you want?" she whispered.

A sigh.

She pressed herself harder against the stones, but there was no place to go.

The shadow moved again.

"Am I dreaming?" she said.

It stretched, tall as a man. Then that shadow man stepped forward. A slant of moon coming through the slit window caught his face. He stared at her for a long while. Then he smiled.

"Cruz?" she gasped. "Cruz?"

He put his finger to his lips. Shook his head.

"What are you doing here?"

She rose to her knees, reached for him.

Vague smell of smoke.

He held out his hand, motioned for her to stay where she was. He shook his head. Then he put one finger near his eye. Tapped his eye.

Look.

Watch this.

She followed his stare, as he turned and looked at the far wall.

The stones there were flickering, as if candles had been lit in the cell.

"Cruz?" she repeated.

He pointed at the wall.

She watched.

The flickers expanded, grew long and bright. They burned blue, red, green, white. Brown. Yellow.

They formed and re-formed, knotting and furling. And, as if they were clouds creating images, the flickers quickly resolved themselves into a picture. It was a mountain valley. A river cut through the center, and small corn patches grew on one side, and across the river, a great cave. Then houses appeared. Then a church. She heard the bell ringing.

She knew this was Tomóchic.

Cruz and his warriors appeared, running with their weapons. The populace, small as ants, hurried about the village. Men clutched their hearts and heads and fell. Women and children and old men were hurried into the church. The big wooden doors closed.

She saw an image of a statue of her.

Fire appeared on the mountain peaks — gouts of flame and smoke.

The tiny houses before her exploded: fireballs bloomed where the houses had stood, and in the hearts of these little firestorms flew chairs and dogs, tables and babies.

She saw the Mexican army ringing the village, troops pouring down the peaks. Small cannons loaded with grapeshot. They fired, but all she could hear were low gasps. And the cannon shots dismembering Tigers —

heads and arms flew from their bodies. The cannons shot balls, nails, coins. Walls flashed from white to red as men evaporated.

She saw Cruz and Rubén in the Chávez house — she knew it was the Chávez house. They fired through splintered windows, fired although they were wounded, starving.

Then the church was burning.

The army had set it aflame. The cries of the burning people within came to her as tiny as the cries of distant birds. Soldiers ran to the doors and broke them open, and Teresita thought they were showing mercy. But as the people ran out, some of them burning, some women carrying burning children in their arms and beginning to burn themselves, the Mexican army opened fire with Gatling guns. Their barrels spit and coughed and cut down wave after wave of people. The bodies squirmed under the impact of the rounds, falling and burning where they were hit.

And she saw that the soldiers had moved in behind Cruz and his men. They climbed the roof and poured burning pitch down the chimney hole. They were burning inside the house. Walls, window frames, doors bursting and splintering with withering fire; Cruz bloodied and shouting rose and fell in the broken windows, firing, firing, smoke curling from his hair.

And she saw the Mexicans send a man forth with a white flag.

He gestured at the burning house, was yelling something to Cruz and his defenders inside. The army ceased firing. Eerie silence of echoes and crackling flames. And the door opened — a billow of choking black smoke furled out. And there was Cruz himself, leaning on a friend's shoulder. Wounded — terribly wounded. His leg was bent, and he had been shot in the side, in the back. A yellow-white finger of bone hung from the red hole in his thigh, splinters of bones like toothpicks stuck to the black clot of blood in his clothes.

The Tigers helped Cruz hobble forward.

The Mexican smiled at him. Took his hand. Offered Cruz a cigarette.

And when Cruz leaned forward to accept a light, a soldier stepped up behind him and shot him in the head.

"No!" she cried.

The lights faded.

Cruz turned to her.

"I am doomed."

"I did this to you!" she cried.

"We did this to ourselves," he replied. "We are doomed to our fates," he said. "But your avengers are strong."

"My avengers?"

"Your avengers gather in the hills."

"Who?"

"They come," he said. "They come. Everyone will die for you."

"No! No!"

She watched blood spread across his face. Dark black blooms of blood sprouted on his shirt, soaked around his ribs, jetted from his leg.

The world was on fire.

She reached for him, Cruz Chávez, the only man who had ever pressed his face against her and listened to her heart.

"Be strong," he said. "All is not lost. Adios."

And he was gone.

Sixty

THE GUARDS MARCHED toward Teresita's cell at dawn. The skinny kid who delivered her food had been found outside the prison with three arrows in his back. The attackers had also cut off his ears. No one had seen anything.

She awoke to the sound of the guardias' boots echoing on the cobbles and between the stone walls. She sat up and listened to them come. They weren't shuffling this time. They were marching. So this is my hour, she thought. Perhaps Cruz Chávez would greet her when the rope snapped her neck.

The thin blooms of crusted blood on her face she wiped away with spit on her fingers. She fixed her hair as best she could in the gloom. The boots approached. She wondered if she would be executed beside her father.

The boots stomped to a halt outside the door. Keys rattled. The lock snapped and the door creaked open on its rusty hinges. Three guards stepped inside and ordered her to turn her back. She put her hands behind her back and waited with her head down. They shackled her. She turned and looked at their faces. She saw that Pepe was not among them.

They gestured for her to step outside. She didn't know how long it had been since she'd seen the sun, walked any distance at all. She stepped out into the brightness, holding her head high, blinking. Even among the fetid stables, the air was fresh and brisk. They grabbed her arms and led her out of the barnyard, away from the gallows.

So.

It was to be the wall.

"Where is Pepe?" she asked.

"I am here, girl," he said.

He was behind her.

"Shoot well, muchachos," she said. "Pepe, aim for my heart. But let my father go."

"Shut up," Pepe said. "Do you know your problem? You never learned to keep your mouth shut."

"Aim for the heart."

"I said shut up!"

She was marched briskly past the wall, and back down the long courtyard where she had entered the prison. Faces pressed to the bars in the windows again, but the prisoners said nothing. She twisted and looked over her shoulder.

They passed a stained, punctured adobe wall.

"Señores," she said. "Isn't that where the firing squad —"

"Quiet."

At the far end, in painful light, she saw others gathered, and a black wagon pulled up and blocked off the opening. It was drawn by a large white horse.

"Where are you taking me?"

"Keep moving."

The crowd was made up of soldiers, Rurales, police. They stared at her as she approached. All of them had heard of her, read the newspapers. They pressed in to get a look. Her guards pushed them aside and shoved her through the narrow gap in their hot bodies. To the back of the wagon. Where Tomás waited.

"Father!" she cried.

His left eye was blackened and swollen, and a slim crust

of blood was stuck to his chin. He was filthy, his shirt half-untucked, and his hair stood straight up in the back. When she first saw him, he was slumped against the doors of the wagon, his eyes closed, and his face gray. He heard her voice and stood tall — taller than all the guards. He smiled.

"Teresita," he called.

She rushed to him and laid her head against his chest.

He rubbed his chin on the top of her head.

"Did they hurt you?" he asked.

"No. I was spared."

"You are thin," he said.

"I have a little fever," she replied.

She leaned back and peered up at his battered face.

"And you, Father? Have they hurt you?"

"I," he said. Then, "I fell against a door, that's all. Nothing to worry about."

She stretched up and kissed his cheek.

"Liar," she said.

"Back," Pepe said, opening the doors of the wagon. He allowed them to put their hands in front, then he relocked their shackles. He grabbed their elbows and roughly helped them climb the metal step. Once they were seated inside, he slammed the doors and locked them.

"Where are we going?" Tomás demanded, but no one answered him.

The whip cracked. The horse lurched forward. They fell against each other and struggled to stay upright as the wagon wobbled away from the prison.

"Are you afraid?" he asked.

"I am."

"Me too."

"Oh, Father."

"Is dying bad?"

"Not as bad as you think."

"But the bullets," he said.

She shook.

"That frightens me," she said.

"Well, girl, at least bullets are fast."

The wagon rattled and banged over the cobbles in the street. Mounted soldiers spread out before and behind it. Guaymas was quiet that morning — the sea breeze that they had been denied in the prison blew down the alleys, carrying with it the smell of salt. Teresita pressed her face to the bars to smell it until a tomato hit the side of the wagon and sprayed her cheek with juice.

People along the way peered in at her, whispered to her, hissed. "Witch," one woman said. Men laughed. Two horsemen rode along beside the wagon, and they pushed people back with the toes of their boots.

"And so we die," Tomás said.

From the street: "Viva la Santa de Cabora!" Followed by the sounds of a scuffle.

Teresita took his fingers in hers.

"Be brave," he said.

"I will."

They passed down an alley, broke out into a sunny boulevard.

"You say death is not so bad?" he asked.

"No, not so bad, Papá. Better than prison."

He nodded.

She leaned her head against his shoulder.

"They might not shoot us," he said. "They might hang us!" He had hoped to be more positive, but being executed was a terrible affront to him. He could not contain his outrage. These fools would forever think themselves his equals, or worse, his superiors. He wanted to kick somebody. "Cabrones!" he said.

"I have had bad dreams about the noose," she whispered.

How could he comfort her?

"Oh," he finally said, "the noose isn't so bad. It breaks your neck if they do it right. You'll probably never feel it."

"Why, thank you, Father. That's the best news any girl could ask for!"

They laughed, for neither of them would weep.

Teresita had never seen a train, but she knew what it was when she saw it. And in spite of the wagon and the chains and the blood-drooling bites on her face, her neck, the terrible burn and itch under her clothes, she was excited to see the great machine stretched out before the station like a grand serpent.

"Look, Father," she said. "A train."

"By God," he said. "A train?"

Tomás was so tired, so very tired. He could barely keep his eyes open. But he raised his head — it could have weighed ten pounds — and smiled.

"Yes," he said. They were going to be shot against the station walls. Witnesses had been brought in to watch. Reporters, no doubt. Military wives.

"We are, apparently, to be the great spectacle," he said.

It was a steam locomotive, and it was attached to a long string of cars, and soldiers stood all along its serpentine length and squinted at their black wagon.

Tomás strained to keep his eyelids open, but his vision was blurred. His eyes felt as if they had sand in them. His wrists were black from the bruises, his fingers swollen and dark from the cuffs' cruel bite.

The wagon jerked to a halt. They listened to the soldiers mumbling outside. It was already so hot in there they thought they wouldn't be able to breathe. The guards left them locked inside for a half hour. When they finally unlocked the back doors and grabbed hold of Teresita, Tomás was asleep again, huddled on the bench like a dog. A soldier took hold of his ankles and hauled him out; his head smacked against the floor.

Tomás opened his eyes and said, "Watch out, pendejo."

The soldier grabbed his collar and pitched him forward. Tomás went down chin first in the dirt.

Teresita said, "Stop it!"

The same soldier turned and spit at her.

"Or what?" he said. "Or what, witch?"

One of the others called out, "She'll turn you into a lizard!"

"She'll feed you to the Yaquis!"

They were laughing at her.

She helped her father to stand. He shook his head, shook the dirt out of his hair.

"Hey! Hey!" Pepe called. He hurried forward. "No need to hurt the prisoners," he said.

"How do I look?" Tomás asked.

"Handsome," Teresita replied.

They smiled at each other.

The train chuffed on the track nearest the station. Soldiers pushed against Teresita's back with their rifles held before them, knocking her ahead as if she were a cow or a reluctant mule. She reached for her father's hand, but they knocked her fingers away with a rifle butt. "Move," Pepe said, and she moved. Her shackles clanked. She could smell herself, and she could smell her father. Dirty hair, sweat. She held up her head as she walked.

"Bastards," Tomás muttered.

Pepe laughed.

"Where are we going?" Teresita asked.

"Judgment day," he replied.

They crunched past the caboose. Soldiers stood on its back platform. Then two passenger cars. In the distance, the locomotive chugged like a vast heart. Its languid double-chuff blew vague steam into the air. *Cha-hump, cha-hump, cha-hump.* Most of the windows of the train cars filled with faces — women and children staring down at her. Atop these passenger cars, sandbag nests held soldiers with more rifles. They stepped up a small stairway onto the station's platform, and they walked across it at eye level with the passengers, walked to the end of the platform, then down three steps to the slippery gravel along the track. Teresita lost her footing once — Tomás grabbed her with one hand, steadying her. The soldiers crunched behind them.

They walked past the passenger wagons, and came abreast of a flatcar. The car's bed was lined with sandbags, and rifles bristled over their heads as the soldiers and guards watched for marauding Yaquis. In the middle of the car, a Gatling gun stood tall on its tripod. In front of the flatcar was another, abandoned passenger car with more soldiers on the roof. And ahead, between this car and the locomotive, yet another flatcar covered with soldiers.

"They expect a war," Tomás said.

The head guard struck him between the shoulders with the butt of his rifle. Tomás fell forward against the side of the car.

"Shut up," the guard said.

An officer stood alongside the empty passenger wagon. His back was to them. His uniform was crisp. His cap sat squarely on his head. He turned and stared at them.

"Enríquez!" Tomás shouted.

Pepe smacked him in the back of the head.

Enríquez turned to a soldier and borrowed his rifle. He stepped up to the leering Pepe and struck him in the forehead with the rifle butt. Pepe let out a startled bark and fell on his back in the dirt.

"Like a sack of beans!" Tomás enthused.

Pepe gargled and writhed.

Tomás turned to Teresita and said, "By God, it's Major Enríquez!"

"A major no longer," said Enríquez.

"Captain Enríquez?"

"Not quite."

"What, then?"

"After our little visit at Cabora," Enríquez said, "I am now a lieutenant again."

He snapped his fingers, pointed at the manacles. A private with a ring of keys stepped over Pepe and unlocked Tomás and Teresita.

"Thank you, sir," she said.

"At your service."

He clicked his heels and gave her a slight bow. He gave Pepe a brisk kick. Pepe grunted and opened his eyes. Enríquez glared down at the prostrate guard and scolded him: "You are a soldier of the Mexican army. You will hereafter comport yourself with honor. We will observe protocol here."

Teresita bent to Pepe and laid her palm upon the black mark spreading across his forehead. He blinked up at her in terror and scrambled away on his back. He got to his knees and scuffled off, his ass churning back and forth in its dirty khaki pants.

"Pig!" noted Tomás.

Among the lieutenant's retinue was a boy of about twelve. He was dressed in a small uniform, his hat cocked crookedly on his head.

"Private García!" the lieutenant said.

The boy stepped forward and saluted.

"Sí, mi teniente!" he shouted.

"Private, see if you can bring the prisoners some water."

"Sir!"

The boy rushed away.

"Yes, yes," Tomás said. "Quite right, Lieutenant. Allow us to die with some respect."

Private García came up with the water in two tin cups. He was very careful not to spill the water.

"Give it to them," said the lieutenant.

Teresita looked at Tomás. Neither of them knew what was happening, but Tomás pointed his chin at the boy and she reached out and the boy gave her the cup and she drank from it. It was warm and tasted like metal. Tomás held his own hands up and the boy handed him his cup.

Tomás smiled at Teresita. "It's all right," he said. "We are in the hands of gentlemen."

Tomás put his hand on Teresita's back and addressed the lieutenant.

"Where would you like us to stand?" he asked.

"Stand?"

"Yes," she said. "I would like to know. Let us do it quickly. We are ready."

"Ready?" Enríquez said. "Ready for what?"

"The firing squad."

The lieutenant looked around at his men. They laughed.

"The firing squad!" he said.

"Sir," said Teresita, "I don't find it very amusing."

"Oh," said Lieutenant Enríquez, "but you will."

He took a proffered document from the hand of a subordinate. He held it out before him and read:

"Miss Urrea has been recognized by presidential declaration to be the Most Dangerous Girl in Mexico."

"Bravo!" said Tomás.

The lieutenant glanced at Teresita and raised his eyebrows.

"Are you?" he asked.

"They say that I am."

"At the moment," he noted, "you are perhaps the dirtiest girl in Mexico."

She nodded slightly.

Enríquez resumed reading the declaration:

"And her father, Tomás Urrea, has been found to be an enemy of the state and a general danger to Mexican society. Political, fiscal, and moral supporter of the indigenous uprisings in the states of Sonora, Sinaloa, and Chihuahua."

Tomás nodded and smiled. "That's me," he said.

"Señor, please."

The lieutenant continued reading. He read of heresies and Yaqui raids, of abetting the enemies of the republic and defying the rule of both the military and the Church. He read to them of their grievous insults to the benevolent regime in Mexico City and to its noble head of state, the great president and general, Porfirio Díaz. He read that they had been found guilty of treason, of fomenting revolution, and that by abetting the recent armed assault on the cavalry by guerrillas led by the outlaw Cruz Chávez, they had earned the sentence of death by firing squad.

Tomás squared his shoulders. "Here it comes," he said.

"I am no longer afraid," Teresita replied.

"However," Enríquez read, "due to the immense generosity of General Díaz and the Mexican government, the sentence of death will be forthwith commuted to expulsion."

They stood there as the lieutenant folded his proclamation and tucked it inside his tunic.

"What did you say?" asked Teresita.

"Expulsion."

"Expulsion?"

"Expulsion, indeed."

"Enríquez, my good man," said Tomás. "Is this a joke?"

Enríquez shrugged one shoulder.

"My dear Señor Urrea, it has occurred to me on more than one occasion, particularly since becoming embroiled in your lives," he tipped his hat at Teresita, "that much of life is a joke."

"Wait. We are being deported?" Tomás said.

The lieutenant gestured at the train.

"Mexico's newest rail line is at your disposal. As you can see, it is a Santa Fe train. Mexico's railroads are in partnership with the Santa Fe line, and this rolling stock has come to us from —"

"Wait!" Tomás said.

"Yes?"

"Exiled?"

"Not to return. I would consider that a good offer."

"But my ranch!"

"Sorry."

"But my wife, Loreto!"

"Perhaps she can join you."

"But Gabriela!"

"Another wife?"

"His beloved," Teresita offered.

"Ah! A complication. Perhaps she can join you as well."

Tomás smacked himself on the forehead.

"Consider the alternative," Enríquez suggested.

"We aren't going to die?" Teresita asked.

Her fever had made her pale — her eyes burned in her white face like the eyes of a lunatic. She unnerved Lieutenant Enríquez.

"Señorita," he said, "you will surely die one day, but this is not that day."

She fell back against Tomás.

"Wait," he shouted. "Wait! Instead of shooting us, you are taking us on a train trip?"

The lieutenant studied his own boots.

"So it seems," he said.

Private García came back to them. He tapped Tomás on the arm.

"Sir?" he said. "I think the Saint has fainted."

Sixty-one

THE SPIES WATCHED Teresita swoon and fall against her father. They counted the gun emplacements on the train cars. They noted the big tripod with the wicked bullet-spitter gun on the flatcar. A Pima rider named Martínez led them, two Yaquis and this skinny Yori boy who insisted he follow. They lay on their bellies in the weeds on a hill a half mile from the train. The boy said, "Let's kill them now!" Martínez put his hand up. His blue bandana was carefully folded along the tops of his eyebrows. Runners were already going north, calling for warriors to come to the prison. But it was obvious to Martínez that there would be no assault on Guaymas, even though the Apaches wanted to set fire to one more Mexican city before they rested. No, the battle was going to be on the rail lines. They had to stop the train. They had to set Teresita free. They had to kill everybody. They ran, bent down, through scrub and berry bushes, cactus and hedionda, until they dropped into an arroyo where their horses waited. They had four of the best horses from Cabora — the Yori boy had brought them. Martínez sped down the arroyo and over its lip and into the redness of the desert without once looking back.

Enríquez ordered four soldiers to carry Teresita onto the empty train car at the front of the train. They were afraid to touch her at first. When they picked her up, one said: "See, boys, she is as light as straw!" Tomás hovered around her like a dragonfly as they moved down the empty aisle. They chose a random seat and laid her across it. She moaned. Her eyelids fluttered. One of the pustules on her neck broke, and ghastly yellow humors drained from it.

"Please," Tomás said. "Bring me warm water and soap!"

Enríquez, who had followed, nodded at them.

They saluted and hurried away.

"Will she die?" Enríquez asked.

"She is strong, Lieutenant," Tomás whispered. "So strong."

"Well," said the lieutenant, "you could pray for her."

"I would have to learn how."

"No one has to teach a father how to pray, Señor Urrea," he replied. "Fathers and mothers know how to pray better than priests."

Tomás put his hand on Teresita.

"I have been . . . so bad," he confessed. "What God would listen to my pleas?"

The soldiers appeared with a bowl of steaming water and a towel.

Enríquez bent to Tomás.

"My friend," he said, "I know little of God. But I do know God loves His prodigal sons the best."

He patted Tomás on the shoulder.

"Men," he said, "let us withdraw and offer these people some privacy."

He posted an armed guard at each end of the car.

Tomás didn't know where to begin, but he opened the top of her filthy dress and wet the towel and carefully mopped at her wounds.

Teresita slept through her bath. She did not stir when

Tomás had a second, then a third bowl brought in. When he went outside to join Lieutenant Enríquez on the first flatcar, she did not open her eyes.

"But why are they sparing us?" Tomás said to Enríquez.

The lieutenant looked at his soldiers, stepped closer.

"If they kill her," he said, "they make a martyr. Do you see? Mexico City could never contain the Yaquis if Miss Urrea were to be executed. That is my opinion."

Tomás nodded.

"You are still prisoners," Enríquez reminded him. "And should Miss Urrea misbehave on this trip, it is my duty to kill her. Until we get to Arizona."

"The United States," said Tomás. "Good God," he sighed, "we're going to be Americans."

The lieutenant produced a silver cigarette case and offered Tomás one. He took it and accepted the lit match and drew the smoke into his lungs.

"Better a gringo than a dead man," the lieutenant sighed, smoke escaping his nostrils.

"Barely! But, yes, hell yes."

"A lucky day for you, Tomás."

They puffed away.

"All these guards just for my daughter?" Tomás said.

"Yaquis," the lieutenant replied. "We do not expect to leave Mexico without a fight." He smiled sadly. "I don't know if any of us will survive this trip, to tell you the truth."

"But," Tomás said, looking back down the length of the train, "those passenger cars, they're full of civilians."

"Es verdad."

"It strikes me as odd that you would transport civilians into a war zone, my dear Lieutenant."

Enríquez spit a bit of tobacco off the edge of the car.

"Really?" he said. "After all you saw at Cabora, are you so innocent?"

Tomás looked him in the eye.

"What are you saying, Lieutenant?"

"Sir," he said. "Consider the advantage to our leaders should the savages assault a trainload of good Mexican citizens."

"What!"

"The civilians are here by official decree."

Tomás flicked away his cigarette. "Díaz *wants* the Indians to attack this train!" he said.

The lieutenant tipped his head and said nothing.

They looked back through the door's window at Teresita.

"By presidential decree," offered the lieutenant, "my own wife and daughters are in those cars."

"Cabrones," muttered Tomás.

"Such gestures," the lieutenant said, "reveal why you and I will never be president."

He whistled for his men to mount up, and he helped Tomás step across the gap and into the car. "Vámonos!" Lieutenant Enríquez yelled: the whistle sounded; a bell as if on a seagoing yacht clanged three, four times; the locomotive lurched and chuffed, and they began to roll.

The rails clacked. The cars swayed back and forth. The wheels sang on the rails and they clacked. Tomás's eyes grew heavy, his head bobbing as he rocked back and forth. He sighed, rubbed his face. The land whipped past like yellow banners. Trees appeared and instantly vanished. He rocked. He swayed. He yawned. The rails clacked some more.

His head dropped to his chest and he began to snore.

It was a surging motion, a constant heaving. They could have been at sea. The train could have been alive. Teresita's leather seat was as hard as wood, but to her, it was soft. Her head rolled back and forth as she dreamed. She was imagining the plum tree and its little purple fruits, and she was seeing the sacred spot where Huila once prayed, and she was walking with the old forgotten she-pig through a valley full of blue flowers. She dreamed that her old friend Josefina was eating breakfast and laughing. She laughed in her sleep. Good old Fina! What had happened to Fina Félix, anyway?

She opened her eyes. For a moment, she did not know where she was. She sat up. Her father snored in the seat behind hers. The train. Going north. To the border.

She pulled her hair back and looked out the window. The land rolled away from her in constant waves, curling from the train as if it were rotating on a great wheel. The land was orange, red, tan. It was pale blue and green and gray and slightly violet. It was white.

She turned and looked out the window on the other side, and the land was utterly still. She blinked. She could hear the locomotive chugging, could feel the sway and hear the clack. But nothing stirred. She turned back to her own window: now that landscape, too, was as still as a painting. She rose, steadied herself on the backs of the seats, and moved forward. The door at the end of the car opened easily enough. She stepped out on the platform at the front of the car. The wind whipped her hair in her face, but the train was not moving. She gazed into the distance, and there she saw a great crow in midflight, caught in the air as if in amber. His huge wings were spread, but taking him nowhere.

Teresita turned around and looked back into the car.

She cried out.

There, sitting in a seat, smiling at her, was Huila.

Teresita pushed the door back open and hurried down the length of the car.

"Huila?" she cried. "Huila? Have you come back?"

Huila turned and looked around her.

"So this is a train," she said. "I don't like it much."

Teresita took her hands in her own and kissed the old knuckles, sinking to her knees.

"Huila!" she cried. "I have missed you so."

Huila patted her head.

"Child," she said, "have you got any beer? I miss beer."

Teresita shook her head, and Huila stood and pulled her to her feet.

"Come," she said.

She took a step into the aisle, and they were outside, standing on a hillside.

"Did you wear your shoes?" Huila asked.

Teresita looked down. Her feet were bare.

"My father must have taken them off," Teresita said.

"How are you supposed to walk in the desert with no shoes?" Huila asked.

"I have walked barefoot before!"

"Your father will be mad."

When Teresita tried to answer, she found herself walking in a blue stream, on smooth white stones.

"Isn't that nice?" asked Huila.

Teresita's three old men stood on a hill a mile away. She could see them like three little balls of snow. There would be snow in America, she thought.

"There are your old cabrones," Huila noted.

Teresita waved to them.

A hummingbird circled her head. Its tiny wings whirred loudly. "You sound like a bee," Teresita told it. It circled her again. She could feel the wind of its flapping on her skin. It chirped its funny little kissing sounds and sped away.

"Which direction?" asked Huila.

"Left," said Teresita.

"Always flies toward the heart, that little bastard."

They were holding hands.

Golden fish tickled Teresita's feet.

They went up a hill covered in white flowers. The water followed them, flowing impishly against gravity.

"Have I been here?" Teresita asked.

"You were always here."

"Huila," she said. "Help me! Help me now! Things are terrible. Things are getting more terrible every day. Help me stop it."

"Oh no, child," said Huila. "I am on this side, and you are on that side. We cannot interfere with you."

"Help me!"

"I am here, aren't I?"

They climbed through a tissue of cloud.

Teresita started to see. Things were brighter here. The cerulean sky was full of stars.

"Look," said Huila.

The stars formed straight lines. Then the lines expanded horizontally and vertically, creating a grid in the sky, spreading out away from her until they became invisible in every direction.

"Look," said Huila.

The stars swelled. They looked like ice chunks melting

in reverse, growing larger. They were silver. They formed small globes, a million, ten million brilliant silver globes above and around her.

"I was not a very good student," Huila said. "I had to die for God to teach me this. But I am teaching you now. Look."

Teresita stared at the silver globes. And each globe held a picture. She turned to the nearest one, which was not at all a star far away, but was close enough to touch. And in it, she saw her own face. And in the next one. And in the next one.

"Look," said Huila.

She looked.

In this globe, she was riding the train. In the next globe, she was a child. In the third globe, she was dressed in fine clothes, walking down a city street. She held children. She was pregnant. She was laughing. She was weeping. She was asleep. She held a weapon. She was naked and washing herself. She made love to a man whose face she could not see. Her wedding day. Dressed in mourning black. Her legs held up and a baby coming forth. Some globes were so far away that Teresita could barely see herself or see herself only as a small dark figure among others. They were all clear to her, though most of them were too small to be seen at all. She was everywhere in the sky. She turned around and saw herself behind herself, reading a book; cooking; preaching; laying hands on a child; riding; sleeping.

"What is this?" she asked.

"Isn't it beautiful?" said Huila.

"Yes."

"It is you," Huila said.

"I don't understand."

"It is you. Every you, every possible you. Forever, you are surrounded by countless choices of which you are to be. These are your destinies."

Huila touched a globe. It rang softly like a chime. In it, Teresita sat on the train.

"This is your next second," Huila said.

Teresita turned and stared.

"All of them. Every moment of your life, every instant, looks like this. Do you see? You are always in a universe of choices. Any moment of your life can go in any direction you choose."

"How?"

"Learn to choose."

"How?"

"Learn to see. This is your life, what it looks like to God. Every second of every day."

Teresita stood in the water and put her hands out to the globes.

"Most of us," Huila said, "trudge in a straight line. All day every day, we march like sheep. Look straight ahead. What do you see?"

She stared into the globe in front of her.

"My own face."

"We spend our lives walking into our own mirrors. All we see is ourselves as we walk down the road."

Huila spread her arms.

"Look to the side."

Teresita turned her head, and looked in the window of the train. Tomás was still asleep. Huila was gone.

"Huila!" she cried. "Where are you?"

"Beside you," Huila's voice said. "Where I have always been."

"Don't go!"

"I must."

"Huila!"

"Look ahead."

Teresita turned.

She saw a Yaqui fighter crouched behind a bush. He was holding a rifle. He was looking at the train.

"Wake up!" Huila said.

Teresita sat up. The train rocked. The rails clacked below her as the wheels passed over them. Her father was snoring. She looked around her, but there was no one else in the car.

❀

"I have ruined us," she said, awakening her father.

"True," said Tomás. "It would have been better for business if you had not met God."

"Forgive me."

He offered her one of the People's sayings: "No bad can befall us that does not bring us some good."

"Do you believe it?" she asked.

"Why not!"

He reached over and patted her knee.

"Look at us now," he said. "This nice train trip!"

Teresita said, "The lieutenant says the Indians will attack at sunset."

"Yes. So he does."

"He says we will enter a canyon then."

"Ambush Canyon," said Tomás. "Picturesque name!"

"We will slow down," she said.

"And they will attack. Yes, yes. Everybody dead. Except you."

They brought lunch in pots. Beans, potatoes. Tortillas, coffee.

After Teresita finished her lunch, she looked up to see Lieutenant Enríquez watching her through the door. He signaled her for permission to enter. She nodded.

"Now what," said Tomás.

Enríquez came forward.

"We have a sick child," he said. He seemed embarrassed.

"Oh?" she said.

"Not again!" said Tomás.

Enríquez ducked his head.

"It is the child of one of my men. He ate bad sausage, apparently. Quite ill. His mother thinks he might not survive the night." Enríquez raised his hands. "I do not know what to do. They asked for you."

"Bring him," she said.

"Are you sure?"

"Bring him."

Enríquez went to the back of the car and stepped out. They could hear him shouting to the soldiers on the flatcar.

"Father?" she said as they waited. "Did you enjoy any of it?"

"Oh, of course."

"What was your favorite part?"

He thought back.

"The plum tree," he said.

Enríquez came forward with a woman and a soldier. She carried a small bundle in her arms. They could smell the vomit and the shit.

The woman fell to her knees.

"Bless us, Teresita," she said.

Teresita put her hand on the woman's head.

"Give me the child," she said.

The woman handed her the baby.

"He is green," the mother said. "Will he die?"

Enríquez and Tomás crowded in. "Watch this," Tomás said, suddenly surprised by pride in Teresita's miracles.

Teresa opened the wrap and looked into the child's contorted face. He grunted and fussed. He waved his little fists.

"He is very ill, mother," Teresita said.

She placed her hand on his brow. She reached into his little shirt and put her hand on his belly. He cried. She passed her hand over him. She prayed. She held him close to her and whispered. He grew still. She looked at him and smiled. "He is asleep," she said. "Give him cool tea. Té de canela, if you have it."

The woman cried.

She grabbed Teresita's hands and kissed them.

"Viva la Santa de Cabora," the soldier said.

"That," said Enríquez, "is all we need!"

※

The warriors were hidden along the entire length of the Cañón de la Emboscada. Martínez and his men had been able to collect more than a hundred fighters. People and Mexicans alike hid themselves behind boulders and creosotes. Riflemen hid on either side of the tracks. There were snipers in the mesquites. At the end of the valley, riders sat on fast horses, ready to rush the crippled train after the first volleys, to attack fast and pick off any soldiers not already dead.

"Kill no man," Teresita said.

"You are insane," Enríquez replied, "if you think I will allow the savages to slaughter the people on this train."

"They will not."

"They will."

"They will hold their fire."

Enríquez laughed.

"Miss," he said, "I have fought Indians my whole life. They will not hold their fire. They will not show mercy. They will spare no one."

"And I," she replied, "have been an Indian all my life. I tell you they will not fire."

He smacked his fist against the wall.

"Miss! You put me in an impossible situation! Must I remind you," Enríquez said, "that my own family is in the back of this train? Would you endanger my children?"

"I will save you and your children," she said.

"Miss!"

"That's it!" Tomás proclaimed. "I have reached my personal limit!"

"I will make the warriors hold their fire."

"I thought pride was a sin," Enríquez snapped.

"Not pride," she said. "Put me outside, on the flatcar. They will hold their fire."

He shook his head.

"You want to die!"

"I have died before. I will die again. I am offering to spare you and your men. Put me out there!"

Tomás had found a bottle somewhere, and he was working hard at draining it.

Enríquez said: "Who do you think you are? You don't give orders here. I do."

"I know who I am," Teresita said. "I know what I am."

Her eyes made him look away. He felt slightly dizzy, as if Tomás had given him a drink. He did not know what to say to this filthy girl. He did not know how to look in her face.

Enríquez flexed his hands. He smoothed his whiskers. He pointed at her.

"Look," he said. "I will give you one chance. I will put you out on the flatcar, if you so wish to be martyred. But the first shot from any savage's gun will lead to a storm. Do you understand? We will decimate them all. No quarter."

"They will not fire."

"One bullet."

"Agreed. One bullet."

Enríquez shook his head.

"Give me a drink," he told Tomás.

Martínez had passed the word down the line. Let the train enter the valley. It will slow as it climbs. Once the train is fully enclosed in the walls of Ambush Canyon, open fire from either side. Shoot at the soldiers first, then through the windows. Do not hit Teresita in the first car.

"Slow the train," she ordered.

"Estás loca," Enríquez replied.

"Do it. Slow the train before we get to the canyon."

"Why?"

"So they can see me."

"I must be as mad as you."

"When we reach the mouth of the canyon," she said, "you must order them to stop."

"What!"

"The warriors," she said. "They want us in the canyon."

Tomás reeled out the door, said, "Are we dead yet?" and slammed back into the car.

"Father is drunk," she noted.

"Who could blame him?"

Enríquez sent word ahead to the engineer. The train slowed. The brakes squealed loudly as the smokestack billowed great clouds.

"Here it comes," the forward lookout shouted. A fighter nearby briefly rose and waved his arm over his head. They all took aim.

Teresita stood in the center of the flatcar. Enríquez himself manned the bullet spitter on its tall tripod. Tomás hid in the train car, crouched between the seats. Soldiers splayed themselves on the roof, and they huddled behind sandbags on the aft flatcar.

"Slow," Teresita said.

"It is slow."

"Stop! Now!"

Enríquez signaled his men.

The train, already crawling, slowed and stopped. It chuffed. Its nose was into the narrow gap between stone walls.

"Ease ahead," she said.

Enríquez signaled again. The train lurched. The loco-motive cleared the gap, then the coal car. The flatcar entered the gap, and she called:

"Stop!"

Enríquez signaled and fell behind his machine gun and yanked back the handle.

"Calma!" he called.

"Don't shoot," she said.

"Calma, muchachos!"

"Don't shoot."

She could feel them watching her. She knew they were there. The bushes all around her were alive with her brothers, her friends, her followers.

She raised her hands and held them before her. Then she stretched them out to either side. She stood there, still and thin and somehow frightening.

They were aiming at the train.

Enríquez saw a warrior rise from the brush and aim at him.

"Hold your fire," he told his men.

"Harm no man!" Teresita called.

The warrior lowered his rifle and watched them, confused.

"Calma," said Enríquez.

One of the People could contain himself no longer. He let out a yell and ran at the train. He was dressed only in a loincloth. His face had streaks painted along the cheeks.

"Harm no man!" Teresita called.

The warrior ran up to the train and smacked it with his palm. He yelled. Smacked it again, and ran back to the brush.

Men yelped. Invisible men. Hooted. Enríquez felt his hair rising on the back of his neck.

Tomás cracked the train-car door and said: "I think I just pissed my pants!"

"Calma!" Enríquez called.

The locomotive double-chuffed as they stood, exposed. *Cha-chuff. Cha-chuff. Cha-chuff.*

"Miss Urrea," Enríquez said, "I believe we are all going to die."

Teresita called out to the hidden men:

"Brothers! It is my destiny to go! I choose to go! Kill no man! Harm no man!"

Silence.

"Move," Teresita said. "Now."

Enríquez waved frantically. His men were hiding in the engineer's cabin. One of them finally looked and pulled his head in. The locomotive gave out one huge chuff and the train lurched again.

"Viva la Santa!"

The cries came from the sage and the creosotes.

"Viva Teresita!"

"Viva la Santa de Cabora!"

The train was moving slowly, slowly — it was agony for Enríquez.

She never moved. Stood with her hands raised, staring into the canyon. Enríquez could not believe his eyes. Ten, thirty, fifty, a hundred armed warriors rose around them.

"Don't shoot!" she shouted. "Don't shoot!"

He did not know if she was shouting to them or to him, and it did not matter. She was shouting to them all. And the warriors came forward. They ran, they jumped down to the tracks. The train slowly accelerated, and the warriors raised their rifles. But they did not shoot. They formed a double line that stretched ahead of the train and vanished around the bend in the tracks. Each man stood silent, staring up at her, and he held his rifle over his head to salute her.

Enríquez stood, made his way to her side. Tomás was on the step behind them, then he came forward to join them.

The warriors stood a silent vigil as their saint passed out of their lives. Tomás saw that some of them were weeping.

The train was moving faster now. The engineer dropped sand through the slots onto the tracks so they could build traction and climb. The train rumbled and howled, sparks swirled around them and smoke, and the whistle shrieked and the warriors never moved.

They climbed and approached the great curve out of the canyon, and the men still stood all along the line.

"There!" Teresita cried. "Look there!"

She pointed.

Tomás looked: sitting on his horse on the last rise beside the tracks, he found Buenaventura. He was laughing. He held his great old idiotic Texan cowboy hat in his hand. He waved it over his head.

And then, as if it had all been a strange dream, Mexico, and Cabora, and the wars, and President Díaz, and the Yaquis and Mayos and Apaches and Pimas and Guasayes and Seris and Tarahumaras and Tomochitecos were gone.

Nothing ahead of them now but night.

Night, and great, dark North America.

AUTHOR'S NOTE

TERESA URREA WAS A REAL PERSON. I grew up believing she was my aunt. Apparently, my great-grandfather, Seferino Urrea, was Tomás's first cousin. She was a family folktale until César A. González, at San Diego Mesa College, showed me the first of many hundreds of articles I would read about her. Although I could claim to have been pursuing her story since my boyhood, my serious research into her life began in Boston in 1985.

Teresita's sermons, her argument in the prison wagon with General Bandála, and Cruz Chávez's heated discussion with Father Gastélum in Tomóchic are all based on Lauro Aguirre's own notes. Although they are difficult to find, you can still uncover microfilms of his writings if you know a helpful librarian. The story the old woman tells Aguirre near the end of the novel is an eyewitness account told by a 101-year-old curandera in Benjamin Hill, Sonora. It was tape-recorded over a decade ago by my brother, Alberto Urrea. This is the first time it appears in any source.

The teachings of Huila are based on the Mayo medicine woman of El Júpare, Sonora — Maclovia Borbón Moroyoqui. Maclovia was the maternal grandmother and teacher of my cousin, Esperanza Urrea. Esperanza was one of my teachers as I learned a few of the secret medicine ways recounted here.

Two other teachers deserve mention: Elba Urrea, aunt
and curandera-hechicera, delivered before her death a trunk
full of documents, letters, pictures, and articles relating to
Teresita. The Chiricahua Apache medicine man, "Manny,"
at Rancho Teresita in Arizona shared much with me.

Please note that these, and many other, sources asked
me to disguise certain details from readers. I was taught
that it would be fun as an author to show off all the Yaqui
and Mayo and curandera secrets I had been shown. But
that kind of showing off would be wrong. So I have
changed certain small details, and I have maintained the
secret names of things. Written formulas are accurate, and
all "miracles" attributed to Teresita are from the record,
witnessed in writing in the archives.

This book took more than twenty years of fieldwork, research, travel, and interviews to compose. The acknowledgments I owe are extensive and would add several pages
to this text. Writers, scholars, clergy, curanderas, and
shamans helped me all along the way.

For those interested in sources and the like, a full bibli-
ography and acknowledgments section can be found on
my Web site (www. luisurrea.com) under the "Teresita"
subheading. Michelle McDonald brilliantly designs and
maintains the Web site.

Several books are quite valuable to the Teresita scholar.
Everyone begins in the same place: *Teresita,* by William
Curry Holden. It's a fine old text, rich in detail. Lauro
Aguirre's *Tomóchic!* (also known by different titles) is in-
teresting, since it suggests it was edited — if not co-
written — by Teresita herself. José Valades wrote the

influential newspaper series on Teresita that appeared to great fanfare in the Southwest in the 1930s; this material went into his slender book, *Porfirio Díaz contra el gran poder de Dios*. For a deeper understanding of Tomóchic, and Teresita's role in the debacle, you must begin with Heriberto Frías's *Tomóchic*. Paul Vanderwood has written the definitive Tomóchic history, *God and Guns Against the Power of Government*. Brianda Domecq will, perhaps, forgive me if I confess I have not read her no-doubt fine novel about Teresita, *La insólita historia de la Santa de Cabora*. Aside from giving me an epigraph for the first section of this book, Ms. Domecq's work remained a mystery to me, since I didn't want any fiction affecting the fiction I was composing. I have read her excellent historical notes and essays, however, in such places as the Arizona Historical Society.

I owe a great deal of gratitude to the Lannan Foundation for their generous support. The award is just a small part of it.

Finally, Geoff Shandler, my careful editor, has walked back and forth through this epic, trimming and shaping an unruly text. I couldn't put my work in finer hands. Along with Geoff, everyone at Little, Brown has been kind and supportive as I've bashed my way through this book — thanks to Michael Pietsch, Liz Nagle, Shannon Byrne, Peggy Freudenthal, copyeditor Melissa Clemence, and proofreader Katie Blatt, among so many others. Everyone at the Sandra Dijkstra Agency watches over me and makes my career possible; Mike Cendejas at the Lynne Pleshette Agency battles Hollywood for me and makes dreams come true.

Cinderella did tireless work in support of the creation of *The Hummingbird's Daughter*. Any husband would be wise to say this, but in my case it's true: without her help, there would be no book.

More Urrea family members than I can name here gave me hours, days, years of their time. Please see the Web site.

Thank you all. Y gracias, Teresita.

ABOUT THE AUTHOR

LUIS ALBERTO URREA is the author of *The Devil's Highway*, winner of the 2004 Lannan Literary Award for nonfiction; *Across the Wire*, winner of the Christopher Award; and *By the Lake of Sleeping Children*. He is the recipient of an American Book Award, a Western States Book Award, and a Colorado Book Award, and he has been inducted into the Latino Literary Hall of Fame. His poetry has been collected in *The Best American Poetry*, and his short-story collection, *Six Kinds of Sky*, won the 2002 *ForeWord Magazine* Book of the Year Award, Editor's Choice for Fiction. He teaches creative writing at the University of Illinois in Chicago.